DIANE JANE BALL

The Austens of Steventon

A catalogue record for this book is available from the British Library.

Cover Design by Tania LaGambina.

Printed by Amazon.

First edition

ISBN: 978-1-73-845310-8

This book was professionally typeset on Reedsy.
Find out more at reedsy.com

*For Janeites everywhere.*

# Foreword

**Note to the Reader.**

Jane Austen was not born famous. It was not until she reached the age of thirty-five that she saw her first novel in print, and she died six years later with no inkling whatsoever of the incredible legacy she was to leave behind. This story takes place long before that when Jane was simply a young girl growing up in a large family.

Opening with her parents' wedding in 1764, the narrative follows Mr and Mrs Austen to their first home in Deane and then on to Steventon. You will bear witness to the births of all eight of their children and discover the individual life stories of them all, as well as their relatives and their friends. This was the time of American Independence and the French Revolutionary Wars and you will see how these international affairs affected even the smallest of rural communities.

Everything that is written on these pages is based on true historical facts and each fact has been thoroughly researched and cross-referenced. The timeline of the story follows the same run of events as recorded in letters, memoirs, and ancestral records. At the back of the book is a reference section which contains the sources of my research which you can use as a starting point should you wish to find out more.

You can also experience the settings from the novel by

visiting them yourself. *The Austens of Steventon* has a sister website which can be accessed at https://www.diane-jane-ball.com. There you can browse photographs and facts about all the important places, together with maps to direct you there and links to external websites. In addition, the site has extracts from the novel for each of the major settings, enabling you to make connections between who lived there in the past, and what remains standing today.

You will find family trees for the Austen, Fowle, Lloyd, Leigh and Cooper families on the website too, including a brief explanation of who each person is to help you identify them within the novel.

I hope you will enjoy learning more about the family who were responsible for giving us such an extraordinary author.

Diane Jane Ball, 2023.

# Who's Who?

If you would prefer to see this information presented in the form of traditional family trees, you will find them freely available on my website at: https://www.diane-jane-ball.com/family-trees

Each tree is too complex to fit onto a page here, but once online you will be able to zoom in and study them closely.

In the lists below, a single date in brackets next to someone's name records their year of birth. It signifies that they are still alive at the end of the novel. Where there are two dates listed, this records the years of their birth and death. These individuals are no longer alive by the end of the novel.

## The Austen Family

**Mr Austen** *(1731)* Reverend George Austen is rector of Steventon and Deane, as well as being schoolmaster of his own boarding school and father to eight children.

**Mrs Austen** *(1739)* Born Miss Cassandra Leigh, Mrs Austen is a mother to eight children and keeps the rectory running smoothly.

**James Austen** *(1765)* Known as Jemmy when he was a boy, James follows in the footsteps of his father to become a clergyman.

**George Austen** (*1766*) George has developmental difficulties and is fostered out to be cared for by Mr and Mrs Cullum at Monk Sherbourne.

**Edward Austen** (*1767*) Known as Neddy when he was a boy, Edward is adopted by the wealthy Mr and Mrs Thomas Knight II of Godmersham Park.

**Henry Austen** (*1771*) Henry is the most charismatic of the brothers and joins the militia before opening his own bank. He marries his cousin, Eliza de Feuillide.

**Cassandra Elizabeth Austen** (*1773*) Cassandra has a sweet and obliging temperament. She is betrothed to Tom Fowle before she learns of his untimely death.

**Francis William Austen** (*1774*) Referred to more commonly as Frank, this brother achieves great things with the navy and reaches the rank of Post Captain by 1801.

**Jane Austen** (*1775*) Jane Austen is a keen writer. She produces all her works of *Juvenilia* and the drafts of three major novels during her time in Steventon.

**Charles John** (*1779*) Charles is the baby of the family and another successful sailor. He reaches the rank of 2nd Lieutenant by 1801.

### The Hancock Family

**Philadelphia Hancock** (*1730 - 1792*) Philadelphia is Mr Austen's exotic sister. She spent her early married life in India where she allegedly had an affair with Warren Hastings. She is a frequent visitor to Steventon.

**Tysoe Saul Hancock** (*1711-1775*) Tysoe is Philadelphia's husband. He is a surgeon with the East India Company and spends most of his time in India. His wife finds him dull and tedious.

**Eliza Comtesse de Feuillide** *(1761)* Known as Betsy Hancock as a child, Eliza is the flirtatious niece of Mr Austen. Her first husband is a Captain in the French Dragoons and together they have a child, Hastings, who suffers from fits.

**Comte Jean Capot de Feuillide** (1751-1794) The Comte de Feuillide owns land and property in the south of France. He is a Royalist soldier for the French army and dies on the guillotine during the Reign of Terror in Paris.

### The Walter Family

**William Hampson-Walter** (1721-1798) William is half-brother to Mr Austen; both men share the same late mother. He lives in Kent and has business interests in Jamaica.

**Susannah Walter** (1718) Susannah is William's wife. She is a close friend of Mrs Austen, and the two women correspond regularly throughout the novel.

**Philly Walter** (1761) Philly is the youngest child of Susannah and William Walter. She is very close to her cousin, Eliza de Feuillide and the news in her letters often serves as gossip for the rest of the family.

### The Leigh Family

**James Leigh-Perrot** *(1735)* Mr Leigh-Perrot is Mrs Austen's elder brother. Like Edward Austen, Mr Leigh-Perrot was adopted by rich relations as a boy and consequently lives a privileged lifestyle.

**Jane Leigh-Perrot** *(1744)* Referred to affectionately as 'dear

Jenny' by her husband, Mrs Leigh-Perrot is notably accused of stealing a card of white lace from a milliner's shop in Bath.

**Mrs Leigh** *(1704 - 1768)* Old Mrs Leigh is Mrs Austen's widowed mother. She comes to live in Deane when Mr and Mrs Austen first marry but dies soon after the family move to Steventon.

**Thomas Leigh** *(1747)* Thomas is the unfortunate son of Mrs Leigh and brother to Mrs Austen. He had developmental issues as a boy and is fostered out to the Cullums in Monk Sherbourne. He is later joined in the farmhouse by Mr and Mrs Austen's own son, George.

**Reverend Thomas Leigh** *(1734)* Reverend Leigh is the rector of Adlestrop in Gloucestershire. He is an amiable character and often tips the children coins. He is host to Mrs Austen and her daughters during the summer of 1794.

### The Cooper Family

**Mrs Jane Cooper** *(1736-1783)* Born Jane Leigh, Mrs Cooper is the sister of Mrs Austen. She lives in fashionable Bath with her husband and meets a sad and untimely death.

**Reverend Edward Cooper** *(1727-1792)* Mr Cooper is Mrs Austen's brother-in-law. After his wife's death, he moves away from Bath to the village of Sonning.

**Edward Cooper** (1770) Edward is the son of Mr and Mrs Cooper (above). He becomes a clergyman, like his father, first taking up the former living of his grandfather in Harpsden, and then moving to Hamstall Ridware in Staffordshire. He is a regular guest at Steventon and is close to his cousins.

**Jane Cooper** *(1771-1798)* Jane Cooper is a frequent child-hood companion to Cassandra and Jane Austen and goes with them to school. She marries Captain Thomas Williams of the Royal Navy, who plays an influential role in the career of Charles Austen.

## The Fowle Family

**Reverend Thomas Fowle** (*1726*) Reverend Fowle is a rector in Kintbury and is a friend of Mr Austen's from Oxford University. He sends his four sons to boarding school in Steventon.

**Mrs Jane Fowle** (*1727-1798*) Mrs Fowle is married to Reverend Thomas Fowle and lives in Kintbury. She is the sister of Mrs Martha Lloyd of Enborne.

**Fulwar Craven Fowle** (*1764*) Fulwar is the eldest child of Mr and Mrs Fowle and the first to attend school in Steventon. He is a clergyman like his father and a lifelong friend of all the Austen family. He is especially close to James Austen.

**Tom Fowle** (*1765-1797*) Tom Fowle also pursues a career as a clergyman and is betrothed to Cassandra Austen. Before they can marry, he sails to the West Indies as a private chaplain and tragically dies on his way back home.

**William Fowle** (*1767*) William Fowle is another student in the Steventon schoolroom. He is later apprenticed to his uncle to study medicine and becomes a doctor. By 1801 he is serving with the army as a surgeon in Egypt.

**Charles Fowle** (*1770*) Charles is the youngest of the Fowle brothers and becomes a lawyer. He frequently attends the same parties as the Austen children and remains close friends with them as they grow up.

## The Lloyd Family

**Reverend Nowes Lloyd** (*1719-1789*) Reverend Lloyd is the rector of Enborne in Berkshire. He was also acquainted with Mr Austen at Oxford University and is a proud clergyman and father.

**Mrs Martha Lloyd** (*1729*) Mrs Lloyd is the widow of Reverend Lloyd. After her husband's death, she is forced to leave Enborne and settle in Deane with her daughters. A few years later, she is forced to move again to the village of Ibthorpe.

**Martha Lloyd** (*1765*) Martha is the eldest daughter of Mr and Mrs Lloyd. She is especially close to Jane Austen and the two are regular companions in each other's homes.

**Eliza Lloyd** (*1767*) Eliza is the first of the sisters to marry. She weds her cousin, Fulwar Fowle, and gives birth to six children during the course of this novel.

**Charles Lloyd** (*1768-1775*) Charles died during a smallpox epidemic which hit Enborne in 1775. He was seven years old.

**Mary Lloyd** (*1771*) Mary had her own battle with smallpox and is scarred with pox marks on her face. She fell in love with James Austen as a teenager and after some disappointment becomes his second wife and bears his son.

# Contents

# Prologue

## 1754
## Oxford.

George Austen stood in the centre of the dusty courtyard looking up at the rising moon. By the time it became a full circle in a few days' time, he would be far away from here.

Today marked his final hours as an Oxford student and tomorrow he would embark upon a tedious journey by stagecoach to his uncle's house. Through hour after hour of winding countryside, he knew he would endure early morning mists so thick that they would wrap around his cloak and he would never get warm. He would be forced to wake from uncomfortable slumbers and traipse up steep hills to spare the horses, and when he finally did reach his destination he knew his body would ache from head to toe.

Even more reason to make the most of this idyllic spring day and the precious time he had left in the city he loved.

He found St John's College tranquilizing. The coarse, honey-coloured walls of the quadrangle offered protection from the discordant sounds of the street outside. He sought strength in these stolen moments of peace engrossed in memories and hopes for the future, appreciating all that he felt right now.

Peace, of course, never lasted long in a university town. The substantial wooden gate of St. Giles rattled open, ushering in a fusion of noises and smells to intrude upon the calm.

"Austen, my friend!"

The young Mr Austen turned to see two men in black caps and gowns like himself striding swiftly towards him.

"Fowle. Good day to you!"

Thomas Fowle was someone George Austen knew he was going to miss. A member of nearby Wadham College, the two men had shared many a merry time experiencing student life together.

Mr Fowle was accompanied by an older man sporting the ecclesiastic attire of a white cravat and wig. This was Nowes Lloyd, a former student himself of St. John's College but now a rector with his own parish. Not yet married, he remained a Fellow of the College and often returned to lecture there.

"Where will you go from Oxford?" Mr Lloyd quizzed. "Do you have a living arranged?"

"Sadly, not yet, Sir. But I have been offered a teaching post at my former school in Tonbridge which I take up next month."

"If you should find yourself in need of a testimonial one day I would be happy to write one for you," continued the senior man. "I have heard good things about you, Mr Austen."

"Thank you, Sir."

Mr Fowle was watching his friend closely and could sense his sadness. "Be sure to call by my room before you go, Austen," he chivied. "I want to be certain I have your correct forwarding address. I expect you to become one of my regular correspondents, you know."

"Good luck, young man," offered Mr Lloyd with a firm handshake. "Be sure to come back and see us when you can."

Mr Austen was so overcome with gratitude at these warm gestures, coupled with a great deal of sorrow because he had no firm plans yet when he would return. Fearing his emotions may betray him, he quickly made his excuses about an appointment in town and exited hastily out of the same gate that his friends had just entered.

# Chapter 1

## 1764
## Mr and Mrs Austen wed.

I t was a dull, cold morning when George Austen stood outside St Swithin's Church in Bath waiting to marry his sweetheart. The date was the 26th of April and the venue was a small, plain structure with little character. There were no welcoming cheers from neighbours to mark this momentous occasion, nor any pretty ribbons to celebrate their joy. Yet it was a well-connected match on both sides and promised as happy a union as any in their wider social circles.

Miss Cassandra Leigh had lived in Bath for two years before the wedding. She had moved there with her parents from the village of Harpsden, near Henley-on-Thames, where her father had been rector of the parish there. The family had not been long in Bath before Mr Leigh was struck down by illness and died. He was buried in this very church.

"Why is it so cold?" complained Miss Leigh, stamping her freezing feet to stop them from going numb. "How much longer will we be forced to wait outside?"

Mr Austen led her to the porch, which offered some respite

at least by blocking the harsh, biting wind on one side.

The officiate for the service was waiting with them and offered his weak reassurance. "We *are* a little early. I'm sure it won't be much longer." This was Tom Powys, a long-standing friend of the Leigh family.

The only other two members of the party were Miss Leigh's brother and sister, who were to serve as witnesses. Mr James Leigh-Perrot was quiet and reflective, remembering the funeral procession that had carried his father's coffin to be laid to rest here a few weeks before. Miss Jane Leigh stood next to her sister in companionable silence, so it was down to Mr Powys and Mr Austen to make conversation.

"Have you seen the plans for the new church yet? I believe they are in circulation," began Mr Powys.

"No. I have not."

"Magnificent, I understand," enthused the vicar. "It will be much grander than this one and destined to become a prominent landmark of Bath, I believe."

Despite this church being only twenty years old, it was not considered large enough to match all the other developments going on around it and an improved version was being commissioned.

Mr Austen thought of his own little parish church at Steventon that was full of holes and leaks. As much as he craved the repairs, he would have been sad to think of it being replaced entirely by one deemed 'much grander'.

"I think everyone is striving to create the greatest landmark around here," considered Mr Austen. "On every corner, I see some new project or other. I have never seen building work like it."

"Yes," agreed Mr Powys. "There is talk of a new bridge

across the river. And have you seen those new houses in The Circus, built around in a circle? Astonishing architecture!"

Thankfully, it was not long before the wooden door of the church creaked open and out stepped the wedding party from the service before their own. When they were gone, Mr Powys led the way into the vacated church and the two sisters followed the gentlemen up the aisle. The whitewashed walls and wooden beamed ceiling were stark and severe and the sound of clicking footsteps over the hard stone floor was a poor substitute for musical bells.

The wind blew against gaps in the windows and whistled around the thin wooden pews, which creaked under the weight of their bodies. When Mr Powys read from his *Book of Common Prayer*, his words were visible on his breath through the little tufts of steam that exited his lips. His voice echoed alarmingly and he was forced to adjust it to a lower pitch.

There was nothing romantic about this moment – and yet Mr Austen was not worried at all. In his career thus far, he had met with people from all corners of society. He knew from experience that an extravagant display of wealth and materialism was no guarantee of happiness. A pretty dress and lots of finery at a service did not automatically lead to a long and happy marriage. It was what the couple felt in their hearts that was important, and he was very secure with what he felt.

In Miss Leigh, he had found a soulmate who would serve him with an intellect equal to his own. She had impressed him with her knowledge on a range of topics and he looked forward to many evenings ahead where he could share his interests and be sure of a fulfilling discussion in return. He pictured a brood of little children sitting around the fire, eagerly listening to him read and always keen to please.

And so it was, on that bitterly cold morning, that this tall, thin-framed young lady, just twenty-four years of age and dressed in a fashionable red riding coat and warm black hat, was joined in matrimony to her angel-faced fiancé of thirty-two years, wearing a formal white wig and a long dark travelling coat in anticipation of the journey he was to take later that day.

The smiling vicar directed the shivering groom to place the golden ring on the fourth finger of the bride's trembling left hand, and the couple vowed to love each other until death made them part.

And then it was done. No wedding breakfast had been arranged and with a hasty goodbye the couple left the rest of the party to walk quickly towards the stagecoach which would transport them to Andover, and then tomorrow conclude their journey through Hampshire on to Steventon.

Their first home was to be a rectory in the village of Deane, where the bride's mother was due to join them in a few weeks' time. It would be wet and it would be muddy; there had been severe flooding in the area for months. But none of those problems were insurmountable. They were everyday obstacles experienced by village folk up and down the land.

When the horses pulled away from Bath the newlyweds snuggled up together in the carriage to keep warm. Mr Austen squeezed his wife's hand and placed a tender kiss on her forehead whilst the other passengers looked tactfully out of the window.

# Chapter 2

**1764**
**Mr and Mrs Austen settle in Deane.**

Deane was as different to Bath as a boot is to a slipper and the new Mrs Austen was struck by the contrast immediately. The higgledy-piggledy rooms of her little rectory were a far cry from the smartly decorated chambers she had been accustomed to.

Throughout her youth, time management had been the backbone of her society. She had eaten at a respectable time, paid visits when predicted and received callers as etiquette dictated. Here, in this friendly little neighbourhood, people stuck to no rules whatsoever. They called when they wished or simply because they were passing. In Deane, folk were ruled by the land and the seasons, not by convention or the clock.

The acquisition of an elegant young couple into the neighbourhood was a novelty. Eager to make them feel at home, the locals came by the rectory every day to offer presents of rabbits, eggs, preserves and handmade gifts.

"What am I to do with all these handkerchiefs?" laughed Mrs Austen when yet another farmer's wife left a lovingly embroidered bestowal at her door. "I must have ten now … at least."

"I'm sure they will come in useful, my love." Mr Austen held the latest addition up to the light to admire it; an intricate flower had been sewn into one corner by a very capable hand. "I think you will be exceedingly glad of them all in this rural wilderness." He smiled tenderly at his wife. "It's their way of welcoming you, my love. They want you to know that they like you."

Mrs Austen decided this unfamiliar fuzzy feeling must be contentment and she hummed a tune to herself whilst she folded up her latest lace-trimmed offering and placed it neatly in a drawer on top of the rest.

Whenever the couple walked around the lanes they were followed by curious children or watched by old maids twitching at the curtains of their cottages.

"Can I carry your basket, Ma'am?"

"Let me help you over that ditch, Mrs Austen."

"My mother says to tell you she will call by later to bring some more butter."

Mr Austen's good looks drew plenty of admiring glances when he gave his sermons and Mrs Austen noticed the young women lingering over the small talk he always made at the church door at the end of a service. Some found it hard to draw their gaze away from his large bright eyes: pear-green with flecks of brown scattered about them like magic dust.

The family that owned the most land and property around Deane was the Harwood family of Deane House. Mr Austen was working alongside some villagers in the rectory grounds when Mr Harwood strolled up.

"Good day to you."

"Ah! Mr Harwood. Welcome." Mr Austen stood up and mopped his brow to wipe away the sweat of his toils.

"Excellent work, I see here. You have made so many improvements already in the short time you have been amongst us."

"Yes, Sir. Lots to do, but it's coming along well."

"You are an asset to our community, Mr Austen. We are very lucky to have you."

"I'm thrilled to be here," affirmed the young rector. "Although I cannot take all the glory for myself. If it were not for these fine men helping me out every day, I would never manage the half of it. And Mr Bond here is a true marvel." Mr Austen placed his arm around the shoulder of the man closest to him - John Bond, his trusty bailiff and the fount of all knowledge in the workings of the countryside. The two were becoming firm friends.

Before summer was out, Mrs Austen's mother came to live with them. She had sent her servants on ahead to prepare her room, wash and air her bedding and hang her clothes in her closet. Her husband's death at the start of the year had jarred her confidence so the young couple were determined that they would do everything in their power to make her comfortable and try to bring some joy back into her life.

Mrs Leigh brought with her a young boy of eight years old by the name of George Hastings. He was the child of an old family friend, Warren Hastings, who was currently out in India and wished for his son to be educated in England. The decision to bring the boy to the rectory made good sense as Mr Austen was already an experienced teacher, having been a master at Tonbridge School before being ordained into the church. The generous allowance offered by the boy's father for his son's education also provided the couple with a grateful source of income.

By the time the nights drew in, a comfortable family ritual had established itself. Young George Hastings occupied himself copying out lines of Latin by candlelight, whilst Mrs Austen found the need to let out the seams of her clothes to make room for the growing baby she had conceived. The gowns she had brought with her from Bath were completely inappropriate for country life in Deane so, with a skilful hand, she found ways of detaching the fancy bustles that adorned them and crafting the plainer material into new panels around the front. This would allow her full stomach to rest comfortably and discreetly and after some initial experimentation, she fell upon a method that worked well. Her new talent, and the reason for it, made her happier than she could have imagined.

As her daughter sewed, Mrs Leigh read from a letter that had arrived that day from her son.

"James has sent word that he is soon to acquire a new home in Berkshire, called Scarlets. His bride's family have been remarkably generous and he is planning a series of improvements to it. He assures me it will be the most splendid residence by the time he has finished."

Mr Leigh-Perrot had himself married a few weeks after witnessing Mr and Mrs Austen's wedding in Bath. His new wife was extremely wealthy from some investments that her father had made in a sugar plantation in Barbados. This lucky young couple would never have to worry about paying their household bills.

"I'm sure it will be the most provocative property around," replied Mrs Austen, full of bitter opinion. "With James's extravagance and his wife's indulgent tastes, I am sure every room will sparkle with the latest fashion."

"That sounds very much like jealousy to me," proclaimed Mrs Leigh, scrutinising her daughter's face with beady eyes.

"Not jealousy," confirmed Mrs Austen with a sigh. "Perhaps a little envy, I do admit. But what a difference even a small amount of money could make to us here in the rectory yet James has so much he hardly knows how to spend it all."

"Let us wait and see what the years bring, shall we?" warned the wizened mother. "Money cannot get you everything you want from life, no matter how much you have."

During these quiet evenings, Mr Austen sat in his study poring over the household accounts. "We will manage," he would reassure his wife whenever she asked if he was concerned. "We have enough for what we need." Then he would furrow his brow again, trying the figures in different combinations to see if he could find a more favourable solution.

It had to be said that old Mrs Leigh was not as easily charmed by country life as Mrs Austen and she found it harder to adapt. Her distinguished breeding made her view the forwardness of their neighbours as impolite and she wholeheartedly disapproved of her son-in-law working the fields like a peasant to assist with the farming. She had imagined a far more refined life for her daughter.

When the weather allowed, Mrs Austen took her mother and young George Hastings on her walks, pointing out the views and relishing the fresh country air. Some days they would head towards Ashe and other days walk to the town of Overton to purchase fabric or thread.

When Mrs Leigh was indisposed, Mrs Austen took the

boy further afield. The walk up to Mr Austen's church of St Nicholas in Steventon was taxing and messy, but the child was interested to see the progress of the repairs being carried out there by a band of cheery labourers. Recent storms had toppled the steeple and damaged the roof, but thankfully the old tower had been restored and the three small bells now hung safely back in their rightful places. The leaky church roof had been patched up and the creaky door, swollen from the rain, had been shaved to close once more with a satisfying clunk.

Back down the hill, Mrs Austen pointed to the uninhabited Steventon Rectory with pride. "That house there is where we are to live soon. Won't it be grand?"

George Hastings looked on blankly at the shambles of a building before him, sunk down on the corner of a meadow. He could see nothing but timber and mud and lacked the capacity to visualise the same grand house his guardian was imagining. Even to his innocent eyes he could detect it needed a lot of work before it would be fit to live in.

"May we watch the carriages now?" he asked sweetly, not really knowing the correct thing to say and eager to do something more active.

Mrs Austen smiled indulgently and took his hand. She loved to watch him when the stagecoaches sped past along the route to London, which crossed their path on the way home. He would laugh at the snorting horses and giggle when the splattering mud touched his cheek.

# Chapter 3

**Mr and Mrs Austen start a family.**

Mrs Austen's first child was born in February. Baby James (affectionately known as Jemmy) was bonny and bright and brought instant disruption to the household. Mrs Leigh had no other choice but to fit around the demands of her grandson and begrudgingly resigned herself to eating before dark, going to bed early and being disturbed in the middle of the night by the sound of his cries.

"I have been making enquiries into a dry nurse," she informed her daughter one afternoon whilst Jemmy was suckling contentedly at his mother's breast. "There is a woman at Cheesedown Farm. I have it on good authority from Mr Harwood that she is to be trusted."

Mrs Leigh had made no secret of the fact she did not want Jemmy to remain at the rectory. There should be some distance between him and his mother if he were to grow up to become a gentleman and, as soon as he was weaned from his mother's milk, she was determined he should be sent away to become more independent.

"Are you sure it's the right thing to do?" Mrs Austen had pleaded when she first heard the idea. She could hardly bear to put Jemmy down in his cradle, let alone hand him over to another woman.

"Of course it's the right thing." Mrs Leigh was in no doubt.

She had enticed her daughter with persuasive visions of her boy running about a farmyard with children of his own age; learning about animals; learning to feed himself; learning to walk and talk quicker than he would do at home.

"You can see him every day on your walks. And he will come back here for visits. He will thrive, I promise you. Not grow up weak and coddled with all the attention that *you* spoil him with."

"I would never let him be weak and coddled," argued Mrs Austen. But her mother was not wrong in her accusations. Mrs Austen loved tending to her baby; the slightest complaint and she picked him up.

"It will give you plenty of time to get your strength back ready for when the next baby comes along."

"That may be what people do in Henley and Bath, Mother, but this is Deane. It's not the same," Mrs Austen continued to protest.

"It is exactly the same," reiterated Mrs Leigh. "The Harwoods did it - Mr Harwood told me so himself." This was a debate the old woman was determined to win and for a principled reason. "You may enjoy living the life of a country wife, Cassandra, but you are not one at heart. You are from a different class, and it is that class which will determine the future of your children. You must never forget that."

Jemmy stirred again and cried half-heartedly.

"Leave him!" commanded Mrs Leigh. "You have only just

fed him so he cannot possibly be hungry. He needs to learn to settle on his own without you fussing."

Mrs Austen scowled. She would count up to twenty and then pick him up – he was her son, not her mother's. She couldn't bear to think of him feeling sad.

Funnily enough, by the time she had counted to eight, Jemmy had quietened himself down. By twelve he had let out a yawn. By twenty his eyes were closing and he was drifting off to sleep. Mrs Austen contemplated the relief she felt at being able to sit in silence for a while: the treat of allowing her exhausted body time to rest. Maybe tough love did work after all.

At three months of age, little Jemmy Austen was bundled off to live in the home of John and Elizabeth Littleworth at nearby Cheesedown Farm. He was to lodge there until he could walk and talk and receive visits every day from either his mother or his father. From time to time he would be brought back to the rectory to stay for a few days and renew the bond with his natural parents.

And he thrived - just as Mrs Leigh had predicted. He laughed and he smiled and grew such a beautiful set of teeth that his mother was delighted. If his sleep routine was aided by a little something added to his sugared bread and water to keep him quiet, then his parents were none the wiser and it did not appear to do him any harm.

\* \* \*

It was a blustery spring morning when Mr and Mrs Austen recalled their wedding, two years to the day.

"Do you remember how nervous we were?" reflected Mr

Austen.

"And so cold," laughed his wife. "That reminds me, I must write to Mr Powys. I have not yet replied to his last letter."

"If you want to write now I can take it to post for you. I'm heading that way shortly, but I can wait a while longer."

"Thank you, I'll do it later. I want to go over to the farm now to see Jemmy while the sun is out."

"Then I will walk with you," decided Mr Austen, picking up his hat. "Can you believe it, my love? Two years ago to this very day, we were taking our vows and now here we are, with one fine boy already and soon-to-be parents again. How blessed are we?"

They smiled at one another in agreement.

Mrs Austen stayed at Cheesedown Farm to play with Jemmy whilst Mr Austen walked on to Deane Gate to collect his post. His cheeks were flushed when he returned and he had already opened one of the letters in his hand. It was obviously good news from the look on his face.

"You look pleased," teased his wife. "Have we inherited an estate we didn't know about?"

Mr Austen laughed. "No, unfortunately not. But it is good news. Philadelphia and Tysoe are coming to stay. You will meet them at last."

Philadelphia was Mr Austen's elder sister who had lived for many years in India. Her husband, Tysoe Hancock, was a surgeon working for The East India Company and they had one young daughter, Betsy.

"How wonderful," acknowledged Mrs Austen. She linked her arm with her husband's and together they headed back down the lane towards the rectory.

The Hancock family's arrival in England had been a painful

14

affair, and not an event the Austens liked to dwell on. They had sailed back from India the previous summer, along with Warren Hastings, young George Hastings' father. The boy had been excited at the prospect of seeing his papa again and had chatted endlessly about the gifts he had been promised from overseas. His anticipation, however, was cut short in the most tragic of ways. Within days of complaining of a sore throat, his voice had become too hoarse to speak. He quickly succumbed to an alarming fever and, unable to catch his breath, passed away in his bed less than a week after first falling ill.

Mrs Austen was distraught and wept for him as much as if he were a son of her own. It fell to Mr Austen to break the news to Warren Hastings when he landed in England. Being the generous-natured man he was, Mr Hastings tried to assure Mr Austen he was not to blame and his kind face looked upon his son's guardian with almost as much pity as he was due himself.

Over the following months, Mr Austen had paid further visits to the Hancocks in London where, understandably, Warren Hastings was often present as he lived in a neighbouring street. Philadelphia was supporting him in his grief, Mr Austen had been told, and he praised her noble generosity. But it was an odd arrangement he confided to his wife, noticing that little Betsy showed Mr Hastings more affection than she showed to her own father and he reciprocated the love in equal measure.

Still, who was he to judge? Betsy was Mr Hastings' goddaughter, so perhaps this was his way of coping with his loss.

"You will adore Philadelphia, my love," Mr Austen declared

one mealtime, unable to stop talking about his beloved sister and the forthcoming visit. "She is so chatty: outrageous even. She will brighten up our little rectory, that's for sure."

Mrs Leigh chewed on her baked herb pie in silence. She would not break the spell now, but she must warn her daughter in private. She did not want to see her as besotted by Philadelphia's charms as her son-in-law clearly was. Mrs Leigh remembered the woman before she had sailed off to India. She was a shopgirl in those days apprenticed to a milliner in Covent Garden, but she had given that up to join a group of women heading towards Madras in search of an advantageous marriage.

The East India Company was a thriving organisation under the care of British shareholders. Using a mix of conflict and negotiation, it was slowly transferring power from the local tribes to meet its own commercial needs. Many of the single men employed there still wanted to marry English brides and so it took little to convince Philadelphia that this lucrative life, far away from London, could soon be one she would enjoy.

Chatty – yes. Outrageous – yes, that too. But not always in a good way considered Mrs Leigh. She would prefer the words flighty, flirtatious and capricious. Men had always been attracted to Philadelphia and she to them. It would be interesting to see if she had mellowed at all in the years that had passed, now that she was a wife and a mother.

It was an exceptionally sultry day in July when the Hancocks arrived and Philadelphia quite literally waltzed into the rectory. Her bright mustard-coloured travelling dress swept through the house, bringing with it clumps of dust and dirt from the road and displacing cobwebs and crumbs along the passageways of the house. She was an impressive sight in her vibrant silk skirt, paired with a beautiful fichu and matching apron of the finest embroidered gauze. Her straw hat was excessively wide and decorated with emerald-green ribbons and she wore black leather shoes with heels and a golden buckle. She was adorned with jewels on every piece of exposed skin and fluttered a carved ivory fan before her face, revealing expertly crafted swirls of flowers and long-tailed birds. Even above the scent associated with hours spent in a carriage, there was an evocative oriental muskiness that wafted when she moved, which Mrs Austen found alluring.

"Cassandra, darling! I see you are every bit as beautiful as my brother describes you." She kissed Mrs Austen on both cheeks and continued to hold on to her shoulders whilst stepping back to admire her. "You look radiant, Sister. The very picture of health. Not at all like I did when I was close to my confinement, I assure you."

Mrs Austen did not feel very radiant next to this exotic flower that had suddenly appeared in her room. In the final stages of her second pregnancy, she felt more like a sack of cabbages than a radiant picture of health.

Philadelphia laughed a tinkling laugh and turned her attention to the room, growing bored when Mrs Austen made no attempt to return the compliment. "What a delightful little cottage. What do you say, Betsy? Come and meet your aunt."

The little girl was a miniature of her mother. Her hair was curled like an adult and she was dressed in a white gown with a broad red sash around her middle. She too wore a straw bonnet with coloured ribbons and had a choker of pearls around her neck.

*'Five years going on fifteen,'* thought Mrs Austen, who was even more dumbfounded when the girl curtseyed before her

and smiled demurely under her eyelids. "Good day, Aunt. I am delighted to meet you."

Mrs Leigh was resting under the shade of a tree when Philadelphia arrived so could observe her without being seen. She quickly concluded that the girl she remembered had not changed at all for the better. Rather, she had developed even more fatalistic feminine flaws than before.

"I must change," asserted Philadelphia, bored again with nothing else noteworthy to comment on. "Come, Betsy, let us get out of these heavy things and put on something lighter." In a flurry of swished skirts, mother and daughter headed upstairs to inspect where they were to sleep and find something more appropriate to wear.

Tysoe Hancock stayed only a few days in Deane before being called back to London on business. Mr Austen accompanied him to act as a witness to some documents, leaving the sisters-in-law at the rectory to become better acquainted on their own. Over cups of tea and simple country fare, Mrs Austen understood Philadelphia more each day. Deep down it seemed she was dissatisfied with love and sought attention. Her husband was dutiful and kind, but he was twenty years her senior and not at all exciting. He was meticulous in his bookkeeping, took his work seriously and had little spontaneity. She craved a man like Warren Hastings, a man who wrote poetry and enjoyed classical literature. He showered Betsy with gifts and made them all feel special.

Philadelphia was still at the rectory when the second Austen child was born in August. He was christened George after his father. Philadelphia made an excellent birthing companion and had the house running like clockwork while Mrs Austen was regaining her strength. She took her fair share of chores with the newborn and even Mrs Leigh could not fail to be impressed by her efficiency.

The new baby was different altogether to Jemmy. George was calm and gentle and hardly made a murmur, whereas Jemmy had been whiny and complaining from the start. George seemed to sleep for hours and not ask for food. He seemed content to simply roll his eyes and lie in his cradle. But he did have little Betsy to fuss over him all day, thought Mrs Austen. Maybe that was the difference?

# Chapter 4

### 1767-1768
### The Austens move to Steventon.

When baby George was old enough to go to Cheesedown Farm, Jemmy came home for good. He was nearly two by now and an active little boy. Betsy had just turned six and assumed the role of his mother. She washed him and brushed his hair and dressed him in his little frocks to run about. She read to him and sang to him and kept him happily entertained.

Jemmy adored her and cried when she went away. His face beamed brightly when she returned, which she frequently did and Philadelphia and Betsy became familiar sights in Deane with their colourful clothes and fashionable styles. They were admired everywhere they went and never missed a service at Steventon Church.

Mr Austen was immensely proud of his family, which was growing by the year, and before they knew it the Austens were in their fourth year of married life. They still lived in the jumbled little rectory at Deane, which was bursting at the seams, and a third son was born the following October. This was Edward whom they addressed as Neddy when he was at home.

Mr Austen could not have been in better spirits. He spent most of his days outside helping his labouring friends with repairs or farming in the fields when he was not required in the church. The fresh air gave him an appetite and he whistled when he made his way back home in the evenings to be greeted by a warm house and a hearty meal. He was insistent that he should kiss his young sons before they were taken off to bed and he prayed for their health with dedication every night.

Mrs Austen's world was slightly different. She loved her children, of course. She loved her husband and her mother without a doubt. But everywhere she turned there was always something to be done or someone that needed tending to. Every minute of her day made demands upon her time and she had not a moment's rest for herself. Organisation was nigh impossible, for every corner and closet was full to overflowing.

Even the gowns that she had so lovingly altered at the start of her first pregnancy were frayed and worn. The finer silks, better suited to a ballroom, were not nearly so hardy when worn to feed her cattle or dig up muddy potatoes. The only material that was anywhere near durable enough was the red riding coat that she had worn for her wedding and which covered her frame every day now like a second skin.

"How are the repairs coming along at the new rectory?" she would appeal to her husband, time and time again. She was desperate for something positive to aim for on those days when the rooms seemed to close in around her.

"Not long now," Mr Austen would reply with a gracious smile, never actually committing to how long he really meant.

A lack of funds was his issue.

Luckily, a timely inheritance from the death of his estranged stepmother saved the day. Mr Austen had lost both of his natural parents by the age of six and his stepmother had made it clear in his infancy that neither he nor his two sisters were welcome in her home after their father died. Instead, she sent them off individually to be raised by different uncles and aunts.

After her death, the terms of the late William Austen's will stipulated that if his second wife were to die before his living children, then the dividends from his estate in Tonbridge should be divided equally between the three of them. This was the inheritance that Mr Austen received.

Philadelphia's share would likely be spent as soon as it was in her purse. The younger sister, Leonora, lived a frugal life with some elderly relatives in London. Her share would probably keep her comfortable for the rest of her days. But for Mr Austen, his sum could not have come at a better time and he knew exactly what to do with it.

"Not long until we can move now, my love," he proclaimed joyfully a few months later. "Only the finishing touches are needed. Our new rectory looks very fine indeed."

Mrs Austen was warming some broth for her mother who was rapidly declining in health. Mrs Leigh had little appetite or energy and her daughter had resorted to spoon-feeding her or else she refused to eat at all.

"That *is* welcome news. I fear Mother needs some peace if she is to improve and there is precious little of that around here."

Mr Austen was too full of optimism for his wife's downcast mood to spoil it. "She will pick up when she's in Steventon, you will see. I will make sure she has the sunniest room in the house where she will never be disturbed." He smiled absently before rushing off on another errand.

Mrs Leigh, however, was not to be jollied by the impending move. "I don't think I can do it, Cassandra. My end is coming soon, I know it. Perhaps it would be best to leave me here with Mary and you go on without me."

"Certainly not!" Mrs Austen was indignant. Mary was her mother's faithful maid, but Mrs Austen would never entertain the idea of her mother being provided for anywhere else but under her own roof.

"It is but a short ride away, Mother, and you shall not have to lift a finger. I will see that you travel there in style, like a queen." She laughed at her comparison, hoping to lighten the heavy atmosphere between them, but Mrs Leigh was not amused. Instead, she spent her last days at Deane writing out her will, labouring over it with her withered hand, convinced she would not survive the journey.

After a flurry of activity to pack everything away, two rickety carts were loaded on a fine July morning, bursting with belongings to take to the new rectory. Anything that did not fit in the carts was packed in sacks or wheelbarrows to be transported by hand with the team of servants. A feather mattress was placed carefully on top of some chairs on one wagon, especially for Mrs Leigh. The plan was to make the half-hour journey as easy for her as possible by transporting her in her bed. Unfortunately, the threat of rumbling wheels rattling over bumpy potholes and ditches was enough to convince her that she would surely fall out. She refused to climb up into the cart and refused to be lifted by the servants. She sat on the ground like a petulant child resisting all help until, in total exasperation, Mrs Austen agreed to lie with her.

What a sight they made! A topsy-turvy collection of furniture and pots and pans jangled and clanged along the rutted roads, with a procession of servants following behind collecting anything that fell off as it moved. On top, the two women sailed past on a glorious feather bed like they were cruising aboard a ship on the sea.

Mr Austen marched off ahead with his bailiff, Mr Bond, both men keen to distance themselves from the embarrassment that trailed behind. Excited children ran alongside the rattling carts, happy to be of help, and a carnival atmosphere began to develop. When they passed by the village green, the gossiping wives standing underneath the maple tree stopped mid-sentence, with gaping mouths, to watch the bewildering spectacle glide past.

Steventon Rectory stood in a shallow valley surrounded by meadows and elm trees. Its position on the corner of two lanes provided excellent visibility from the windows, front and back. There was a pond on the grounds and, best of all, the wash house out back boasted its own water pump. This meant that the servants would not have to traipse through the village with their buckets but could simply nip out the back door and collect what they needed in a fraction of the time. There was plenty of space to grow vegetables and flowers, along with lush pastureland for the cows. There were two parlours, two kitchens, a study for Mr Austen and multiple bedrooms and attics. It really was a stately house compared to the smaller rectory at Deane.

No soon as the carts pulled up on the large sweep driveway, the servants set to work forming a human chain. Furniture was lifted, sacks unpacked and before the afternoon was out

Mrs Leigh was sitting up much more serenely on solid land. Her feather mattress was now upon its rightful bed frame and she sipped a peaceful cup of tea in her sunny, airy room.

"This is nice, is it not, my love?" reviewed Mr Austen later that evening. He placed his arm around his wife's waist and surveyed his new home as darkness fell around them.

Mrs Austen was exhausted but for the first time in months, she could see real potential. Just the walk from the parlour to the kitchen took more steps than made up the entire downstairs at Deane. Their old furniture looked small in the vastness of the rooms and by daylight, the sun had streamed in from every angle. The heavy scent of grass at twilight was sweet and there were no other sounds to disturb them except for the occasional bleating of sheep.

"Yes. 'Tis very nice," agreed Mrs Austen. "I think I shall like it here."

# Chapter 5

**1768-1769**
**A Family Secret.**

Mrs Leigh's predictions about her health were tragically accurate and within weeks of the move to Steventon, the feather mattress that had carried her on the cart was destined to become her deathbed. Time was running out in front of her and she was agitated. She had witnessed her daughter's rise in the world at long last, with the acquisition of this fine house, but the old woman knew of a secret that could threaten it all.

"There are stories, Cassandra, about Philadelphia. Stories that you should know."

Mrs Austen remained silent next to her mother's bed.

"Stories of Philadelphia and Mr Hastings," the frail woman repeated, insistent that she should be heard. "I have heard from Lady Clive's mother," she croaked. "There was a scandal in India. Lady Clive has been instructed by her husband to have nothing to do with Philadelphia. He says her reputation will be harmed if they are seen together."

Lord and Lady Clive were highly influential in the East India Company; if they were involved it was likely the gossip had already spread far and wide.

Mrs Austen shifted uneasily in her chair. She did not wish to hear any more, yet simultaneously respected her mother's desire to speak. Mrs Austen's sister, Jane Leigh, was also in the room having been summoned a day earlier because of their mother's rapid decline in health.

"Everything I am telling you is true, Cassandra," Mrs Leigh battled on bravely. "You must heed what I say." She coughed on her words and Jane Leigh helped her with her tonic. "There are rumours that young Betsy is not her father's child."

She coughed again and Mrs Austen appealed with her eyes to her sister to stop her mother's ramblings. But Jane Leigh only returned a look to confirm that their mother was speaking the truth.

"It is Mr Hastings. People say that *he* is Betsy's true father. Everyone who knew them in India suspects it was so. Philadelphia is a silly fool, Cassandra. Mr Hastings will never be loyal to her."

The coughing fit worsened and Mrs Leigh lay back down to rest. James Leigh-Perrot then entered the room, having also been summoned to be with his dying mother and the topic was dropped. But as she sat staring into the darkness of the night, Mrs Austen replayed the conversation in her mind. Everything made sense now: Philadelphia's behaviour, Mr Hastings' attention, Betsy's devotion to her godfather who spoiled her a little too much...

Mrs Austen matured that night and looked at the world in a new and perplexing light. She thought of the harsh lectures that her mother had given her during her adolescence and the unbending insistence that rules of class and respectability must always be adhered to. *She* had that responsibility now to instil the same values into her own children. It was imperative that she become a better judge of character to determine the intentions of anyone her children befriended. She must teach them how to avoid bringing scandal to their own door.

When the maid entered the room to bring some tea at daybreak, Mr Austen accompanied her to check how things were. He stroked his wife's shoulder as tears pooled in her eyes. The sadness, he thought, was down to the grief she was feeling for Mrs Leigh, but for Mrs Austen, there was more to it. Had her husband heard the whispers about Philadelphia and Mr Hastings she wondered, or was he as innocent as she had been before her mother spoke? Should she reveal the truth to him or were some things better left unsaid?

\* \* \*

Meanwhile, in London, Tysoe Hancock was troubled. When he had come to England three years previously he had meant it to be a permanent move. He had accumulated substantial wealth from his time with the East India Company and had looked forward to a quiet and comfortable retirement. But his intentions had not gone to plan and his money was running out faster than he liked.

The reason for it was that Philadelphia was extravagant, Betsy was demanding and their good friend, Warren Hastings, was immensely generous with his gifts. What else could poor Tysoe do but spend?

Now though, he faced serious debts unless he found more of an income. Begrudgingly, he resigned himself to going back to India for two or three more years. His opportunities would be far easier to come by in Bengal than in London.

"When I come home next time we must be more careful," he warned his wife before sailing off. "We have had our fun, but money does not last forever. I can't afford to squander what I bring back on my return."

Philadelphia had not even bothered to acknowledge her husband's remarks. Life was for living and that's what she intended to do. It was only by mixing in high society that she could ensure Betsy would make a good match. It was this that motivated her above everything else.

"I will keep a good eye on them both in your absence," Mr Hastings had reassured Tysoe as the travelling trunks were loaded onto the carriage. "You can depend on me."

Tysoe made no reply.

\* \* \*

Mrs Leigh died at the end of August with her children at her bedside. She could not have wished for a more peaceful ending to her life of sixty-two years and was laid to rest three days later by Mr Austen in the chancel of Steventon Church.

As was the custom, no ladies were present at the funeral, so it was not until the next day that Mrs Leigh's two daughters could pay their final respects at her resting place. They made plans for a smart stone tablet to be inscribed as a lasting memorial to their mother and took as much comfort as they could from the fact that she was now reunited with their father in heaven.

It had always been a subject of contention with Mrs Austen that the church sought to separate mourners by their sex.

Surely this was the time when unified support was needed more than any other when the loss was most raw. But, in honour of her mother's scrupulous attention to respectability, she abided by the tradition without complaint.

Life had been put on hold at the rectory whilst Mrs Leigh was ill and Mrs Austen had ventured nowhere beyond Cheesedown Farm or St Nicholas' Church since moving to Steventon. She had not yet had the chance to feel properly integrated into the community, but this was remedied once she changed into her black mourning attire and the villagers came by to offer their condolences. Like Deane, Steventon was a neighbourhood where everyone looked out for one another. Everyone had a purpose where farming dictated the need and the humans filled the gaps. Travelling workers added variety from time to time but otherwise, life was quiet and uneventful. Mrs Austen was touched by this show of support, just as she had been when she first arrived in Deane after her marriage.

When autumn turned to winter, the youngest of the Austen boys came home from Cheesedown Farm and the rectory rang out with the sounds of all three sons: Jemmy, who was four and a half; George, who was three and Neddy, who had just turned two.

Philadelphia and Betsy continued to be regular visitors and the young girl had her cousins dancing to her every tune. "Play with me. Fetch that for me. Walk with me." Like a mother duck with her little ducklings, she would lead the brothers around the meadows in a line.

Warren Hastings followed in the footsteps of Tysoe Hancock and returned to India. The offer of a promotion lured him there and, considering that he had also lived far beyond his means in London, it was not a hard decision for him to make.

Mrs Austen never did find the courage to enlighten her husband on her mother's revelations about Betsy's parentage, but the knowledge of it made her less tolerant of her sister-in-law's sighs and complaints whenever she bemoaned her married state.

One morning, Philadelphia received a bundle of letters that had been delivered from an East India ship accompanied by a large wooden box. Letters from abroad always came in a bundle because no matter when they were written, they could not be dispatched until a suitable ship sailed to bring them to England. Philadelphia was growing increasingly frustrated as she read them and it was obvious they contained disagreeable news.

"Insufferable man!" she exclaimed, stamping her foot impatiently as she scanned the cursive writing.

"Whatever is the matter now?"

"I told my husband that I was intending to bring Betsy back to India. And he has refused us! Can you believe it?"

"I'm sure he must have his reasons," said Mrs Austen, jumping to her brother-in-law's defence.

"Here. Read it for yourself." Philadelphia handed over the letter, which was crumpled from where she had gripped it so tightly and Mrs Austen perused the carefully scribed words.

Tysoe was worried about the danger of the journey and made an excellent case to his wife that Bengal had changed considerably since the time they had lived there together. It had degraded dramatically in his estimation and he declared it now to be lewd and inhospitable. There was no mistaking his message that nothing could induce him to introduce his young daughter into such a society.

Mrs Austen did not consider Tysoe's explanation unreasonable and expressed her opinion so. But Philadelphia was in no mood to listen.

"What is the good of us staying here – all alone – with nothing to do? He cares nothing for *our* feelings and what *we* may want. If he will not allow us to go to India, then I shall have to find something else to keep us entertained." She stormed out of the room without a word of apology and Mrs Austen stood confused.

It was normal to hear her sister-in-law grumble about Tysoe's tedious character, but one thing the two women usually did agree on was that Tysoe always had Betsy's best interests at heart. He evidently loved his family and would do anything to protect them, be that in his own mundane way. It made no sense that Philadelphia should be so suddenly enraged when Tysoe was only displaying the same stuffy devotion he always did. Intrigued, she picked up a second letter that lay discarded beside the first. This note contained news of Warren Hastings who was once more lodging near Tysoe in India.

Mr Hastings had a new lady friend. Her name was Mrs Imhoff, and the two had met on the ship that had taken him over to India. Tysoe was very complimentary of this stranger and made no secret of the fact that Mr Hastings was very fond of her.

'Oh dear, that must have hurt,' sympathised Mrs Austen, placing the letter down. The words of old Mrs Leigh came back to her: *'Philadelphia is a silly fool, Cassandra. Mr Hastings will never be loyal to her.'* At least now she understood the reason for the outburst.

An hour after she had taken herself off, Philadelphia reappeared in the parlour looking more composed and proceeded to unpack the wooden box that had arrived with her letters. Trying not to make it obvious she was watching, Mrs Austen glanced from the edge of her vision to see Philadelphia unpacking luxurious gift after luxurious gift. Tysoe had sent his wife's favourite fragrance oil accompanied by several bolts of silk, brightly coloured in rich, warm shades. Next out of the box were softly patterned muslins, refreshingly cool in contrast. The fabrics held the scent of aromatic spices which wafted tantalisingly around the room and wrapped in amongst them were jars of preserves containing oddly shaped fruits.

It was funny, thought Mrs Austen cynically, how Philadelphia despised her husband and yet she never once complained about the generous gifts he continued to send her.

For the rest of her stay at the rectory, Philadelphia kept her temper at bay by writing to various tutors whom she intended to engage for Betsy on their return to London. She was determined that her daughter would beat any other female in a competition for the best performer – be that in music, horsemanship, languages or the arts.

She would not rest until Betsy was the most accomplished young lady in England.

# Chapter 6

**Extended Family.**

Another family member close to Mr Austen was his half-brother, William Hampson-Walter. Both men shared the same mother, with William being the product of her first marriage and Mr Austen, Philadelphia and Leonora being the result of her second. Mr Walter lived near Philadelphia and Betsy in London with his wife Susannah. Most of their offspring were grown up, but the youngest child, Philly, was the same age as Betsy and the two girls were regular playmates. Their eldest boy was ordained into the church, another had expressed a desire to teach, and a further two sons were being educated to help run their father's business interests in Jamaica.

Susannah was an amiable woman with an empathetic nature. When her husband was away in the West Indies, she was invited for a stay in Steventon. It was a pleasure for Mrs Austen to have another female to talk to who was different in every way from Philadelphia. Young Philly was a contrast to Betsy too, and no trouble at all.

One afternoon in June, an impending storm confined all

the children indoors. The air was warm despite the rain and the windows of the rectory had been left open to blow in a breeze. Thunder threatened from the oppressive, darkening sky.

Jemmy and Neddy took little notice of the weather and settled themselves down to play a game with their marbles. Philly sat on an armchair, casually turning the pages of a book. George, meanwhile, looked up in angst at the open window and pointed towards it, grunting incomprehensibly. He was four years old and yet Mrs Austen still found his actions frustrating; she could never understand what he wanted to say and he could never make himself clear.

"What do you want?" she snapped. "'Tis too warm to close the window. Why do you point so?"

The boy continued to gesture and grunt and Mrs Austen looked to Susannah for support.

"I do wish he would hurry with his words. I can't understand a thing that he asks."

"Has he ever spoken?" probed Susannah gently.

"He tries," began Mrs Austen, wanting to believe it true. "He tries to copy his brothers, but Neddy is so much further ahead and he's a lot younger."

It was something Mrs Austen had always avoided speaking about. When Philadelphia had suggested George was thick-headed she had changed the subject and assured her he was fine. But now she could not deny it. The series of niggles she had kept locked away were about to cascade free.

"There are other things too," she continued. "You see he is still not dry, even though Neddy is. And he cannot properly feed himself without my help."

Susannah continued to watch the boy, still nervously

looking out the window. His eyes rolled to the ceiling before coming back into focus.

"Sometimes he has fits. He trembles and I can't wake him. They may be only momentary but they do frighten me."

"Yes," soothed Susannah. "I can see he's different from his brothers. Different to how my boys were too. Do you find he plays well?"

"No," admitted Mrs Austen heavily. "That was the first thing Mrs Littleworth observed of him when he went to stay at Cheesedown Farm. He never played with the other children - would not even look at them, she said."

Mrs Austen's speech dried up and Susannah stayed still. Her own children had their quirks and ailments, but she could see that this was something more.

"I fear ..." started Mrs Austen again and then stopped.

"Go on," urged Susannah. "It's best to talk about it. How else can we make it better?"

"I fear he's an imbecile. The same as my brother, Thomas. He had fits as a boy and they only got worse as he grew. My mother had to send him away when I was a girl and he never came home again."

A child with an affliction brought shame upon a household, everyone knew that. If a respectable suitor knew there was a history of madness in the family, they would withdraw their interest immediately and move on to someone new. Young George could not stay hidden for long in the rectory; he must be put discreetly out of the way.

Grateful for Susannah's sympathetic ear and the cosy atmosphere developing in the sitting room, Mrs Austen called for tea. Several refreshing cups later and feeling much lighter than she had in a long time, Mrs Austen thanked Susannah for listening.

"That's what mothers do, Cass. We listen to each other and share our wisdom. I don't know how I would have brought up my own family without a friend helping me to make sense of my mind sometimes. I'm delighted to be of help, but we must make a plan; we must consider what's best for George."

Using the word 'we' as opposed to the word 'you' made Mrs Austen feel less alone. George was ultimately her responsibility, but knowing Susannah was there for consultation and support was heartening.

"So," considered the practical mentor. "Do you know whatever became of your brother after he went away?"

"Yes. He went to live with a couple in Monk Sherborne. Their details were with my mother's papers when she died. He still lives there, I understand – Mrs Cullum continues to receive an allowance to care for him."

"Well, that's where we'll start," decided Susannah. "We will write to Mrs Cullum and ask after your brother. If the lady is experienced in looking after him, she will be happy to engage in a conversation."

"Oh no," retorted Mrs Austen, clamming up uncomfortably now that real action was a possibility. "She's a stranger to us. I wouldn't want her knowing all our business."

"She's not a stranger though, is she?" pointed out Susannah. "Your mother chose her especially to look after your brother. She must be discreet or else he wouldn't be there after all these years. Think of her as extended family – like me." She smiled warmly at Mrs Austen and carefully removed the cup and saucer from Mrs Austen's lap that she had been gripping on to tightly. "I'll help you draft the letter if you like, Cass," she offered. "We have to start somewhere."

Mrs Austen smiled back. "You're right," she accepted.

"Good. Now let us make a list of your observations ready for when the good woman replies."

\* \* \*

When the time came for Susannah and Philly to leave Steventon, Mrs Austen accompanied them back to London. Her sister, Jane, was due to have her first baby and she had specifically asked for Mrs Austen to be her birthing companion. It seemed sensible under the circumstances to share a carriage as they were all heading in the same direction.

Jane Leigh had married Reverend Edward Cooper two years previously and the couple–lived with his mother in Reading. This was the first trip that Mrs Austen had taken to visit her there and she was excited to experience life in a different household. She first planned to take the coach to London and stay with Philadelphia for one night, then leave the next morning for her sister's house. But the news that greeted her arrival was not what she had expected and Philadelphia was not at home. Mrs Cooper had gone into labour early and when the call had come to seek Mrs Austen's help, Philadelphia had gone instead to assist with the birth.

Mrs Austen's heart pumped rapidly and she felt flush with sudden heat, but all was well confirmed Clarinda, the Hancock's housekeeper whom they had brought back with them from India. Word had already arrived from her mistress that Mr and Mrs Cooper were the proud parents of a son. Mother and baby were well and the boy was to be named Edward, after his father.

\* \* \*

The trip to London reignited in Mrs Austen a desire to travel. She had enjoyed staying with her sister immensely, although it had made her realise how much she missed her own children when she helped with baby Edward. She had also enjoyed day trips around the city with Philadelphia and Susannah, and she warmed to the thought that her old independent spirit had not disappeared entirely: it was simply locked away.

"We must take our boys to see their relations," she petitioned her husband soon after arriving back in Steventon. "If they are to grow up to be gentlemen, then they must see more of the world."

Mr Austen smiled. "You sound like your mother, my love. That is exactly what she would say if she were alive."

"Yes, she would," laughed Mrs Austen. "God rest her soul. She never failed to remind me of my obligations."

December was the chosen month for the trip and everything was planned precisely. First, they would stay with the Coopers in Reading and then later travel to the Leigh-Perrots at Scarlets. Poor afflicted George was unsuitable for travel, so he stayed at Cheesedown Farm. Unfortunately, a nasty cough kept Neddy at home too, meaning only Jemmy could accompany his parents to meet his new baby cousin in Reading.

Neddy recovered sufficiently for the second journey and Mr and Mrs Austen left Steventon with two excited boys to keep entertained on the long road to their rich uncle and aunt in Berkshire. Mr Austen packed books and maps to show his sons where they were going, and Mrs Austen ensured there was food and spare clothes enough to keep them happy and clean.

They had a wonderful time. The upper-class touches that were out of place in a rural rectory were well and truly appreciated by them all. When the new year came around, Mrs Austen felt a renewed sense of optimism.

By the end of January, she discovered she was with child again and, coincidentally, so was Mrs Cooper. In their frequent letter exchanges, they compared the progress of their pregnancies and speculated which sister would be first in their confinement. Both were due around the same time.

In the end, Mrs Austen was first. Henry Austen entered the world on June 8th, two weeks before little Jane Cooper. Both babies were fit and strong and that was all that mattered.

Mrs Cooper had more exciting news to announce shortly after - her family was moving to Bath and they would be in their new house by Christmas. Mr Cooper's elderly mother had died and he had used his inheritance money to purchase a property on the brand-new Royal Crescent. It was still being built and to be the most fashionable of addresses once complete.

"Why does everyone else have money and we have none?" moaned Mrs Austen one night, thinking of her brother and her sister in their luxurious houses. "Where did we go wrong?"

"Wrong?" contested Mr Austen. "What makes you think we are the ones in the wrong, my love? I wouldn't swap our life here in Steventon for twenty houses on Royal Crescent."

"Hmmm," seethed Mrs Austen, stubbing her toe on the unyielding bed frame in the dark. What would she do with such a choice?

# Chapter 7

## 1772-1773
### Broken Hearts.

Philadelphia was ever present at Steventon. Betsy even referred to the rectory now as 'my home in the country', which Mr Austen found presumptuous and amusing in equal measure. She was ten years old and growing into a provocative young lady. Even at that age she understood the reaction a pitiful face and pretend tears could evoke in her male cousins. She wore sprays of her mother's perfume so that Jemmy would tell her she smelled nice. She wrapped the shawls her father had sent her from India loosely about her shoulders, knowing full well they would slip off when she ran and the boys would be obliged to pick them up and chase after her.

Jemmy couldn't wait for his cousin to come and play and he did whatever she asked of him. Some days they ran to the village, some days they played spillikins or building blocks. On other days, they made dens under the trees in the orchard.

"You're my favourite," she whispered to him as they sailed leaf boats together on the pond. "Neddy is so dull. I have much more fun with you."

Jemmy felt he would burst with pride.

When he was called to church one morning to help his father, Betsy stayed at home with her aunt. She watched Mrs Austen feed and change baby Henry and was fascinated by every movement her aunt's hands made.

"Would you like to help?" Mrs Austen asked, seeing the wonder in Betsy's eyes at the baby's tiny moving limbs and fingers. "Come, let me show you what to do."

She directed the girl on how to tie the bows on Henry's frock and showed her how he laughed and blew tiny bubbles when they played peek-a-boo. She sat Betsy down on a big chair and encouraged her to hold him and sing him a lullaby. Henry gurgled and smiled most contentedly and soon fell asleep in her lap. She was still staring at him in awe when Jemmy rushed through the door, freed from his errands and eager to play outside.

"Shhh!" she instructed angrily when his noise threatened to wake the sleeping infant. "Go away," she hissed.

Jemmy was stunned by her words and could not believe his eyes when he watched her kiss Henry's forehead. "Not you, Henry," she whispered to his baby brother. "I didn't mean for you to go away. You're my favourite."

Jemmy ran off, and his father found him later crying by the pond.

"I fear Jemmy has experienced his first broken heart," Mr Austen informed his wife when he came back indoors.

"Poor child," she sympathised. "But I can't say I'm surprised. Betsy has been toying with his affections for weeks without a care in the world for his feelings. It would mortify Tysoe to see the way she behaves."

"Yes," agreed Mr Austen. "She has become a frivolous tease

this past year. I fear she will break many more hearts before she's done."

\* \* \*

When Mrs Austen delivered her fifth child in January, she was delighted to find it was a girl.

"At last," gushed her husband. "We have our beautiful Cassandra to name after you, my love."

Mrs Austen stroked her daughter's crumpled cheek, content that the hard labour was over and she had several days of bed rest to look forward to. With a perfect, pretty daughter to add to her collection of handsome sons, she had every reason to feel proud of her achievements. But a huge black cloud still hung over the rectory in the form of afflicted young George, who was soon to depart for his new home with the Cullums in Monk Sherborne.

Mrs Cullum had been all kindness and help since receiving Mrs Austen's first letter and the two women had kept up correspondence. Little by little, Mrs Austen had been convinced that it was the right thing to do, to put her troubled child under the care of this more experienced woman. After indulging herself to keep him at Steventon for his sixth birthday, his departure beckoned at the end of August. All his clothes and possessions were sent onwards by cart, but Mrs Austen wanted to walk there, hand in hand with her boy, for one last time.

They left the house quietly after breakfast, carrying a basket of strawberries and a selection of George's favourite treats. To passers-by they looked like any other mother and son going about their daily visits and Mrs Austen maintained this pretence the whole way there. "Look at how plump those damsons are," she pointed out as they passed by a row of fruit trees. Then a little further on, "Let us sit here a while and take some refreshment."

No amount of dawdling and distraction, however, could prevent the inevitable and it was obvious that George was ready for a nice long rest when they reached the Cullum's farm.

Mrs Cullum was there to greet them, simply and without fuss as if they came by every day. She took them straight to George's room on the first floor, which was across the landing from the room where Mrs Austen's brother, Thomas, had lived all these years. He paid them no attention when they walked past.

Mrs Austen could see instantly that her brother was secure, recognising that whoever came and went through the house meant him no harm. He sat humming to himself, gazing cheerfully out of the window, with a small picture book of birds on his bedside table and a cup and ball laid down neatly beside it. He looked so reassuringly happy that Mrs Austen was engulfed by a wave of confusing emotion which she could not label. Whatever it was, it made her heart giddy and her eyes sting.

Young George's room was a duplicate of the other, with a similar picture book and cup and ball on the bedside table. It was silent and calm and George sat down to test the bed. 'So much space,' he seemed to say mutely, looking around in astonishment.

He had been used to sharing a room with his brother in the rectory, where the noise of his companions had always been his biggest source of frustration. Immediately, he was drawn to the large window, which was all his own, and he smiled at a cockerel chasing a hen. The sun shone down on the water butt, making it sparkle and shine, and its reflection made dancing patterns along the wall.

After a minute, Mrs Austen placed her hand gently upon her son's shoulder. She told him softly that she was going downstairs, but he did not even turn around, so fascinated was he by his new sanctuary.

It was probably best he hadn't looked, realised Mrs Austen as she made her way down the wooden stairs clinging on to the rail. No matter how much she had been desperate to look upon George's face for one last time, he would never have understood the pain he would see in her eyes, nor the tears that streamed uncontrollably down her cheeks.

Mrs Cullum led her to the bright farmhouse kitchen and offered sweet tea and cake to energise her. Mrs Austen was grateful for how easy this woman was trying to make the whole sorry experience; she was a kind and generous soul, as well as a soundly capable woman. She promised repeatedly that she would send word should George become distressed, but even more forcefully she assured Mrs Austen that she was certain he would not.

It would be better, the new guardian asserted, that Mrs Austen did not return to see her son again. It would only confuse him, she explained in the kindest possible way, knowing that he would soon forget her quite naturally and that would be for the best.

Before the women parted, Mrs Cullum promised faithfully that she would make the boy happy and, after seeing her brother looking so well, Mrs Austen could not dispute that this would surely be true.

When she arrived back at the rectory that evening, with sore feet and a throbbing head, Mrs Austen was extremely fractious. She instantly picked a fight with her husband when he asked after George; she scolded the cook for burning the chops and she smacked Jemmy about the head when he carelessly spilt some cream on the tablecloth. As if that were not enough, she broke the handle of the cream jug when she insisted on clearing up the mess herself.

Everyone in the house gave her a wide berth, instinctively understanding what was wrong, but nothing could give her consolation. The only task she found she could submit to, was to write a letter to Susannah:

*'He was not in the slightest bit upset. In fact, I think he was enjoying being there as far as I could tell. His room was peaceful and spacious, and he was watching the chickens in the yard when I left. He did not concern himself at all that I was going, and Mrs Cullum was very kind.'*

She sobbed hysterically as she wrote the words, her quill flowing absently around the wicked thoughts that troubled every breath. Nothing could describe adequately the shame and guilt she felt about what she had done that day. How would she ever be able to forgive herself?

# Chapter 8

**1773**

**Mr Austen opens a school.**

Mr Austen was presented with the living of All Saint's Church in Deane, in addition to his church at Steventon. He was busier than ever with two parishes to run, but money in the growing household was still tight. The latest concern was for the boys' education and how he was going to afford to pay for it.

"I think I will tutor them myself, my love," he announced to his wife after a few days' contemplation. "I still have my books from Tonbridge and can follow the same curricula to prepare the boys for Oxford."

"But when will you have the time? You are out all day as it is. Who will do the work when you're teaching?"

"I will employ another man."

Mrs Austen sighed, forever the realist. "And how are you going to pay for another man?"

Mr Austen looked pleased. He had been expecting this question and had his answer ready. "I thought I might open a school in the rectory. We can take in boarders to help cover the bills."

"A school? Here?"

"Yes, my love. A school. Right here. Where Jemmy and Neddy can learn alongside other scholars. Henry too when he's old enough. What do you say?"

Mrs Austen did not know what to say, having the idea sprung on her like that, but she could not dispute that the idea had merit. In fact, the more she considered it, the more she felt it could work. Jemmy and Neddy would certainly be more inclined to study harder with peers to learn alongside them, and now that poor George was no longer living there, and Henry and Cassandra were still at Cheesedown Farm, there was plenty of space for lodgers.

"I suppose now would be a good time to do it," she conceded, inwardly grateful that a new project may distract her from the depression she had fallen into since young George had moved away. "We can use the attic rooms as lodgings, and I will have some free time myself until the little ones come home. I could help the pupils settle in."

"My thoughts exactly," replied Mr Austen, somewhat surprised at how easy it had been to gain his wife's approval.

"But you must promise me you will only take in respectable boys. Our sons must have the very best of classmates to model themselves on."

"Without question, my love. I already have my first pupil in mind."

Nobody could complain about the credentials of this boy; Viscount Lymington was the son of the 2nd Earl of Portsmouth, the Honourable John Wallop. He was five years old and displayed erratic behaviour that his parents wanted Mr Austen to correct. They felt that a quiet boarding school in the country would be just the place to do it.

A schoolroom was duly set up in the back parlour of the rectory and laid out with a long wooden table and chairs. A globe and a microscope sat at one end, whilst bookcases filled the walls with manuscripts of History, Classics, Mathematics and Religion. Mr Austen dressed in his university attire of white wig and black gown to teach and addressed each boy by his full name. This helped his sons to differentiate when he was their schoolmaster, and when he later became their papa.

The daily lessons commenced soon after breakfast. First, they said their prayers then began with either Mathematics or Natural Philosophy. According to the topic, this could be an explanation of algebra or sums, or observations of plants, animals and rocks.

During the morning, Mr Austen gave the boys a break in the yard, where they would devour bread and butter or a piece of pie made especially for them by Cook. They would eat it sitting on a wall, watching Mrs Austen tending to her ducks and turkeys and she would quiz them about what they had learned that day. She feigned silly ignorance so they would explain something more fully, and it always made them laugh how little she knew compared to them.

Before lunch, it was the turn of Poetry, History, Geography or Languages. After a hearty mid-day meal, the boys then moved on to practical tasks such as Agriculture, Woodwork or Art.

It was a well-rounded curriculum, designed to prepare the boys for the university entrance exams they would face in the future and introduce them to the skills which a respectable gentleman would be expected to possess when he was out in society.

Jemmy and Neddy had always been receptive to learning, but Viscount Lymington found it hard to settle. He was a delicate child with silky blond hair that grew long past his shoulders. His limbs were loose and limp compared to the sturdiness of the Austen boys and he made the most bizarre remarks.

One morning the boys were studying a passage from Virgil's *Aeneid* and Neddy was reading aloud. He spoke with a firm, scholarly voice and Jemmy and Viscount Lymington were following the text silently in their books.

*"For what offense the Queen of Heav'n began*
*To persecute so brave, so just a man;"*

"Persecute!" shouted out the viscount without warning. "Persecute! I like that word."

"It may be a fine-sounding word, but do you understand the meaning?" asked Mr Austen, bemused.

"Of course. To hurt people you don't like. To be cruel because you can. Because you have the power."

"Hmm, so not a very nice word after all?" suggested Mr Austen.

The viscount would not be silenced and repeated the word over and over.

"What is the antithesis of that word, James Austen?" Mr Austen demanded, grasping for distraction.

"To be tolerant, Sir," replied the scholar, making his father relieved and proud at the same time.

"Quite right, boy. We need to be tolerant of everyone, regardless of our differences. Now you remember that all of you." He spoke in a raised voice, aiming to put an end to the discussion.

"But not if we don't like them," persisted Viscount Lymington, refusing to take the hint. "Then they deserve to be persecuted."

It took several minutes before Mr Austen could resume control of his classroom and move on to something new, but he was growing increasingly concerned by the behaviour he was noticing daily in this troubled pupil.

He was not the only one to see it either, and things reached a climax when Mr and Mrs Leigh-Perrot were on a visit to the rectory in June. Mrs Austen was entertaining them in the smaller of the two parlours, now that the schoolroom occupied the larger one, and they looked quite out of place sat amongst the dust in all their finery. Mr Leigh-Perrot was discussing a portrait that he was soon to sit for, to be painted in oil by a distinguished artist.

"His works are exquisite," confirmed Mrs Leigh-Perrot. "He has been invited to all the great country houses, so it is quite an honour for Perrot to be chosen as his next commission," she bragged.

"I seek your advice, Sister," bumbled the gentleman. "Shall I wear my dark blue jacket or my light blue, do you think?"

"I think dark every time," replied Mrs Austen, as if she were an expert in art. "A gentleman in a dark colour always looks more refined in my opinion."

Mrs Leigh-Perrot smiled triumphantly. "That is my view exactly." Her sharp, narrow features contrasted pointedly with her husband's soft, doughy face. "He was insistent it should be the light blue," she revealed to Mrs Austen. "But now you see, Perrot, both of us women cannot be wrong."

"Very well," he conceded good-naturedly. "But I did so want to wear my buff breeches. They are more stylish than the black ones. More on the edge of fashion, I think." He looked quite dejected at not being allowed to choose his own clothes and his bottom lip protruded beyond the top one.

"You can still wear your buff breeches. And your buff waistcoat," interjected his wife. "Why do you always think otherwise?"

"Yes, I agree. Buff and navy go well together," supported Mrs Austen.

Raised voices from the schoolroom broke through their conversation and they all stopped to listen.

"That is enough! James Austen, Edward Austen, to my study now. Viscount Lymington, you may pack away your things and go outside. Lessons are concluded for this morning."

The viscount trotted out with a self-important air and Jemmy and Neddy stood shamefaced outside their father's study, waiting for him to come and admit them.

"Whatever has gone on in there?" wondered Mr Leigh-Perrot, amused. "Someone has been a naughty boy," he chuckled.

It was most unusual for Mr Austen to lose his temper like that, Mrs Austen explained diplomatically. She hoped very much that Jemmy and Neddy were not picking up bad habits from Viscount Lymington.

"He's a funny little chap, isn't he?" remarked Mr Leigh-Perrot. "I was watching him yesterday in the yard and he has some very odd behaviours. He purposely ignored me when I tried to speak to him and I'm sure I heard him curse when he walked off."

When the adults sat down together in the evening after the boys had gone to bed, Mr Austen told his guests about the commotion in the schoolroom. Viscount Lymington had been reading aloud but seemed to have some difficulty with his pronunciation. He repeatedly misread a word, making it sound like something vulgar the boys had heard the farm workers use in the fields. Neddy had sniggered and the viscount had repeated it.

Mr Austen relayed how he had tried to ignore this immature behaviour, but then Jemmy had joined in too. Before long, all three boys could not stop laughing and that was when Mr Austen had abandoned the lesson. He was humiliated by his sons' behaviour and would not tolerate them making fun of anyone. They were to be punished with no play breaks, no treats from Cook and extra homework for a week.

Jemmy and Neddy bore the punishment well and apologised to both their father and the viscount without having to be prompted. But when they deemed their father was in a more receptive mood, they felt it was imperative he should learn the truth. Viscount Lymington was the one who always laughed at them, they explained to him; it had never been the other way round. He was also cruel to the animals. They had seen him throw stones at a bird in its nest and chase after the goslings to kick them. Only yesterday he had pulled the legs off a spider, one after another, and laughed as he plucked them away. They felt he was a most frightening child.

When Lady Lymington came to collect her son for the Christmas holidays, she was dissatisfied with the progress he had made and disappointed that his manners had not improved. The young viscount did not return to Steventon again.

# Chapter 9

1774-1776
**A Plaything for Cassy.**

T he absence of Viscount Lymington was not mourned
by anyone, and a new boy quickly replaced him in
the schoolroom: William Vanderstegen. Mrs Austen
was acquainted with his family from her days in Harpsden
and welcomed him warmly. Everybody liked him from the
start. He was thirteen years old, a studious scholar, and had a
pleasing and friendly personality.

The babies, too, kept coming and another son was born to
Mr and Mrs Austen in April, whom they christened Francis.
As rewarding as motherhood was, Mrs Austen could not
help but sometimes be short-tempered. In her ten years
of marriage, she had borne six children and her body was
tired. Her own privileged upbringing was a distant memory,
and on top of her children's demands, her current life was
augmented by the growing of vegetables and the farming of
poultry and cattle. The letters she received from her family
only ever relayed how her sister was living a magnificent life
in Bath, or how her brother was growing richer at Scarlets.
Philadelphia had taken a larger residence in London and now

kept her own carriage. Mrs Austen could not imagine any of them experiencing the bone-aching weariness that she did. Consequently, petty arguments were commonplace when she was in a bad mood, although the milder-natured Mr Austen generally refused to let them bother him. Until that is, a letter from Tysoe Hancock provoked the worst disagreement of their married life.

"My word! Betsy is a lucky girl indeed…" muttered Mr Austen as he read.

Mrs Austen was spreading some bed sheets over the bushes to the side of the rectory whilst Mr Austen lingered in the garden with his post. It was wash day and there was much to do. If she was to stay on top of things, Mrs Austen had no choice but to help the washerwoman who came in one day a week.

"Mr Hastings has bequeathed a large sum of money on his goddaughter to be put in a trust until she comes of age," explained Mr Austen, sharing the contents of his letter. "Tysoe has asked that I be one of the trustees."

"How much will she get?" huffed Mrs Austen.

"Ten thousand pounds. Enough to bring her four hundred a year if she's lucky. And then, of course, she will have her own father's legacy on top of that when he dies."

"Pah!" The overburdened woman felt a fury rise inside her that she had no means of stopping. "Do they not realise she will fritter it all away without a care in the world, just like her mother?"

Mr Austen recognised his wife's familiar wash day grumpiness and refused to be drawn in. He continued to peruse the letter in silence, but Mrs Austen's rant was not done.

"Don't you think it suspicious to give her so much? Another

man's daughter? No wonder people talk!" She was struggling with the enormous expanse of a cotton sheet, which was continually snagging itself on a prickly branch.

"I dislike what you are insinuating," replied Mr Austen slowly, forcing down his own fury.

"For heaven's sake, George. You cannot tell me you have never had your suspicions. Philadelphia worships Mr Hastings, as does Betsy. Why else would he give the child so much money?"

"If you are suggesting what I think you are, then it is best that we end this conversation right here." He folded up the letter and looked directly at his wife's sweaty face. "Let me make myself perfectly clear on the matter. Philadelphia is my sister and Betsy is my niece. I will not hear either of them spoken of in such a way."

He turned to walk away and then stopped and paced back. Mrs Austen had never seen him look so angry. "I will pack directly and catch the evening stage. I shall be at my sister's house until I complete the arrangements, should you need to contact me. My brother-in-law has entrusted me with this task and I will not delay it a minute longer by listening to your vulgar insinuations!"

Mrs Austen continued to fight with the sheet, but all she could focus on was the sound of her husband's footsteps clomping up the wooden staircase, heading towards their bedroom where he was going to collect whatever he needed for the journey. Her vision blurred with tears and she blinked hard, taking deep breaths to calm herself. She was torn between running upstairs and begging his forgiveness or pulling out another sheet from the basket and taking her anger out on that instead.

In the end, Mr Austen's crunching steps on the gravel at the front of the house decided it. He was striding away from her so quickly that she would never catch him now, even if she tried.

He returned home a fortnight later in much better spirits than when he left. The children were delighted to see their papa and the husband and wife made no mention of the bitter argument they had both had time to regret. Instead, Mrs Austen disclosed the reason for her erratic behaviour - she was expecting their seventh child.

"You would think it would get easier by now," she sighed in early December. "But this waiting is unforgiving. There is so much to attend to and all I can do is lie here and wait." It was an especially bitter end to the year and the garden weathervane creaked incessantly in the wind, night after night.

"You promised me November, my love," Mr Austen teased tenderly, turning his anxiety into a joke. "Do you think we have gotten such bad reckoners in our old age?"

"I think we must have done," agreed Mrs Austen, rubbing her belly with her hand. "Maybe this little one is too comfortable and does not want to make an appearance until the weather warms up."

There were tears of relief from both parents when they finally held their new mewling bundle on the 16th day of December.

"She looks like Henry," declared Mr Austen, staring into his new daughter's eyes. "A plaything for Cassy. She can be her little doll," he quipped.

"How she will love her!" agreed his wife.

Whilst the maids tended to the cleaning of the baby and

the changing of the bed, Mr Austen used the time to write to Susannah and inform her of his latest arrival. He dutifully asked if there was any news from Jamaica and passed on a message about a ploughing match to his half-brother. He was used to writing family announcements by now, and the birth of another daughter no longer commanded the cost of a letter all to itself. He sealed the paper with wax and handed it to his manservant to take to the post. Then, as was his custom with all his children, he collected the bottle of holy water which he kept locked away in his study, and returned upstairs to his wife.

Jemmy, Neddy, Henry and Cassandra were ushered silently into the bedroom where they watched their little sister being privately baptised. Jemmy held the special candle while his father swaddled the new baby in a fresh blanket. Holding her delicately in his arms, he spoke the familiar words by heart, sprinkling holy water onto her forehead as he did so.

*"Jane Austen, I baptise thee In the Name of the Father, and of the Son, and of the Holy Ghost. Amen."*

"Amen," repeated the dutiful bedroom congregation and Mr Austen made the sign of the cross on little Jane's forehead. Her brothers and sister gazed curiously at their new pink sibling before leaving the room and then baby Jane was put to her mother's breast to feed.

The days and weeks that followed brought the worst winter storms for years. The whole family was trapped indoors by dangerous snowdrifts and the rectory was colder and draughtier than ever, even with blankets covering all the windows and fires lit in every grate. All the homes in the village were the same, with thick plumes of black smoke wafting up from every chimney in the neighbourhood.

Outside, the biting air caused ponds to freeze and milk in the dairy to turn to ice. In the attics of the rectory, the water in the wash basins froze every morning and Mr Austen had to go out several times each day to break the ice in the animals' water troughs with a pickaxe. It seemed to take forever for the ice to finally thaw and the roads to clear.

When the days eventually turned warmer, baby Jane (who had spent every day up to now tucked up warmly beside her parents' big wooden bed) was taken on her first proper outing to St Nicholas' Church. The cosseting and snuggling she had gotten happily used to was a stark contrast to the alarmingly cold hands she felt now, dipping her head in the chilly water of the font for her formal christening.

If that was not enough to make her cry, the following week brought even more distress and confusion to her little brain - she was sent to live with the Littleworths at Cheesedown Farm!

# Chapter 10

1776-1777
**Bad News for the Hancocks.**

S ummer saw Mr and Mrs Austen once more on their
travels, and they took a trip to London to stay with
Philadelphia and Betsy. Whilst they were there, a letter
arrived from India; it was not in Tysoe's usual hand and was
sealed with a black wax stamp. It could only mean one thing;
Tysoe was dead.

Philadelphia gasped and held her fine lace handkerchief
to her mouth. She handed the letter wordlessly to her
brother, the colour draining from her face, and he took in
the importance immediately. It had been written by a Mrs
Bowers who was an acquaintance of Tysoe's in Calcutta.
Philadelphia and Betsy had known her before they had come
to England.

Mr Austen's professional manner was calming from the
moment he grasped what had occurred. He had a way of
offering comfort above and beyond anyone else: a true proxy
of God in tragic circumstances.

"Last November…" he whispered, relaying the contents
of the letter to his wife. "A fever. A long illness. Buried in

Calcutta. Attended to with dignity..."

Mrs Austen felt a heavy sadness. She had not known her brother-in-law that well, but she appreciated how he must have suffered. She knew how difficult Philadelphia was as a wife and felt sorry for him. She remembered all the cruel things Philadelphia had said about him, and the parcels of generous gifts that came as regular as the clock chimed, sent aboard the East India ships.

The next day, the entire household began their period of mourning dressed in black. They welcomed Tysoe's lawyer, Mr Woodman, who promised to sort out his client's financial affairs. Mr Woodman was a familiar face to the Austens and they trusted him absolutely. He was married to Warren Hastings' sister and was a joint trustee of Betsy's generous trust fund together with Mr Austen. Proceedings were therefore more relaxed with him in charge than they would have been with a stranger. A few days later he was back again.

"Good day, Mr Austen, Mrs Austen." The lawyer stood up and shook Mr Austen's hand. He had been waiting on purpose for them to return from their morning walk. "I am afraid Mrs Hancock has received another shock," he spoke quietly. "Will you be able to stay with her for a while?"

"Yes, of course," agreed Mr Austen readily. "What is it?"

Philadelphia was sobbing loudly into her handkerchief; Betsy sat stony-faced beside her, rubbing her mother's shoulder.

"We have been made aware that Mr Hancock ran up a large amount of debt before he died," explained the diplomatic lawyer. "Unfortunately, Mrs Hancock and Miss Hancock cannot now be granted the large legacy they were hoping for."

This, it seemed, was worse news to Philadelphia than the realisation that she would never see her husband again. Betsy's reputation was at risk if their current lifestyle could not be maintained.

They all met again two days later to complete some more documentation and Philadelphia joined Mr Austen and Mr Woodman in an animated discussion about the wars in America. Betsy spoke of the scarlet uniforms she had seen in town. Did they really think America could become an independent nation? Would the king even allow it?

If it were not for the black clothes, Mrs Austen beheld, no one would guess there had been a bereavement at all. No one reflected on what they were doing last November when Tysoe had taken his last breath. No one pondered about the events they had attended since then, ignorant at the time that Tysoe was lying buried in his Indian grave. They all talked of battles, of soldiers, of Mr Hastings instead.

It seemed wrong to Mrs Austen that since Tysoe's passing had occurred out of sight in India, it was treated with less importance than if it had happened here in England. The poor man, she felt, deserved more respect.

* * *

If Philadelphia had hoped that Warren Hastings would be more affectionate towards her now that Tysoe was dead, then she was in for a disappointment. Word arrived from India that he had married another; the same lady whom Tysoe had written about and who had provoked such a jealous outburst from Philadelphia in the rectory. The new bride relinquished her rather grand-sounding name of Anna Maria Appolonia

Imhoff to become Mrs Marian Hastings instead.

Warren Hastings' career in India was flourishing. Since his return there five years before, he had worked to introduce a new system of justice into Bengal and had made many changes to the tax collection system. He assumed the title of 'Governor General of Bengal', which brought him great power, but also led to conflict. His interventions meant Calcutta was now under complete control of the British Government, which divided local opinion. With some of his British peers, he was a popular leader, while others disagreed with his decisions. Similarly, some of the Indian tribal leaders respected him, while others saw him only as a threat. The actions he took at this time would not be forgotten and would continue to haunt him in later life.

His communication with Philadelphia was at the lowest point it had ever been and without his dominant influence, or Tysoe's stability to keep them at home, Philadelphia and Betsy planned a trip abroad.

*'We have paid our last visit to Steventon for the foreseeable future,'* Philadelphia wrote to Mr Austen in September. *'Eliza and I are to leave shortly for the Continent and will take Clarinda to serve us. We will stay first in Germany, then plan to move on to Belgium and France.'*

Mr Austen was taken aback and most upset by this news. He knew his sister was a restless soul, but he felt he deserved more of an input into her thinking before she took herself and her daughter out of his life for who knew how long. And what was this about Eliza? Why had she changed her name from Betsy?

Mrs Austen felt sorry for her husband and was sympathetic towards his annoyance. She was determined not to antagonise him further and desperate to avoid a repeat of that terrible row from a couple of years before.

"Do you think the fact that Mr Hastings has wed again has something to do with the trip?" she suggested casually, trying not to sound critical while she scattered food for the chickens.

Mr Austen was cleaning some farm tools in the yard alongside her and the sloppy splashes of water from the bucket served as a buffer to allow each of them time to consider their next exchange.

"Perhaps so," he conceded gracefully. "I expect Philadelphia is lonely without Tysoe, and seeing someone else happy often makes grief harder to bear, I find."

"I wonder if she will seek a husband for Betsy while they are there?" speculated Mrs Austen in a measured tone, tying up the sack of chicken feed with some rope.

Mr Austen flinched at the suggestion. He was silent as he continued to wipe down the blade of a scythe with a rag. He did not disagree with his wife's rational reasoning, but it was uncomfortable for him to think of his niece as a woman, mixing in an adult world.

Mrs Austen placed the sack inside the barn and then helped to put the clean tools away in the tool house. "If Betsy wishes to take the name of Eliza from now on, that is a clear sign to me that she is growing up. She's sixteen, after all. It can't be long before she's someone's wife."

Times may have been unsettled with war brewing between England and France, but this did not stop the determined travellers and they made no plans to return home any time soon. The finery and high society of Europe suited them admirably.

# Chapter 11

**1778-1779**
**A new boy joins the school.**

M r Austen's school in Steventon was thriving. His distinguished reputation in the neighbourhood was recognised by the local authorities and he was invited to become one of the commissioners to oversee the construction of the new Basingstoke Canal. He took on the role with relish, bringing the intricacies of canal design and its use to form new topics of learning in the schoolroom.

He explained how canal transport would benefit local farmers, who would soon be able to transport their food more easily to destinations further away. He shared his excitement at the labyrinth of routes that was spreading throughout the country and he expressed his pride at being part of such a significant enterprise.

"Gentlemen," he announced to his class at the end of another busy morning, "I am pleased to inform you that a new student will shortly be joining us. He will arrive on Thursday, and I trust you will make him most welcome."

Four polite heads assented to do so with positive nods as they continued to look up at their master. Jemmy was now twelve, Neddy was ten, Henry was eight, and William Vanderstegen was the most senior at fourteen.

"James Austen, I would like you to accompany me to Deane Gate when I go to meet him. I wish for you to be his companion for the first few days, to help him settle in, show him around, that kind of thing. I know you will get along splendidly."

"Yes, Sir," confirmed Jemmy, willingly. "Where is he from, Sir?"

"He presently lives in a place called Kintbury. His name is Fulwar Craven Fowle and he is the son of a very old friend of mine from Oxford."

Neddy smiled. "I have heard you speak of Mr Fowle often, Sir."

Mr Austen returned the smile. "Yes, you have. We were good friends together at university and I am honoured that he has chosen to send his son here to be educated. I rely upon you all to show him what hard workers you are."

A frenzy of activity ensued over the following days, making space for the new boy to sleep in the attic and an extra plate to be served at mealtimes. Mrs Austen thrived on such domestic arrangements and was as excited as her husband at the prospect of a new face. His trunk arrived by the carrier's cart the day before he did and was placed in his room, ready to be unpacked.

Fulwar Fowle was a confident young man with a shock of blond hair and striking blue eyes. He had mixed feelings about leaving home, which his fourteen-year-old brain was still trying to process. Bored by the halfhearted lessons he had received from his tutor in Kintbury, he was eager to learn at a higher level and understood the importance of a good education. He had a natural ability to write and speak well and knew he would be a clergyman like his father. He also enjoyed being the eldest of four brothers and felt the importance keenly of being the first one to be sent away to school. He reminded himself of all these things on the long stagecoach journey to Steventon and generally, they kept him in a positive frame of mind.

Yet, as he came closer to his destination, he was struck by just how rural a setting it was. In Kintbury, his home was the hub of the village, where visitors called on his father and mother at all hours of the day and night. He was also used to riding his horse over to the neighbouring village of Enborne where his close relations, the Lloyd family, lived. He felt a pang of sadness that he would not be doing that again until the holidays and thought fondly of his Uncle Nowes, Aunt Martha and their friendly housekeeper, Mrs Stent, who always made him welcome.

He thought of his cousins: dear, sweet Eliza; kind and helpful Martha; even the irksome Mary would be a welcome distraction today. And he had still not gotten over his grief for poor little Charles – the sweetest-natured cousin anyone could ever wish for, who had been cruelly taken by smallpox at seven years of age.

The memory of that time made Fulwar feel guilty. Charles's death had come so suddenly that Fulwar did not know when they played together, that it would be the last time he would ever see him. This thought (which recurred regularly in his mind) put his own life into perspective and he gave himself a scolding. A solo journey by carriage like this may seem frightening, but it was nothing compared to the suffering that poor Charles and his family had been forced to endure.

No matter how hard the young scholar tried to ignore his negative emotions, however, he could not fight the overwhelming sense of anxiety that this new experience was bringing. His limbs were heavy and his breathing was pained. He had never understood what homesickness was before now – but a sickness it most certainly was.

Jemmy and Mr Austen were there to greet the stagecoach as promised and they both stood with broad, welcoming smiles. Jemmy was a few inches taller than Fulwar, but the new boy held his head high and pointed his long nose upwards to compensate. He was tired, impatient and preoccupied with everything that was happening, but he remembered his manners and was under strict instructions from his father that he must be on his best behaviour and make the best impression on his old friend. He bowed respectfully to Mr Austen and nodded courteously to Jemmy.

"Welcome Master Fowle. Welcome to Steventon." Mr Austen rambled on in jumbled words about how delighted he was to know him, what a wonderful man his father was, and he hoped that his mother and brothers were well. They traipsed quickly along the road, past the maple tree and the village green and along the lanes to the rectory. Jemmy made companionable conversation whilst Mr Austen proudly led the way.

"Do you like cricket? Do you ride?" enquired Jemmy, wanting to get to know his new classmate. Then, when his father was conversing with a neighbour and out of earshot, "Latin is so tiresome, do you not think?" with a cheeky conspiratorial grin.

The fresh country walk, after a long time confined in a carriage, helped to put Fulwar in better spirits. Combined with the friendly conversation, he arrived at the rectory grateful that the new school did not appear to be as daunting as he had formerly feared.

Mrs Austen clucked over him like a mother hen and Cook plied him with a plate of cold meat, bread and butter and apple pie. Within an hour of arriving, Fulwar had decided that things were not so bad after all.

He spent the afternoon being shown all the important spaces by Jemmy and then joined his classmates, who were being taught how to join two pieces of wood together by Mr Bond. Another substantial meal followed in the evening and by the time Fulwar retired to the little attic he was to share with William Vanderstegen, he could barely keep his eyes open. William chatted away cheerily and helped him unpack his belongings into the dresser, concluding his first day at Steventon with a sound and solid sleep.

Before long, William Vanderstegen was taking his entrance exams for Oxford. Pride in his success was shared by everyone in the rectory and they packed him off to St. John's College with genuine good wishes, like a true member of the family. His vacancy in the schoolroom was filled by Fulwar's next youngest brother, Tom Fowle. He arrived just as politely and well-mannered as his brother and settled in as quickly. Three more boys came too: Gilbert East, Frank Stuart and George Deane. Together with the Austen boys, the schoolroom was a vibrant and exciting place to be.

Mrs Austen played as equally important a role in the school as her husband. She was quicker to pick up on a boy's unhappiness and very often anticipated a problem in the making, which she would then tactfully resolve. All the boys loved her for it and when she became pregnant again they rallied around chivalrously to help her fetch and carry, dig and lift. Every boy vied for her attention, complaining if she favoured one over another, and they shared many happy evenings in animated discussion.

In return for their goodwill, Mrs Austen wrote poems to amuse them. Following a long absence from the schoolroom by Gilbert East, the boys speculated if he would ever return. They joked he was spending his days dancing when he should be learning and Mrs Austen took this as her cue to compose a new little ditty which she read aloud for approval at mealtime the next day. Every boy laughed and clapped at Mrs Austen's sterling effort, causing the skin on the back of her neck to tingle.

Next came the turn of Francis (Frank) Austen to join his elder brothers in the schoolroom and he earned the nickname of 'Fly' amongst his peers for being fast and agile in every task; the most daring of riders on horseback.

Even the girls, Cassandra and Jane, joined in the games when the boys took a break from their studies. On sunny days, they would play cricket or blind man's buff together or, if it was raining, they might clamber around the microscope and take turns looking at butterfly wings, fish scales or insects under the lens.

Baby Charles was born on June the 23rd to complete the Austen family and the seven siblings lived side by side with all the pupils that came and went. The bonding that occurred between these young people during their formative years secured several friendships to last their whole lives long.

# Chapter 12

## 1779-1780
### Edward Austen is favoured.

D uring the summer holidays, life took on a more relaxed pace at Steventon Rectory. Breakfast was served later and the Austen boys spent their days performing chores around the village instead of poring over their school books with furrowed brows.

Jemmy passed his entrance exams for Oxford at the impressive age of fourteen and set off eagerly for St. John's College to follow in the footsteps of his father. His infant name was abandoned with this rite of passage and from then on, he was addressed by his baptismal name, James.

His absence from the rectory gave his younger brothers a chance to step up their responsibilities and Henry became the chief helper in the church. Neddy and Frank were encouraged to work on the farm and Cassandra and Jane assisted their mother in the running of the household. It was never too early to learn how to sew when there was always a shirt that needed mending or a stocking to be darned.

A letter arrived one day from a distant cousin of Mr Austen's. He was on his wedding tour and wrote that he would shortly call at the rectory to introduce his new wife. His name was Thomas Knight II, a Member of Parliament for Kent and in line to inherit a considerable fortune. His ancestry was a rich one, coming from a family where hereditary estates were passed down from one generation to the next. It was this man's father, Thomas Knight I, who had been responsible for presenting Mr Austen with the living of St Nicholas' Church, and it was this cousin who owned much of the land around Steventon where Mr Austen farmed and kept a share of the profits.

Mr Knight's new wife, Catherine, was also from a well-respected family and Mrs Austen was keen to make her acquaintance. She was an elegant lady, with a slim and beautiful face that she did not flaunt. She had a mound of auburn hair piled high on her head and she wore a travelling gown made of ivory linen. It would be easy, given her status, for the lady to wear sumptuous silks, but she had been raised to oblige a varied company and Mr and Mrs Austen were charmed by her understated elegance. They were even more pleased to find, after a little conversation, that she possessed a modest character too and was every bit as keen to make a good impression on her hosts as they were to her.

Mr Knight was a slim man with long, thin cheeks and a pointed chin. His voice had a nasal quality and he was clearly used to being listened to. He knew exactly the right turn of phrase to use and cleverly steered the conversation to ensure it flowed smoothly.

When the tea had been taken, Mrs Austen addressed her eldest child in the room. "Edward, will you take our guests for a turn in the gardens while the weather is fine?"

"How delightful," agreed Mrs Knight, clapping her hands

together like an enthusiastic little girl. She had been charmed by this sweet, easy-going boy with his soft blond curls and curious mind.

They stepped outside into the bright sunshine, broken by a string of threatening clouds pulled along by a brisk breeze. Mr Knight held his wife's arm and helped to wrap her shawl a little more securely around her shoulders.

Neddy led the guests first to the gravel walk, which was bordered by neat rows of strawberry plants. "These should turn red in three to four weeks, depending on the rain and the sunlight," he announced confidently. "When they are ripe enough, we will pick them and then Mother and Cook will turn some of them into preserves to store for the winter." He strolled with his hands behind his back, as he had seen his esteemed neighbour, Squire Digweed, do when showing visitors around his land. "The smell is quite divine when they are fermenting," continued the young boy. "Do you like strawberries, Ma'am?"

"Oh yes, very much indeed," replied Mrs Knight. "But my husband is not so keen. Can you believe it, Edward? That someone cannot like such a delicious fruit?" she teased warmly. Mr Knight gave her an indulgent smile.

"Especially when they are very sweet," continued the child with his contagious enthusiasm. "And if there is cream … mmmm … I think they taste better than anything else in the world!"

They made their way further along the path and turned a corner. "Be sure to stay on the gravel walk so that your feet remain dry," he instructed authoritatively, causing Mrs Knight to bow her head in order that the child did not see the wide smile which was spreading across her face.

73

Neddy skipped up to the sundial and moved his head at a jaunty angle to assess the dark and the light. "The time is now a little after three o'clock. You see, here, where the shadow falls on the dial. That is how we know what time of day it is."

Mr Knight humoured him with questions as if he had never stumbled upon a sundial before in his life.

"And I must apologise for that frightful noise," grimaced the boy as they approached the weathercock, groaning and swishing in front of them. "It makes a frightful din on a stormy night when we are all trying to get to sleep."

The Knights chuckled and agreed that it must do.

"Let me show you the walled garden next," he continued merrily. "There are cherry trees and apple trees and pear trees. We are even attempting to grow cucumbers in a frame in there." He bent his head solemnly and spoke in an undertone, "Please remember us in your prayers for them to be successful," he added, repeating another phrase he had heard Mr Digweed use.

He showed every part of the simple garden to the visitors and they were sorry to reach the end of their tour. Potted herbs and marigolds adorned every corner with splashes of colour and abundant fragrances led them back to the house.

"What a delightful family you have, Mrs Austen," Catherine Knight complimented when leaving. "All of your children are a credit to you and Edward has inspired us with tips for our own garden. It has been a pleasure to meet you all."

The whole family responded with similar admiration and bowed and curtseyed as they should whilst wishing the guests farewell. Mrs Austen was overjoyed by the good impression her children had made and she could not quite believe her luck when Mrs Knight continued to speak. "I would be most obliged if you could bring Edward over to walk with me around the gardens of the Manor House. We stay there for a week longer and I am desirous to seek his opinion on the fruit growing there."

Mrs Austen accepted the invitation readily and took him for the visit a few days later. Once again, Neddy charmed the lady with his natural inquisitiveness.

"You never know when a good connection may be useful," Mrs Austen pointed out to her husband, recounting the events of the afternoon. "Your cousin may be able to help our sons one day with a living or introduce our daughters into society. You must ensure you maintain a regular correspondence with him so that he does not forget you."

But even her most fanciful imaginings could not prepare her for what happened next.

The Knights were travelling onwards from Steventon to their estate in Chawton. They planned to stay there a month before returning to their home in Godmersham, Kent. "We would be honoured if you could spare Edward to accompany us to Chawton," Mr Knight requested. "There will be lots for him to do there, which we feel certain will keep him entertained. There is a full stable of horses to ride and a vast library of books from around the world. What do you say, Cousin?"

Mr Austen was truly surprised, but Neddy's eyes lit up at the prospect of a trip and Mrs Austen's heart flipped.

"Just as long as Edward will be home in time for school in the autumn," Mr Austen agreed.

After a day of frantic packing and lectures from his father covering all eventualities, the excited young Neddy Austen sat up straight and tall in the Knight's grand carriage to embark upon the first big adventure of his life. When he returned four weeks later, he brought back books for his siblings and was full of tales about his visits to Alton, Basingstoke and Winchester. He described his bedroom at Chawton, which had great red and gold drapes on the windows to match the warm velvet curtains around the bed. He talked of the billiard room, where he was allowed in the daytime with Mr Knight and a pony he had become attached to that he rode every day. He told his family how he had been out hunting pheasants with the gamekeeper and how the food he had eaten in Chawton was beyond anything he had ever tasted at home.

Mr Austen soon lost patience listening to his son's rec-ollections and removed himself to his study. Neddy was speaking of a world beyond the family's boundaries and he resolutely felt it was wrong to encourage such grand ideas. Mrs Austen felt differently. She longed for a contemporary insight into the world she had seen as a girl and enjoyed every remembrance that Neddy shared.

The following summer, the boy was invited to Godmer-sham Park. There were still no children to bless the Knight's marriage, and none hinted at for the future. The whole circumstance reminded Mrs Austen of her own brother's situation; James Leigh-Perrot had been of a similar age to Neddy when the rich and childless Mr and Mrs Perrot had taken a liking to him. They had invited him to stay at their fine home and eventually made him their heir. Was it possible the Knights were planning something similar for Neddy?

Mrs Austen kept her thoughts firmly to herself, hardly daring to hope for such an outcome, but with every day her son spent at the grand estate in Kent, the prospect became more of a reality.

Mr Austen's uncle Francis also lived in Kent, so when Henry was taken by his parents to visit the old man, they called into Godmersham on their way back home. It did not surprise Mrs Austen that Neddy and Henry were encouraged to go out riding one morning, leaving the adults alone to broach the all-important topic.

"We would be extremely obliged if Edward could stay on at Godmersham for a while longer. With your generous permission, of course," ventured Thomas Knight. "He is the most delightful boy and has completely captured the heart of my wife. It would please us enormously to give him all the things that we would wish to give a child of our own. He would be extremely well looked after."

Mr Austen returned the civilities with the flattery they deserved but assured his cousin that it was out of the question. Edward could not afford to miss any more school and was already falling behind with his Latin. He thanked the Knights for their kind offer, but that was an end to it.

The two women exchanged a look.

"We will say no more for the moment," suggested the hostess, standing in anticipation of leaving the room. "But I would be grateful if you would take some time to think it over while you remain here. Please, take a tour of the grounds; the entire house is at your disposal and Mrs Driver will answer any questions you have about the housekeeping." After a brief pause, she added, "I promise with all my heart that Edward would be exceedingly well cared for if he were to reside here and we would ensure he has the very best education that London can offer."

"Come, let us take a walk," urged Mrs Austen to her husband.

"We will see if we can spot Neddy and Henry on their ride."
It was a beautiful day with a perfect blue sky puffed up with
majestic white clouds. "There they are," she pointed.

In the distance, they could see two specks galloping off
beyond the trees. Full of fresh air in their young lungs, the
two boys were in a continual race: overtaking one another,
then falling behind, then overtaking again. Mr Austen smiled
a thoughtful smile, almost melancholic, and Mrs Austen knew
he was deliberating what Mrs Knight had said.

"Shall we walk to the church?"

They passed through the back gate of the park, past the
sounds of chickens in the vegetable garden and beyond the
granary, where sacks of milled wheat were being offloaded
from the back of a horse-drawn cart.

The churchyard was dotted with stones, like crisp, white
handkerchiefs and at the bottom of the slope, a glistening river
wound its way peacefully like a silken ribbon. They watched
the silvery fish for a few moments before taking the path
back up to the church door and entering the old, comforting
building that had stood on the same sacred ground for
centuries. Mr Austen sat in the Knight's family pew at the
front of the nave and Mrs Austen let him contemplate in
peace the image of Neddy taking that seat as his very own in
years to come. She walked towards the chapel, which led to a
bell tower, and waited there while her husband sought God's
help and guidance alone. When she heard him stir, she moved
again towards him, her soft soles making only a whisper on
the hard stone floor. It was wonderfully cool and peaceful
inside this precious haven.

Wordlessly, the couple walked outside into the scorching
sun, retracing their steps through the back gate of the

park until they found the welcome shade of a prudently planted, tree-lined path. There was no denying the house was magnificent, but it was the grounds which impressed the visitors the most - they were absolutely stunning.

"This really is a most handsome place," disclosed Mr Austen. "Do you think I am wrong to keep Neddy away from here?"

Mrs Austen chose her words carefully. "No. You are not wrong. You are a good father, George. 'Tis only natural you want to protect your son by keeping him close to you." Her tone of voice suggested the contradiction that followed. "But there are many ways to be a good father. I know you want to guide all our boys to follow your example and teach them right from wrong. Yet we had to let little George go, did we not? We both knew it was cruel to force him to stay in such a busy home when the noise upset him so. Sometimes as parents, we must make sacrifices we dislike, but which we know instinctively will benefit our child."

Mr Austen still felt the guilt and shame of what had happened with young George and he did not like to speak of it. Over the years, he had purposely ridden past the cottage in Monk Sherborne to catch a glimpse of his son in the farmyard and had sometimes heard him singing or seen him running around collecting eggs with Mrs Cullum. It reassured him to know he was safe and well.

"You are right," he acknowledged sadly.

They were now in sight of the great house, stretched out before them across the velvet green grass, like a palace from a fairy tale. Mrs Austen breathed in the air. "I have never known a place so fresh as this. You can barely hear the world beyond the gates."

"What are they doing now?" Mr Austen chuckled, spotting

Henry and Neddy lying flat on their backs on the grass, pointing their gangly arms up to the sky. The horses were grazing contentedly under some nearby trees.

"Finding shapes in the clouds, I suspect," guessed their mother. "I used to love doing that when I was a girl."

"They couldn't do that at Steventon," admitted Mr Austen philosophically. "There is no stretch of grass clean enough to lie upon."

Mrs Austen sensed her husband was wavering and seized the moment without delay. "I would never consider such an offer you know if I thought Neddy would be unhappy. But the Knights obviously adore him, and I cannot think of one thing that would not be to his advantage if he were to come and live here."

Mr Austen sighed, that melancholy mouth returning and the sadness settling again behind his eyes.

"And we will always be his parents," Mrs Austen continued. "Nothing can ever change that." The Knights had been quite firm in their assurances that they had no intention of making Edward break off relations with them.

"I know, my love."

"I think, my dear, you had better oblige your cousins and let the child go," soothed Mrs Austen.

"Yes," he sighed, defeated. "I think, perhaps, I should."

# Chapter 13

**1780-1781**
**Kintbury and Enborne.**

When the horses trotted off through the gates of Godmersham Park, a cloud of misery enveloped the Austen's carriage. Mrs Austen was taken by surprise at the intensity of emotion that engulfed her when she watched her precious boy turn back into the great house quite naturally, holding his new mother's arm. The outpouring of jealousy and grief this incited made her sob huge, ugly tears for miles.

Mr Austen stared impassively out of the window, making no attempt to speak or to comfort his wife. He squeezed his hands into tight fists, accepting that the pressing of sharp fingernails into his palms was a pain he thoroughly deserved.

Poor Henry watched them both with horror. He squirmed in his seat, his mouth flooding with bile from the back of his throat, and he felt as if he might be sick. He certainly hoped he would not, because there was always such a fuss when he was unwell and the last thing he wanted to do now was to make his parents angry.

The coach came to a stop outside the Hampson-Walter's

house, where they had arranged to break their journey. It was with a heavy heart that Mrs Austen reached out to greet Susannah, her prime source of comfort when she had left young George in his new home seven years before. She hardly knew where to begin, having come away from Godmersham Park and doing the same thing again.

"But how could you refuse them, Cass? You had no choice," Susannah assured. "Any good mother would have done the same. Neddy will live a life we can only dream of."

And that, Mrs Austen knew, was the sting. By encouraging Neddy away from his little rectory home, she was giving him the chance to experience things that her humble circumstances could never equal. The world did not seem fair.

Naturally enough, once refreshments had been taken and the travellers were revived, the conversation turned to Philadelphia and Eliza, who were now living in Paris. Susannah's daughter, Philly, was the only family member to be kept regularly updated on their progress through her frequent letter exchanges with Eliza.

"How are they both?" asked Mr Austen. "My sister writes very little these days other than on matters of business. How do they like Paris?"

Philly passed on their news without censure. "They are having a marvellous time," she began. "Although I get a sense from Eliza's complaints that her bills are rather excessive."

Philly had always been prim and plain compared to Eliza and usually overlooked when the two were in company together. Today she had centre stage, proud to be the messenger to deliver her cousin's news. She took her time to select her words carefully and pronounced each one with dramatic effect.

"Their maid, Clarinda, has suffered some ill health and has been under the care of a surgeon. This undoubtedly has put a strain on their finances."

The trust fund Warren Hastings had set up for Eliza when Tysoe Hancock was still alive, remained firmly in the hands of her trustees and was only accessible to the women on request. They may have been free to enjoy French society, but financial independence was not within their power.

"It must be very dull for them, not able to afford to go out in such a vibrant city as Paris," Mrs Austen reasoned, imagining them bored in some shabby apartment, longingly looking down from an upstairs window.

"Oh, not at all," contradicted Philly merrily. "The last I heard they had been to Versailles and seen the Royal Family. Eliza wrote at length about the beautiful queen and her magnificent attire. I would say they sound very happy!"

When the Austens arrived back in Steventon, a package was waiting for Mr Austen from France. Eliza had written her uncle a very sweet letter full of kind regards and sent him her latest miniature as a gift. The painting depicted her wearing a low-cut white dress with blue ribbons, complemented by more ribbons in her heavily powdered hair. She looked mature beyond her years and no longer recognisable as the fun-loving little girl he remembered.

He handed the tiny oval frame to his wife with a heavy heart, before heading towards his study and closing the door behind him.

\* \* \*

James Austen concluded his second year of university with a

visit to Kintbury to stay with his friend Fulwar Fowle. Fulwar was soon to join him at St John's College and James was keen to enlighten his former classmate on all that he could expect from student life in Oxford.

James had never had a best friend before he met Fulwar, but the two had become close in their later school years. Fulwar was more self-assured than James and exuded an air of self-belief that he would be successful and influential one day. James had looked up to him and admired his determination, but Fulwar had been equally enamoured by James' down-to-earth attitude and his ability to find pleasure in the simplest of rural encounters. Together they had shared long walks, cold swims in the river and clear nights of stargazing. It was liberating for James, when they were together, to test out his opinions on his friend to give them validation and learn more about other people's worlds.

He had heard much about Fulwar's family and was looking forward to meeting them. He was charmed by the manners of Mr and Mrs Fowle from the moment he walked through their door and could not have been made more welcome.

Fulwar's brothers came and went from the room exchanging handshakes and snippets of news, then Fulwar took James for a tour of his father's church of St. Mary's. He made no secret of the fact that it would become his own living one day and he talked as if he owned it already.

"This statue here is of my grandmother Elizabeth," explained Fulwar.

James was impressed by the white marble bust and carved tablet of stone that stood ominously in front of him. He smoothed his fingers over the contours of pale, cold rock to admire the sculpture of a rather fierce-looking woman.

"And this figure next to her was her second husband, Mr Raymond. There was a special service when these monuments were unveiled and everyone in the village came to see them."

It surprised James to learn Fulwar was part of such an important legacy; he had not spoken of these notorious ancestors before, but now he was on home ground he chatted openly and casually.

"My true grandfather died before I was born," he continued. "So I never met him, but my grandmother lived near to here when I was little. She was a formidable character," he let slip before turning away with no further explanation.

They silently wandered around the rest of the church and dutifully prayed at the altar before stepping back outside into the cool air.

"Shall we ride to meet my cousins now? You can take Tom's horse if you like."

James had heard so much about Fulwar's cousins that he felt he knew them already. Martha was the eldest, but he knew Eliza was Fulwar's favourite. Charles had been the next but had died a few years ago from smallpox, and Mary was the youngest.

"We'll stop off on the way so you can see my father's other church," shouted Fulwar over his shoulder. "It's a beauty!"

They fled along the track towards Enborne, with James barely able to keep up. Fulwar stormed ahead of him, his coat tails flying behind him and his horse striding effortlessly through the puddles and brambles in its path. James was a proficient rider enough, but nowhere near as accomplished as Fulwar, who was something else. He rode with the wind, at one with the horse, the king of the saddle.

When they stopped at St Mary's Church in the tiny hamlet of Hamstead Marshall, Fulwar was down on the ground and patting his horse before James had cornered the last bend in the road.

"Where did you learn to ride like that?" James asked breathlessly.

Fulwar shrugged off the praise. Everyone told him he was the best rider they knew, so he was used to it.

The young men walked up the steep path towards the church door and Fulwar pointed out the different landmarks that lay before them. It was a smart little church raised high on a hill and bordering Lord Craven's estate. The weekly congregation boasted many influential figures from the Craven family and their aristocratic guests who came to stay with them.

They reached Enborne just as the rain became persistent. They pulled up outside the vicarage of Fulwar's uncle's church and tied up their steaming horses to the posts. Mr Lloyd's stable boy came out to lead the animals away and brush them down and feed them like he always did when the Fowles came to call, ready for a good gallop home

James's attention was drawn to a slight figure tending one of the graves in the churchyard.

"That's Mary," revealed Fulwar quietly. "At Charles's grave."

"She will be soaked through. We should help her."

Fulwar hesitated a moment, then agreed. "You're right. Come. But don't be surprised if she doesn't thank you. She can be a little abrupt."

The young gentlemen walked towards the pathetic little figure, who was desperately trying to secure some floppy flowers so that they would not blow away in the beating rain.

"Let me help you." James picked a long reed from a nearby plant and wrapped it securely around the stems of the flowers. Then he took another reed and tucked it just below the petals to help them hold their heads straighter. It was something he had done many times in his father's churchyard to preserve the offerings on the graves before a storm. He thought everyone knew how to do it.

Mary watched James in silence, her eyes focused on his hands tying up the flowers. When he was done, he looked up at her with a smile, but she looked away uncomfortably and addressed her cousin instead.

"Your friend is very kind. I am grateful. Thank you."

Used to her strange responses, Fulwar introduced James. "This is James Austen, Mary. My friend from school. He will be staying with me in Kintbury for a few days."

"I've been looking forward to meeting you for a long time," interjected James clumsily. "Your cousin talks of you and your sisters constantly when he's at Steventon. I'm so very sorry about what happened to Charles."

Mary's face snapped up automatically. Hardly anyone outside the family talked of her brother these days, and it was gratifying to hear his name spoken out loud.

James's eyes strayed to the scars that covered Mary's face. They spread over her skin in unsightly blemishes, resembling mould growing on fleshy fruit. This must be the result of her own battle with smallpox, realised James, and he felt sorry for her. He hastily tried to cover his shock and talked about the rain instead, but it was too late. She had noticed how horrified he had been when he looked at her – the same reaction she received from any newcomer.

James had a kind heart and was not to be put off. "Your

flowers will be quite safe now," he chattered as if nothing else mattered. "If you tuck them here, next to the wood of the cross, and put a stone against either side of their heads like this, then they will stay upright. When the sun comes out again, they will naturally reach for its rays and open up."

"What good fortune I brought him here, eh Mary?" said Fulwar, holding his arm out for his younger cousin to be led away from the cold churchyard. "Time to go inside now."

James smiled at Mary and walked alongside them. He could not be sure, because it was such a tiny movement of her lips, but he thought Mary may have tried to smile back.

Inside the vicarage, the Lloyd family were every bit as welcoming as the Fowles. Nowes Lloyd held a quiet authority in the room and was clearly an intelligent and deeply religious man. He spoke of Oxford and how he remembered James's father as a young man. James very much hoped that his answers in response to a discussion of the doctrine met with the senior man's approval.

Mrs Martha Lloyd was lovely. Practical and warm, James could see the sisterly resemblance to Mrs Fowle. She guided her daughters with quiet efficiency to look after their guests and their housekeeper, Mrs Stent, was treated like a friend.

The eldest daughter, Martha Lloyd, was like her mother. She also had pox marks, but she was less conscious of them than Mary. She quizzed James on his life at Steventon and about all his brothers and sisters of whom she had heard Tom and Fulwar speak a great deal.

Eliza was the most interesting to observe, especially around his friend. Fulwar softened when he was with her and became less opinionated. Eliza was pretty and delicate and whatever she said, Fulwar agreed with. There was clearly an affection between them and James would often see them whispering together, sharing confidences. James had known for a long time that Fulwar missed Eliza the most when he was away from Kintbury and now he understood the reason why.

The biggest surprise from James's visit was seemingly the change he had brought about in Mary. Normally reclusive and unwilling to trust, Mrs Lloyd informed James that she was delighted how much Mary had opened up to him in conversation. "She is so conscious of her scars," she relayed when they were preparing to say goodbye. "She finds it hard to look people in the eye. But I can tell she is comfortable with you. It is a pleasure for me to see it."

"What are a few scars," replied James, poetically. "Does not beauty in a person come from within?" Mrs Lloyd smiled as he talked on. "I'm pleased you feel Mary can trust me. We have had some excellent conversations."

"Rest assured you will always be welcome in our house whenever you are passing this way again," enthused Mrs Lloyd, taking James's hand. "I do hope we shall see you again."

"I hope so too," agreed James. "The pleasure has been all mine."

# Chapter 14

There was a lot to catch up on when James returned home following his term at Oxford and then his visit to Kintbury. His mother could not stop admiring how much he had grown since the last time she had seen him and was eager for him to sit with her in the parlour while she darned some gloves.

James could never be described as sturdy, but he made up for it by holding his slender frame with elegance. He had learned from watching his university peers that if you walked with an air of importance, then you were more likely to be admitted into popular circles than if you stood timidly by on the sidelines. He dressed with care and wore his hair brushed back fashionably from the centre of his forehead. A set of whiskers lined each of his cheeks and his large brown eyes and thick lips offset his sharp nose handsomely. He had a likeable appearance, which pleased his mother's pride well.

Mother and son talked over the events of the previous summer and how Neddy was now fully integrated into life at Godmersham Park. James understood instantly the advantage that this alliance would bring, not only to his brother but to the rest of the family. He had no hesitation in agreeing with his mother's views.

"Now it has been decided that Neddy will be educated here during school time, then your father is happier about the arrangement too," she explained.

Neddy split his time between Steventon and Godmersham by amicable agreement. Mr Austen was to remain responsible for his son's education, then when that was complete, the boy was to be formally adopted and become the legal heir to Thomas Knight II.

James and his mother chatted about the younger children and what they had been doing whilst James had been away.

"Frank was barely breeched when I left for Oxford. I had to look twice when I saw him galloping across the field yesterday."

"Oh yes, he is quite the horseman now," confirmed his mother. "He would ride that pony all day long if your father let him."

As for the babies, Jane and Charles, they were babies no longer. They were noisy and vibrant and had developed strong personalities of their own. James listened fondly to his mother's tales of how they would run down the lane laughing to meet their father's chaise, so they could climb aboard to ride back with him and steer the horses.

"Is there any news of Aunt Hancock and Cousin Eliza?" James asked his father at the end of his welcome-home meal. He hoped his cheeks were not as red as the burning suggested, and he spoke as casually as he could, but he longed to speak of Eliza again. He had thought of her often while he had been away.

"Hmm." Mr Austen spoke in a disapproving tone whilst wiping his mouth with a napkin. "Your cousin is shortly to marry a Captain of the Dragoons in the Queen's Regiment in France. He is far too old for her and I fear nothing more than a fortune hunter."

The room fell silent. None of the children dared interrupt their father when he spoke in a tone like this.

Mrs Austen attempted a good-natured reply to ease the tension. "His family own a small estate in the south of France, so he may not be such a bad prospect. We know nothing more at present."

James could sense the disappointment in both his parents' voices and realised that this was not an easy topic for either of them. Nevertheless, he was keen to show his knowledge of the world and contribute to the family discussion.

"Are we not in conflict with the French?" he asked, knowing from his understanding of current affairs that the two countries had been involved in battles at sea for two years or more.

"We are indeed," confirmed Mr Austen. "And Monsieur Jean Francois Capot de Feuillide may even now be planning an assault against our great nation." He spat out his words with true malice.

More silence followed and the table emptied. The household dispersed into its familiar after-dinner routine and James was invited to join his father in his study.

"Do you know?" he confided to his son, sinking down in his chair, "Your aunt has asked me to release your cousin's trust fund: I assume so that it can be transferred into French money. I have refused, of course, but I am most unhappy about it."

James took a seat opposite his father, who looked deflated.

"I feel like I hardly know my sister these days," he offloaded. "It would not surprise me to learn she has renounced her faith and joined the Catholic Church!"

"I am truly sorry, Sir," mumbled James, as much for himself as for anyone else.

\* \* \*

When James went back to Oxford, he was accompanied by his friend Fulwar Fowle at St. John's College, then a year later, by Tom Fowle too. In the Steventon schoolroom, three new boys were enrolled with Henry and Frank: the two youngest Fowle brothers, William and Charles, and the son of another friend of Mr Austen's, George Nibbs. The school had achieved an impressive reputation in the neighbourhood for producing a steady stream of successful students and soon enough the baby of the family, Charles Austen, started lessons as well.

This led Mrs Austen's thoughts to turn to her girls. Cassandra was ten and Jane had just turned seven. They had been taught their letters and numbers by their mother and had picked up snippets of history and geography from their brothers. Both girls were avid readers and were supplied with a ready stock of books from Mrs Knight, who sent them as gifts via Neddy. But that was as far as their education went; otherwise, they pottered along, day by day, helping with household chores and mending the endless holes in their brothers' shirts and breeches. If they were to become as accomplished as their cousin, Jane Cooper (who had the advantage of Bath's society quite literally on her doorstep) then they really needed to be exposed to more of the world outside Steventon and Deane.

"What am I to say to my sister about Mrs Cawley's offer?" pestered Mrs Austen for the umpteenth time to her husband.

Mr Austen was being intentionally evasive, as he always was when he wanted to avoid a difficult subject. He would use his sermon writing, his marking, or his meetings about the canal to get in the way of a proper conversation.

"Must we decide now?" he replied, irritably. "I need to finish this report for the bishop."

Mrs Austen sighed. "Yes, George. We must decide now. My niece has already been accepted at the school and my sister urges that if we don't take up the places soon, they will go to some other girls."

Mr Austen put down his quill, knowing he was defeated. "So, my love, what do you think is best?"

Mrs Austen silently fumed. If her husband had bothered to listen in the first place, or indeed during any of the numerous discussions she had tried to have with him on the matter, then he would be in no doubt whatsoever what she thought!

She began again, patiently. "Well, I believe the school to be reputable enough, or else my sister would not be sending her own daughter there."

Mr Austen nodded.

"And even though I am not acquainted with Mrs Cawley personally, my sister obviously is and trusts her well enough. And my brother-in-law is a sensible fellow, which bodes well."

"Yes, yes," Mr Austen agreed some more.

The family connection to this particular girls' school was through Mrs Austen's brother-in-law, Edward Cooper. The Mrs Cawley in question was Edward Cooper's sister. She was the widow of a former schoolmaster and by taking in girls as lodgers and schooling them herself, she could earn sufficient income to maintain her status in society. Mr and Mrs Cooper's daughter, Jane, was already enrolled in the school and Mrs Cooper had canvassed her sister for many weeks now to encourage her to send her own Cassandra and Jane as well. It would be more fun if the cousins learned together.

There was no doubt the Coopers were good role models for the Austen girls. They had already outgrown their fashionable townhouse on Royal Crescent in Bath and had moved to a larger property in the neighbouring Bennett Street. This bragged of bigger rooms for entertaining and was a stone's throw from the Upper Assembly Rooms. It was inevitable that Cassandra and Jane would be invited to stay.

If these were not reasons enough, Mrs Cawley's school was in Oxford, an ideal location in Mrs Austen's mind because James was already living there and could keep an eye on his sisters if needed.

"It sounds as if your mind is made up," presumed Mr Austen, after dutifully sitting through his wife's application. "I believe we can afford the fees, so if you're sure it will benefit the girls then I wholeheartedly give my consent."

"So, I can write to say they can go?"

"Yes, I think you may," confirmed Mr Austen.

Mrs Austen kissed her husband impulsively on his cheek. "Thank you," she beamed. "They will be such accomplished young ladies before the year is out, you will see." She skipped off brightly in search of Cassandra and Jane to break the happy news.

Her daughters' absence, however, left a surprising hole in Mrs Austen's world. She had not realised how much trivial tittle-tattle they talked during the hours of chores that they shared together. Any one of them might bring up a snippet of overheard conversation or an observation of a passer-by to help the time tick pleasantly along whilst working in the dairy or shaking out the beds. So when a new family moved into the neighbourhood, Mrs Austen found that relaying the news to her daughters in a letter was not nearly as enjoyable as sharing the gossip face to face.

*'I called upon the newcomers today. Madam Lefroy is a most gracious woman, and longs to meet you when you return home.'*

The new family that had moved into the rectory at Ashe was headed by Reverend George Lefroy and his wife Anne. They had two young children and Madam Lefroy was expecting another. But words on a page simply did not do the meeting justice. Mrs Austen fretted as she sealed the letter with her red wax stamp and slipped half a crown under the seal to cover the cost of the post for her girls at the other end. What she really wanted to say was that Madam Lefroy was a very attractive woman. She was spirited, clever and witty and such a refreshing change to the slower farmers' wives they were usually forced to converse with. When she had called that morning, Mrs Austen had been greeted by a lady dressed in an elegant blue gown, with powdered hair arranged impeccably on her head. It was obvious that she would bring a touch of class and finesse to the otherwise rustic neighbourhood and Mrs Austen looked forward to associating with her some more.

She planned to take her best embroidery to work on when she made her visits, to show Madam Lefroy that they were both of a similar mindset and she had already decided that the Lefroy children would be invited to the rectory during the school holidays as playmates for her own.

# Chapter 15

**1783**
**Typhus.**

While the girls were at school in Oxford, a worrying measles epidemic swept through the university town. Mrs Cawley thought it wise to move her young charges far away and settle instead in Southampton. The thought of living by the sea on the south coast of England was far more appealing than staying in an infected city inland.

Southampton was an amusing place to be, where tall ships sailed by every day from the naval base in Portsmouth. But even the open blue sea had its dangers when sailors brought back unwanted diseases from their voyages. The lice they carried slipped into overcrowded houses and their tiny bites spread typhus.

All the girls succumbed to the disease one after another, with a headache, high fever and a rash. Mrs Cawley and her servants took on the duties of nursemaids until Jane Cooper and Cassandra improved. But seven-year-old Jane Austen got it bad and her fever continued to rage.

"When will our mothers come?" Cassandra asked Mrs Cawley, with all the politeness she could muster. At nearly

98

eleven years of age, she had the wisdom to know this was serious and the knowledge to know she was scared.

"There's no need to worry them," cajoled Mrs Cawley. "I see no cause to alarm them. Your sister will be as right as rain in no time."

Jane Cooper, at thirteen, was not so sure about this advice. She could not stand by and do nothing when Cassandra sobbed constantly over her barely conscious sister, holding the wash bowl under her chin whenever she was sick. It was time to act.

Jane Cooper wrote a note to her mother and slipped it out with an errand boy she had befriended. She gave him some coins from her purse and instructed him to take the letter to the post. It was vital, she assured him, that it be dispatched urgently to Bath.

Thanks be to God, the errand boy did as he was bid. He ran straight to the coaching inn, where the letter was loaded onto the evening mail coach and by the next morning it was in Mrs Cooper's hand. She showed it to her husband and no time was lost in swiftly packing a bag and dispatching the family carriage. Within two hours of the notification, she was speeding her way towards Steventon to break the news to her sister.

Mrs Austen was working on the vegetable patch when the visitor arrived and ran across the drive to greet her. "Sister? I thought it was your carriage. Whatever is the matter? What on earth has happened?"

Mrs Cooper was woozy and weak with distress, causing the gardener to come across and offer his hand. Mr Austen came out of his schoolroom, as baffled as his wife regarding this unexpected visit, but they were not kept in suspense for long.

"Oh Sister, I have had a letter from Jane. The girls are all ill and your little Jane is at death's door! My Jane begs that we go there immediately to collect them. We must make haste. We must get there before it's too late."

Mr Austen called for a drink for the visitor and sat her down in a chair.

With an uncontrollable flow of curses, Mrs Austen ran upstairs to collect some things for the journey. The boys came out of the schoolroom, eager to offer their assistance and some went out to help with the horses. Cook took some bread and boiled some eggs, then prepared a jug of small beer; she placed them carefully in a basket and tucked them in with a piece of white muslin. The boys placed the basket inside the carriage ready for later, when it would be needed.

Mr Cooper had sent a note via his wife to inform Mr Austen of the preparations he had already made that morning. He had engaged two of the best coachmen from Bath to drive the ladies. Both drivers were carrying pistols, which would enable them to travel on the shortest route to Southampton. They had been supplied with an adequate supply of coins to hire the fastest horses en route and pay whatever turnpikes were necessary. Everything had been thought of and there was no time for talk other than to wish the two women well and pray that they would reach their destination in time.

On the open road, Mrs Cooper showed her sister the letter she had received from Jane. She had read it so many times by now that she knew every word and tried to convince her companion that her daughter was being over dramatic. But deep down, both women knew they would never have been summoned like this if there were any other way.

"How long have they been ill? Why did Mrs Cawley not write to us herself? Was the physician in attendance?"

These questions batted back and forth across the seats of the carriage like a tennis ball. The Cooper's carriage lurched this way and that over rutted roads, with the stench of mud and manure turning their stomachs.

When darkness fell the women opted to carry on through the night. Their bodies ached and the air inside the carriage was stale. Outside the mud-spattered window, a crescent moon could be seen blinking fleetingly between the trees. Clouds flew through the sky in some places and stars twinkled down in others.

The leaves on the twisty branches of the roadside trees reminded Mrs Austen of the Indian necklaces that Philadelphia liked to wear, laced with dangling green sapphires and fluttering gold leaf. She chided herself for thinking such an irrational thought at a time when one (or both) of her precious daughters may at this very moment be dead.

When the sun rose again, the ladies revived a little. The bread and eggs in the basket were warm by now and tasted like the smell that lingered from the seats of the coach. But desperate times called for desperate measures and the women knew that they had to keep up their strength. They would be no use to their girls if they were to faint away with hunger.

After a very slow plod up a very muddy hill, at which point the two women got out to walk behind the carriage, they finally saw the sea. Black smoke billowed from the industry below and the port of Southampton was alive with movement. They watched tiny figures run in all directions, on the land and on the decks of the ships on the water. Mrs Cooper and Mrs Austen slumped back in their seats and prepared themselves for the worst, while the horses traipsed their final steps toward the crowded streets of Southampton. Street urchins ran alongside the carriage; ragged girls and women stared with pitiful, doleful eyes as it drove past; tears fell from Mrs Cooper's eyes.

The coach eventually pulled in at The Dolphin - the coaching inn that signified the end of their journey. One of the coachmen went inside to seek a guide to take the women to Mrs Cawley's address. The other coachman informed the ladies that he would stay there to await further instructions. He promised them the horses would be ready whenever he received word.

It was not far to Mrs Cawley's lodgings and the women followed their guide hastily past the merchants who were opening their shops, towards Bargate and on to the house. The sea breeze that ruffled their hair and displaced their bonnets was far from refreshing. It brought with it a pungent smell of raw sewage and rotten fish and the guide gagged as much as the women. Mrs Cooper had never felt so wretched in her life. She thanked the guide for his kindness and handed him a coin while Mrs Austen knocked on the door. She knocked twice and still, there was no answer but looking up at the windows she saw a curtain pull back and a little pale face peer out.

"Cassy? Is that you?"

Footsteps came running down the stairs and a bolt was released. Jane Cooper sank into her mother's arms and wept with relief.

"Oh Mama, we have been so worried! Thank heavens you are here. I knew you would come. I knew you would make everything right."

"And my little Jane?" asked Mrs Austen, placing far too much responsibility on the poor girl's shoulders than was appropriate for her age.

"She's upstairs. Cassandra has been up with her all night. Oh! Thank heavens you're here!"

The women made their way up the shabby wooden staircase that smelled of damp and mould. The bedroom smelled terrible. The chamber pots had not been emptied and vomit littered the floor.

"Open the window," commanded Mrs Cooper, although in all honesty the smells coming in were no better than those they were trying to let out.

Mrs Austen pulled out some fresh clothes from her bag and, after giving her eldest daughter a brief kiss and a hug, instructed her to get changed. "Bring back your soiled clothes and we will use them to clean this floor. Bring any water you can find."

She rolled up her sleeves and sat on the bed next to little Jane.

"Mama?" Jane's eyes rolled, but she was conscious at least. "Mama," she said again and clung on to her so tightly that it was now the turn of Mrs Austen's tears to flow fast and strong.

When Cassandra returned in her fresh clothes, carrying a jug of water and a bowl, Mrs Austen ripped up the old garments into rags. The two women and the two older girls wiped and cleaned and tidied as best they could and helped to release little Jane from her dirty bed sheets. They dressed her in a fresh nightgown and her mother reached for the bottle of laudanum that she always carried with her in her hidden pocket. She placed a drop on Jane's tongue. "That will help you to feel more peaceful, my darling," she whispered, attempting to stroke the tangled hair off her face.

"I must dispatch a message to George," she spoke suddenly. "I must tell him we will need the physician as soon as we arrive back at the rectory. And we must get word to the coachmen. We cannot stay here any longer."

"I can help," assured Jane Cooper eagerly. "I know where to find an errand boy, he will make sure your word is sent. He was the one who took my letter yesterday, so you can be sure he is to be trusted."

She turned towards the door to go, but Mrs Cooper pulled her back by the arm. "Here," she said, wrapping three gold coins in a handkerchief. "Give these coins to your friend for his help. Thank God, he helped you when he did, or we may never have got here soon enough."

Cassandra looked a little sprightlier for seeing her mother and packed her and Jane's things into their trunk. She directed Mrs Cooper to where her cousin kept her belongings and everything needed for departure was soon collected and ready. No words were required to state that none of them ever wanted to return to this filthy place again.

"And where is Mrs Cawley all this time?" questioned Mrs Cooper, her anger rising to the surface now that she had a firmer grip on the situation. "How dare she leave you girls in such a state and all alone!"

"She often goes out in the morning," Cassandra replied sheepishly. "But she will likely return soon with the apothecary, to check on Jane."

"Do you mean to tell me that the apothecary has attended your sister before and no one thought to tell me?" Mrs Austen was fuming.

"I tried to make Mrs Cawley write to you, Mama," pleaded Cassandra with tears in her eyes. "I promise you I did. But she told me not to worry you. She told me Jane would soon be well again."

"Come here, my child." Mrs Austen scooped Cassandra into her arms and kissed the top of her head. "I'm not angry with you, my precious girl. Not one little bit. And I'm so grateful for how you have looked after your sister. I think she may owe her life to you, my darling."

Cassandra was somewhat pacified, but Mrs Austen realised she must choose her words more carefully to avoid alarming the young girls even further. "But if we had known how poorly you all were, we could have got here sooner to help you. And you would not have had to do this by yourselves. That's the only reason I'm upset."

Jane Cooper returned shortly after, having found the errand boy and paid him handsomely for his task. "He will stand under the window when he has delivered the letter and spoken with the coachman. Then we'll know what time we can leave."

Mrs Cawley eventually did return with the apothecary and was shocked to find the girls' room occupied by their mothers. Mrs Austen barely gave her a look, preferring to focus her energy on her youngest daughter instead. She spoke with the medical man for reassurance and discussed a plan of care. In exchange for a little more gold coin, he reluctantly handed over the concoction that he had intended to dispense over the coming days.

On the other side of the room, Mrs Austen could hear the bitter exchange between her sister and Mrs Cawley. "But we are family, not some paying strangers! What if one of them had died? How can you possibly live with that on your conscience?"

Mrs Cawley tried to placate her in the same foolish way she had tried to placate her pupils, but Mrs Cooper was having none of it.

"Save your words for Edward. He will be furious when he learns how you have treated these girls. I have no doubt he will write to you directly when we are safely back home!"

Jane Cooper had been keeping a watch out of the window and left the room quietly when she spied the errand boy waiting with his message. "The coachman says to wait for ten more minutes while he secures the horses," she repeated when she came back in. "He says we are not to attempt to leave until he arrives. He will come up himself to carry Jane down the stairs and settle her in the carriage. We will be off before the clock strikes mid-day," she finished, the relief obvious in her breaking voice.

"Let me get you some refreshments before you leave," spoke Mrs Cawley harmoniously, trying to make amends.

"We want nothing more from you, I assure you," spat Mrs Cooper. "I would be obliged if you could leave us now, to wait for our carriage in peace!"

The apothecary bowed and both ladies thanked him politely for his help in attending to their daughters. He looked as if he would like to stay and sympathise with their plight but knew only too well who paid his fees, and it was not worth upsetting his clients in Southampton, no matter how unworthy they were.

At long last, thanks to the excellent teamwork from all concerned, the carriage and horses were trotting out along the outskirts of the city when the church bells chimed mid-day. Jane Cooper and Cassandra snuggled up against Mrs Cooper on one side of the carriage, whilst little Jane Austen lay across her mother's lap on the other. The girls slept like babies almost all the way back home, whilst the mothers wearily contemplated what might have been.

When they pulled into the gravel sweep at Steventon Rectory, Mr Austen and the boys came out of the house to offer their services.

"Thank God we got there in time," the two sisters echoed when the Cooper's carriage departed the next morning to take them back to Bath. Jane Cooper had been checked over by the Austen's physician and was declared to be out of danger.

It was only little Jane Austen now, who gave cause for concern.

For four days and four nights, she tossed and turned at Steventon until her fever broke. Extremely weak and frail, she was unable to leave her bed, but the threat to her life had gone. In time, her mother was assured that she would make a full recovery.

For four days and four nights, Mrs Cooper tossed and turned in Bath, but her fever never broke. Extremely weak and frail, she never left her bed again. Typhus may not have killed her daughter, but in making the rescue attempt to save her life, Mrs Cooper lost her own.

This was the first close family bereavement that any of the Austen children were old enough to understand. Their kind and generous aunt was someone they loved; someone they had hugged and kissed and who had played with them again and again whenever they had met. It was impossible to comprehend that they would never see her again.

# Chapter 16

## 1784-1785
## Unrest at the Rectory.

I t was the wonder of nature that helped to soften the grief hanging over Steventon Rectory. Through the dark days of winter, life remained subdued, but the distraction of a rooks' nest in early spring eased the conversation from Mrs Cooper's death on to happier observations of chicks learning to fly.

Jane Austen continued to gain strength, but it was a slow process and she did not stray far from home. Jane Cooper and her brother, Edward, became regular house guests at Steventon whilst Reverend Cooper struggled with his loss and made plans for a future without his wife. He left Bath and rented out all but a few rooms of his large house on Bennett Street. He moved from the city to take up a new living in the village of Sonning, not far from his wife's childhood home of Harpsden.

In moving away, he was faced with the painful process of clearing out her possessions. He gifted Cassandra one of her rings: an emerald stone encased in diamonds, and for little Jane, he gave her a pretty headband. He offered them both with a heartfelt wish that the girls should treasure these tokens in remembrance of their aunt.

Fourteen-year-old Edward Cooper was enrolled at Eton College and Jane Cooper was sent to The Abbey School in Reading. Mr Cooper felt that with no mother at home, boarding school was the best option for both of them.

Neddy's lucky situation, beneficial in many ways, was still a source of friction at Steventon. When Mr and Mrs Knight went on a tour of Europe, they invited Neddy to accompany them to Calais and generously offered for one of his brothers to come along with him for company. Henry did not need to be asked twice and the two boys sailed over the English Channel, full of tales of daring and high seas to share on their return.

Mrs Austen was thrilled to witness these opportunities for her children under the influence of the Knights, but Mr Austen was worried about the impression Neddy's situation was having on his younger sons, Henry in particular. He was the closest in age to Neddy and the one where the difference in circumstances was most pronounced.

"Where are they now?" Henry constantly asked his brother, regarding the Knight's location on their travels. "When are they coming back? Shall we sail to Calais to meet them again?"

"Henry will be so disappointed when Neddy goes away for good and he realises he has been left behind," Mr Austen warned his wife.

And sure enough, he was right.

A few months later, when the Knights returned to England, Neddy took Henry with him again to greet them at the port of Dover. Both boys were presented with lavish gifts and treated to a splendid meal at a hotel. Henry heard tales from Europe that awakened a desire to see it for himself and made his own experiences of Hampshire seem very dull indeed. They saw the castle at Dover and watched some soldiers marching with guns. Henry imagined himself aboard one of the ships he could see in the distance, bobbing up and down on the waves, off to do his patriotic duty for his country.

When it was time to depart, Neddy went back to Godmersham with his hosts and Henry returned to Steventon alone. He was not in good humour when he reached the rectory, so was allowed two day's grace by his parents to recover from the journey and sulk away his misery in his room. On the third day, he was summoned downstairs by his father to assist his younger siblings with some French.

Frank, Charles and Jane were sat at the table with a book of French fables and a French dictionary in front of them. Cassandra and her mother were out on an errand, which meant Mr Austen was left in charge of the children to oversee their work.

Henry was in a bad mood and not inclined to be much help; his father was growing more displeased with his attitude as the afternoon progressed. It was unusual for any of his children to answer him back, but Henry's courage had developed with his little excursion to the sea and he was feeling bold.

"Why should I teach them," he grumbled under his breath. "Neddy doesn't have to. Neddy can do anything he pleases."

Mr Austen pretended not to hear his son's mutterings.

It was hard work translating the stories into English and none of the children around the table had much motivation. Instead of looking up the words in the dictionary, as they were meant to do when they were stuck, they passed the time doodling on the cover page instead.

Charles began with a series of lines at the foot of the page, building them up into a haystack, lost in his thoughts. Frank wrote his name in different sizes and styles, beginning at the top and working his way down the page. Now seemed as good a time as any to perfect his signature.

'*I wish I had done,*' scrawled Jane on her side of the page, becoming increasingly uncomfortable at the unpleasant exchange she was picking up between Henry and her father. She wished Henry would just get on and help her so that they could all be released to play outside, and she squirmed to hear her brother continue with a topic she could sense was upsetting their father.

"Neddy rides every day at Godmersham, Sir. I wish I were allowed to ride more."

Mr Austen inhaled deeply. "You know exactly what the situation is regarding Neddy. We have explained it to you often enough. Now please assist your sister and brothers. You are good at French, Henry. Now is the time to show it off." He was trying to be as reasonable as he could, fully aware of the point Henry was making.

"But if Neddy doesn't have to spend the holidays studying books, then why do we, Sir?"

This, in his father's mind, was impudence and he was not going to tolerate it.

"You know very well it is not in our power any longer to tell Neddy what he can and cannot do when he is not under our roof. But it is still in my power to ensure that *you* have the best education, and you will not challenge me again on the subject!"

Henry's face reddened and he looked down. Mr Austen

feared he was about to cry and regretted he had been too harsh.

"You will be glad of the discipline you are learning now when the time comes to take orders for the church," he continued, trying to make amends. "A strong education will see you through many an obstacle ahead of you, believe me."

Henry was not to be consoled so easily.

"Papa, I have been thinking very hard about that," he wagered. "I know that I do not have the patience that you have, and I'm not sure I am best suited to a life writing sermons. I would like to do something more active, Sir."

Now that was a surprise.

"Another career?" quizzed Mr Austen. "I thought you were happy to become a clergyman?"

"I was. At least, I thought I was," the boy bumbled. "But now I think I prefer the military, Sir."

There. He had said it. He could not quite believe he had found the courage, but the words had tumbled out of his mouth before he could stop them.

Mrs Austen and Cassandra could be seen out the window walking up the drive, but the three younger children sat as still as statues. Tension engulfed the room.

"The military!" Mr Austen's voice was uncomfortably loud. "What on earth has put that idea into your mind?"

Henry opened his mouth to speak, wanting to explain further, but was denied the chance. Mr Austen raged on.

"Is this because of your visit to Dover? Seeing all the smart uniforms? Is that what did it?" He stood up, looking more menacing than any of the little faces looking up at him had seen for a long time.

Henry was caught out. The trip to Dover was precisely what

had put the idea in his head, but he was scared to concede it now. "No, Sir."

"So where else has this silly notion arisen from?" Henry was beginning to regret having raised the subject at all.

"I – I – just thought …"

"I will tell you what you thought," bellowed his father. "You saw too many fine sights with too many fine people and wanted a piece of it for yourself. I am sorry to disappoint you, my boy, but I can tell you now that our future is not destined to be one of rich clothes and adventure. This family's destiny is to live a humble life and you will do well to be grateful that you have the opportunity of an education at all!"

Henry began to sob and Mr Austen quit the room, brushing past his wife and daughter in the doorway without a word of acknowledgment.

"What in heaven's name has gone on here?" shrieked Mrs Austen.

Henry broke down completely at his mother's entrance and cried proper tears of anguish. Frank, Jane and Charles looked dumbly up at their mother, not knowing what to offer in the way of an explanation, and Cassandra hovered by the door with a basket in her hand, trying to decide if it was safe or not to come inside.

"I am away for less than two hours and I come back to this!" Mrs Austen cussed. "Am I never to get any peace!"

Henry got up and ran outside, embarrassed, humiliated and ashamed. His mother followed him out, tutting as she lifted her skirts to avoid the basket that Cassandra had just that moment placed on the floor.

*'mothers angry fathers gone out'* wrote Jane, resuming her doodling at the top of the page of her textbook. Frank bent

his head low and signed his signature even larger this time, with an extra flourish.

Mrs Austen trailed Henry to the water pump where he was tilting the handle to fill up a bucket. He was just like his father, in so many ways. Not only was he his model in looks, but he would always find some distraction to avoid a difficult conversation. Thankfully, his anger dissipated just as quickly.

"I'm sorry, Mama," he sniffed, with his head focusing on the water to avoid looking her in the eyes. "It was wrong of me to provoke Papa like that."

"What happened?"

"I made him angry. I told him I didn't want to study for the clergy. I said I wished to join the military instead."

"Ah…" Mrs Austen could imagine the rest for herself.

"There were lots of soldiers at Dover, were there?" she enquired. "You thought you might like to join them?"

Henry looked into her eyes and gave a nod; he was amazed how she had so easily guessed. But her smile reassured him she was not as angry about it as his father.

"It must be hard for you seeing your brother being taken away into a life of splendour, and you being stuck here with us?"

Now this was getting strange, thought Henry. He had never admitted that to anyone, so how could his mother possibly know what he was thinking?

Mrs Austen took the water bucket from Henry's hands and put it down on the floor. She walked outside to a small wall in the garden and sat down, patting the space next to her for Henry to join her.

"When I was about your age, some very rich relations of your grandmother came to visit and took a liking to my brother, your uncle Leigh-Perrot. He went to stay with them often like Neddy does now with the Knights, and we all went to dine at their big house with magnificent paintings on the walls and more bedrooms than we could count."

Henry listened intently.

"I didn't think much about it at the time, because my mother and father were always so pleased to go there. But after a while, your Aunt Cooper - God rest her soul – pointed out to me that our brother always had better clothes than we did; he was allowed to attend balls that we were not invited to and he stayed away from home for longer each time he went."

This was sounding familiar to Henry and he waited patiently for the rest.

"And then he changed his name. He was no longer just a Leigh, like my parents, or your aunt, or me. He became James Leigh-Perrot and heir to their family fortune. You must see it for yourself when we go to Scarlets, that his lifestyle is different to ours."

"Yes. Yes, I do," agreed Henry, remembering some of the pastimes he had heard his uncle talk about. He was beginning to understand his mother's message.

"I used to be so jealous of him," admitted Mrs Austen with a smile. "Especially when we moved to Deane before any of you were born. Money was scarce for such a long time before your father set up the school, and I could not stop thinking of my brother having a big house and a fine carriage."

She put her arm reassuringly around Henry's shoulders and pulled him near. "So, you see, I do understand what you're feeling. It's normal to be angry about what's happening to Neddy. Even I envy the beautiful grounds he gets to walk in every day. But he's still your brother. And none of this is anyone's fault."

Henry nodded, trying hard to believe it.

"It's the way of the world," his mother continued matter-of-factly. "And we have no choice but to accept it. One thing we can be sure of though, is that his good luck will have an impact on all of us, one way or another. At least I hope it will. Just as I expect your uncle Leigh-Perrot's good fortune will benefit you and your other brothers when you are older since he has no children of his own."

They chatted a little while longer until Henry had aired all his concerns and Mrs Austen had made sure he understood why his father had been so angry.

"I really would like to join the military rather than the church," Henry admitted bravely, as they headed back to collect the bucket of water and take it into the house.

"I'll tell you what I think best," suggested his mother. "You go to Oxford and study for your degree as planned. Once your education is complete, if you're still sure you don't want to take orders, then I will find a way for your father to listen to your reasons. How does that sound?"

It was as good as Henry could hope for and seemed like a fair compromise for now. In the meantime, he promised to continue to help his father and pray that his outburst would be quickly forgiven.

# Chapter 17

**1785**
**Mrs Austen is displeased.**

I n a large family like the Austens, whenever one child was pacified there was always another one to tip the balance. Henry, to his credit, settled down charmingly to his filial duties and made no more mention of joining the military. Harmony reigned in the household until a visit from Reverend Cooper and his daughter disrupted it once more.

They had come to appeal to the compassion of Mrs Austen. Jane Cooper was doing well at her school in Reading, but she missed her cousins terribly and her father feared she was becoming melancholic. Their mission was to persuade Mrs Austen to spare her dear Cassandra to join Jane Cooper at the boarding school for the new term.

It can only be imagined how Mrs Austen reflected on her previous experience of sending her girls away, where that fatal brush with typhus had killed her sister. But Mr Cooper was not to be put down. The brother and sister-in-law held an honest and frank discussion and through persuasive strong will and determination, the gentleman was able to reassure the lady that The Reading Ladies' School was different altogether to the one run by Mrs Cawley.

He was emphatic that this was a highly reputable establishment, and he could vouch for several of the parents whose daughters went there. He could not be more satisfied with their respectability and even offered to assist with Cassandra's fees if that should prove to be the barrier. It meant so much to him that his daughter would have the company of her cousin.

It was not an easy decision to come to, and much contemplated by Mr and Mrs Austen. When the girls had come home from their disastrous experience at Southampton, they had decided to find alternative ways of ensuring Cassandra and Jane would become accomplished without being sent away again. A watercolour artist was engaged for a while to give drawing lessons to the girls, which they enjoyed immensely. It was evident that this stimulation was good for them and Cassandra had bloomed with this new skill. Perhaps it was unfair of them to deny her the opportunity to develop her talents further.

The factor that decided it in the end, was the promise that Cassandra would soon be invited for a stay at Godmersham. Mr and Mrs Austen did not want her to feel out of place amongst such influential people so agreed she could go to the school.

"Do not make me go without Jane," Cassandra begged her mother. "I will not go without my sister." She was being uncharacteristically stubborn.

"Jane is too young for such learning. The work will be too hard for her at the Ladies' Boarding School," appeased her mother.

When that did not work and Cassandra continued to

protest, her mother tried a new approach. "Jane will join you in a year or two, but for now you must be a brave girl and go by yourself. Your cousin will look after you."

But her cousin was equally as determined. "I can look after Jane too, Aunt," she assured. "I already know how clever she is from when we studied together before. You don't need to worry."

Day after day they campaigned a little more and nine-year-old Jane Austen did everything she could think of to prove she was mature enough to go too. It wore her mother down.

"If Cassandra's head was about to be cut off, Jane would have hers cut off too!" she grumbled. So off they went again to school, the three girls together.

Six months later, on a crisp, winter's day, Edward Cooper and Neddy were sent to check on them. They trotted up the driveway of Steventon Rectory on their return, with a brisk wind in their faces and their fingers numb from the cold.

Mrs Austen had been waiting anxiously for over an hour before they arrived, repeatedly popping out the back kitchen and round to the side of the house by the stables to check for any sign of them. She was desperate to know how her girls did and be reassured they were healthy.

A mutton stew simmered noisily on the stove in anticipation of the young men's welcome, filling the warm room with the thick scent of boiled meat and onions, carrots, potatoes and rosemary. A rich, golden-crusted apple tart was baking in the oven, and Mrs Austen was impatient it should not burn.

A little after one o'clock the welcome crunch of gravel alerted her, and she placed her sewing down in the basket beside her chair to give the boys her full attention.

Edward Cooper was sixteen now, maturing into an extremely respectable young man from his time at Eton College. Neddy was almost three years his senior and would soon be leaving to live with the Knights permanently. The rest of the household was out hunting, and Mrs Austen relished this opportunity of having Neddy and Edward all to herself for a few precious hours of maternal fussing. Since the death of Mrs Cooper two years before, Mrs Austen had maintained a special duty of care towards her nephew and indulged him with the same love and kindness that she bestowed upon her own sons.

As soon as their horses were attended to and their coats hung up, the fire was stoked some more and dinner was served. The two young men had taken their sisters out for a meal the night before at an establishment in Reading. They had been required to seek special permission first from the Head Mistress, as her pupils were not normally allowed out.

"Little Jane was quite the young lady with her napkin and her wineglass," Edward Cooper relayed jovially, devouring his second plate of mutton stew with gusto.

"She is old beyond her years, that is true," agreed Mrs Austen. "It must have been such a treat for them all to dine out at an inn. How did they seem to you? Are they happy?"

"My sister has much improved with her cousins alongside her," confirmed Edward Cooper, still chewing heartily. "She has more colour to her complexion since the last time I saw her and appears much happier."

Neddy nodded in silent agreement. His table manners were impeccable and he ate slowly and precisely next to his companion.

"Cassy is delightful company," continued Edward in praise of his cousin. "It does my sister good to be around her."

Mrs Austen felt her breath catch and a pang of sadness pull at her heart; she was reminded how much she missed her eldest daughter with her sweet face and happy chatter.

"Tell me about the food. What did you all eat?"

"There was so much choice!" beamed Edward. "We tried a bit of everything between us did we not, Neddy? Salmon, trout, eggs, chops, bacon. There were three cheeses and cucumbers with the salad. But I must say the apple tart was not anywhere near as tasty as yours, Aunt."

Mrs Austen was only too happy to indulge him and she cut both boys a large piece of pie when the stew was finished. She took a piece for herself, licking her lips at the buttery pastry crust and tangy apple slices.

Edward had always enjoyed his food, which could be guessed from the stoutness of his frame; he was turning into the model of his father. After the dishes were taken away, Mrs Austen presented Edward with a pair of slippers. "I made them myself," she told him.

She was an avid reader of *The Lady's Magazine* and had been inspired by a sewing pattern for the embroidery of a shoe. Using some leftover silk that Tysoe had sent over from India some years before, she adapted it for her purpose. The drop-leaf design of the pattern was easy for someone with her level of competency and the whole project had taken her less than a week to complete. She was very pleased with the result and even though she could not provide her nephew with much in the way of material possessions, it fulfilled her to demonstrate her love and kindness in this small way.

"I thought they may help to keep your toes warm under your night shirt when you're in your dormitory at school."

Edward took them from his aunt's hand and his fingers slid

121

over the smooth material, the colour of rich, red wine. The soft sheen of the silk changed with the direction of the light and an intricate pattern was embroidered in gold. They were shaped like mules, with no back and no heel, meaning they would easily slip onto a stockinged foot at the end of a tiring day.

"How did you know these were just the things I needed?"

"I know how fast you boys grow," laughed Mrs Austen. "It's what we mothers worry about. Your own mother would have been exactly the same."

Edward was touched and grateful. "Thank you, Aunt Cassandra," he managed.

They moved away from the table and settled themselves down in front of the parlour fire.

"So, tell me," continued Mrs Austen, brightly. "What are the girls enjoying best about school?"

"Hmmm...I would say they are extremely good mimics."

Neddy burst into laughter at his cousin's frank response and his mother looked confused.

Neddy explained. "You should have seen them, Mama. You would think Mrs Latournelle herself had entered the room. They had all her actions down to the last detail."

The boys laughed compulsively, unable to disguise their amusement, but this was far from the news Mrs Austen had been hoping for. Mr Cooper had promised her that standards were high and she was alarmed to hear the Head Mistress being spoken of so disrespectfully. She was mortified to imagine her polite little girls mocking the woman in public.

"Surely," she persisted. "Surely by now, they must seem more accomplished to you?"

"Worldly wise, perhaps," suggested Neddy, honestly. "They

did talk of their needlework and their spellings. They have been learning new dances and spoke a good deal about art. We had some very intellectual discussions," he concluded, deciding that was what his mother wanted to hear.

But Mrs Austen was not convinced. She could read her children well and knew that Neddy was trying to placate her.

"What about their manners?" she persisted. "Would you regard them as having the air of a lady?"

Edward Cooper thought about how the manners of all three girls had shocked him: how they had joked and flirted with the waiting staff.

"I fear the rules on etiquette seem rather relaxed in Reading, Aunt," he stated sympathetically. He could not lie.

Neddy tried to turn the conversation into a positive. "They enjoy acting," he continued gleefully. "They will have picked up their skill for that, no doubt, from the plays we have put on here in the barn."

Mrs Austen's perplexed brow creased some more. She had not sent them to school to become better actors.

"And music? French? What did they say of those?" She was desperate now for any hint of progress.

Neddy played back in his mind his sisters' mimics of the French mistress, which had made his eyes stream with laughter. And with regards to music, the girls had boasted proudly how they often 'forgot' their appointments with the music master, because he was simply too tiresome. They had confessed that if they hid behind a big tree at the side of the grounds, then nobody came to look for them.

"No. I don't recall that we talked about those," replied Neddy, in fake contemplation. "Do you remember Edward?"

Edward Cooper looked back at Neddy, exaggerating the

puzzled look on his face too, pretending to search out some distant memory in his brain.

"No, no ..." He shook his head in over-compensation for the lie. "We were so busy with eating and talking of home that we never spoke of music at all."

Mrs Austen's sharp eyes missed nothing, but now was not the time to discuss it. Neither was it the fault of these two young men. She would save herself until later when Mr Austen was home; he would be told about what she thought in no uncertain terms!

A welcome interruption brought the arrival of tea and a plate of Edward Cooper's favourite seed cake. The topic of the girls' education was dropped for now and the rest of the cosy afternoon was taken up with talk of Eton, Mr Cooper's new parish and Neddy's plans for his forthcoming Grand Tour of the Continent.

# Chapter 18

**1786**
**The Call of the Sea.**

A t twelve years of age, it was time for Francis Austen to consider his future.

Since Henry's shocking outburst at not wanting to become a clergyman, Mr Austen had reviewed his stance on the way he offered career advice to his sons. He had mellowed in his demands, detracting from the view that his offspring should blindly obey what he thought best. His own father had been a surgeon; the uncle he lived with when his father died was a bookseller. It did not signify that the same occupation must follow through a household. Mr Austen invited Frank into his study, which was a clear indication to the child that the discussion he was about to have would be important.

"So, my boy, tell me more about this passion of yours for the navy." He smiled warmly, sitting opposite his son in his favourite high-backed chair.

Frank explained his ambitions to become a sailor and Mr Austen listened attentively. He had heard Frank speak to his brothers of this desire before.

"I can see how keen you are," his father assured him. "And I have been making enquiries into the Naval Academy. Is that somewhere you think you might like to go?"

"What would I do there, Sir? Would I go onto a ship?"

"No, not straight away. If we knew someone at sea already, then that may have been an option. But because you have no patron to vouch for you at present, then you will need to take a different route."

Frank looked disappointed.

"But in my opinion, I would say this way is better," proceeded Mr Austen, enthusiastically. "It will mean that you continue with your regular lessons like I teach you here, but on top of that you will learn about sailing and the jobs that need doing at sea."

A crease in Frank's brow showed he was considering the idea. His quick, dark eyes lit up and his curly black hair wobbled up and down when he nodded to show he was listening. "That sounds very well, Sir."

"And you will be taught how to dance, how to fence, and improve your French. You will become an officer one day, you see, and these things will help when you entertain your guests from around the world. You will become a gentleman - like Neddy - but on a ship instead."

"Am I not too short, Sir?"

This had always been a sensitive point for him, having been teased about his height for as long as he could remember by the tall and gangly Henry and James. Frank was still embarrassed to be shorter even than his sister, Cassandra.

"Nothing to worry about there." Mr Austen brushed away the concern with a wave of his hand like he was batting away a fly. "You have exactly the right build to become a sailor. You will have all the advantages over your brothers when you need to climb a rigging. And you have always been the bravest and most daring of our party out hunting. Those are excellent qualities, my boy, and will prove very useful."

Frank, like all his brothers, was not used to receiving praise from his father and he was flattered by the compliment. His self-esteem had rocketed since the start of the conversation and he was starting to believe he may be a good sailor after all.

"You will be required to take an entrance exam before you can join, which will demonstrate that you are good enough. But I have no worries on that score. Take some time to think about what I've said. Talk to your mother and your brothers if you wish, although I warn you now, your mother thinks it a fine idea too."

"I think I like the idea already, Sir," replied Frank.

"What do you say we meet again a week from today? If you still feel the same after thinking it over, then I will write to the Master of the Academy."

"Yes, Sir. Thank you, Sir." A week later, he had not changed his mind.

The Naval Academy was based in Portsmouth and for the first three years after joining, a boy's schedule was predominantly reserved for study. Only after that was he deemed suitable to sail away to sea.

"If you prove yourself a worthy scholar, you may be able to set sail sooner," hinted Mr Austen and Frank was determined to prove him right. Following an easy success in the entrance exam, it was arranged that he would join the Academy in April.

Only the higher ranks of the navy were required to wear official uniforms, but it was still important that the garments worn by lower ranks were practical and durable. Tailors made up their own patterns for this purpose and Mrs Austen went shopping to acquire what she needed. Day after day, she lovingly cut and sewed broad-fitting shirts from yards of tightly woven white cotton with narrow blue stripes. Next, she made sets of matching trousers, unusually wide in shape, to allow her young boy's legs plenty of wriggle room for manual work. Finally, a set of fuzzy flannel waistcoats made up the collection to keep her boy warm on the waves. It was a rewarding time for any mother to kit her son out in this way as he prepared for his national duty.

"Be sure to write to us every week," she pleaded, pulling Frank into one last embrace before he climbed into the carriage with his father to be taken to Portsmouth. "I will be excited to hear all your news." She wiped the tears brimming from her eyes with her frilly lace handkerchief.

"Of course, Mama," Frank agreed readily. "I promise I will make you proud."

\* \* \*

Meanwhile, in the city of Oxford, James Austen was falling in love.

His best friend, Fulwar Fowle, talked constantly of his cousin, Eliza Lloyd, mapping out a future with her quite clearly. James had felt jealous at first, remembering that he too had a cousin he had once thought he might like to marry, but she was now the wife of a Frenchman. The news had hurt him deeply, leaving him no choice but to seek out someone new and more worthy of his admiration.

His first choice was Lady Catherine Powlett, the daughter of the 6$^{th}$ Duke of Bolton. She had soulful brown eyes and glossy brown hair and lived in Hackwood Park, a significant estate not many miles from Steventon. James flattered himself to be considered amongst her friends and it did not seem to occur to him that he was being rather ambitious, given the lady's wealth and background against his own. James was a romantic and felt it impossible that any woman could turn down the advances of a suitor who declared his love with true passion.

He had practised the art of poetry since he was a boy and encouraged by Miss Powlett's politeness (all be it formal and indifferent) he wrote her a flowery sonnet, comparing her to Venus walking amongst the wondrous Hampshire woods. Much to his mortification, it was not well received, and Miss Powlett made her distaste for his advances abundantly clear.

Defeated in this first attempt at courtship, he turned his attention elsewhere. The Lefroy family, as Mrs Austen had long proffered, added colour and charm to the rural Hampshire landscape and as luck would have it, Madam Lefroy had a sister. She had come to settle in Deane Rectory with their brother, Samuel Egerton Brydges, who was a writer. James called on him when he was back in Steventon and the two men sat up late discussing politics, books and history. It was impossible not to cross paths with Miss Charlotte Brydges during these intellectual visits and it did not take James long to appreciate her beauty. He gazed at her soft features enhanced by the candlelight of the supper table, thinking that she resembled a pretty, porcelain doll.

"Oh Lord!" exclaimed the lady one morning, walking down the lane with Madam Lefroy. "There's Mr Austen again! I swear he knows my every movement."

The two sisters were walking back to Ashe Rectory follow-ing a visit to Overton. Madam Lefroy had purchased some ribbon and some lace and she and Charlotte were planning a productive day sitting by the rectory window, altering some old ball gowns to make them new again.

"Good day to you, Madam Lefroy, Miss Brydges." James stepped down from his horse and dipped himself into a low bow.

"I have just called at Deane Rectory, Miss Brydges, in the hopes of seeing you, but I was told you were visiting your sister."

"As you see," replied Charlotte through gritted teeth.

"I would ask you in for refreshments, Mr Austen, but sadly we have a prior engagement," lied Madam Lefroy. "My husband is preparing for an important meeting and does not wish to be disturbed. So, we are only returning to put down our purchases and then we must be off again."

Charlotte said nothing, focusing her gaze on the lane beyond.

"In that case, please allow me to accompany you," offered James a little too eagerly.

"There is no need for that," gasped Charlotte, quickly. "Please do not trouble yourself. We would hate to keep you from your business."

It was true that James really did have some business to attend to, but he would gladly have given it up for the opportunity of gazing into Charlotte's cool blue eyes.

Charlotte avoided his stare.

"As you wish," he conceded. "But perhaps I may be allowed to call on you tomorrow, Miss Brydges?"

"Oh, Mr Austen," interrupted Madam Lefroy again. "I am afraid you will be most unhappy with me. I must steal Charlotte away for myself for the coming days. There are so many matters to attend to before the ball at the end of the month, I simply cannot spare her."

Charlotte nodded dumbly. How she loved her sister!

James was deflated, but he had no reason to believe the ladies were not telling him the truth.

"That is a pity. I must postpone my visit until a more convenient time. But of course, I will see you at the ball?" There could be no mistaking his intentions now.

Charlotte shuffled her feet uneasily on the ground and squeezed her toes into tight curls inside her boot to distract herself from saying something impolite. Only a few days previously, James had written her a poem which she had not acknowledged; his ardent declarations of love and desire had alarmed her.

'This must not continue', she told herself, sternly. 'I must rebuke this man's advances before he accepts my silence as consent.'

"I must satisfy myself with my pen until we meet again," James continued to ramble. "I have been composing some more verses. I will leave them for you the next time I call on Mr Brydges and perhaps you would be good enough to let me know what you think?"

Charlotte felt sick at the thought and two weeks later, poor James Austen was heartbroken again.

'What is it with women?' he asked himself in the mirror soon after. 'Why is it so hard for them to like me?' He was attractive enough, he figured and he knew he had a kind soul. His mouth was not so bad when he examined it from different angles and his eyes were bright enough. Why was that not

131

enough?

Tracing his hands through his hair to experiment with the style, his thoughts took him back to Betsy, and the way she used to tie ribbons into his blond childhood locks. How they had laughed all those years ago; he would do anything to speak to her again. Romance between them was impossible now, he knew that, but maybe if they simply talked together in the easy way they always had, then she would help him feel better about himself. She might even have an unattached friend.

Mr and Mrs Austen were surprised when they saw an envelope addressed to 'Comtesse Eliza de Feuillide' at her latest French address. "You are writing to your cousin? For what purpose?"

"I was hoping I may pay her a visit and introduce myself to her husband. I have some time before I am deaconed and have a mind to see something of France."

James was twenty-two years of age now and his parents could hardly stop him. He was a devoted son and had readily accepted his mission to follow his father's footsteps into the church. They had little choice but to keep their misgivings to themselves.

Three weeks later Eliza's reply came and James tore at the seal hungrily.

*Dearest Cousin,*

*I would be delighted to receive you in France. I have missed you so much! I often recall the fond days of our childhood and the games we played in the meadows at Steventon.*

James felt himself shaking. It was as if he could hear her voice whispering in his ear.

*But I fear we must postpone our meeting a little longer. I am planning to leave France myself soon, and our paths will surely cross along the way if you sail on the dates you propose. I am happily expecting a child, and my husband is keen for our baby to be born in England. I will therefore be returning with my mother to London in the spring.*

*The Comte de Feuillide is keen to make your acquaintance (I have told him so much about you!) and he bids me to offer you an open invitation to visit him whenever you desire. He will not accompany me to England as he is working on the drainage of some land around his property. If you are interested in seeing the project in operation you are most welcome to join him.*

All of James's energy left his body and he slumped down in his chair. His mood switched from elation to gloom in an instant. How many rejections could a man take? James could not recall a time in his life when he had felt so low.

No one wanted to be courted by him.

No one understood how inferior he felt next to Neddy and Fulwar, with their easy charm and good fortune.

Even Henry, on occasion, was more popular than he was and Henry was six years his junior.

His next letter was addressed to the Comte.

*I would be delighted to make your acquaintance, Sir. I am most interested in learning about the drainage of your land...*

Perhaps he would have better luck in France.

# Chapter 19

## 1786
### A Steventon Christmas.

The afternoon service at St Nicholas' Church on the third Sunday of Advent concluded in much the same way it always did. Mr Austen positioned himself at the church door to converse with his parishioners, whilst Mrs Austen busied herself inside with tidying the box pew and sweeping away clumps of mud and leaves blown in by the congregation.

It was bone-chillingly cold with a light mizzle outside and Mr Austen shuddered when he eventually closed the wooden door behind him and stepped back inside. Immediately, the bitter draught was replaced by a weighty silence that warmed the church.

"Everyone seems to be looking forward to Christmas," he informed his wife, his deep voice resounding around the empty chasm. Darkness was falling fast outside.

"It will be strange for us to celebrate without James and Neddy this year," Mrs Austen reflected with a hint of sadness, extinguishing the tiny orange flames along the nave with a gold-handled candle snuffer.

"Yes, it will. And they will miss our little gatherings too, I'm sure. But we should not feel so bad for them, my love. What an opportunity for them both. How magnificent those snowy mountains must be at this time of year."

Neddy had recently embarked upon his Grand Tour of the Continent. A few weeks previously, he had sailed across to France and then ambled his way by travelling chariot over the mountain passes to Switzerland. He had initially settled in the town of Neuchatel on the shores of a lake, where he had befriended some other young gentlemen who were also on tours. Together they had designed an itinerary to visit every Swiss town they could get to, taking in as many museums and concerts they could cram in along the way.

James had sailed down to southern France to stay with the Comte de Feuillide. Despite being a lover of poetic flourishes, James could also be a man of very few words when it suited him, and his letters up to now had revealed little of his state of mind.

"Not to worry, we shall have a full house regardless," Mr Austen forecast. "It will be like the old days with Philadelphia and Eliza coming to stay."

Mr Austen was looking forward to hosting his sister and niece in his home once more, and he smiled whilst he straightened his leaflets and prayer book on the lectern.

"Our girls will love having the new baby to fuss over," Mrs Austen volunteered. "I wonder how Eliza enjoys being a mother?"

"More than Philadelphia enjoys being called Grandmama, I'm sure," chuckled Mr Austen mischievously.

The child had been born in June and even though the Comte de Feuillide had wanted his wife to give birth in England,

Eliza had not made it far enough in time. The baby boy had arrived whilst she was still in Calais. Thankfully, there were no complications and by the end of the summer they were all safely settled in London, accompanied by a collection of servants who had travelled alongside them from France.

The first visitors to offer their congratulations at the hotel when they arrived in England were Warren Hastings and his wife Marian. Mr Hastings had not long returned from India himself, determined this time that it would be for good. Any animosity between him and Philadelphia was soon forgotten and Mr and Mrs Hastings invited the family to be guests in their home. They helped them to secure permanent lodgings in London and in return, the baby was christened Hastings. Eliza was eager to resume a close relationship with her godfather.

When all was in order in Steventon Church and every candle had been snuffed out, Mr and Mrs Austen stepped outside, locking the door and placing the key in the hollowed-out trunk of the old yew tree for safekeeping. Their eyes were still adjusting to the dark when a pheasant squawked in front of them, flapping its wings and scurrying off into the hedge. A glow of candlelight in the windows of the Manor House opposite guided the couple along the lane to where they could just about make out the tufts of smoke curling from their own rectory chimney in the meadow below.

"I cannot wait to see Frank," admitted Mrs Austen, trying to avoid the muddy puddles as she went. "It seems an age since we saw him last."

Frank was a good correspondent and wrote regularly from the Naval Academy. He was enjoying himself there enormously and was looking forward to telling his parents all about it during his few days back home over the Christmas holidays.

"He has done well this year," confirmed his father. "His reports have been outstanding. I must be sure to tell him how proud we both are."

Cassandra and Jane were also due to return home from the Abbey School in Reading, but Mr and Mrs Austen had been disappointed by the whole experience of sending them there. The cost of financing such an education far outweighed any progress they had made, and it had been decided that their daughters would not be returning as pupils next term.

In the lead-up to the twelve days of Christmas, both kitchens of the rectory were hives of activity. The servants were constantly up to their elbows in flour and the sweet smell of sugar paste wafted through every room. No one escaped their duties without red glowing cheeks or a dewy forehead, shiny with perspiration.

It had been more than six years since Mr Austen had seen his sister and niece and on their day of arrival he awaited their carriage with a mixture of excitement and trepidation. He need not have worried; within minutes of them arriving it was as if the old familiarity between them had never been disturbed. Warm embracing hugs were passed from one to another accompanied by squeals of joy and excitement to be together again after such a long period of time. Constant mutterings of 'How much you have grown!' 'How pretty you have become,' fell in a continuous flow from Eliza's lips as she made her way along the line of her cousins.

Henry was shocked when he saw her. He had been a young schoolboy the last time they had met and she had been of no more consequence in his life than any other guest who came to stay. But now, Eliza, Comtesse de Feuillide, struck him as every bit as magnificent as her name implied.

Her almond-shaped face was radiant, her deep brown eyes sparkled with wit and with life, and he was captivated by the slow, teasing curl that formed around her commanding, rouged lips. Her sumptuous dark hair tumbled about her ears like a waterfall, cascading from a shimmering jewelled headband to land on her daringly exposed bronzed shoulders. She smelled of zesty wild herbs and citrus; Henry thought he had never met anyone so breathtakingly beautiful in the whole of his life. He could not comprehend why he had never noticed her before.

She was also very proud of her baby. Hastings was six months old and completely indulged with whatever he demanded. His rosy cheeks creased with dimples and his chubby little fingers flexed in and out. The girls fussed over him like he was a puppet, swinging him high and low, first one way and then another.

Philadelphia was little changed and dressed as elegantly as ever. Her gown shone like a raindrop, made from light grey silk. A slim, fitted bodice was drawn tight at the neck and waist and then opened out wide at either side. Her shoulders looked bonier than they used to, next to her wide fan-shaped sleeves and she stooped more when she walked. Otherwise, her sing-song voice rattled around the rectory as gaily as it ever had.

Life in France had aged her, thought Mrs Austen to herself, but judging by her animated recollections of visits to Versailles, accounts of her dashing son-in-law and remembrances of the splendour of southern France, it was an experience she had enjoyed.

On Christmas Eve the family woke early. Tradition dictated the tasks which everyone must fulfil and there was no time to spare. The children may have been adolescents and keen, at any other time of year, to show off their maturity and independence, but Christmas was a time for each of them to regress. They had fond memories from their early years that none of them were ready to let go.

Mr and Mrs Austen's task was to decorate the church. The plain and simple nave was transformed into a theatre of colour, with fresh new candles placed in clusters to magnify the warm, golden light. They placed holly, ivy, mistletoe and laurel upon the windowsills and tied silver ribbons around sprigs of rosemary on the pulpit. Each pew was carefully adorned with red and silver ribbons.

The effect was mesmerizing; it looked like they had taken a plain wooden box and covered it in a rich, regal blanket. Every straight line was softened, every cold stone was warmed, and every shadow became a summer's afternoon.

Outside in the frosty meadows, the girls and Charles collected greenery to decorate the rectory. They chopped the best holly with the juiciest berries and plucked the brightest ivy with the prettiest leaves. Later they would form them into wall hangings and table decorations, but for now every child's pocket was stuffed full of woodland foliage and every pair of arms groaned under the weight of their treasure.

A little further on, Henry and Frank were collecting the Yule log. It had been chosen the week before by Mr Austen and cut down by Mr Bond. All it required now was to be brought into the house.

It had originally been the branch of an old oak tree and its thick, ridged bark was already starting to peel away from its trunk. Dark circles spanned out from its centre like the ripples on a pond and it took a great effort to lift. The boys tied a netting of hazel twigs around the log and dragged it back breathlessly to the house, making their fingers sticky with sap and sore from splinters. Tonight, it would be lit to mark the beginning of the festivities and then burn continuously until Twelfth Night, when its softened cinders would be all that was left.

Back in the house, Philadelphia and Eliza were in charge of filling the wassail bowl. It was customary for a wandering choir of neighbours to call upon every household on Christmas Eve to sing for them and play tunes. They would raise their cups to toast the health of the family inside, and in return for the entertainment, their empty cups would be replenished with an offering from each household's wassail bowl. In the rectory, this meant a heavy, warm negus made up of port wine and water, generously sweetened with sugar and garnished with lemon and nutmeg.

On Christmas Day itself, everyone got up early for church. The bells rang out proud and long, and a full congregation buzzed with kind wishes.

Church was followed by a grand roast turkey dinner and there seemed no end to the plum pudding and mince pies that the family devoured afterwards. They chatted happily and companionably late into the evening, roasting chestnuts on the fire.

The next day, the Austen family gave gifts to their servants, packed in little brown paper boxes tied up with string. It was the time of year to thank them for their loyalty, followed later in the day by the distribution of food parcels and coins to any neighbours facing hard times.

Dancing was not forgotten either, and when Edward and Jane Cooper arrived on New Year's Day, Mr Austen borrowed a pianoforte from the Digweed's manor. Eliza played her repertoire of fashionable tunes whilst her young cousins laughed and pranced their way around the parlour. Then they sang songs together and played charades.

The seasonal message of peace and goodwill has forever been poignant in its ability to heal rifts and appease relationships, and in Steventon Rectory this was no exception. To everyone's joy and satisfaction, Philadelphia and Eliza were welcomed warmly back into the bosom of the family as if they had never been away.

# Chapter 20

**1787**

**Cupid calls at the rectory.**

E arly in the new year, Henry Austen was invited to London. Philadelphia and Eliza had taken a house in Orchard Street, a stylish location near to Portman Square. Having spent such a pleasurable time together over the Christmas holidays, Eliza was desirous to show her charismatic young cousin the sights.

Mrs Austen thought it a splendid idea, deciding that Henry was exactly the right age to appreciate the fine theatres and museums. It would do him no harm at all to make some influential acquaintances whilst he was there.

Henry was politely gracious in his acceptance and wrote a well-mannered letter to his aunt, but privately his emotions were in turmoil. It was a miracle no one could hear his heartbeat banging out of his chest. At sixteen years of age he was at his most impressionable, and the prospect of spending time with his beautiful, provocative, flirtatious cousin filled him with enough nervous excitement to intoxicate him.

Cassandra and Jane waved him off disconsolately, knowing that their own travelling days were over. Thanks to their parents' decision to take them out of school, the only reason they would leave the rectory now would be for some well-meaning relative to parade them up and down an Assembly Room to attract a husband. At fourteen and eleven, that remained a long way off.

Now that Frank and Neddy had left home for good, and James was absent more often than not, the rectory had more space. The girls were afforded the luxury of another room for their own particular use, in addition to their bedroom. It became their dressing room and a place to talk and speculate away from their mother's earshot. A place for Jane to enjoy her writing and Cassandra to practise her art.

Today, the young author was writing a short story in letters. It was meant as an entertaining charade, whereby three different couples would all be matched together by the end. Cassandra was painting a landscape, dipping her brush in and out of her water glass to mix an array of colours from her paintbox.

"What are you working on?" enquired Cassandra to her sister. "Are we to discover at last what will become of Mr Clifford?"

Jane had been writing about her fictional Mr Clifford the day before but had struggled to come up with a satisfactory conclusion to his adventures. "No. Mr Clifford is still at the bottom of Basingstoke Hill. I'm not sure where I shall put him next. I am working on something new, for Mama."

She dipped her quill into the inkpot and looked up. "I think it will meet with her approval: two sisters and one brother will marry within the week."

They both burst into giggles.

"Respectable marriages, I hope?" questioned Cassandra,

the smile still on her lips.

"Of course."

"Then I agree that she will like it very well."

"Would you like me to read what I have so far?" offered Jane, picking up her manuscript.

"Yes, please." Cassandra sat up straight and wiped her brush on a rag.

Jane cleared her throat and began. "My dear Amelia. You will rejoice to hear of the return of my amiable brother ..."

The sound of horses on the driveway made her stop.

"Are we expecting visitors?"

"Not that I'm aware."

Both girls rushed to the window to see who had arrived and watched a slim, blond-haired gentleman dismount nimbly from his imposing black stallion. He was accompanied by another man, slightly taller, standing by a chestnut mare and attempting to pat down his mousey-brown hair with his hands before replacing his hat.

The blond man made a joke and straightened his companion's cravat for him, but the words were inaudible through the glass of the window.

"It's Fulwar," squealed Jane. "And Tom!"

"What are they doing here?" mumbled Cassandra, trying unsuccessfully to control her shaking hands as she wiped them on the rag. She could feel the flush on her cheeks whilst she fumbled to change her old cap for one that complimented her better. "Surely they know James is away in France?"

"Of course, they do. But why should they not come to call on us? Hurry, let's go down."

Jane's logic was just. When Fulwar Fowle and his brother Tom were pupils in the schoolroom, they had all been friends together. It was true that James and Fulwar had become close, but not to the exclusion of anyone else. And Tom had been amicable with everyone, partnering both girls in impromptu dances and siding for the same teams in sports.

"COME ON!" ordered Jane, grabbing her sister's hand and pulling her through the door.

They entered the parlour as sedately as they could manage, deploying their best feminine charm. But finding herself face to face with such dear, old friends was too much for Jane and she failed to maintain her composure.

"Fulwar! Tom! How wonderful to see you!" Both men stood and walked towards her, placing kisses on both of her cheeks.

"Whatever has happened to you?" flattered Fulwar. "What have you done with little Jane? I see only a fine young lady in her place."

Jane laughed, as did her mother and father who had already welcomed their guests and were seated.

"Cassandra. Even more beautiful than I remember." This time Fulwar admired his former playmate's face and figure with genuine appreciation.

Tom Fowle made the perfunctory greetings, blushing as he did so, and unable to hide the fact that he was completely captivated by Cassandra's charms.

"Fulwar has just been telling us his news," stated Mrs Austen, looking pointedly at the young man for him to repeat his tidings.

"Yes. I am to be married!" he effused. "My cousin Eliza and I are betrothed."

Jane, who had still not sat down, clapped her hands together and rushed over to him once more. She shook his hand with

145

vigour and everyone laughed at her impulsiveness.

"We have set the date," he continued. "The service will be at Enborne, in my uncle's church, and I very much hope that James will be back from France in time to attend. I have written to him with an invitation."

James would not be the slightest bit surprised to learn of the engagement.

When Fulwar's happy news had been discussed to the full, Mr Austen turned the conversation towards Tom.

"How long until you graduate, Tom?"

"Next month, Sir. I will attain my Bachelor of Arts and then hope to continue at Oxford to study for my Masters. Presuming I achieve the correct standard," he added a little uneasily. "Some days I doubt I am clever enough for any of it."

"I will hear of no such nonsense. You are an excellent scholar, always have been."

Tom nodded his appreciation and blushed some more.

"Papa has often told us that your understanding of Virgil is amongst the finest he has ever known," Cassandra relayed warmly to her old friend.

"Quite so," agreed her father. "I still bring out your essays even now, when I need an example of quality work to show the new boys."

"So, you see, you must be a little bit clever," teased Cassandra.

Tom's gratitude shone out. It was not because he had been told he was clever, but because Cassandra had been the one to praise him.

The Fowle boys stayed for the whole day, dining with the family and taking a stroll around their old surroundings.

News flowed fast between them, including the fact that Fulwar had almost finished his Masters and was awaiting an audience with Lord Craven, to learn which living was to be presented to him when he wed.

William Fowle, the latest of the brothers to leave Steventon, was moving to London to become apprenticed to his uncle and begin a study of medicine. Only the youngest of the Fowle family, Charles Fowle, was left in the schoolroom now.

It had been the best of days, reflected the girls when they prepared for bed that night. It had been a surprise that the men had called, but extremely welcome all the same.

"He still likes you, I can tell," insisted Jane, before lying down to sleep.

"I don't know what you mean," replied Cassandra, gratified that darkness was hiding the smile creeping along her lips.

"You know very well what I mean," chided her sister. "If Tom Fowle does not ask you to be his wife one day, then I'm a kangaroon!"

# Chapter 21

James Austen returned from France without telling anyone he was on his way. He took a coach from the port and travelled up to Steventon, alighting at the inn on a misty, autumn morning.

In the rectory, the servants were attending to their daily duties with their usual quiet efficiency; Mrs Austen had long ceased paying attention to their clicking footsteps as they moved back and forth along the passageways. Her head was bent intently over a needlework pattern, trying to work out how to correct a careless error she had made in her embroidery.

Mr Austen was in his schoolroom, explaining some complex mathematical formula to his boys. So it was easy, under the circumstances, for James to creep indoors unnoticed. He was in his mother's parlour and almost seated upon the armchair opposite before she looked up.

"Good morning, Mama. How are you?"

A satisfied smile beamed across his face as he took in her shocked features, knowing he had achieved the very surprise he had intended.

"James!"

Her vexation at dropping the stitch was instantly forgotten and her needlework fell to the ground. The stretch of muslin toppled at her feet, but she made no attempt to retrieve it, preferring the joy of embracing her eldest son instead.

"I was only thinking about you this morning!" she blinked.

"And here I am!"

The commotion of his mother's fussing soon alerted the servants to his presence, followed by his sisters and then his father. Finally, Henry and Charles came crashing through the door, delighted to shake his hand.

After dinner, nobody wanted to go up to bed, preferring instead to stay downstairs and listen to James's tales. He told them of France and the kindness of the Comte de Feuillide; he talked of a trip to Spain for the Festival of San Fermin, where bulls had run loose in the streets, and he spoke of a stop he had made in Holland before crossing the Channel back home.

He was in extremely good spirits, with a tanned body and a mind full of happy memories. The trip had done wonders for his morale.

Mr Austen wasted no time in involving him in the church and James threw himself into his new calling with zeal. He was ordained as a deacon in St David's Cathedral in Wales and took on his own responsibilities during the services at Steventon and Deane. He was welcomed warmly when he visited the poor and brought fresh energy and ideas to parish meetings. He busied himself preparing for the family Christmas by organising a play. He was saddened to hear that the traditional theatricals the family normally enjoyed together had not been performed last year in his absence and was determined to put it right.

Acting was always a pleasurable affair for the Austens and James took his role of director seriously. He oversaw the making of props and the setting up of the barn for the performance. He ensured there were enough parts for all his brothers and sisters, and wrote extra lines for his cousins and friends, or any neighbour who wanted to join them.

His reunion with his cousin Eliza was another success. When they met over the holidays, they chatted at length about the Comte de Feuillide and the French landscape. He felt empowered to be able to speak of places that only they knew because, apart from Philadelphia, no one else in the household had ever been there. Eliza confided to him her worries for her son, who she revealed had lately been having convulsions. James extolled the benefits of sea bathing and Eliza vowed she would take her boy to the seaside in the spring in the hopes he would get better.

Back home in London, Eliza and Philadelphia dined frequently with Warren Hastings. He was buying an estate in Gloucestershire that had been associated with his family for centuries. He was joyous at the prospect of settling down with his wife in the pretty village of Daylesford, where he had fond memories as a boy.

Over a meal one evening, their talk turned to the disturbing news from France.

"My husband writes that in every town there is unrest," explained Eliza. "He says that people are desperate because of the rising cost of food. They protest at the taxes which they say are unfair and he is waiting to be recalled to his regiment to help maintain order on the streets."

"Will that prevent you from returning to France as you had planned?" questioned Mr Hastings with a frown. "You really should not go if there is a threat of danger."

"You are very sweet to worry, but I think my husband is being over dramatic. Perhaps the reality will not be so bad when we get there. I do hope so because I know he is desperate to meet his son."

"Which is quite understandable," asserted Philadelphia, putting an end to any hint of ambiguity. "Speaking for myself I cannot wait to go there. I feel my health deteriorate every day that I spend here in the smoke of London and I crave some mountain air."

"In that case, I wish you both safe travels when the time comes," conceded Mr Hastings gallantly.

When dinner was over, he put forth a topic that had been playing on his mind all evening.

"You may read some unpleasant news about me shortly in the newspapers. I thought it best to warn you that there are some people who wish to slur my reputation. I beg that you keep an open mind, rather than condemn me straight off when you read what they have to say."

Eliza leaned forward like an eager child about to be told a secret. "Whatever have you done?" she asked, her eyes widening with anticipation.

"Nothing you need concern yourself with," the gentleman replied, trying to play down the gravity of the accusation. "Merely some messy business from when I was Governor of Bengal. In my view, it is nothing more than nonsense and bad feeling, but these things always tend to be exaggerated when they appear in print."

"It sounds most distressing," sympathised Philadelphia. "If

we can be of assistance in any way then you must speak up."

Marian replied on her husband's behalf. "Thank you. We know that the king and Mr Pitt are sympathetic to the case and pray that their intervention will be enough to get the allegations overturned."

The news did soon reach the papers, and the accusations against Warren Hastings provoked animated debates in every club in London.

Eliza and Philadelphia were fierce in their public support and accompanied him when he walked around Kensington Gardens with their heads held high. They dined with him in the city's restaurants and sat proudly in his box at the opera.

The trial itself was held in Westminster Hall, and soldiers on horseback lined the streets to keep order whilst the rich and the famous flocked from all over the country to witness the spectacle.

For the opening speeches, Eliza sat between her mother and her cousin, Philly Walter, whom she had invited especially to watch the proceedings. They were joined on the front row by Marian Hastings and all eyes in the chamber strained to watch their reactions. Unfortunately, with the hall packed to the rafters, and a constant murmur of voices overshadowing the official formalities, it was difficult for them to hear clearly what was being said.

It was uncomfortably hot and stuffy in the chamber and the pungent air grew thicker and staler as the hours progressed. Some ladies in the audience cried out behind their fluttering fans and others wept into their embroidered handkerchiefs when the alleged atrocities were read out loud. One woman was so overcome that she had to be carried out.

The prosecution announced a stream of charges, which Mr

Hastings bore with dignity. He attempted to remain calm and expressionless, but sitting alone before a sea of opposition gave the impression he was more isolated than he would have liked to appear.

His perfectly manicured hair was a symbol of the very privilege he was being accused of. His smart black jacket, with its shiny brass buttons and silk waistcoat, was an emblem of the wealth that people despised him for. Jeering faces taunted him to confess what he had done.

Far from being a formality, the repeated stories of violence, corruption and cruelty spoke for themselves. Instead of being sent home a free man by the end of the week as he had expected, Prime Minister Pitt called for Mr Hastings to be impeached; he was to face a trial of long duration. His image appeared in national newspapers, drawn by satirists who covered him in jewels to mock his wealth. He became an object of ridicule, and public opinion turned against him.

"This is outrageous!" fumed Mr Austen, finding one such account in his daily newspaper. "Hastings would never break the law. These men are jealous he will take their seats, that's all. That's the real reason for slandering his name."

Mrs Austen listened obediently and murmured agreement where she felt it appropriate, but she was not entirely convinced. *The Lady's Magazine* that she took contained an account of the opening of the trial too, and she read it for herself when her husband had gone out. She could not profess to know if the allegations were true or false, but what she could say with some certainty was that the evidence presented against the man was damning.

# Chapter 22

**1788-1789**
**With age comes responsibility.**

"I pronounce that they be man and wife together, In the Name of the Father, and of the Son, and of the Holy Ghost. Amen."

Reverend Nowes Lloyd proclaimed these time-honoured words in his church of St. Michael's and All Angels in Enborne to his pretty daughter, Eliza, and his nephew, Fulwar Fowle. It was a warm August morning and his paternal pride shone out over the bountiful congregation of family and friends who looked on.

Both mothers shed joyful tears before the blessed young couple stepped out onto the flagstone pathway strewn with a carpet of wildflowers and lavender. Even the birds in the trees twittered their congratulations by singing in unison high above their heads.

Mrs Lloyd linked arms with her two other daughters while they waited outside in the sunshine: Martha on one side and Mary on the other. Her heart felt fit to burst from the huge, fizzing ball of gratitude which expanded inside her chest to see her middle daughter married. They were soon joined by

Reverend Lloyd and each, in their own way, affirmed it to be the most perfect day.

Fulwar's parents strolled up next to them, equally revelling in such a merry occasion and brimming with compliments for the beautiful bride. Whilst Fulwar and Eliza chatted with their well-wishers, the groom's brothers positioned themselves in a group to the side of the church door, making a dashing sight dressed in their elegantly cut suits and dapper top hats. They were oblivious, making small talk, to the many admiring glances being cast in their direction and were joined in their gathering by James Austen, who had travelled on purpose to support his friend on his special day.

Martha and Mary were impatient to escape the sentimental gushings of their mother and aunt recalling their own wedding day memories, so they walked over to join their cousins instead. They laughed at a joke someone made, and their long locks of chestnut hair glistened when they tossed their heads back into the rays of the light.

"I wish it were possible to capture this moment in a painting," sighed Mrs Lloyd, wistfully. "Then we could look at it every day to remember."

Mrs Fowle was busy observing James and studying how he spoke with the girls. She was pleased with his manners and his willingness to prove himself a keen listener.

"I find James Austen a most likeable young man," she chanced. "He will make an excellent catch for some lucky girl."

Mrs Lloyd laughed out loud, understanding her sister's intentions only too well. "You are impossible, do you know that? Will you never give up trying to match my daughters to every newcomer that passes by?"

"Ah, but there you are wrong," teased Mrs Fowle with a playful twinkle in her eye. "James Austen is not a newcomer. We have known him many years now and Fulwar thinks the world of him."

Mrs Lloyd was not to be cajoled into a response, but Mrs Fowle was far too invested in her plan to let it go without a fight.

"You can't tell me you have never thought of him for Martha. Or Mary?"

Mrs Lloyd formed her lips into a shy grin. "Perhaps," she confessed.

Fulwar and Eliza moved away from Kintbury and Enborne to start their new life together in the village of Elkstone in Gloucestershire. Fulwar had been presented with the living of St John the Evangelist by Lord Craven, and the newlyweds were excited at the prospect of living in their charming little rectory built from honey-coloured stone.

\* \* \*

In December, it was customary for Mr Austen to receive a report from the Naval Academy to inform him of Frank's performance over the year. These reports were always complimentary in their findings and so the boy's father was not at all surprised to read of his excellent achievements.

But this year it went further. At the tender age of fourteen, Frank had completed his mathematical learning 'quicker than normally expected'. He had shown 'uncommon assiduity and excellent conduct' in his studies. In short, he had completed all the academic learning required of him in two years instead of three and was ready to take to the seas.

He was granted a brief home leave to say his goodbyes, where he was duly fussed and fretted over amidst a whirlwind of patted backs and anxious tears. He was set to sail in the new year as a volunteer under Captain Isaac Smith on the *Perseverance* heading to the East Indies. He was thrilled by the prospect, not believing himself to be in the slightest danger, leaving his parents to absorb that obligatory worry on his behalf.

Mr Austen withdrew voluntarily from the hysterics in the parlour, giving space for his wife and his daughters to give the new sailor a farewell he would not forget. He used the time instead to write his son a letter. In it, he offered guidance on the scriptures he felt Frank should read and the importance of frequent prayers; he gave advice on how the young man should behave and how he should apply to his father for money when required. Beyond that, he urged Frank to write to his senior officers as soon as he could and thank them for the benefits they were bringing to his career, signing off with best wishes aplenty.

"Read this when you are on your ship, my boy, and think of me as you do so. I want you to know that I am extremely proud of you and rest assured I will pray every day for your safe return."

On board the ship, Frank had no private space to call his own. The only safe place to store his letter was in the pocket of his trousers and he took it out every day to read again. By the time a week had passed, he knew every word by heart.

'I will never let this letter out of my sight,' he vowed to himself, folding it once more into its well-worn creases. 'Wherever I sail in the world, this will always keep me close to my family back home.'

\* \* \*

Life was much quieter in Steventon with everyone gone. Henry had matriculated to Oxford where he lived alongside James, and Philadelphia and Eliza were back in France. Madam Lefroy's brother, Mr Brydges, left the neighbourhood to move to Kent, taking his entire household with him including the delightful Charlotte. Deane Rectory was vacant again, giving Mr Austen the task of preparing an advert for the newspaper to seek a new tenant.

The mood in the rectory was miserable with so few of the family left and it was not helped when a black sealed envelope was delivered at the end of January addressed to Charles Fowle. Mr Austen took his pupil into his study to present him with the letter and to be on hand to offer whatever assistance was necessary when the letter had been read.

"My Uncle Nowes has died," explained the boy with trembling hands and a shaky voice. "My father wishes me to go home to attend the funeral."

"Of course, you must go," agreed Mr Austen. "I am very sorry to hear it, my boy. Your uncle was a good man."

Charles simply nodded, fighting to contain his emotion. Mr Austen had no desire to upset him further and ushered him quickly towards Mrs Austen who, he knew, would organise his departure and keep him bright enough until it was time to make the journey.

Within the week, Reverend Nowes Lloyd was buried in his own sacred churchyard in Enborne, on the same spot he had stood only a few months before to celebrate his daughter's wedding.

Life certainly was contrary.

After the funeral, Charles Fowle was escorted back to Steventon by his eldest brother, who looked extremely sombre in his mourning attire. It was with some visible effort that Fulwar Fowle held up his gaunt and drawn face above the black silk cravat that framed his throat. His unruly blond hair had been tamed beneath his raven-coloured hat, and his grief was yet more pronounced by the addition of a thick satin band wrapped tightly around its rim. His slight figure looked pitiful and vulnerable in his oversized dark suit and he was weighed down with black from every angle, finished with heavy, black gloves to protect his cold hands.

Not half a year had passed since he had been the sprightly young bachelor with a life full of dreams ahead of him. Now, he was bearing the responsibility of a whole family in grief, as was his duty to his wife.

When Fulwar had sat with his little brother and Mrs Austen in the parlour for half an hour, Mr Austen invited him into his study for a reviving glass of brandy in front of the crackling fire.

"My father-in-law's illness was not a long one, thankfully," Fulwar revealed, by way of explanation. "Although for his final weeks, Eliza tells me that he became a sad and nervous invalid. He kept to his own room and on some days was equal to nothing."

"He was the best of men," reflected Mr Austen. "He always had a kind word for everyone in Oxford."

"I could not have wished for a more benevolent uncle and father-in-law," agreed Fulwar. "I miss him a great deal already."

"I will call for some refreshments," Mr Austen decided, ringing the tiny bell on his desk. "You must not venture out into the cold again until you have eaten something warm."

Fulwar looked at him despondently, his thoughts elsewhere.

"Be assured we will keep a good eye on Charles. He will be allowed to grieve in his own way, and we will support him with whatever he needs," Mr Austen offered by way of consolation.

Fulwar leaned forward in his chair and cleared his throat. "I have no doubt of that, Sir. And I thank you for your kindness."

Mr Austen could see something else was troubling the young man, greater even than the well-being of his brother.

"I hope we are old acquaintances enough by now that I may be allowed to speak freely?" said Fulwar, attempting a confidence it was obvious he did not feel.

"Certainly, my boy. Go ahead."

"I have been thinking, Sir. When I received word from James at Christmas, he wrote that the rectory in Deane had become vacant. Does it remain so?"

"Yes," replied Mr Austen, a little confused as to the question. "I have advertised it, but these things often take time."

Fulwar looked relieved and Mr Austen thought for a moment that he wished to take it for himself: but why, he could not imagine.

"You will understand, Sir, that my aunt and my cousins are now in need of a home. If it is not too presumptuous of me, I wonder if you may consider them to be your next lodgers?"

Mr Austen let out an exclamation of surprise and took a moment to gather his thoughts. "I certainly have no objection to the idea," he conveyed. "But do they not wish to stay close to Enborne - or Kintbury even – to be nearer to your own mother and father?"

"I'm sure they would, Sir, if it were that easy. But there is nothing suitable to be found in the village. We have tried, I assure you, but nothing can be practically done for them there."

"Yet they will be strangers here in Deane. And under such terrible circumstances."

"They will be strangers wherever they go, Sir, when they are forced from the rectory in Enborne. These situations are impossible to resolve happily."

Mr Austen could only agree. It was the way of the world that once the man of the house died, the women he left behind were at the mercy of whichever relation could provide for them.

"The truth is, Sir," Fulwar continued, now flushing slightly. "I do not consider Deane to be wholly foreign to our family. My brothers and I have spent some of our best days in this house and the neighbourhood is familiar to all of us. I believe it would be a far better prospect for my aunt to relocate here than to somewhere none of us has ever been."

Mr Austen acknowledged this reasoning and respected Fulwar's logic.

"I think more importantly, Sir, I am encouraged by the fact that you will be the person to oversee the affairs of Deane Rectory. I cannot think of anyone I trust beyond my own parents, more than yourself and Mrs Austen."

Mr Austen was humbled by this declaration and folded his hands in his lap to give the matter his full consideration.

"You have been the very best of guardians to me and my brothers – indeed all the boys in the school - and I know that my aunt would be in no better place than under your guardianship during these dark times for her. I do not forget your kind daughters either, Sir, who I know will be the most excellent companions for my cousins."

Fulwar's tone had lightened a little for his passionate speech and he was finding it cathartic to share his concerns.

"Martha and Mary are used to hearing about Cassandra and Jane whenever any of us are home for the holidays, so there is a connection there already. I am certain they will become friends."

Mr Austen was reminded of the exchange he had witnessed between Cassandra and Tom Fowle the last time they had parted from each other; neither could he ignore the growing friendship that was developing between Jane and Charles Fowle this very year. Fulwar was right, the two families shared a bond already.

Emboldened further, Fulwar raised the topic of money.

"You may be assured, Sir, that my aunt has been well provided for by my uncle, so there is no question of relying upon your charity. And she is of good social standing; you will not be disgraced by the acquaintance."

"I do not doubt your honour for one moment, my boy," Mr Austen replied with sincerity. "If you are certain that is what your aunt and your parents would like, then I am happy to oblige."

"Thank you, Sir. Thank you." Fulwar's face reddened and he took in a deep breath. Then, just as quickly, he seemed to cave in on himself, deflated by the effort the discourse had caused him.

"Come," guided Mr Austen, standing to move towards the door. "Let us eat now and break the news to Mrs Austen. She will be ecstatic at the prospect of an agreeable new neighbour to call upon."

Fulwar smiled too and the two men shook hands to seal the

agreement before heading towards the dining room, where they were tempted by the enticing aroma of a spicy winter soup and freshly baked bread.

# Chapter 23

**1789**
**New Neighbours.**

T he Lloyd ladies arrived at Deane Rectory in the spring to a very warm welcome. They looked tired and pale when they alighted from their carriage, but regardless of how they must have been feeling, they each tried in their own way to appear amicable.

Martha was the tallest of the three, towering by a head over her greying mother. She wore her long brown hair tucked into a tight bun beneath a black bonnet and she stretched out a graceful hand to greet her new neighbours.

Mary's face was concealed underneath a hood, which she wore low to hide the pox marks on her face. Her senses had reached the point of overload on the journey with all the new sights and smells and her wary eyes flitted from one face to another.

Mrs Lloyd made an incredible effort and thanked everyone wholeheartedly for their kindness in allowing them to stay at the rectory. She took Jane and Cassandra's hands in her own and kissed Mrs Austen on both cheeks. She was a true inspiration to her girls, remaining calm and serene and insisting that God was her guide and as He had brought her to Deane, she had no fears about setting up home there.

Most of the servants from Enborne had chosen to accompany their mistresses and so for the first couple of days, the Lloyds asked to be left alone to get organised. On the third day, Mrs Austen and her daughters went to call.

Once inside her old home, Mrs Austen could not resist offering her new friend advice on the layout of her furniture. "I think the best place for your screen is over here because the draught can blow alarmingly from that passage. And if you position your armchair here, like so, then you will be quite comfortable even on the coldest of days."

Martha and Mary were quick to establish a cosy parlour, setting up a side table with a pretty lace cloth on which to place the tea things. Both daughters were exceedingly well-trained in etiquette and Mrs Austen admired their manners immediately. They allowed their mother to be the centre of attention, taking care of the pouring and the serving, and handing out teacups and plates discreetly to their guests.

They both wore matching oval lockets on simple gold chains which caught the light when they moved. The lockets had glass fronts, to display a lock of their father's white hair, tied with the finest slice of silk ribbon. Mrs Lloyd wore a similar locket as a brooch, larger than the girls', but with the same sample of wispy hair plaited together like one might weave a straw basket. She touched her fingers to it unconsciously when she spoke, seeking comfort from its presence next to her heart.

Mrs Lloyd and her daughters were dressed from head to toe in black, as were the servants, but the mood in Deane Rectory was deliberately cheerful and upbeat. "We cannot choose when we are laid to rest," was a common theme in their discourse. "All we can do is strive to serve God in the best way we can until the time comes when we are called to Him ourselves."

Martha was twenty-three at the time of the move and Mary was eighteen, so there was quite a difference in ages between Cassandra and Jane who were sixteen and thirteen. Nevertheless, the Austen girls proved capable guides to the newcomers. They went together to Overton where Cassandra and Jane showed them where to collect their post along the way, and where to find the best purchases in the shops. They informed them about the different families in the neighbourhood and a friendship soon blossomed.

Mrs Austen stayed close to Mrs Lloyd when her neighbours came to call. Her familiar presence helped to lessen the awkwardness of a new acquaintance and her knowledge of the individuals ensured that addresses to the widow were based on safe and neutral topics.

When six months had passed since her husband's death, Mrs Lloyd felt ready to return the calls in person. She still sought Mrs Austen's company, requesting that she remained by her side for moral support, but it was hardly necessary for such a popular woman who was welcomed wherever she went.

Mary preferred to stay home if she was able and took on the organisation of the rooms. She was an anxious soul and meticulous in her arrangements, wanting everything to be in perfect order. The servants had gotten used to her fastidious ways a long time ago and were generously accepting of her demands.

Martha took charge of the dressmaking. The mourning

clothes they had all worn up to now had been hastily cut from bombazine, a heavy silk with winter in mind. Now that the days were turning warmer, crape garments would be a more comfortable alternative.

Martha unpacked their dresses from the previous summer and sought out those that could be easily dyed; she aimed to turn the lighter shades of muslin into grey or lavender. It would be quite acceptable now for the grieving daughters to be seen in garments of colour, so long as the earthen shades were paired with a dark apron or shawl.

Martha joined Cassandra and Jane several times a week to sit with them in their dressing room at Steventon. The blue wallpaper and blue and white striped curtains bore witness to their intimate conversations, and rainbow-coloured threads toppled haphazardly from their work boxes onto the chocolate-coloured floor.

It became quite the centre of industry and the three young ladies shared patterns, cut fabric, made caps, and picked flower petals to colour the clothes. Their efficient teamwork brought swift results and not a month had passed before they marvelled at how they had ever managed without one another.

"I am quite determined for you to marry my brother, James," decided Jane one day, addressing Martha as she sewed. "You are of a similar age and height. You would make an excellent match, I think."

Martha laughed. "Oh no, I couldn't possibly. It would break poor Mary's heart."

Jane and Cassandra looked up in unison with the same surprised expression. "Mary and James? Surely not."

"Oh yes," returned Martha, still smiling. "I believe her

preference towards him stems from the very first time he stayed in Kintbury."

"But she is so quiet and …" Jane wanted to say strange, but knew it would sound like an insult. "She is so shy," she corrected herself.

"She is shy with strangers," accepted Martha. "Yet once you get to know her better you will find she is far more intelligent than I am and considerably more disciplined. She and James have much in common and she is very fond of him, I have no doubt."

"Well, well…" plotted Cassandra. "We shall have to see what we can do to throw them together."

"We certainly will," agreed Jane, looking forward to the prospect of some matchmaking.

"So," continued Jane. "If it is not to be James, then who will you marry? One of your cousins, perhaps?"

Martha was amused by her young friend's insistence.

"No. It was clear from a very young age that Eliza and Fulwar would marry. They have been inseparable for years. But for me, my cousins are like brothers. I share no romantic attachment with any of them."

Cassandra concentrated extra hard on stabbing her fabric with her labouring needle, grateful that Martha had no designs on Tom Fowle.

"Besides," continued Martha. "I understand Tom is already spoken for. He would not have me even if I wanted him."

She expressed herself so simply and plainly that Jane felt the need to slip a sideways glance at Cassandra. What could Martha mean?

Their friend was enjoying watching the exchanges between the two sisters, prolonging the silence for as long as she could to see who would be the first to speak. In the end, it was Cassandra.

"I had no idea. I had not heard he was betrothed."

"I don't believe he has asked her yet. But I do know his brothers tease him about her all the time in Kintbury."

The joke was not playing out as well as Martha had intended; she had expected Cassandra to understand her meaning and join in the fun.

"Will you not ask who she is, or shall I be forced to tell you?" Martha asked, looking for a way to resume the jollity.

Cassandra kept her cool, still looking down at her needle. "You may tell us if you wish."

"My dear Cassandra, it is no other than you! I thought it would be obvious to you both or I would not have tormented you so."

She reached for Cassandra's hand whilst her own face blushed with shame. "I'm sorry to have jested with you. I meant no offence."

Cassandra smiled back and blushed prettily too.

Martha was relieved. "Believe me, dear friend, Tom thinks you are the most beautiful and sweet-tempered girl he has ever met."

Jane picked up the cushion that was supporting her back and threw it at Martha's feet. "What a terrible prankster you are, Martha Lloyd. Why could you not say so right at the beginning!" Yet despite her protectiveness towards her sister, Jane was laughing too.

"Is that really what he says?" asked Cassandra bashfully.

"Yes. That is really what he says," confirmed Martha. "And knowing you as I do now, I completely understand why."

# Chapter 24

**1789-1790**
**The Loiterer.**

James Austen was enjoying life in Oxford as a bachelor, oblivious to the fact that he had a secret admirer in Mary Lloyd.

The city coffee houses were his friends and, amid the smoke, sweat and steam that always greeted him inside, James would engage in long debates with peers and strangers alike. The coffee itself was no attraction (it made him think of ink every time he tasted it) but what really enticed him into the crowded corners was the opportunity to thump his fist down on the long wooden tables when he wanted to emphasise a point. Then he held the attention of all the fellows in the room.

James had recently become the editor of a successful periodical magazine called *The Loiterer*. He had named it after his procrastinating peers whom he knew would take it to read every Saturday morning over their leisurely breakfast muffins.

He had begun its publication rather tentatively, enlisting only the help of his brother Henry at first, then soon after recruiting their friend from Hampshire, Benjamin Portal.

The purpose of the paper was a humorous glance into academic life and a satirical, light-hearted discussion of current affairs.

There was much enthusiasm amongst the three young men to produce a quality product, but there was also much secrecy. Each writer was identified by only a single letter of the alphabet and their editorial meetings took place in different coffee houses around the town. The men were charged a penny each to enter, but that was soon paid back through the plentiful supply of daily newspapers they could access when they were in there, and the never-ending stream of conversation they could listen in to.

"We must include some correspondence soon," stated Henry, pointing to the letters page of a well-known newspaper. "Our articles must appear authentic; people should react to what we say."

"They should complain too," supplemented Mr Portal. "People need to show anger. That way our loyal readers will feel the need to come to our defence."

"Clever," smirked James. "I like your logic."

They each took fresh sips of their coffee and grimaced as they forced the bitter liquid down their throats.

James took charge of the proceedings. "Let us consider some of the fellows we know; perhaps we could draft a letter based on something they might say? Whom do we know who is outspoken?"

Henry furrowed his brow in concentration; James looked around the room listening for words he could steal as his own; Benjamin Portal swirled the final dribble of grey liquid around the bottom of his cup, trying to get a stubborn clump of sugar to dissolve without success.

"Why not a woman?" he prompted.

James looked blank, but Henry liked the idea. "Why not indeed?"

Benjamin continued in a mock high-pitched voice: "I am frightfully sorry to be presumptuous, Sir - but I feel I must point out an error ..." He acted out a fluttering of eyelashes and waved an imaginary fan in front of his face.

Henry laughed obligingly but James was not convinced.

"Honestly, Portal, how many women do you know who speak like that? I've never met such a helpless damsel in my life!"

Benjamin thought some more. Images circulated around his mind of women who had left a strong impression on him. "What about Madame de Feuillide? She would be an excellent choice. I'm sure a letter from her would reveal a magnificently colourful character."

James and Henry were hesitant. Each of them still considered Eliza to be their own personal property (notwithstanding the fact that she already had a husband and a child). They were uneasy about releasing her conversations into the wider world and reluctant to share her with anyone else.

"What about Jane?" Henry clapped his palm down on the wooden table making his saucer tilt and clatter. "Do you remember in the holidays, James, when we were talking about setting up *The Loiterer*? Jane was determined we should include some romantic stories in its content."

James and Benjamin laughed and Henry took this as encouragement.

"A foolish idea, I agree. But you see, our sister writes stories of her own," he explained for the benefit of his friend. "I'm certain she would be able to put something together for us if we asked her."

Benjamin was silent, remembering Jane as a rather silly girl running about a meadow from his last visit to Steventon.

James took up Henry's inefficient explanation. "The point is, many of the stories she writes are in the form of letters." He was following his brother's pattern of thought and liked the idea. "Her characters can be ridiculous it's true, but she does have an assertive style and I would say her work is largely entertaining."

Henry illustrated the theory to his friend. "How dare you, Sir! I will take no nonsense from you so off I go! Your publication is diabolical!" The three friends laughed.

"Sounds amusing enough," agreed Benjamin.

"Well?" persisted Henry. "Shall we ask her?"

"Yes, let's do it," decided James. "She can criticise our periodical: tell us we are a disgrace to women everywhere - that sort of thing. Are you planning to go home before the end of term?"

"I could go next week if it will help," offered Henry.

"Excellent. Then take this piece with you ..." He fished out a script that Henry had written from a pile of papers that were laid on the table in front of him. It was about a curate who had gone to live in Yorkshire. "Tell Jane to use this as the basis of her complaint. We can publish your piece on week eight, and the letter on week nine."

The plan of action was taking shape. "Be sure to oversee what she writes, Henry. It must fit the style of our magazine."

"We shall need a suitable name for our dear lady," reminded Benjamin Portal when the preparations of the two brothers had run their course. "She must be a sentimental sole if she is to represent the fairer sex."

The plans were executed with precision and an engaging letter was provided. James sent a copy of the printed magazine to Steventon so that the family could read it aloud after dinner, and everyone agreed with a chuckle that Sophia Sentiment expressed her point very well indeed!

\* \* \*

By mid-summer, the coffee shops were dominated by more disturbing news from France. Mobs were taking to the streets and calling for the monarchy to be overthrown. At first, it seemed ridiculous to the privileged young men of Oxford that such a thing should occur, and it was initially greeted as a form of compulsive entertainment. But after a while, the gruesome reports made folk uneasy. Riots were happening in every town on a progressively grander scale and the graphic reports were terrifying.

"Papa writes that Aunt Philadelphia, Eliza and the boy have set sail," James informed Henry after reading his post. "The Comte will obviously remain with his regiment for the time being, but our aunt and cousin are to lodge with Mr Woodman in London until it is safe for them to return."

One week later, newspapers were reporting the most catastrophic events in Paris yet - the Bastille had been destroyed and its prisoners set free; the Governor had been beheaded and his severed skull paraded around the streets on a pole; King Louis XVI and Queen Marie Antoinette had gone into hiding amid the anarchy.

Alarmingly for the English nobility, unrest grew in London too. Debates raged day and night about who was to blame, and pockets of activists became inspired to plot a similar revolution against King George. Tension settled over the country.

It was time, decided James, to leave Oxford and return to Steventon. He felt the need to offer protection to his parents and his siblings and return to the place where he had always felt safest as a boy. Who knew what these frightful scenes in France might lead to?

He completed his ordination and took up his first living as curate of St. Mary's Church in Overton, not two miles cross-country from the rectory at Steventon.

Nobody in Oxford was interested in a humorous periodical at such a time as this, so *The Loiterer* was no more.

# Chapter 25

## 1790-1791
### A Wedding Rehearsal.

One of the first services James was tasked to perform in his new parish was a wedding. "Can I confirm with you, Sir, that I read the passage up to here before I lead the prayers?"

He was not new at officiating weddings, but now the responsibility lay to him alone, he was anxious to do it right. He knew that the vows taken from the *Book of Common Prayer* were legally binding and so he had come to seek his father's more experienced reassurance.

Mr Austen was happy to be of assistance and pleased that his adult son still needed him. "In my mind, the best way to remember what to do is to have a rehearsal. Come, I will open up my church and you can practise what to say." He remembered only too well his own sleepless nights of worry in those early days when he was new to the clergy.

James donned his hat and coat while his father skipped upstairs to knock on his daughters' dressing room door. "I need your help girls. James is to rehearse for a wedding and we need a bride and a groom. Would you like to play along?"

"Oh, yes!" beamed Cassandra, wiping her paintbrush and reaching for her bonnet. Jane was as willing as her sister and the two were soon ready.

"Perhaps we should fetch MARY," suggested Jane, clomping noisily down the stairs. She placed a heavy and unnatural emphasis on Mary's name, loading the word with enough intonation for Cassandra to understand her meaning. Neither of them had forgotten the promise they had made to Martha to try and match James with her younger sister.

"No time for that," dismissed Mr Austen with the familiar wave of his hand. "I'll call your mother and then we must be off."

The women of the impromptu wedding party followed James and his father compliantly up the lane to St Nicholas' Church. Once inside, Mr Austen issued out everyone's roles.

James was the officiate, Cassandra was the groom, Jane was the bride, and their mother was a witness. Mrs Austen sat down in her pew begrudgingly going over, in her mind, the list of tasks that needed completing before supper. She could have done without being dragged away to come here when she had so many chores that needed completing over the course of the afternoon.

Mr Austen had become an expert over the years in tactically ignoring his wife's disapproval and continued to organise the proceedings without comment. He would double up as the second witness when the time came.

Cassandra and Jane found the scenario highly amusing. They grinned their way through the service like silly little schoolgirls and thought James sounded funny when he put on his officiate voice. It was hilarious for them to declare their undying love to each other in front of their brother and not even their mother's tutting from behind could spoil the game.

"The relevant parties sign the register here," Mr Austen persevered, pointing to the thick leather-bound book that documented every event. "You must make sure it is open at the correct page before the service begins, and that there is a quill and sufficient ink for the purpose."

James nodded. He was loathed to admit it, but this idea of a rehearsal had been just what he needed, and he was feeling much more relaxed now about the task ahead.

Mr Austen then turned to the specimen page of the Parish Register. He had intended for James to fill it out as part of the tutoring, but Jane greedily snatched up the quill instead.

"I assume the banns are all in order for your service?" Mr Austen checked with his son.

"Yes, that was organised before I took over. This will be the third week of them being read."

"Excellent. Well then, when you receive your next request for a wedding, this is where you record the banns first, at the top of the page, like so."

He pointed to the appropriate place with his forefinger.

Now that his nerves were calmer, James was sufficiently at ease to indulge his sister's playful mood. "What names shall we give to our happy couple?" he asked Jane, who sat poised with her quill.

"Henry Frederic Howard Fitzwilliam of London," she announced regally.

"My goodness!" laughed her brother. "You will need to write very small to fit all of that on one line."

Jane wrote quickly and neatly in the register.

"And who is he to marry?"

"Miss Jane Austen of Steventon," she replied. "I feel I am well suited to become a future Mrs Fitzwilliam."

Her mother expressed her annoyance with a sigh, but the others enjoyed the joke.

Mr Austen indicated what to do with the next section in the register. "You will complete this with the bride and groom when you are sat in the vestry after the vows have been exchanged."

Jane was already filling in the blanks with another fanciful name.

"Finally, the two witnesses sign here, and here," concluded their father patiently.

Mrs Austen was uncompromisingly irritable now. "Stop being silly, Jane. James knows perfectly well what he must do. You are wasting everyone's time."

Her mother's berating dampened Jane's spirits like water drenching a fire. She completed her task by signing two of the shortest and simplest names she could think of.

"It will be best to leave the register open in order for the ink to dry," Mr Austen battled on. "I will put it back on its rightful page in the morning."

To avoid looking her mother in the eye, Jane read through what she had written one last time:

The banns of marriage between *Henry Frederic Howard Fitzwilliam* of *London* and *Jane Austen* of *Steventon*.
*Edmund Arthur William Mortimer* of *Liverpool* and *Jane Austen* of *Steventon* were married in this church.

This marriage was solemnised between us, *Jack Smith* and *Jane Smith* late *Austen,* in the presence of *Jack Smith, Jane Smith.*

She would experiment with those names, she decided, in her future stories.

\* \* \*

James settled quickly into his new role at St. Mary's in Overton and actively ingratiated himself with his parishioners. He dined out wherever he was invited and joined the local hunting pack to show off his athletic prowess. There, he knew, he would meet with the cream of the neighbourhood elite.

"I was only speaking of you last night in Basingstoke," said a delighted Mr Austen, happy at the coincidence of bumping into James on the High Street after settling an account with his mercer. "I was at the campaign launch of Mr Chute and your name came up in conversation."

William Chute was a prospective Tory candidate in the forthcoming General Election. "I didn't realise you were so well acquainted with the man," Mr Austen probed his son.

"Yes," replied James easily. "We hunt together. I think it fair to say we have become good friends."

"Yes, yes," agreed his father. "That was my impression too. I could tell he has high regard for you. He has a mighty fine house, too."

Mr Chute lived at The Vyne in the nearby village of Sherborne St John. It dated back to Tudor times and was one of the grandest mansions for miles.

"Yes. I have dined there on a few occasions."

Mr Austen was impressed.

"There was another fellow who expressed an interest to know you better too, when he realised we were related, a General Mathew. He was new to the neighbourhood and I'd not met him before. Just come in from Grenada where he was Chief of the British Indies out there."

"Yes, I know who you mean," confirmed James with a slight blush. "He has taken Laverstoke House."

"That's right. You certainly are well informed," smiled the proud father.

"I met the family last week," James revealed, "when I became acquainted with his daughter at a ball."

The involuntary blush that had rushed to his cheeks when he spoke of the General's daughter was no mistake. The lady in question was Anne Mathew, six years older than James and unattached.

She had a slender frame that made her look vulnerable, and James had felt protective of her in the ballroom, sensing a quickening in his pulse when she looked up at him with her shy, dark eyes. She had a pale, heart-shaped face and favoured wearing a white wig covered with rolling curls. If anything, the wig made her face look like a child, yet she met the gaze of her admirers with a woman's dignity and charm.

No number of coincidental meetings set up by Cassandra and Jane, to throw Mary Lloyd in their brother's direction, could alter his preference for Miss Mathew, and Mary was cruelly cast aside in James's blissful ignorance of the plan.

Anne's father, General Mathew, had accumulated substantial wealth from his distinguished military career and his wife was from an aristocratic background. There could be no denying that marriage into this family would secure a step up the social ladder for any young curate.

As the months progressed, another factor in James's favour helped him to be accepted as an eligible suitor: this was his friendship with Mr Chute. Visitors of influence were always in attendance when James dined at The Vyne and in honour of the regard he held for his new friend, Mr Chute invited

James to become rector of St Andrews Church in Sherborne St John.

With a living of his own, on top of his resident curacy, James Austen was in the ideal position to support a wife.

# Chapter 26

**1791**
**A Visit to Portsmouth.**

Edward Austen returned to England from his Grand Tour of Europe and came to Steventon in the spring. He was now twenty-three years old and pulled up on the sweep driveway of the rectory in his black carriage, embellished with the Knight's Coat of Arms on the door. His four hale and hearty horses snorted noisily, their neatly plaited manes as glossy as any to be found in the kingdom.

Mr and Mrs Austen were nervous before his arrival, fearing that he may have changed in personality, but they were soon put at ease. The inspiring sights Edward had witnessed on his travels had taken nothing away from the affection he still held for his natural parents and his humble childhood home.

"James looks well," he affirmed after the preliminary greetings were over. "He has already engaged me for a dinner party later this week."

Edward had met his elder brother briefly on the driveway, before coming into the house.

"Yes. You will find him a social butterfly nowadays," verified Mr Austen. "He even hunts with the Prince of Wales when he's up at Kempshott."

"We are hoping for an announcement soon," clucked his mother excitedly. "He has become attached to the daughter of General Mathew in Laverstoke; no doubt you will be introduced to her while you're here."

"Good for him!" Edward was genuinely pleased for his brother and his sun-kissed face beamed with goodwill. "I will enjoy the dinner even more now, with that knowledge!"

"And how is Henry?" he asked, moving down the males of the family in order of age. "Still at Oxford, I assume?"

"Yes," confirmed Mrs Austen. "He's grown very tall of late, and always has some tale to tell when he comes home for a visit."

"I must call on him soon," pondered Edward. "There were many days in Italy that I thought of him. He would have loved the old ruins and the sculptures out there. And Frank?"

"A midshipman now," informed his proud father. "Remarkable at such a young age, I feel." Frank had successfully completed his first year aboard his ship as a volunteer and deservedly earned his promotion to the ranks. "His letters are full of cheer when he writes home. He seems very happy on the seas."

After being updated on Frank's career thus far, Edward turned his attention to his youngest brother, Charles, who was watching him with awe. With an age difference of twelve years between them, they had barely been in each other's lives as they grew up. This richly clad, worldly-wise, finely-spoken young man was still a bit of an enigma to the eleven-year-old country boy.

"Tell me, Charles. What are your plans for the future?"

"The navy, definitely," he answered without hesitation. "I

am to join the Academy this summer."

"Then how proud we shall all be," returned Edward kindly.

After pausing to stare around the room and marvel at how little had changed since his last visit, he finally addressed his sisters.

"I was reminded of you both many times on my travels and chose my gifts with the young girls in mind that I remembered. Had I realised what graceful young ladies you have become, I would have bought you jewels and perfumes instead," he admitted.

"We are still the same young girls deep down," Cassandra assured him. "We are not good manners and politeness all the time, you know."

"I venture I can still catch you out in cricket," Jane challenged good-naturedly. "We must put a team together while you're here, and you will see I have only got better."

"Yes. I would like that."

Matters then moved on to farm news, the neighbours and crops. A special four-course meal was eaten in Edward's honour and plans were made to get up early for a shooting party the next day.

Jane could not help but feel disappointed when she prepared for bed that night. Although Edward had been charming and courteous to a fault, he had not spoken seriously to her or Cassandra other than to admire their beauty. He had spent a good deal of time discussing their brothers' prospects and capabilities, but he had given no consideration to the fact that his sisters had worthy minds and intelligence too.

She and Cassandra were working on a book together about the kings and queens of England. Jane was cataloguing the facts in her familiar, sardonic style whilst Cassandra was providing the illustrations. It was a major project that was taking up much of their time, and the more it progressed, the prouder they felt about its completion.

Jane would have liked the opportunity for that to be acknowledged.

\* \* \*

When the time came for Charles to join the navy, Mr Austen arranged for his wife and his daughters to accompany them to Portsmouth. His youngest son's entry into a life of service was to be marked with a holiday by the sea.

Portsmouth was like nothing the girls had known before and they found themselves buffeted and blown by the bracing, seaside air. Initially, they had been nervous about coming on the trip, thinking back to the filthy streets of Southampton and their fateful encounter with typhus on their last visit to the south coast.

But Portsmouth was different altogether; the air was invigorating and fresh, and their windswept faces held a permanent expression of joy. The family walked together every day along the fortifications and across the common. Each gust of wind and splash of waves produced smiles from ear to ear.

Their greatest wonder was the blueness of the sea. It was not a dirty green as they had expected – but the bright sunshine produced a turquoise bed of diamond-studded waves. The white fluffy clouds floating across the sky made the water twinkle and the salty air sizzled on their tongues and on their lips.

Jane and Cassandra's light summer dresses billowed in the

wind and their bonnets pulled in all directions. At first, they placed their hands firmly upon their heads to hold them, but in the end, they submitted like every other young girl and cast them off to carry in their hands. They trotted behind their parents like liberated ponies with flowing manes, whooping excitedly as the wind ruffled their crowns.

All along the pathways, little pockets of people stood admiring the water and the ships. Invalids were assisted with sticks or in chairs; frail children were encouraged to take deep breaths; hypochondriacs took up every space along the seating areas, claiming them for their health.

It was easy to see, thought the girls, why so many people came to the seaside for their constitution, and it began to make sense why Eliza was always taking her son to some resort to try and make him better. The whole experience was exhilarating!

The highlight of every day for Cassandra and Jane was when they climbed atop the Square Tower to watch the ships. They had never seen a tall ship up close before, and no amount of pictures in a book could prepare them for the thrill of being next to one in real life. Each morning they played the same game; they turned their backs away from the dock and positioned themselves to where they could only watch far out at sea. By monitoring the water in front of them, they would try to guess when a ship was on its way.

The build-up began with the tide gently rippling and slowly agitating. Little frothy crests formed on the water's surface and the soothing slap, slapping against the rock transformed into louder rhythmic claps.

The most thrilling part came when the gigantic ship appeared alongside them, out of nowhere like a huge monster.

Timber creaked from every crevice on its deck and the frantic sea sprayed up in all directions to tickle the girls' faces and drop great dollops of water on their clothes. They squealed and laughed shamelessly, relishing the pleasure of such an unfamiliar and extraordinary feeling.

The hull of the ship bounced effortlessly over the fermenting stretch of sea, cutting through its path like scissors on lace. Tall masts stood up pencil straight, holding square white sails that bulged in the wind. It was tempting for the girls to wish they were on board themselves, to be taken on some great, faraway adventure.

'*Frank will be on a ship like that,*' thought Mrs Austen, every time a new vessel caught her eye. She knew nothing of the difference in designs, or the artillery that made up each boat, but the fact that a gigantic sailboat was leaving port full of eager young sailors was enough for her to make the comparison.

"Look how smart those uniforms are, girls," she pointed out to her daughters. She was watching a group of naval officers dressed in dark blue coats with golden buttons down their fronts. They wore the same gold and red belts around their waists, and matching gold epaulettes on their shoulders. Their hats were shaped like triangles. The men's faces were brown from the sun and months of exposure to nature's elements. They were an attractive sight to behold.

"Let's go down," Mrs Austen pronounced impulsively, deftly tripping her way down the sandstone steps with the girls following daintily behind. If they hurried, they would intercept the path shortly before the officers got there; it would be gratifying to watch how Cassandra and Jane would be admired when the gentlemen were forced to step aside to allow them to pass.

# Chapter 27

**1791**
**The End of an Era.**

Edward Austen planned to visit all his favourite relations over the summer months and took the opportunity to pay a surprise call on his aunt and cousin when he found himself in London.

"I'm sorry to keep you waiting," Eliza apologised, greeting Edward in the drawing room where he had been instructed to wait by a servant at least a quarter of an hour before. "My mother is not well and I was helping her to settle."

"I hope it is nothing serious," acknowledged Edward, more from politeness than concern. He was used to the females in his circle fussing excessively over their health for no other reason than to seek his attention.

Eliza did not respond.

"I am on my way to the northern lakes," Edward resumed joyfully. "And have broken my journey to collect a keepsake from a miniaturist only two streets away from yours. I could not leave without asking if you and Aunt Philadelphia would do me the honour of dining out with me this evening."

Edward had much news to tell, having recently become

190

engaged to a pretty girl by the name of Elizabeth Bridges. Her family lived at Goodnestone Park, a short distance from the Knight's home in Godmersham. The keepsake Edward referred to was a miniature likeness of his fiancée, which weighed heavily now in his pocket in his eagerness to show it off.

Eliza had heard of the engagement from Mrs Austen's letters and had written already to congratulate Edward on his good fortune. Only now did she recall that she had offered an open invitation for him to call whenever he was next in London.

Unsurprisingly, it had slipped her mind. Her mother was sick and a mere shadow of her former self. She was nursing an uncomfortable swelling which she had tried to ignore, but the lump had grown at such an alarming rate on her breast that she could no longer hide her pain and discomfort.

These days Philadelphia was unable even to dress herself and had secluded herself from all society. She was embarrassed at the shame of being unwell and refused to see any callers to the house. It was better to lock oneself away, she reckoned, than to be whispered about behind one's back.

"I'm sorry, Cousin," Eliza apologised once again. "We cannot possibly dine out with you. Mama does not feel up to it and it would be unforgivable for me to leave her."

She tried desperately to hide her sorrow and mask the nervous exhaustion that was consuming her.

"I trust she is not so unwell that she is in danger?" queried Edward, intuitively picking up on the catch in her voice.

Eliza was hesitant to answer.

"Betsy? What's wrong?"

All formalities disappeared as soon as Edward recognised

that he had walked into a family crisis. He searched Eliza's face for a flicker of understanding and noticed how grey her complexion had become. He observed her hair lacking its former glamour, and her dark-rimmed eyes without their familiar sparkle. Her whole demeanour suggested despair and defeat.

"Is my aunt very ill?"

Eliza nodded and slumped down ungraciously into a chair. The room was warm and the burning oil from the freshly lit lamp was making her light-headed.

"Oh, Neddy. You do not know the half of it!"

Edward sat down in the chair opposite and leaned forward to take her hand. He had come with such joyful news to share and this sombre welcome was the last thing he had expected.

"Mama's health has been failing for some months now," Eliza told him. "She will not go out anymore and she talks only of dying."

No sooner were the words out in the open than her sobbing began.

"She refuses to let me tell my uncle. She does not want anyone to know the extent of her weakness - except for Mr Hastings - and only then because he is organising her affairs."

Loud, ugly sobs dripped spittle onto her fine clothes.

"What can be done?" asked Edward, full of concern. "Let me fetch the physician. I can walk this very minute to summon whomever you choose."

"You are most kind, but everything has been tried already."

She went on to reveal her mother's treatment thus far. Philadelphia had been bled with leeches, purged with potions, cupped to create blisters and her skin bathed with herbs. Cordials, barley water and every water cure imaginable had been attempted. And everything had failed.

"Mr Roops is the only physician she will let in the house now. He has told her the truth of the situation, that it is unlikely she will be well again. He has urged her to write her will, which is the reason my godfather is allowed to attend her."

Edward listened carefully, trying to come to terms with this sudden shock.

"I had no idea," he answered grimly. "You say my father does not know?"

"No. Nobody does except the servants, and they have been sworn to secrecy. Mama would be mortified to think of our neighbours knowing."

Edward frowned deeply.

"May I see her?" he asked gently.

"She is sleeping at the moment," said Eliza, wiping her tears and forcing herself to stand up. "She will not know you are there, but I see no harm in you going in for a moment."

She opened the door of the drawing room and led Edward along the hallway to the stairs. Everything was quiet in the house and the servants were carrying out their duties in hushed undertones. Doors were closed silently, and no one spoke above a whisper.

They passed by an open room on the landing which was being used as an airing room. Bed sheets and pillowcases were draped next to a small fire and the sharp smell of potash drifted to the back of Edward's throat and made it dry.

The door to Philadelphia's bedroom was closed and Eliza paused before she opened it. She looked up at Edward as if to speak, then thought better of it and turned the doorknob instead.

The room was stifling. There was a full fire, despite it being summer, and droplets of sweat formed on Edward's upper lip. The air was suffocating with the pungent smell of lavender mixed with the bitter-sweet tang of laudanum.

Edward had to bend directly over his aunt's face to make out her features, so dark was the room, and he looked for any sign of the exotic charm and larger-than-life personality he remembered. He found neither in the woman that lay there, with her mottled skin and wispy strands of hair.

Edward kissed his aunt tenderly on her forehead and stroked her hand with the tip of his finger. He was consoled to see that she looked restful, at least. He made his way wordlessly back down the stairs behind Eliza and they both resumed their positions in the same drawing room chairs as before.

"You must write to my father. He must be told," insisted Edward.

"But Mama begs I do no such thing," pleaded Eliza.

"Then I will write," he replied firmly.

Eliza did not contest her cousin's words, but neither did she agree to them.

"My father must be given the opportunity to offer his blessings to his sister before it's too late. You must see that."

Eliza gave the slightest nod of her head.

"Come," urged Edward, taking control as was his duty as a senior male in the family. "Write the letter now and I will call into Steventon on my way up to the lakes. I will personally hand it to my father and explain the situation to him."

When Eliza still did not move, he became sterner in his instructions.

"I am obliged to tell my parents what I have witnessed today,

Betsy, with or without your consent. But you know as well as I that the truth would be better coming from you, and not from me."

Eliza had no fight left in her under such duress and assented to her cousin's demands. It was arranged that Edward would go for a walk and return in an hour. He would then dine at Orchard Street that evening where Eliza promised to enlighten him on everything that had passed.

When she took up her quill, Eliza could not stop her hands from shaking. Her words began formally and with difficulty, but the more she wrote they flowed into a stream of remorse and regret.

She begged her uncle to come quickly and prayed that he would forgive her secrecy on the state of her mother's health. She urged that he understand it was her mother's express wish that no one be told and that was the reason she had not written before. She openly thanked God that Neddy had come to call when he had, and that he had made her see sense while there was still time.

Edward returned as agreed, having passed an agitated hour striding about Hyde Park.

"You have done the right thing," he confirmed, hugging Eliza tightly to his chest when he prepared to leave later that night. "You are not alone, Betsy. I hope you know that everyone in the family will help you."

Eliza kissed her cousin on the cheek.

"I will call upon you again on my return from the north," he concluded. "Please tell Aunt Philadelphia I have been asking after her when she wakes."

Eliza broke down completely when he left and swallowed three substantial drops of laudanum for herself. She slumped down in the chair next to her mother's bed and fell into the longest slumber she had experienced in weeks.

# Chapter 28

**1792**
**Funerals and Weddings.**

Philadelphia Hancock died in February and was laid to rest in the churchyard of St John-at-Hampstead. Eliza was heartbroken, but she had some small consolation in that her husband had managed to obtain leave from his regiment in France, and he was by her side when the fateful time came.

Young Hastings babbled away in his mix of French and English words, not really understanding what his grandmother's passing meant. His five-year-old innocence provided a much-needed diversion for everyone in the household.

The Comte was not able to stay long in England, so following some miserable weeks alone, Eliza headed to Steventon. Mr Austen chaperoned the journey and for the most part, it passed in silence. But when they came upon the familiar Hampshire landmarks, Eliza's emotions betrayed her.

"I'm sorry, Uncle," she apologised, dabbing her eyes with her handkerchief. "Mama and I always used to observe these sights together."

"Yes," he comforted, his own eyes smarting too. "It is strange for me not to see her sitting alongside you. I think it will take some getting used to for the both of us."

Eliza smiled up at her uncle's compassionate face. "You share a strong resemblance to her," she noted. "I did not see it before, but now it is as if her eyes are looking straight back at me."

"It was often remarked upon when we were younger, how similar we were," reminisced Mr Austen. "We could be a pair of rascals when we wanted to be!"

The rectory was quiet when they arrived, with only Jane and her mother waiting to greet them. Cassandra was away in Kent, staying with Edward and his new wife.

Edward had wed Elizabeth Bridges the previous December in the bride's church at Goodnestone. It was a double wedding, with two sisters marrying their new husbands at the same time. Edward and his wife had taken a house on Sir Bridge's ancient family estate of Goodnestone Park called Rowling House, and Cassandra was the first of the siblings invited to stay there.

Edward was not the only son married now either. James had wed General Mathew's daughter Anne, in the village of Laverstoke, in March.

"Tell me about James's wedding," requested Eliza, settling down comfortably and purposely speaking only of happy events.

"It was a truly marvellous day," praised Mrs Austen. "Was it not Jane?"

Jane nodded readily.

"Mr Austen took the service, as you know, and we were all there. The bride had two attendants and the General put on a most generous wedding breakfast for the guests."

"I wish I could have seen it," replied Eliza honestly.

"You were remembered in our prayers during the service," assured Mrs Austen. "Your husband and your mother, too."

"Thank you," choked Eliza. "What is Anne like?"

Anne was a prominent figure amongst the society ladies in the area; she kept her own carriage and was very well-bred. She was not unlikeable, but at the same time, Mrs Austen could not feel completely at ease in her presence. She had racked her brains to try to understand why this was and wondered if it was nothing more than a simple prejudice against her wealth.

Anne's family had been made rich partly due to the profits of a sugar plantation. Many people were of the opinion these days that the trading of slaves for this purpose was unchristian. It had never occurred to Mrs Austen to think of it before, but the more she read on the topic, the more faults she found in people who took such wealth for granted and looked down on the poorer classes.

Eliza was able to judge for herself what she thought of Anne when James brought her to call the next day. The two women talked about London and its sights; Anne was familiar already with many of its famous museums and landmarks.

James asked about the Comte.

"He is as worried as the rest of us about the state of his country," confessed Eliza, referencing the violence throughout France that was showing no signs of abating. "Believe me, Cousin, nothing that you read in the newspapers is an exaggeration."

* * *

Everyone's mood lifted when a letter came to say that the Coopers would shortly be in the neighbourhood. Edward and Jane Cooper had been holidaying on the Isle of Wight with their father and his close friends, Mr and Mrs Lybbe-Powys. They were breaking their journey in Steventon on their way back home to Sonning.

Mr Lybbe-Powys was the brother of Tom Powys - the vicar who had officiated at Mr and Mrs Austen's wedding - so there was much news to be exchanged when the party eventually arrived. The Austens had been forewarned to expect notice when the travellers were in the area, and sure enough, when the sun sank down on a warm Tuesday evening, a messenger boy ran up to the house with an invitation for them to breakfast at The Wheatsheaf Inn the following morning.

There was much excitement when they stepped out early, taking no refreshments before they left. The sun was already out and its bright beams were starting to warm the earth. The hedgerows were damp with dew, and finely crafted webs from busy nocturnal spiders were spread over the bushes like intricately spun silk. The worn soles of Jane's boots soon soaked up the water and she cringed at the uncomfortable seep of cold moisture around her toes when they passed over a field. Mrs Austen began to grumble how shoddy they would look with their soggy hems, but Mr Austen and Eliza strode ahead unconcerned, marvelling at the wonder of nature. The countryside was at its most magnificent at this time of day.

Jane's hunger made her miserable, and she regretted not taking a cup of milk before dashing out of the door. She really must plan things better, she told herself. Cassandra would not have been so impetuous; Cassandra would have worn the right shoes. She trudged on wearily beside her mother, who sympathised with her plight and made her feel better with complaints that she, too, had a headache brought on by a lack of food.

It was not a long distance to the inn, and they were soon immersed in the frantic comings and goings of strangers finding themselves mid-journey. A heavily laden stagecoach was just about to depart, and a cluster of servants ran to and fro to secure the baggage and attend to the continual demands of the ringing bells. Doors opened and closed at the entrances to the inn; horses were led away and new ones brought forward; bags flew from hand to hand through the air. Everywhere they looked, someone was in a hurry to either arrive or depart.

Mr Austen and his family made their way to a peaceful area inside the inn, where they were welcomed by a friendly man who was expecting them. The best dining parlour had been hired out by Mr Cooper, and the waiter showed them to a pleasantly set table laid with a clean white cloth and gleaming silverware. They were the only guests in the room, and there were relieved smiles all around when the serving girl brought in tea.

The floor was covered with rushes which had been laid out fresh that morning, with fragrant lavender sprigs and herbs. A row of potted plants along the window ledge added a touch of class and a wooden grandfather clock ticked loudly in a corner. When its tinny chimes struck eight o'clock, footsteps came clipping down the stairs and Jane Cooper entered the room. She looked radiant and fresh and was soon followed by the rest of her party.

"How well you look, my dear," complimented Mr Austen,

kissing his wife's niece on the cheek. "Edward, my boy! How wonderful to see you again." Warm embraces were exchanged all around.

The smell of bacon wafted enticingly when the tureens of food were brought in, and the guests' mouths watered in anticipation of the feast. They each scooped up thick salty rashers onto their plates, the rind still sizzling and glistening with fat. Puffy poached eggs shone like jewels on another tray: soft white balls revealing sunshine yellow yolks. Their runny liquid seeped tantalisingly over the bacon and slivered out across their plates.

The remainder of the breakfast was made up of two long racks of toast and a bowl of creamy butter. The bread was thickly cut and singed around the edges where it had been smoked over the open fire. Each delectable bite was accompanied by an equally satisfying crunch.

Everyone ate heartily apart from Mr Cooper who, Mrs Austen observed, was picking at his food more with gritted determination than pleasure. Whilst the conversation flew back and forth in time with the passing of sugar and milk, Mr Cooper coughed discreetly into his handkerchief. If red jam had been on the table, that would have accounted for the stains that Mrs Austen's sharp eyes picked out on the plain white cloth. But no jam was to be seen.

'Dear God, not you too ...' she protested silently to herself as she sat alongside him, her own appetite now quelled by a nauseous sense of foreboding. She was growing weary of death taking her cherished relations before she was ready to let them go.

Mr Cooper's encouraging smiles and nods in his children's direction indicated strongly that he wanted no fuss. When breakfast was over, he took a newspaper from the stand and moved towards a large leather chair by the window. "The young people have some news for you," he announced cryptically, before slowly shuffling off.

"You have more news?" laughed Eliza. "My goodness, how many more things could you possibly have found time to see?" They had already told of multiple day trips; sights they had seen whilst riding; thrilling tales of sailing, and vivid descriptions of their walks around the modest little island where the sea was constantly at their toes.

"There are many more places worthy of note," replied Edward warmly. "But it is my sister who has the news."

All faces turned expectantly to Jane Cooper, who was blushing profusely. "I am to be married!"

Squeals of surprise rang out. Mr Austen and Mr Lybbe-Powys settled back in their chairs, happy to observe the proceedings through the actions of the females who all leaned in a little closer to capture Jane's joy.

"Why did you not say in your letter?" asked Mrs Austen, dumbfounded.

"It is so recent that I wanted to tell you in person. It only came about on the final day of our holiday, so it is still new even to me! But the wedding will not be long. My fiancé is a naval captain, and we wish to marry before he sets sail again." Jane Cooper was positively gleeful.

"I declare I did not expect anything of the sort when I set out this morning," proclaimed Mrs Austen. "I wish you all the joy in the world, dear child!"

Jane Cooper got out of her chair and flung herself into her aunt's arms, where they exchanged happy kisses on their cheeks.

"His name is Captain Thomas Williams," continued Edward on his sister's behalf, now that she was being engulfed in embraces from the entire family. "We first met him when we dined with the Admiral and I believe it must have been love at first sight - from that day on he never left my sister's side."

Everyone agreed it was a most romantic tale and that he sounded a wonderful man.

Mr Austen was eager to learn more about him, curious as to whether Captain Williams may have met Frank in their shared lines of duty.

"I do not believe he has," explained Jane Cooper to her uncle. "His last commission was out in the North Sea and next he is to join the *Lizard,* which is presently being kitted out in Portsmouth. He is not due to sail until the new year which is why it is so convenient for us to marry this autumn."

"Then maybe he will come across Charles in Portsmouth?"

"Yes, perhaps he may," agreed Jane amenably, seeing how much such a connection would mean to her uncle. "I will ask him to seek Charles out on the pretence of passing on a message from me," she decided.

Mr Austen smiled at the thought. "Shall you join your husband when he sails?" He felt a sudden surge of admiration for his young niece who now presented herself with such maturity before him.

"Not initially, no," replied Jane. "The *Lizard* is to patrol the south coast of England and so after the wedding, I will reside with his mother at Ryde. But we have discussed the possibility of me joining him when he is abroad. It will be something to decide when the time comes."

"It can be difficult living away from your husband." Eliza mused. "But it does not have to be forever. And the anticipation of being together again is certainly a nice thing to look forward to."

A loaded look passed between the two women, containing a thousand sympathetic words which were not appropriate to share in this public place and whilst the mood was so gay.

"Perhaps you could write to me when I am married?" Jane asked quietly of Eliza, whilst the others were distracted by Mrs Austen discussing her latest correspondence from Tom Powys and the fact that he was now chaplain to King George. "I would be glad of your advice," Jane pressed further in her quiet undertone.

"Certainly," agreed Eliza warmly. "I too will be grateful for your letters. We shall be companions for one another."

Jane Austen wrote immediately to Cassandra when she returned home, to inform her of the news. Mr Austen went out to check on the haymakers, whistling his way down the lane, and Mrs Austen and Eliza were left to contemplate the morning's encounter over their sewing and a fresh pot of tea.

"What happy news!" they trilled.

"I hope my uncle Edward improves in health before the ceremony," said Eliza. "Let's hope it was nothing more than the strain of a long journey which made him look so tired."

"No doubt the prospect of a wedding will lift him," assured Mrs Austen, sounding more confident than she felt. "He would do anything for his daughter and will not want to let her down."

It came as a shock when a black-sealed letter arrived from Jane Cooper three weeks later. Her father had passed away suddenly, soon after arriving home to Sonning. His body was being transported to his former living of Whaddon for him to be buried alongside his late wife.

Jane Cooper confirmed that Mr and Mrs Lybbe-Powys were doing all that they could and were being exceedingly helpful, but under the circumstances, she longed for the company of her aunt and cousins. She asked if she could stay with them in Steventon whilst her brother stayed on in Berkshire to sort out their father's affairs.

Her wedding to Captain Williams was postponed.

# Chapter 29

## 1792-1793
### A New Generation.

J ane Austen spent the summer being angry at her brother. When James had married Anne, Mr Austen had gifted him the curacy of All Saints Church in Deane. Jane did not mind that at all, but what had enraged her now was the fact that the newlyweds had chosen to move from their home in Overton, and into the rectory next to All Saints.

Jane reasoned that the house they had before was perfectly adequate, with ample room for James's pack of hunting dogs and in a central location for the two parishes that he served. It was already closer to Deane than to Sherborne St. John, and Jane had never heard her brother complain about the distance he had to travel there each week in order to preach at the church of Mr Chute.

No, huffed Jane, James was more concerned with making a good impression on his rich friend than worrying about the miles it took to get there, so why was it so vital that he live on the doorstep in Deane?

Her anger was understandable. After Fulwar Fowle's heartfelt plea to Mr Austen three years before that Mrs Lloyd and her daughters be allowed to lodge in Deane Rectory, the three women had made it their home. Now, because of James's desire to better himself, they were being forced out.

If that were not enough to throw Jane into a tantrum, she watched her brother purchase an obscene amount of furniture from the local auctioneer. He was making Deane Rectory unrecognisable from the place that Jane had always considered perfectly lovely the way it was.

Mrs Lloyd took the news of her eviction uncomplainingly and relocated to the village of Ibthorpe. It was a peaceful and pretty place, she reported back - but even the prettiest place in the world was a problem to get to when it was eighteen miles away.

Jane missed seeing Martha and Mary every day, and being a single young woman she did not have the freedom to travel without a chaperone. Thankfully, despite her enduring sulks and sighs, the friendship between the girls still thrived by letter and it was not long before an invitation arrived from Mrs Lloyd requesting Cassandra and Jane come to stay.

Jane pestered James to escort them as soon as Cassandra was back from Kent, and she felt some small sense of victory over the injustice he had caused when she saw a flash of envy cross his face. He looked most put out when their carriage drove up a neatly maintained driveway, to stop before a handsome, square house.

Ibthorpe House was bigger than the rectory at Deane. It was double-fronted and had two large windows on either side of a white front door. A smart row of windows on the second floor reflected the clouds passing swiftly by, and there were many signs that the ladies enjoyed their ample garden; tall herbs lined the clean pathway and a pretty orange rose rambled its way upwards towards the chimney to dress the front of the house with a rich warmth.

The air was fresh and carried scents of wood smoke and pine and Jane and Cassandra took invigorating gulps to cleanse their lungs from the journey. The village was peaceful and they heard only the sound of their brother's footsteps striding over the gravel to announce their arrival.

Mrs Lloyd opened the front door herself, and her daughters ran out from behind to clasp their old friends with joy. The first task, as always, was to sit down politely and take refreshments. They all remained dignified until a reasonable amount of time had passed for James to respectably take his leave. Then the fun began.

Frantic footsteps ran across the landing, with the opening and closing of doors accompanied by whoops of laughter and squeals of delight. The four friends were clearly ecstatic to be once again in each other's company. The summer had been a busy one for Martha and Mary as their sister, Eliza Fowle, was at Kintbury for the birth of her second child and the young women had just returned from a visit to see her. Fulwar and Eliza were now proud parents of a son and a daughter.

"Edward's wife is with child," added Cassandra, whilst they were on the subject of babies. "A little after Christmas I believe is the anticipated date."

James's wife Anne had also announced she was expecting but was still in the early stages of her pregnancy. As James had not chosen to share this news with Mrs Lloyd earlier at tea, Jane and Cassandra did not mention it either.

The four girls changed for dinner when the candles were lit, and Cassandra tutted to discover a stitch had come loose on her gown. She got up to fetch her sewing box, but Mary sprang into action and reached for the needle case on her dressing table instead.

"I still use the gift you gave me," she showed Jane, quickly untying the string of a little pouch and taking out a dainty set of needles and thread.

The small white housewife bag, with its gold and black patterned border, had been Jane's gift to Mary when she left Deane. Along with all the normal accessories, Jane had also placed a poem inside which she had written especially for her friend. She was delighted to see how fondly it was still appreciated.

The weeks spent at Ibthorpe that autumn were idyllic. Some days they ambled into the neighbouring village of Hurstbourne Tarrant and then shared a delicious meal at home with Mrs Lloyd. On other days they tended to the garden, where the trees were a rich russet red. One afternoon they harvested some apples and their cheeks glowed and blushed like the flushed skins that they placed in their baskets.

On one grand occasion, they attended a ball at Enham. The Austen sisters were introduced to all the Lloyd's new neighbours and friends, and Jane and Cassandra felt very daring to still be out in society after midnight with none of their brothers present to watch over them.

The best times, however, were when they all sat together in Martha and Mary's workroom with a sewing pattern between them and the conversation flowing freely wherever it went. This was how the friends had secured their close acquaintance in the first place and it was where they felt most at ease.

"I'm so sorry to hear that," sympathised Mary when Cassandra told them of Jane Cooper's ill-fated wedding plans and the death of their Uncle Edward.

"I don't know how she bears it," empathised Martha when the topic turned to the Comte de Feuillide, and the sorrow of Eliza not knowing the next time she would see her husband.

"We saw William when we were in Kintbury," Martha relayed next. "I would say that marriage suits him very well." William Fowle had completed his medical studies and was now a qualified doctor. He had married on completion of his training and was practising medicine in Wiltshire.

"He is hoping to produce a paper soon on the use of mercury in the treatment of smallpox," Mary went on, knowledgeably. "He is translating it from the work of a gentleman in France who has been conducting experiments. He truly believes these findings will prevent deaths from the disease in the future."

Cassandra was humbled. "We are so lucky to have clever men like William and his colleagues to investigate these things for us. If their work can save just one family from the pain that you were forced to endure when you lost your little brother, then it will be a good thing."

Martha and Mary nodded vigorously.

"And how is Charles enjoying law school?" asked Jane, who was fondest of Charles Fowle out of all the brothers.

"You know Charles," laughed Martha. "Happy to joke his way through his lectures and then spend his study time in the coffee houses. Anything to avoid his books."

"James told us that Tom officiated at William's wedding," tested Jane. Tom Fowle had hardly been mentioned up to now and she knew that Cassandra would not be the one to ask.

"Yes, that's right. He has taken quite a few wedding services, but I think marrying his brother must have been his proudest moment."

"Until the time comes when he weds himself ..." gambled Jane, playfully.

Tom was starting out his clerical career with a curacy in the church of St. John the Baptist at Allington. He was patiently awaiting the time when Lord Craven would offer him a permanent living of his own. His income was presently low and not enough to support a wife, but that did not stop his well-meaning relatives and friends from speculating who that wife should be when the time came.

Little did the girls know, but a secret plot was being schemed at that very moment through a series of letters between Fulwar and James, for Tom to officiate at the wedding of Jane Cooper.

The recently orphaned Jane was planning to marry from Steventon, where she was still staying with her uncle and aunt. If Tom Fowle could be persuaded to take the service, then he would have to stay with James in Deane. If he was staying with James in Deane, then he would see Cassandra every day. Fulwar and James were both convinced that this little intervention was all that was necessary for Tom to finally pluck up the courage and ask for Cassandra's hand.

Happily for all concerned, the plan worked.

Jane Cooper and Captain Thomas Williams married at St Nicholas' Church in Steventon in December, and Tom Fowle took the service. Jane and Cassandra were witnesses and Edward Cooper took on the duties that would have befallen his father. After the event, Tom Fowle requested a meeting with Mr Austen, and the felicitous engagement was agreed upon.

"We cannot marry just yet," Cassandra explained to Jane, by way of easing the pain that would inevitably come when they would have to live apart. "Tom must wait for his own living, so we are not declaring the engagement officially at present. It is more of an understanding between us."

Nevertheless, Cassandra's joy was unmistakable, and Jane could not have been more thrilled.

Charles Austen had also been home for his cousin's wedding, with it being Christmas holidays at the Naval Academy. Captain Williams appreciated Charles's enthusiasm for his chosen career, and amongst the frenzy of activity that surrounded the celebrations, he made sure to carve out some time to talk to the eager young boy about his life at sea.

"Let me know when you have finished your studies and are ready to set sail," he reminded Charles before leaving with his new bride for the Isle of Wight. "I will see what I can do to get you aboard my ship. You are just the type of keen fellow a captain needs on a long voyage."

\* \* \*

Edward and Elizabeth's first child was born at Goodnestone in January. She was a perfect little girl named Frances Catherine, who would be addressed as Fanny by the family. Edward wrote to inform his parents directly, but his erratic writing was far from his usual elegant hand. Mrs Austen smiled to herself as she imagined her son scrawling out his frantic note in a hurry so that he could rush back to marvel over his precious baby girl.

More happy news followed from Edward Cooper, who had become engaged to Caroline, the daughter of Mr and

Mrs Lybbe-Powys. Their wedding was to be in the spring, whereafter he would take up the living of St. Margaret's Church in Harpsden. The bride's uncle Tom Powys - now infamous in the family for serving the king - was to officiate the ceremony.

Mrs Austen was delighted for her nephew and duly sent her blessings, but if she was being perfectly honest, she was more excited by the happy coincidences that this union had thrown together. Not only was her nephew to be wed by the same life-long friend who had officiated her own ceremony, but St. Margaret's Church in Harpsden was the living her father had held when he was alive. The rectory where Edward and Caroline would live was the very same house that Mrs Austen had grown up in with her brother and sister.

She could not stop chattering about how much she looked forward to visiting there again and seeing Edward settled in the house that had once been the dwelling of his grandparents. She promised to tell him all the childhood tales from the old rectory that she could remember, and she educated him on the features of each of its rooms. She urged her nephew to make the most of the tranquil surroundings, where peace and beauty were in abundance, and she could not have wished for a better outcome than to see him walking in the same footsteps trod by his late mother.

* * *

Anne Austen's pregnancy was proving problematic and arguments bubbled up daily over preparations for her confinement. Jane and Cassandra frequently paused what they were doing to eavesdrop on the disputes being battled out downstairs.

"I will not have you walking the lanes alone in the dark," boomed the voice of their father. "How many more stories of violence do you need to hear before you understand it is simply not safe!"

"I will come myself, then, instead of sending a boy." This was James, shouting back in exasperation. "I will come in the carriage if it helps!"

"I have walked those lanes a million times, come rain or shine," asserted their mother. "It will take no more than half an hour and I will take the new lantern with me. You know how well that lights up the way."

Mrs Austen's wish for independence, it seemed, was the cause of the conflict.

"It matters not how bright a lantern is when you are alone on a lane with an attacker," roared her husband. "Who will see you then to come to your rescue?"

"Stop being so dramatic! I swear you go looking for trouble." With that, they heard their mother slam the door and walk outside on the gravel.

Mr Austen knew there was no point going after her when their words had become heated, but he was determined not to back down. There was no way in the world he would agree to his wife walking alone to Deane Rectory in the dark to assist with the birth. 'Day or night,' she had promised James; 'I will make myself available whenever you send word that the child is on its way.'

James was in a quandary now. On the one hand, he wished he had never asked for his mother's help if it was going to cause such unhappiness. On the other hand, who else was there better than she to ensure that his wife's labouring went to plan?

In years gone by, the short distance between Steventon and Deane would not have been a problem. Nowadays, unrest was commonplace even in the countryside. A servant of Reverend Lefroy's had been robbed and beaten in Overton at ten o'clock at night, and newspapers were always writing about incidences of jewellery being taken from ladies in their carriages.

Times had changed since the French king had been executed by the guillotine; the Republican Government that ruled France with such terror was affecting life across the Channel too. England was at war with its closest neighbour, which meant that the threat of invasion from French troops was a reality they must face up to. Mr Austen was not wrong in his declarations that they must all be on their guard.

When Anne's labour pains started, James sent two of his burliest men to fetch his mother. One rode on horseback in case of trouble, and the other walked alongside her and carried her lantern. Tactfully, they conveyed her safely to her destination where she assisted with Anne's labouring deep into the night.

Her efforts were rewarded with a bonny baby girl who was to be Anna, from her full name of Jane Anna Elizabeth. Mrs Austen loved her from the moment she saw her face.

Weary, but euphoric, the same burly men delivered Mrs Austen safely back to her door where she told her waiting husband and daughters the happy news. Their fretful quarrels were, for the moment, forgotten.

# Chapter 30

## 1793-1794
## La Guillotine.

S oldiers in uniform became a common sight around Hampshire. The king decreed that all inland regiments must make their way to the coast, as this was where the threat of invasion was at its highest. Passionate cries of 'God Save the King' rang out as troops passed through the towns, enticing swarms of boys and men to join up along the route. Henry Austen was amongst them and wrote to his father to explain.

*Sir,*

*I write at present from St John's College, but by the time this letter reaches you, I will be gone from here on my way to the coast. Last evening, the Oxfordshire Militia arrived in the city on a recruitment campaign. As I am still a year away from completing my studies, I have accepted a commission as lieutenant with the regiment and travel today towards a garrison in Southampton.*

*My duties are yet unclear, but I know that my artillery training will take place in Portsmouth. I intend to make myself known to my brother Charles whilst I am there to check on his welfare: an obligation I willingly undertake on your behalf.*

*I hope you are not too disappointed in me, Sir, for taking such a decision, and I urge you to understand that this is not an abandonment of my clerical career, but merely a postponement. I am not alone in accepting this commission and am joined by many of my Oxford Fellows. The Master of the College has already expressed his willingness to hold our positions open for when we are able to return, and we will be invited again to complete our education.*

*I hope you will understand the strength of patriotic duty which guides me forward, and I flatter myself that you would have done the same, had you been faced with a similar fate before your own ordination. I could not live with my conscience if I chose to do nothing.*

*I will write to you as often as I can to keep you updated with my movements, and I pray each day that you and my dear Mama remain safe.*

*Please be assured,*

*I remain your faithful and humble servant,*

*Henry Austen.*

"I am not in the least surprised," sighed Mr Austen, handing the letter to his wife. He took off his glasses and placed them down on the table before rubbing his eyes. "What else is the boy to do at such a time?"

He was immensely sad.

Henry partook in various camps to learn his soldiering skills and then took up his first official role as a prisoner escort. French prisoners of war were arriving on ships at Southampton and needed to be transported forward to Bristol. Henry's company served the route from Southampton to Salisbury, where cheers and flags from well-wishers lined the roads. The autumn saw him move to Brighton, eventually settling in West Sussex for the winter.

Frank, meanwhile, was on his way home. His naval service out in the China Seas for the East India Company had earned him another promotion and he had been granted his first leave in five years. "We shall have two lieutenants together," exclaimed Mrs Austen with a joy she could barely contain. "I cannot wait to see my boys standing side by side once more in the same room!"

This wish was soon realised, and her soldier and sailor sons were often in each other's company. The war did not appear to be encroaching on anyone locally, so most people in the neighbourhood carried on with their business as usual.

In December, Frank accompanied his sisters to Southampton where they stayed with the Butler-Harrison family, who were distant relations on their father's side. The obliging hosts were well respected in the city and introduced them to the rich of Southampton's society at an Assembly Ball at The Dolphin Hotel. Jane stayed on for a while to assist her hostess who had given birth whilst she was there, becoming godmother to the child. Cassandra came back home to Steventon and was chaperoned by Henry to a ball in Basingstoke, where she danced with Mr Chute.

Mr and Mrs Leigh-Perrot spent the season in Bath, and Edward Cooper hosted his sister in Harpdsen whilst her husband was away at sea. When the weather turned warmer, the invitation was reversed, and Edward and Caroline went to stay with Jane on the Isle of Wight. Babies continued to be born and Edward and Elizabeth provided Fanny with a little brother at Goodnestone, naming him Edward after his father.

This mundane domestic life was all very well for a short

while, but too many days attending dinners and playing cards was making Frank restless. He longed to be out at sea once more and doing something useful. "I am to join the *Lark*," he informed his father when news came through of his next commission. "I will serve under Captain Rowley, and we will patrol the Downs and the North Sea Station."

"That is good news," interposed his mother. "You will not be too far away from us this time."

"Of course, that is the bonus," replied Frank diplomatically. "Yet I fear I may find it all rather dull. I would have preferred a posting in France. After my experience in the East Indies, I am more than capable of helping in battle." He was most disappointed.

Henry, on the other hand, was unconcerned about forfeiting his share of action and returned to Oxford to resume his studies. Months of repetitive training were leading nowhere and he was granted a leave of absence from the army until his services would be required again.

Eliza, Comtesse de Feuillide took this as an encouraging sign. She felt a renewed sense of optimism that France may be a less dangerous place for her husband too, if the war was not causing a problem for her two serving cousins.

She could not have been more wrong.

\* \* \*

Life in Paris was unbearable. It had been a bitter winter, where suspicion fell as thick as the snow. Being a former Captain in the Queen's Regiment, the Comte was not welcome; there was no place for aristocratic landowners in this new Republican world and he could trust no one.

Hateful rivalry had torn the country apart and old supporters of the Royal Family were being obliterated – quite literally
limb from limb - by the new Republican movement. Bribery
and corruption were rife, and everyone led lives of secrecy.

One dark afternoon in February, the Comte made his way
to a coffee house in the centre of Paris. He had arranged
to meet a man called Morel, who worked for the powerful
Committee of Safety - the group of individuals who now
ruled France in place of the king.

As he made his way through the filthy streets, strewn with
rotting animals, urine and scurrying rats, he held his head
up high and forced his shoulders straight. He desperately
wanted to appear calm although his heart was throbbing hard
behind his ribs. He feared at any moment he would be slain
by a knife from the shadows.

He pushed open the door of the coffee house and weaved
his way through the crowds seated at wooden tables, where
multiple debates rang loud in his ears. He reached a small
table in a shaded corner underneath an alcove, where Morel
was already waiting.

"I took the liberty of ordering you a drink." Morel smiled
broadly.

"Thank you." The Comte sat down opposite Morel and
loosened the buttons of his overcoat. He was warm from the
oppressive hot air in the room and knew that the smell of
his own disgusting body odour would soon be swallowed up
unnoticed, amongst the hundred other foul smells fighting
for dominance.

The two men eyed each other carefully and made small talk
whilst they sipped their drinks. They were testing out each
other's reactions and the tone of their voices in the crowd.

They speculated on the latest news with delicate phrasing, keeping a watchful eye on everyone around. When they were sure no one was paying them any attention, they got down to the business at hand.

"You are a friend of the Marquise de Marbeuf," began Morel.

"An acquaintance," corrected the Comte.

"Ah," nodded Morel. "So, you do not stand to gain from her property?"

"No, I do not," confirmed the Comte. "I gain nothing by my intervention other than my honour. But I am told that you share my sentiments. You too would not wish to see the elimination of wealthy landowners?"

Morel had been introduced to him as a sympathetic Royalist. The Comte had been assured that this man's role for The Committee of Safety had transpired merely as a coincidence, due to him being a superior man of business. The Comte was not sure he believed it, but Morel was the only option he had left to protect himself, and had been known to take a bribe before.

The Comte's mission on this cold day was to persuade Morel to free an influential aristocratic figure, the Marquise de Marbeuf, who was currently being held in prison for planting some non-edible plants in her fields. She had been instructed by the new government to plant edible crops instead. The Republican leaders had charged her with creating famine and using her power as a landowner to starve the innocent people of France. Initially, she had denied the accusations, but when the proof against her was indisputable, she declared that as it was her land, she would plant whatever she liked.

The Comte, although not necessarily agreeing with her

actions, was wise enough to recognise her influence within the former royal hierarchy. He knew that being in her favour today would be a valuable card to reveal in the future. She would be obliged to him when rightful order was restored and would help his former privileged lifestyle to be reclaimed. He intended to charm the crooked Morel into securing the release of the Marquise in exchange for a substantial sum of gold coins.

"I am afraid Monsieur Robespierre is a very stubborn man," bewailed Morel when the Comte set out his first offer of 20,000 livres. "It is difficult to do anything these days without our leader knowing."

The Comte had expected some resistance to his enticements and increased his offer. At the sum of 24,000 livres, and when Morel sensed that he would get nothing more, the bribe was discreetly accepted.

"We will meet again tomorrow afternoon," the Comte muttered. "I will bring part payment with me. For the rest, I will need a permit for the Marquise's Man of Business to obtain her signature in jail."

Morel silently assented, and the plan was put into action. The permit was given, and a gentleman's agreement was shaken on whereby Morel would free the Marquise, then the Comte would see to it that Morel got all his money.

It was with these thoughts swimming in his mind that the Comte tried to settle down to sleep. A sudden commotion snapped him from his slumber and, before he had time to even reach for his gun, the door to his lodgings burst open and a band of Republican guards rushed in. Morel had betrayed his trust.

Events from there transpired quickly. The Marquise de

Marbeuf was sentenced to death and the Comte de Feuillide was put on trial. He denied every charge made against him and even denied his own identity in his desperation to be saved. He claimed that he was a valet to the Comte, not the real man himself. He told the judge he had murdered his master when he discovered his corruption.

But nothing he said could save him.

With no opportunity to write to Eliza or send his last fatherly advice to his son, the Comte lost his head to the guillotine on a raw February afternoon.

Two weeks later in London, Eliza summoned Warren Hastings to visit her urgently.

"Read this!" She thrust a smudged newspaper into her godfather's hands, which had been smuggled in by her servants. She was pale, tear-stained and shaking.

"Condemned to death …?" Mr Hastings could hardly believe what he was reading, even though the Comte's name was clearly printed there before him, in black and white.

Eliza needed to escape again. She was weary of the challenges life was constantly throwing up for her and this time she needed somewhere even further away than Steventon. She needed a place where there would be no well-meaning questions from people who knew her too well, so she went to stay with some friends in Northumberland who were discreet people and led a quiet life.

This was where she must contemplate what to do next.

# Chapter 31

### 1794-1795
### Family Ties.

The brutal execution of one of their own clan came as a complete shock to the Austens in Steventon. James was affected most of all. He knew the Comte personally from the months he had spent with him in France, and he was dumbstruck that such an ordinary man should be swept up in such extraordinary circumstances, to meet his death in such a gruesome way. He repeated to anyone who would listen that the Comte only ever spoke of his country with affection and wanted nothing more than for Eliza and his son to join him there. That it should end in such a way was incomprehensible.

The terrors abroad caused English newspapers to rouse their readers into a patriotic fervour. Prime Minister Pitt was certain that the country was on the verge of attack and was uneasy about his defences. With the whole of his regular army now deployed along the nation's coasts, a new force of yeomanry was needed to backfill the gaps inland and each region was ordered to provide volunteers for a local defence force. These men would serve as security in the event of invasion, and law enforcement in the event of civil unrest.

Steventon and its neighbours became part of the Basingstoke Troop: a division of the North Hampshire Yeomanry Cavalry. Mr Chute was put in charge of recruitment and had no trouble enlisting members. James Austen signed up willingly, as did Reverend Lefroy and Deane's leading landowner, Mr Harwood. Many other men joined up, too, attending group training once a week to learn how to use different types of weapons and practise a combination of scenarios through drills.

Morale was important, and extravagant celebrations were encouraged for any victory of national importance. When Admiral Lord Howe returned to Portsmouth with six French ships that he had taken in battle, the Knight family hosted a celebratory parade in Godmersham. Local soldiers paraded through the streets accompanied by a band playing 'God Save the King' and 'Rule Britannia'. Several local dignitaries came out to wave their flags and handkerchiefs and the entertainment culminated in the Knight family throwing open their grounds to offer food and drink to all. When darkness descended, a fireworks display was put on by Mr Knight for the villagers to enjoy.

Charles Austen finished his schooling at the Naval Academy and joined Captain Thomas Williams' ship as he had been promised at his cousin's wedding. He wrote home with great pride that he was soon to be aboard the *Daedalus* as a midshipman, based in the North Sea.

Frank remained frustrated on the *Lark*. He was keener than ever to defend his nation against its ruthless enemy, and he was annoyed beyond politeness to find himself part of a fleet transporting Princess Catherine of Brunswick to England so that she could marry the Prince of Wales. Bad weather was the only hazard he faced on this meek and powerless mission, causing his appetite for battle to grow stronger by the day.

His former patron - the Master of the Naval Academy - had died, which meant there was no one now to personally look out for him. He was invisible within naval circles, with no one to recommend him for a new commission or to further his career. His parents were worried when they received their son's letters, which were gloomier than they had ever known.

"Is there nothing we can do to help him?" fretted his mother.

"I can write to Warren Hastings, I suppose," considered Mr Austen, thinking out loud. "He has spoken to me of Admiral Affleck before, who has had some acquaintance with our family in the past. Perhaps that may be a route we could try?"

Mr and Mrs Austen were not known for being pushy, but when it came to the welfare of their children they did not hold back.

"I was thinking I could ask my cousin in Adlestrop," offered Mrs Austen. "He is familiar with Lord Hawke, which could be a path of influence. I will take the girls for a visit," she decided there and then. "It's high time they met their Gloucestershire relations."

With Cassandra's future secured by her engagement to Tom Fowle, Jane was now the focus of attention. Her mother was on a mission to find her a similarly fortuitous match and in taking her to a new neighbourhood, it would bring about new introductions.

Adlestrop was the place where Mrs Austen's father had been born. She had visited there often as a young girl, but had not returned at all during her thirty-one years of marriage. She was delighted to find the local roads were little changed from her youthful recollections and was as excited as a child to recount her memories to her daughters along the way.

"Now remember, you must not seem overbearing, but neither must you be too reserved," she babbled nervously when they were nearly there. "We want to be spoken of for the right reasons after we leave, not the wrong ones. Our hosts must be left with a desire to know you some more."

"Yes, Mama," chorused the girls obligingly, bored from the same message they had heard multiple times before.

The three females were to stay in the rectory with Mrs Austen's cousin, Reverend Thomas Leigh. He was a likeable man and not a complete stranger to the girls; they had met him a few times before when he had called in at Steventon on his travels. He was a firm favourite with their brothers, who always followed him about, as it was his custom before he left to present them each with a coin to spend as they wished. He had even called in on the girls when they were at school in Reading with Jane Cooper and gifted them each a guinea.

"Come, come, make yourself at home," he urged, ushering them into a comfortable parlour the minute they arrived. "Refreshments are already laid out, as you see. I thought you might be hungry after your long journey."

Reverend Leigh was married to Mary, who was as congenial as he was, and his unmarried sister, Elizabeth, lived with them too. Both women were old friends of Mrs Austen from her youth and they had all remained in contact by letter over the ensuing years; Reverend Leigh was Henry Austen's godfather, and Elizabeth Leigh was godmother to Cassandra.

In her eagerness to catch up on the latest gossip, Mrs Austen became distracted with her friends, leaving Cassandra and

Jane to eat the finger sandwiches and fancy cakes without censure. They were entertained by the humorous anecdotes of the flamboyant Reverend Leigh and enjoyed themselves immensely.

The church of St Mary Magdalene was opposite the house, on a slope overlooking the street. It was of sturdy build that seemed to offer the same hearty and friendly welcome that mirrored their host. It was straight and solid, made from amber-coloured stone with an attractively maintained pathway leading up to its door. Reverend Leigh told the girls he had been rector there for a very long time.

"Yes, I remember," recalled Mrs Austen when they went inside after tea. "I remember when you were presented with the living, just before George took up his own in Steventon, even before we were married."

She gazed around the neat and bright church in awe, her head tilting upwards towards the high rafters on the ceiling. Sunlight streamed through the window to brighten her face. "So long ago, and yet it feels like no time at all that I stood here last!"

Relations in the subsequent years between the different strands of the Leigh family had been difficult. There was a question over who was to inherit the large ancestral seat of Stoneleigh Abbey. Its current resident had no heir, nor was likely to produce one, and there had been much infighting amongst the younger Leigh generation to claim it for themselves. Mrs Austen's brother, James Leigh-Perrot, had made himself a nuisance with his own claims and Mrs Austen had been worried that this may taint the way she was received. But her old friends placed no blame on her at all; they were used to the squabbles and preferred not to dwell on such displeasure.

"I see no likelihood of Stoneleigh becoming imminently vacant," stated Elizabeth plainly. "And none of us know what situation we will find ourselves in a few years from now. Let us value the comforts we have today and leave the future to unfold as it will."

The Leighs of Adlestrop really were the most delightful of hosts and nothing was too much trouble for their guests, whom they treated like royalty. Reverend Leigh was a theatrical character with an elaborate personality and everyone he met on the street was his friend.

In years gone by, he had been the guardian of a boy who was another of Mrs Austen's relatives, and who had since grown up to inherit Adlestrop Park, the large estate that bordered the church. Consequently, Mrs Austen and her daughters were invited to dine there too and enjoy its magnificently landscaped gardens.

Warren and Marian Hastings' home of Daylesford House was only a short walk away, and a happy day was spent in their company exploring their luxurious mansion and marvelling over the exotic fruits they were attempting to grow in the orangery.

Mrs Austen was most optimistic when she returned home to her husband. Her cousin had promised that he would follow up on her request to investigate Frank's prospects, and Mr Hastings had told her that he would do the same. The girls had made the best of impressions; the only downside being that Jane had still not found a suitable suitor.

Not to be defeated, Mrs Austen sent her daughter next to Kent. When Cassandra was invited to stay once more with Edward and Elizabeth at Rowling, Jane went with her. She was guided in the conventions of upper-class society which consisted of (as it appeared to Jane) entertaining the children and painting flowers by day; then dancing by candlelight in the parlour of Goodnestone House by night. It was not the same relaxed and jovial society that they had found at Adlestrop, but the pleasure of being together with their brother for a substantial length of time made up for the formalities they were forced to endure.

Cassandra observed Jane closely during their stay and decided she was showing signs of attachment to an acquaintance of Edward's wife who lived close by. His name was Edward Taylor, and he spent a good deal of time in Jane's company.

"She thinks he has handsome eyes," Cassandra confided to her mother when they were back home in Steventon. "She talked with him almost every day we were there, and he was most attentive to her."

"In that case, I will write to Edward and see to it that she is invited back very soon," plotted her mother.

Her plan was scuppered, however, by the tragic death of Mr Thomas Knight II, who suffered a paralytic seizure when visiting his estate in Chawton. It was wholly unexpected and much lamented, actuating Edward Austen to assume his filial duty of escorting his adopted father's body back to Godmersham for burial. Thick with grief, he led the mourners in a trance for the funeral procession, which saw the streets lined with hundreds of villagers who had gathered to pay their respects to this highly esteemed man.

Mr and Mrs Austen freely admitted that Mr Knight had turned out to be an excellent guardian for their son, and their gratitude towards him swelled even more with the reading of his will. As expected, he left his three substantial estates to his wife, to be passed on to Edward after her death. But a stipulation had also been added that if Edward's line of succession was unsuccessful, then the properties should transfer to Edward's brothers in turn. In short, if Edward did not have a living son at the time of his own death, the estate would be passed on to James Austen. If James were not alive, it would fall to Henry Austen, and so on. Cassandra and Jane were not forgotten either and a gift of money was left for them both.

"God was looking down on us that day your cousin called on his wedding tour," pronounced Mrs Austen when the news of the will reached her ears.

Deaths like this in a family put the anxieties of war into perspective. Even though the nation was still under threat, it did not mean that every other problem simply went away. A particularly bad winter brought devastation to Hampshire and days of heavy snow were followed by flooding on an epic scale. Huge numbers of livestock were lost, including a selection of James Austen's prized pigs who drowned in the swelling streams.

Water seeped into every home and people became trapped. For two days the Austens were unable to come downstairs in their rectory because the ground floor was underwater. It took weeks before it was properly clean and dry again and the spoiled food could be replenished.

Jane spent most of her free time writing. Her father had bought her a little desk made from nut brown mahogany wood, with a drawer underneath to store her papers and a pretty glass inkstand on top. Cassandra had never once complained about the fact that Jane forever hogged the table they usually shared, nor did she reveal there was never any room for her own seals and notepaper amongst Jane's littering of manuscripts. But her father, it seemed, had noticed.

Now that she had a workspace to call her own, the nineteen-year-old authoress was more productive than ever. "I have decided that my next work will be a romance," she revealed to her sister whilst sharpening the end of her quill.

Cassandra was kneeling on the floor cutting out a length of fabric from a pattern she was making up as part of her wedding trousseau. Tentative plans for her marriage to Tom Fowle were being talked of openly and James had secured himself to lead the service when the day came.

Cassandra looked up from the ground and blew away a loose strand of hair that had fallen over one eye; her face was flushed from being bent double.

"Do you mean to tell me that the likes of Lady Susan are no more," she contested with mock horror. "You intend to truly make your characters fall in love properly?"

Jane's response was as dismissive as ever. "Lady Susan is perfectly capable of finding her own way in the world now."

Cassandra was inwardly amused at her sister's newfound interest in romance and wondered if the handsome eyes of Mr Edward Taylor from Kent had anything to do with it.

"I have decided that my next heroines will be sisters," Jane resumed.

"Very well," grinned Cassandra. "But I beg that the one you base upon me will secure the happiest marriage."

"Of course, you need not fear. I intend for one of them to act most irrationally with an ill-fated match, and I know that one could never be you."

"My little sister, a romantic!" Cassandra mocked affectionately. "I never thought I would see the day."

"It will be my characters who are romantic," retorted Jane, blushing. "I only create them."

"Come down girls, your cousin is here!"

Cassandra and Jane both rolled their eyes at their mother's shouting up the stairs. They had been expecting the interruption, knowing that today was the day when Edward and Caroline Cooper were due to arrive to introduce six-month-old Edward Junior to the household.

"We will speak more about your romantic sisters later," Cassandra assured Jane as they combed their hair. "Do they have names yet?"

"Hmmm..." Jane tidied her curls with a clip. "Definitely Elinor for one, I am quite decided on that. And I thought perhaps Marianne for the other. What do you think?"

"Perfect," agreed Cassandra, opening the door for them to go down. "I think they sound just the kind of girls to fall in love."

# Chapter 32

**1795**
**James Austen is widowed.**

After many years of waiting, Warren Hastings was finally cleared of all the charges brought against him in his Westminster Trial. The jury had sat for one hundred and forty days, over a span of seven years, to reach the 'Not Guilty' verdict. His supporters were elated.

"Listen to this, my love…" Mr Austen read the report from the newspaper to his wife. "Did I not tell you right from the start that he was innocent?"

James appeared at the rectory door shortly afterwards, having ridden over on purpose from Deane to share the glad tidings with his father, and Henry wasted no time in Oxford, writing directly to Mr Hastings with an effusive letter of congratulations. He liked Mr Hastings as much for his association with his cousin Eliza, as for the man himself, and was eager not to be overlooked should there be any kind of celebration.

Eliza had never doubted that her godfather's honour would prevail, but she could see how the trial had affected him. The result may have settled in his favour, but the accusations

235

and evidence against him had harmed his reputation beyond repair. The cost of defending himself financially had been excruciating and he left the city of London permanently to settle away from the glare of public scrutiny on his Daylesford Estate.

Talk of the trial was a hot topic following the acquittal, and debates dominated the after-dinner conversations at social gatherings. James Austen was a sought-after guest through his personal association with the man and his ability to offer more insight into his true character than any newspaper could.

He was looking forward to one such event at the beginning of May when a friend of General Mathew's was hosting a dinner party; James had been invited to join the guests for drinks after the meal. He dined early at home with his wife, and over their simple supper, Anne recounted their daughter's antics from that afternoon.

"She was watching the bird so intently that she didn't see the stick and tumbled right over it! But she didn't cry for long; you would have been so proud to see how quickly she picked herself up."

James smiled agreeably before popping a small potato into his mouth with his fork. "Such a pleasing child."

He always replied with a broad statement when it came to Anna because, in truth, he could not say convincingly if she was a pleasing child or not. He rarely spent time in her company, leaving her care entirely to his wife. But the fact that Anne doted on her was recommendation enough that she must be a very sweet girl.

Anna resembled her mother in looks and in personality, with large brown eyes and a slender frame. She had the grace of a fairy, toddling through the woods with wonder and attracted by every insect and flower. Constantly inquisitive, her hands forever reached out to take a closer look at some pretty sign of nature's splendour.

"Are you not hungry?" James was disturbed to see his wife was not eating. "You have hardly touched your meal."

Anne usually fussed over the table with dedication, keeping James's glass topped up with wine and serving out the vegetables to meet his demands. Today she looked unusually tired and listless.

"I don't think I can eat any more," she apologised, placing her knife and fork down next to her plate and leaning back in her chair. "I seem to have lost my appetite."

"Perhaps you should lie down," suggested James. "You do look rather pale."

Anne assented and made to stand up but was immediately forced to sit back down again when a sharp pain bit into her stomach.

"You are unwell. I will call someone. I will not go out and leave you like this."

"No. You go. I will be better with some rest. 'Tis only a twinge."

James was not convinced and called Anne's maid. Between them, they helped her up the narrow, crooked stairs and lay her down on her bed.

"What has she eaten?" questioned the maid, drawing the curtains briskly around the bedposts and shouting for some smelling salts to be brought in.

"The same as I," replied James, perplexed. "She barely touched a morsel. It can't be that."

Anne's skin looked yellow in the light of the bedroom, and

she groaned grimly from the pain. She clutched her side with both hands and grimaced with discomfort.

"Do you think I should call for the surgeon?" James asked the maid, clueless about how best to proceed.

"Yes. And quickly."

James ran back downstairs to dispatch a messenger, leaving the maid to deal with the sounds of vomiting which were now travelling down from the sick room.

He sent one man in the direction of the surgeon, and another to inform Anne's father. Then he returned upstairs. His wife was now in a state of confusion; the pain and sweats he watched accompany her groans reminded him of what he knew of childbirth, but Anne was not in the family way.

He had never had to deal with a situation like this as master of his own household and was at a complete loss for what to do next. The servants awaited his commands with eager expectation, and he flailed about with instructions to fetch more water and build more fires, whether they were needed or not.

The creak of a door off the landing attracted his attention and he turned to see little Anna peeping out of her room. She was crying at the frightening sounds around her. "Mama?"

"Back to bed," ordered James sharply, giving a disapproving look to Anna's nurse who swiftly scooped her up and shut the door behind them. Defeated, he sent yet another messenger to alert his mother and father; they would know what to do.

The surgeon arrived promptly and quickly assessed that he was powerless to help. "I fear a rupture of the liver." His words slurred in and out of James's ability to concentrate. Recognising that the husband was in no fit state to hear such news about his wife, the medical man instructed James to sit down on a chair and reached in his bag for a reviving tonic. This was followed by the strong smell of opium drifting down the stairs, which had been administered to ease Anne's pain: the only remedy on offer.

James felt as if he was looking down upon himself, watching the events unfold as a stranger. One by one his house filled with people, and he had no control over what was happening. General Mathew came with Anne's sister, and they went straight upstairs to see the patient. Within a few minutes, they came back down, wearing the gravest of looks. Anne's sister wept hysterically, and another tonic was called for and administered.

When Mr and Mrs Austen arrived, James was jolted back to reality. His father's calm command and his mother's empowering presence made him acknowledge that there really was something very wrong happening here.

"You should go to her now." Mrs Austen's voice broke through his thoughts like she had woken him from a dream. One foot in front of the other, James's legs carried him up the wooden stairs.

Their bedroom was peaceful by this time and a lamp flickered softly by the bed. The drugs had done their job and the servants had made the room respectable. Anne lay on a clean and tidy bed, barely conscious.

"I will wait downstairs," whispered the surgeon, vacating his chair for James to take his place. He placed Anne's frail, cold hand in James's substantial palm before heading towards the door. "She may still be able to hear you, but it is doubtful she will reply."

The end came quickly. Before an hour had passed, Anne Austen was dead.

Folk in the neighbourhood were used to rallying around when death took one of their own and the capable network of specialists engaged themselves discreetly into action. Black baize was delivered and draped around the dining room walls; black ribbon was administered for wrapping around arms and hats; buckets of sawdust and herbs were tipped out onto the flagstone floor and the table was scrubbed for Anne's body to rest until the day of her burial.

A carpenter brought a coffin on his wagon and the servants lined it with black crape and more sweet-smelling herbs. Anna's nurse, dexterous with her needle, ruffled a border around the coffin's edge to soften the harshness of the wood, and the elm casket was lifted gently onto the table.

James's wife of only three years was lovingly dressed by her maids for the final time, lying on the bed where she died. They wept as they teased the brush through her raven locks and wrapped her body in a woollen shroud. From there, the men lifted her reverently and carried her to her casket.

James Austen sat numbly on a mahogany chair, whilst his friends and neighbours filtered through the room by candlelight to pay their last respects. Why any of this was happening to him, and however he was going to recover, he could not fathom.

Anne's funeral took place at Steventon Church a week after she died. Her coffin was collected from her home in Deane and transported in a glass-sided hearse pulled by two stately black horses. Each horse had a plume of black feathers attached to its mane that swayed in time with the rhythmic brush of their muffled hooves.

The horses walked sedately in front of the mourners, with James and General Mathew in the first chaise behind.

More chaises followed them, tailed by a trail of manservants bringing up the rear. All was silent except for the sound of the tolling bell that called them forth to Mr Austen, who was waiting at the lychgate to greet them.

When Anne's body was carried along the pathway into the church, the sun glinted off the golden plaque nailed to the top of her coffin. It was a simple inscription with her name and date of death, embellished by the figure of an angel and a sprig of flowers. It offered hope to the followers that she would be granted eternal life and implied a welcome was awaiting her in heaven.

When her feather-light body was laid inside the bricked grave on the south wall of the chancel, her stoic mourners stood tall. Each one fought to suppress his emotions in a display of public unity because it was unseemly for men to cry.

Poor Anna did not know what to do without her mother. She had known nothing other than being folded into her warm, welcoming arms every day. Now she was alone, and her world was shattered. Her father was no comfort at all, in too much of a daze himself to think about what a two-year-old girl could possibly need to feel better.

"Bring her to us," suggested Mrs Austen after witnessing the hopeless situation for herself. "We can look after Anna at Steventon until you feel more able to manage. Then you can take her back."

"Yes. Yes," replied James. "I agree, she will be happier with you and my sisters while she pines for her mother. I will visit her every day, naturally. But yes, that is a good idea."

James never mentioned Anna's mother again, in his conversations with his daughter. The child was swallowed up by

241

the love of her grandparents and aunts instead. That became her new life.

# Chapter 33

**1795-1796**
**Confessions of the Heart.**

M r and Mrs Austen loved having their granddaughter stay with them and decorated a bedroom, especially for her. They bought her a little cherry wood chair designed with a child's frame in mind and she settled in easily.

Frank was happier too, out on the seas. Following his parents' intervention to find a suitable influencer, he had been invited across a range of vessels and was currently serving on the *Glory* as part of a convoy of nineteen thousand men sailing towards the West Indies to take on the French. There was unrest from some slaves on the plantations there, who had been incited by the French to rebel against British rule. A mission such as this was far more to Frank's liking than chaperoning a princess.

Henry was fretting over his career with the militia. He had barely seen live action since taking up his lieutenancy, but a sight he was forced to witness when on duty had disturbed him greatly. Some members of his regiment had broken the law and, as a deterrent to show their comrades that this type of behaviour would never be tolerated, they were shot dead by a firing squad in front of all their fellow troops. The images of the men's faces as they fell to the ground had haunted Henry ever since.

It made him question if a soldier's life was for him and he turned to Eliza as his counsellor and confidante. She was back in London and out of mourning for the Comte and both she and ten-year-old Hastings looked forward with eagerness to Henry's frequent calls.

Hastings was still a weak child and suffered from long bouts of illness, but fighting over mock battles with Henry and a set of wooden toy soldiers gave him the opportunity to become noisy and boisterous, if only for a short while.

There were two career choices open to Henry which he discussed openly with Eliza once Hastings had gone off with his nurse. Firstly, he had been made acting paymaster of his army regiment. This was no bad thing and earned him a level of respect. It removed him from the threat of front-line duty, although did not guarantee he would avoid the battlefield altogether.

The alternative was pursuing a future in the church. When Thomas Knight II had written his will, he had stipulated that Henry Austen should be offered the living of Chawton, if the first choice rector, Mr Papillon, decided to turn it down. Henry was genuinely tempted by this idea and became curious as to his rival's intentions. It would be too presumptuous to approach the man directly, but after some investigation, he discovered that the Papillon family was known to Madam Lefroy. She agreed to make some enquiries on Henry's behalf and see what she could find out.

"I have wanted to be a soldier since I was a boy," Henry

told his cousin, "But the clergy is in my blood and is what my father expects of me. How am I to know what to choose?"

Eliza placed her hand on Henry's arm and squeezed it. "Follow your heart," she breathed, those sparkling eyes drawing closer and implying something far deeper than his choice of career.

The sense of her touch on his arm sent a tingle through Henry's body and his mind became distracted. It was not the first time she had implied an intimacy between them, and he was swept up in the intensity of the moment, all thoughts for his career momentarily forgotten.

"My heart, Eliza, is yours. It always has been." He took her soft white hand in his own.

Eliza smiled slowly, knowing exactly where this conversation was leading. "We have always been the closest of friends, Cousin," she warned. "Is it not best that we keep it that way?"

Henry gazed deeper into her eyes. He could almost taste the sweetness of her lips, so near was he to her face. "We can be the closest of friends as husband and wife, can we not?"

Eliza pulled away. "Just because the Comte is dead, it does not follow that I must marry again," she replied coldly.

She averted her gaze and looked towards the window to compose herself. She too had been weakened by the intensity of the moment but was the quicker one to recover. No matter how strong her feelings for Henry were, she could not risk becoming attached to anyone again whilst the pain of losing her husband and her mother was so raw.

Henry coloured profusely at her obvious rejection. He had not come here today with any prior thoughts of a proposal and profoundly regretted what had just passed between them. He loved Eliza fiercely, but he was growing exceedingly weary

245

of her fickle personality. One minute she was tempting him: looking into his eyes like no other woman ever had. The next she was distant: mocking him like he had broken some unknown rule of etiquette.

"I beg your pardon," he spoke brusquely. "I will take my leave immediately."

"Do not let this come between us, Henry," laughed Eliza playfully as he stood up to leave. "Our friendship is too valuable to break in such a silly quarrel. You must stay for dinner as we had planned."

"I'm afraid I must not."

Eliza was shocked at his assertiveness and perturbed by the offence she had caused.

"I shall return to my regiment directly and will not disturb you again." Henry marched out of the room and out of the front door without a backward glance.

'Never again will I embarrass myself in her company,' he repeated to himself as he stomped off down the street. He swore under his breath for allowing himself to be taken in by Eliza's compulsive game. He scolded himself with insults for openly revealing his feelings and vowed that from this day forward he would find someone to love who deserved him better.

True to his conviction, a few weeks later (and much to everyone's surprise) he found a fiancée.

The lady in question was Mary Pearson, the daughter of a knighted naval captain whom he had met whilst camped with his regiment at Sheerness. She was pretty and vivacious, with many admirers and a suitable social match. An alliance with her family promised Henry a life of gaiety, filled with parties and fun.

To validate this whirlwind romance, he obtained Miss Pearson's miniature portrait. Her gentle eyes stared lovingly back at him and she wore a low-cut sheer white gown. On the back of the ivory watercolour was a plate of her copper brown hair weaved together, set within an oval gold-rimmed frame. Henry took this love token to show his bewildered family at Steventon. Obviously, they offered their congratulations, but privately they were puzzled and concerned. It was all so sudden and unexpected.

\* \* \*

There was no such worry over Cassandra's engagement. The love between her and Tom Fowle was true and real and she was invited to stay with his family in Kintbury over the Christmas season. He was due to sail overseas in the new year with the 7th Baron Lord Craven and he was keen to spend as much time as possible with his sweetheart before he left.

"Lord Craven has promised that I will be presented with a living in Shropshire upon my return," he informed his fiancée as they strolled through the village. "Then we can finally set the date for our wedding."

"I cannot wait," agreed Cassandra. "But honestly Tom, all I can think of for now is the danger you will be in on your voyage. Please promise me you will keep safe."

"I will promise anything you wish," Tom replied, giving her his best loving gaze. "I am as eager to return home as you are, so for that reason alone I will not let myself come to any harm."

The voyage was headed to the West Indies where every

ship, it seemed to Cassandra, was sailing these days. He was to accompany Lord Craven's regiment as part of the huge convoy following behind her brother Frank.

"I will not see any conflict," Tom stressed. "I have been assured on that many times." Lord Craven's private yacht was to sail a little way apart from the main troops and Tom was travelling as his private chaplain. The threat to his safety was minimal.

"I will write to you every day," he promised. "And whenever I meet a ship heading back to England, I will hail the captain and pass him all my correspondence. Then I will tell him to make sure it is delivered to you the minute he is back on dry land."

He kissed Cassandra on the forehead, and she laughed at the image his words had painted in her mind.

"You will have so many bundles of letters from every ship," he continued jovially, "that everyone in the navy will know how much you are in my thoughts!"

They turned to walk back towards the house in silence, both enjoying the closeness of their linked arms, which pulled them together, side by side. Tom was thoughtful, wondering if he should speak of the one thing that pressed on his mind.

"I was not sure if I should tell you this, but now that our separation is near, I feel it should not be kept a secret."

Cassandra was alarmed at how solemn he had become and watched his chestnut brown eyes seek stability in the middle distance. For the first time since they had been together in Kintbury, she recognised how vulnerable he was. He was fresher-faced than all his brothers, and his innocent features had still not lost their boyhood appeal. How was it right that he should be allowed to travel on such a perilous voyage?

"It is nothing so terrible," he sought to placate her, catching the fear in her eyes. Cassandra stopped walking to give him her full attention.

"It is regarding my will. I want you to know that I have named you as my beneficiary."

Cassandra gasped and the colour drained from her face.

"My estate and belongings shall be dealt with by my father, but my money I will leave to you. It is not much, but it pleases me to know that you will be comfortable, should I not return."

This made Cassandra cry. She was unable to find the words for such an abrupt announcement; she busied herself wiping her eyes with her handkerchief, whilst Tom wrapped her in his arms and soothed her as best as he could.

"Please don't upset yourself, my sweet Cassy. I say this only because I love you and I want you to know how very much."

"But I don't want to talk of your will. Or your money. I don't want you to go away at all!"

Tom continued to hold her whilst she sobbed into his shoulder.

"The way I feel now, Tom, I don't care if we never get married. I only want you to be safe. I would sacrifice all the money in the world to walk by your side like we are doing now and stay poor as we are if it meant you would not leave me."

"I promise you we will walk side by side for the rest of our lives. We will wear out the soles of our boots together until the time comes when we can no longer leave our chairs."

His last remark made Cassandra smile and she fought to compose herself.

"You mean everything to me, sweet Cassy," he continued. "I have only done what any man would do to provide for the woman he loves. It is a common business transaction and nothing more than God would expect of me."

"Well, in that case, I thank you for being so kind." She tried her utmost to replicate her lover's tone and force the conversation away from her morbid imaginings. "I assure you that your gesture is appreciated. But please, from now on, let us talk only of happy things."

"Agreed." Tom took Cassandra's arm once more and they resumed their walk.

"So blue for the kitchen, you say?" He stumbled on as if the prior fit of passion had never taken place.

"That's right," confirmed Cassandra, with a false ardour. "It is the best colour to repel the flies."

"Very well, blue it is. What do you say for the parlour...?"

The days they spent together in Kintbury were truly wonderful but passed all too quickly. When the morning arrived for Tom's departure, Cassandra fought to remain calm. She clutched his hand tightly, pushing her prayers into his skin. When she was forced to let go so that he could take leave of his mother and father, all she could do then was watch him leave.

She had so much wanted to be brave and to wish him well with a happy smile, but her tears streamed freely, regardless. Mrs Fowle stood by her side and rubbed her back as they both watched the horses into the distance.

"We must bear it the best we can," she instructed her daughter-in-law-to-be. "We must look forward to when that carriage returns, and not dwell upon it leaving."

Cassandra attempted a smile.

"And if I am not mistaken, we have a wedding to prepare for. That will keep us busy!" Mrs Fowle was being exceedingly kind, but somehow this only made Cassandra feel worse. "What if he never comes back?" she sobbed.

# Chapter 34

## 1796
### Mr Lefroy.

Cassandra's absence was duly felt while she was staying in Kintbury, but her seat at the table in Steventon was soon filled by a guest. John Warren, a former pupil of Mr Austen's and a good friend of Henry's, had been invited to stay. Henry was home too.

It was the season for balls and dinner parties, which the young people threw themselves into with pleasure. Speculation over whom they might meet at their next gathering was a popular thread of conversation between them.

"We saw Madam Lefroy this morning in Overton," Henry told to his companions. "She is bringing her nephew with her to the ball this evening."

"Is that the lawyer over from Ireland?" queried James, who was now out of mourning for his late wife. "I heard he was staying in the neighbourhood but I've not seen anything of him yet."

"That's the fellow. Tom Lefroy. An amiable chap was he not, Warren?"

"He seemed decent enough," agreed John Warren. "Although I thought him a little shy."

The ball was to be at the Basingstoke Assembly Rooms, a regular event on the Austens' calendar. On this cold December night, a frost had formed on the ground before they even left the house.

"You must dance with Mr Lefroy, Jane," Henry decided as the horses lumbered over the uneven roads, making the carriage tilt from side to side. "He knows no one in Hampshire apart from his aunt."

Jane gave a non-committal nod, but inwardly she was pleased. She was curious to meet this nephew of her neighbour whom she had heard so much about. Madam Lefroy was very fond of him by all accounts.

The carriage pulled up with ease outside the Assembly Rooms, which Jane took as a bad omen. When there was a queue, it meant that the ballroom was busy; being able to park without difficulty meant not many people had ventured out. She lifted her dress to avoid soiling the hem and stepped daintily over a pile of manure. Fortunately, the path to the entrance was well-lit by the torches on either side of the door, so she was able to keep her slippers clean all the way inside.

Jane conditioned her mind to remain optimistic; perhaps they had been fortunate in their timing and had missed the early rush. There was still a chance that once inside, it would be busy. The cold air was welcome and refreshing after an hour of enduring her brothers' cologne at close quarters and she wrapped her cloak closely around her frame. She took James's arm, to be led up the stairs and along the narrow passageway towards the ballroom of the Angel Inn.

The sound of tuning violins lifted her spirits yet more, and a nervous anticipation warmed her veins; the musicians were getting ready to take their places so it would not be long now before the dancing began.

Expectantly, she peeked into the room to see who was there. It was half empty.

Her heart sank and she resigned herself to the prospect of a very dull evening. There were far more ladies than gentlemen, and far too many vacant seats. The space on the floor was cavernous and draughty, and she held little hope that the mood would brighten.

Wishing she had never come, Jane put on a brave face and applied her best smile, taking a seat next to James and feigning interest in watching Henry and Mr Warren circulate the room. She hated small talk at the best of times, finding nothing more tedious than commenting upon the weather with people she had no wish to converse with, in order to pretend she was having an agreeable time.

Luckily, the musicians did their best to liven things up. She was gratified that the dancing soon began and relieved when John Warren led her to the floor. He was not the most attentive of partners, but Jane found it amusing to watch his eyes flit from one female dancer to the next. She envied him slightly, as for him the room was full of unfamiliar faces and any number of new acquaintances were ripe to be made. Jane, on the other hand, knew everyone. She could recite where they lived, who were their brothers and sisters, and the breeds of pigs and geese they kept in their yards.

Warmed from the exertion of the dance, her mood improved. The dismal walls were transformed by a pleasing golden glow dripping down from the glass chandeliers above. Jane's steps became lighter, and she skipped around the room with more enjoyment. The place looked livelier still when she passed by the long oval mirror above the fireplace, throwing the reflected images of her fellow dancers far into the distance.

Even the hearths were more cheerful from the activity and their amber flames licked up high. Henry was laughing, and James had found himself a partner. Everyone exchanged affectionate smiles with their neighbours, and she was heartened by the thought of fresh snippets of gossip over supper.

A flash of red and black in the doorway alerted her to the fact that Madam Lefroy and her husband had finally arrived. Immaculate as ever in a bright red gown with a black fur wrap, the lady's presence was welcomed. Her magnetism was attractive wherever she went, and Jane was not the only one watching her from the corner of her eye. Reverend Lefroy was all smiles and warm greetings as he walked towards an empty row of seats, addressing everyone in turn on his way.

Behind him was the elusive nephew.

Tom Lefroy was tall and slender with fine, fair hair parted down the middle of his scalp and brushed back neatly in the most sensible of styles. His face was narrow, fronted by a long sharp nose, but his eyes and mouth were friendly enough. Overall, his appearance was rather pleasing, thought Jane.

The young stranger greeted each nosy onlooker with a nod or a bow as he was introduced around the room by the Master of Ceremonies. Jane sympathised with his plight; how daunting it must be to be thrown into a room where so many people were eager to stare at you.

Henry and Mr Warren soon made their way over to him and chatted like old friends, their introduction that morning in Overton giving them a common ground to build upon. Jane braced herself as they headed in her direction, intending to act demurely and calm; but unfortunately, the warmth of her cheeks told her she had not managed to contain the blush she had wanted to hide.

"Allow me to introduce my brother, James," said Henry and the two men shook hands. "And this is our little sister, Jane. I can vouch you will not stand up with a better dancer all evening."

Jane curtseyed and lowered her eyes.

"In that case, perhaps you will grant me the pleasure of the next dance, Jane?"

Her breath caught in her throat at the directness of his address, but when she looked into his eyes, she could see a twinkle of mischief: something she had not expected from Mr Warren's earlier description of him.

From their first turn around the room, Jane was convinced he was not shy at all, and he was clearly used to dancing. He relaxed in time with the music and his politeness shifted quickly into friendly conversation. Jane was sad when the dance ended, and they were forced to begin the next with fresh partners. All evening she studied him, but try as she might, she could not determine which face out of all the pretty ones in the room, had appealed to him the most.

This Irish nephew of Madam Lefroy was the talk of everyone in the insular neighbourhood the next morning, giving Mrs Austen the perfect excuse to pay her friend a visit. She took the chaise to Ashe, with Jane as a happy passenger, to meet him for herself.

"There he is," pointed Jane, her voice flat with disappointment as she saw Tom Lefroy striding off at speed when they pulled up. "It looks like he's going for a walk."

"That is a pity," replied her mother, squinting at the decreasing figure. "A minute earlier and he would have still been in the house."

Another ball followed shortly after at Basingstoke, this time a little livelier than before and allowing a repeat performance of civilities. By this time, Henry and Mr Warren had become regular companions of Tom Lefroy and he was more at ease in their company. When the invitation arrived for the end-of-season ball at Manydown, Tom Lefroy was a secure member of their party.

The setting of Manydown was spellbinding. The greenhouse had been lit with hundreds of candles which, set against the inky black of the sky, added tints of gold to the sprinkling of snow on the ground. The green leaves of the tropical plants transformed the room into an enchanted fairyland and Jane was in a magical mood to match.

She wore her best ivory gown for the occasion, made up from embroidered muslin with a small train. Her headband was of matching fabric, twisting tantalisingly through her curls and catching the light with its tiny beads. It complemented perfectly a string of decadent pearls she wore around her neck. She felt like she was floating on air and wished that Cassandra could see her now, so sure of herself and full of confidence. She felt beautiful, in a way she had never felt before, for no other reason than that Tom Lefroy was in the same room.

He, presumably, felt the same because he followed her everywhere. At every opportunity he found her a chair, fetched her a drink, and accompanied her onto the terrace when she needed some air.

She sensed that James disapproved. He did not say so openly but she often caught him scowling at her, along with Madam

Lefroy. Both of them made it obvious they were not pleased with her conduct.

The problem was, that Jane could not help herself. Tom Lefroy seemed to be able to see right through her and read her innermost thoughts. He chose exactly the right words to make her laugh and she felt like they were twins, knowing instinctively what each other was going to do next. She enjoyed his company exceedingly.

Henry was not concerned about their behaviour and neither was Mr Warren. As all three men rode out regularly together, Jane took this as proof that Mr Lefroy could not possibly be an unsuitable companion. If he was, she knew Henry would have warned her.

"The 86th Regiment is my first choice," Jane could hear Henry telling a family friend in an alarmingly loud, slurred voice. "They're due to set off for the Cape of Good Hope in the spring. I'm waiting to hear if I can join 'em."

"What about Miss Pearson?" asked the friend. "I doubt she will want to be left alone to pine after you."

"Oh yes, Miss Pearson," repeated Henry with an unbecoming laugh. Not only did he seem to have forgotten his obligation towards her, but sometimes Jane thought he had forgotten her altogether.

Henry bumbled on, in his embarrassingly drunken stupor. "No. I suppose that would not do..."

In recent months, Henry had changed. Jane still could not fathom what had brought about his sudden engagement to Miss Pearson, but more than that it had coincided with a curious desire to join the army regulars, and an equal willingness to take orders for the church. He was simultaneously trying to impress army generals, whilst Madam Lefroy and their brother, Edward, negotiated with Mr Papillon over the living at Chawton. Jane was worried about his state of mind.

"Come, Jane, let us dance." Tom Lefroy took her hand and pulled her towards the dance floor.

"Again?" she beamed with shame. "What will people say?"

Tom made no answer, which mattered little to Jane as she had no intention of refusing him anyway.

The next day was Cassandra's birthday, which she was spending in Kintbury. A pang of sorrow interrupted Jane's blissful wakefulness when she was reminded how much she missed her sister. Before she even dressed, she began to compose a letter:

*In the first place, I hope you will live twenty-three years longer. Mr. Tom Lefroy's birthday was yesterday ....*

What a thrill it gave her to write his name!

*I am almost afraid to tell you how my Irish friend and I behaved at the ball last night...*

Would Cassandra laugh, or would she be as disapproving as James?

Jane's pen flowed with its usual light efficiency to dispatch her innermost thoughts. Everything she wrote was of Tom Lefroy. Every thought was of Tom Lefroy. And when he stood at the door of Steventon Rectory to pay his obligatory morning call the day after the ball, Jane wanted to sing from the rooftop that he was there.

Mr and Mrs Austen said nothing about her impulsive behaviour, and for that she was grateful. They knew perfectly well that the flirtation would amount to nothing. Madam Lefroy had already made it clear that her nephew would soon be leaving for his law school in London and had no intention of returning.

For all her generous charm and friendship, Madam Lefroy could also be a woman of cold and calculating principle. Tom was starting out on a promising career where a country girl like Jane would never be allowed to distract him. It was just as well they were destined to attend no more balls together.

In the same way that Cassandra had wept for Tom Fowle when he had ridden out of sight, so did Jane weep when she wrote her last words regarding her irresistible friend.

# Chapter 35

**1796-1797**
**Love will find a way.**

Edward and Elizabeth invited their Steventon relations to Rowling for the summer. Even three-year-old Anna was included in the party for the long journey into Kent, travelling with Mr and Mrs Austen, Cassandra, Jane and Frank, who was lately home on leave.

One topic alone dominated the discourse when they arrived, which was that Jane Cooper's husband, Captain Thomas Williams, was to receive a knighthood. He was to be honoured by the king for his command of the *Unicorn*, which had captured two enemy ships in a long chase around the Channel, without a single loss of life to the crew. The accolade was even more poignant for the family because Charles Austen had been serving on board at the time and had played his own part in the action.

Everyone felt a level of pride by association apart from Frank, who was more restless than ever. He was desperate to be back out on the waves following his mission in the West Indies and was impatient for his next commission. He took up the art of woodturning to pass the time and whiled away

261

his days in Edward's outbuilding, crafting toys and gifts for his young nieces and nephews.

Henry Austen took stock of his own situation and slowly unravelled the burdens he had imposed on himself the year before. First came the abandonment of his plan to join the army regulars. Instead of travelling to the Cape of Good Hope for a full-time posting, he opted to continue as paymaster with the Oxfordshire Militia and stayed on in the south of England.

His plans to take orders for the church in Chawton were also dismissed when it became clear that Madam Lefroy's coaxing, and Edward's financial incentives, were not enough to entice Mr Papillon to give up the lucrative living.

The only outstanding conundrum left for Henry to solve now was his unfortunate engagement to Miss Pearson.

His initial feeling of triumph in securing a life partner so soon after his tiff with Eliza had long ago vanished. Henry felt no romantic attachment towards the woman he had chosen and there was no indication that she was especially drawn to him either. Both were in the unenviable position of knowing that, since they had made their engagement public, they must continue to stumble their way through their social obligations and make the best of a bad situation.

Despite the engagement being of many months' duration, Miss Pearson had still not been introduced to Henry's family. She made her first appearance when he took her on a day trip to Rowling where Frank and Jane had remained in Kent after the rest of the party had gone home, so were able to meet her when she arrived.

"Delighted to meet you," curtseyed Miss Pearson as she entered the cosy hallway. Her eyes emitted no warmth when she spoke and, after quickly skimming over her new acquaintances, she attached herself only to Elizabeth. Edward's wife's attire implied she was still in vogue, whereas the homespun garments worn by the rest of them demonstrated a pitiful lack of interest in buying the latest fashions.

"You mean to tell me you milk the cows yourself?" guffawed Miss Pearson when they were seated in the drawing room getting to know one another. She found it too amusing to think of Edward getting his hands dirty when he was in charge of the whole estate.

To his credit, Henry was as irritated by his partner's patronizing ways as his siblings, and the tension between the betrothed couple was obvious. "Tell me, Mary, where else do you expect my sister to obtain eggs for her breakfast if she is not to go near the hen house? Have you never been on a farm?"

Miss Pearson stayed only a few hours at Rowling before she was taken home, and Henry spoke little about her when he returned to join them again the next day. Instead, the three brothers entertained themselves with a trip to Godmersham Park, where they charmed Mrs Knight with their company.

When Henry left for Yarmouth and returned to his duties, Edward and Frank took Jane to London. They could not be faulted in their attentiveness to ensure their sister would have much to speak of in the company of a potential beau, introducing her to a series of exhibitions and a circus.

The former interest Jane had expressed in Mr Edward Taylor (of the handsome eyes) on her last visit to Kent, did not develop into anything more. She did not even meet him during this stay, getting no closer to his company than driving by his house in a carriage. Disappointingly for her mother, the opportunity for an attachment there had passed.

"I have so much to write and tell Cassandra," Jane twittered to her brothers after her brief excursion to London. "But do you think I should warn Mama about Miss Pearson? I fear she will be most disappointed when Henry brings her home; she is not nearly as handsome as her portrait, and has a prickly personality indeed."

Edward and Frank laughed affectionately at their busy body of a sister but could not disagree with her sentiments.

When he did eventually take Mary to Steventon, Henry could tell instantly that his father did not like her. His mother struggled on admirably to make her feel welcome and find a mutual topic of interest to debate, but it was painful for everyone to witness the rude and stunted responses Miss Pearson gave in reply. She made no effort to endear herself to her future parents-in-law and, just as at Rowling, nobody was sorry when she left.

When Henry announced sheepishly at the end of summer that he and Mary had called the engagement off, no one encouraged him to reconsider. They were more gratified to see him happy again, with the old sparkle returned to his eyes. They put this down to his relief at escaping marriage, and a recently attained promotion with the Oxfordshire Militia. He was now a captain lieutenant and adjutant, in charge of a significant amount of money for the regiment's payroll. It was unsurprising he walked a little taller.

The main reason for his transformation, however, nobody guessed.

He had overheard from his father's letters, that Eliza had taken new lodgings in London. His work took him regularly to the capital, and on one sunshine-filled day, he found himself walking in the direction of her street. Fate, it seemed, was egging him on because he passed by a conveniently placed bookstore along the way, displaying a multicoloured book of maps in its window. On impulse, Henry went inside to buy it. It was exactly the kind of book he had enjoyed sharing with young Hastings the year before, quizzing him about his countries and telling him about the world. Before his courage deserted him, Henry marched up to Eliza's front door and rang the bell. He would leave the book as a gift for the boy if his entry was refused.

The welcome he received was warmer than he had hoped for, and he was assured by catching them unawares that both mother and son were genuinely pleased to see him.

Eliza had undergone some serious self-reflection of her own, which first began when she had gone on holiday to Brighton with her cousin, Philly Walter. Painfully aware that Henry was gallivanting about town with his fiancée, Eliza had taken Hastings to bathe in the sea. On their wind-blown strolls along the promenade, Philly had been amused by Eliza's vicious attacks on the character of Miss Pearson. She had called her an 'intolerable flirt' with 'wicked eyes', which Philly knew was nothing more than Eliza's jealousy speaking as she barely knew the poor woman she was blaspheming.

Philly had long ago dismissed the idea of a match between Eliza and Henry, due to him being ten years her junior and a soldier. His military career meant that he would never be able to offer Hastings a stable home. Philly urged Eliza to think of James Austen instead. Both of them had been recently widowed, both were single parents to a child, and both were of a similar age. Furthermore, Eliza had spent almost half her life staying in the neighbourhood where James was settled;

the match, in Philly's humble opinion, had everything to recommend it.

Eliza took this advice to heart and seriously considered her friend's proposal. The next time she went to Steventon she tried hard to see the benefits she had been persuaded of. But in the end, she could not convince herself that marrying James would be a wise undertaking. For one thing, he was not as attentive to her as he used to be, and Eliza was put off by his small-town ways. It thrilled him to receive a dinner invitation from the Honourable Mr Chute, yet Eliza could think of a dozen more interesting figures in London she would rather spend the evening with.

The deciding factor that clinched it was when she studied James with his daughter. He was one of those distant breeds of fathers who showed little affection for their offspring and preferred it when they were quiet. Eliza was the complete opposite, loving her hands-on role as mother to Hastings and proud to be seen with him on her arm.

She wrote to Philly when her mind was made up.

*'I assure you, dearest Philly, that I seriously considered your recommendations whilst I was in Hampshire and saw many attractions to a quiet life in Deane. Yet the moment I arrived back in London, I knew that I could never be happy as the wife of a country clergyman.'*

What she did not confess, however, was that her feelings for Henry ran far deeper than her feelings for James.

\* \* \*

There was good reason for James's lack of attentiveness towards Eliza when she tried to flirt with him in Steventon.

He had been stung by her fickle personality too many times in the past and had learned to be more guarded when she was around. He was not going to fall for her flattery again, only to be made to regret it before the week was out.

His head was turned instead by the presence of Martha and Mary Lloyd, who had both come for an extended stay at Steventon Rectory. Martha's influence filled the rooms with warmth and wholesome goodness, and everyone was drawn into her contagious project of collecting recipes. She was compiling a book she had called *Cookery Interest* and had neatly copied out her mother's old family dishes into a new parchment notebook. Now she was eager to fill the rest of the pages with the favourite tastes of her friends.

It was a project everyone wanted to be a part of and which brought them all together around the table. Food was given an extra zest with the resurrection of best-loved meals and Mrs Austen made everyone smile when she presented her trusted recipe for a pudding in the form of a poem.

Mary used the opportunity of this happy distraction to slip away from the rest of the family and walk with James to Deane. On the way there, she offered to help him in his church, to sort out his account ledgers and organise his diary. It was what she had enjoyed doing for her late father in Enborne and she proved supremely organised and efficient. James was grateful; Anne had always been the one to direct his days when they were married and he still felt her loss having to do it alone.

Mary, of course, had always been fond of James, and their shared friendship of several years was well-established. What made her stand out now in James's affection was the attention she paid to him as a man. His daughter was an endearing little girl, and he was used to being overlooked in her presence; most people did not give James the time of day until they had fussed over little Anna first. But Mary was different. James liked the way she gave him her entire focus, the only person to pay him such unique attention. A new brightness to her eyes seemed to dim the scars on her face and James began to notice the charming way she blushed when she spoke to him.

He found himself increasingly looking forward to the days she was due to come and help him, and his mother was ecstatic when he eventually made her an offer of marriage. Mrs Austen wrote Mary a heartfelt letter to welcome her into the family, stressing that she could not wish for a better wife for her son.

James and Mary were married in St Peter's Church at Hurstbourne Tarrant, near to Mary's home in Ibthorpe. Snow fell the night before the wedding to greet the cold January day, but a cheery sun glistened off the tips of the hills regardless. Twinkles of shimmering light danced over the bubbling streams they passed on their way to the church, and everything they saw on that bright winter's day promised a long and happy life together.

# Chapter 36

**1797**
**The Worst News.**

James and Mary's wedding quite naturally led to thoughts of the next one to come. April was the month Tom Fowle was due home from the West Indies and Cassandra was jittery with nerves each time her father went to collect the post. Tom had promised to write the minute he arrived home.

The bride-to-be had finished making up her wedding trousseau and had even sewn the gown she would wear on the day. Knowing it would not be long, she was making up a pretty new dress for Anna, who could not possibly grow much taller in the few weeks before it would be worn.

They were happy days in the dressing room, with the fresh spring breeze blowing in through the billowing curtains around Cassandra, who sewed, and Jane, who wrote. Jane had finished her story of *Elinor and Marianne* and put it to one side to read over later. She was now concentrating on a new work she had entitled *First Impressions*.

Character profiles were important to Jane and she fretted over each one; she worried if her readers would find the traits she attributed to them believable or not. Once her plot had

THE AUSTENS OF STEVENTON

been decided, the characters grew a life of their own inside her head.

"Miss Bingley reminds me of Miss Pearson," she confided to Cassandra, placing the profile she had written for this lady on top of a neat pile to her left. "She cannot tolerate life in the country because she considers herself to be above it."

This revelation was followed by a sigh. "But her brother is the opposite. Mr Bingley is generous and kind and she is so selfish. Do you think it unreasonable they differ so?"

"Not at all," replied Cassandra. "Brothers and sisters do not need to have the same personality merely because they are related. Look at how differently we all act from one another."

"Yes," hesitated Jane. "But none of us are as disagreeable as Miss Bingley." She bit her bottom lip and furrowed her brow to give the matter more thought.

Cassandra returned to her sewing, recognising the signs that Jane needed some quiet time to reflect.

"Who loves Mr Bingley?" came a little voice from the corner of the room. "I have forgot who you said."

Jane's mouth gasped open, and Cassandra stifled a giggle. Anna had been given the task of sitting quietly on a cushion and rolling up all the stray pieces of ribbon from the ribbon draw. She had conscientiously placed them in neat little circles and arranged them in a long line. Being all consumed by her story, Jane had forgotten she was there.

"When did you hear me say such things?" Jane asked aghast. "You are not meant to be listening! I thought you were tidying the ribbons." Anna's remark was a stark reminder that the ears of a four-year-old girl missed nothing.

The young girl was shocked by her aunt's reprimand and tears sprang to her eyes. "I *am* tidying the ribbons," she whimpered and Cassandra went over to placate her.

"I can see we must save our conversations for when some-one has gone to bed," Jane said in a cross undertone. She could not risk her work in progress being revealed to the world before she was ready to share it.

She continued with the rest of her character evaluations in silence. *Lydia Bennet*, she smiled to herself, when she was once more engrossed in her task. Jane was rather fond of this teenage girl whose creation had been inspired by her own outrageous behaviour with Tom Lefroy. She enjoyed thinking of outspoken lines for Lydia to say, knowing what an embarrassment she would become to her family. Jane would never be allowed to act like that in real life.

Not for the first time, she was gratified by the power she held as an author. Where else did she have the freedom to correct the injustices of society? Still sore from the way Madam Lefroy had put a stop to her friendship with her nephew, Jane knew that in fiction, at least, she could join a poor girl to a rich man despite the disapproval of an aunt!

After another half an hour of sewing, Cassandra broke the silence with a yawn. "I think I will call for some tea," she said, standing up and stretching. "I feel quite sleepy all of a sudden."

"That's James and Mary's fault," complained Jane, cattily, but this time so quietly that there was no chance Anna would hear. "They left far too late last night giving their lectures on the Scriptures - even Papa was getting bored. I think Mary has become as tiresome as James since she married him."

Cassandra could not think of an adequate response, never wanting to speak ill of anybody if it could be helped.

"It's a pity our brother has made her so dull," Jane persisted to whisper, not done yet with her rant. "Promise me you won't change for the worse when you marry Tom."

Cassandra glowed at the thought. "I promise. Although Tom is different altogether to James. His sermons are full of kindness, not criticism."

Jane was consoled by this, remembering that even as boys together in the schoolroom, James' and Tom's personalities were not alike.

"Here they are again." Jane spotted James and Mary out of the window, walking determinedly up the drive. "I wonder what they want so early?"

"Perhaps they left something behind," suggested Cassandra, equally as baffled. "Maybe they have some news for Papa. They do look rather solemn."

Surprisingly, the girls were not called down to greet the visitors as they had expected, but James and Mary came upstairs themselves to knock on the dressing room door.

"It must be Anna they have come for," Cassandra concluded. "Come sweetheart, your papa is here." The time they understood it must be something very serious was when Mrs Austen took Anna's hand and led her away, leaving James and Mary behind.

"Whatever is the matter? Why do you look so severe?" Cassandra was frightened.

"I think you should sit down," commanded James.

Jane and Cassandra sat dumbfounded in their chairs whilst James and Mary delivered the news, repeating themselves many times over until they were sure that the words had sunk in. An express had arrived from Fulwar within the last hour and they had wasted no time before coming directly here. It was Tom, dear, precious, deeply loved Tom; he was not coming home. He had died from yellow fever in Martinique on the 13th of February: over two months ago and they had not known! His body had been buried at sea; the news had only just arrived; they were so frightfully sorry to be the bearers of such tragic news.

For weeks after the announcement everybody everywhere was sorry. But what good was sorry, thought embittered Jane. What good was anything now that Cassandra's only hope of happiness had been snatched away?

It was the worst news imaginable for all of them and yet Cassandra remained the calmest of them all. She had felt so ecstatically overjoyed by her good fortune in finding love with Tom, that she had often asked herself how she would bear such happiness. She knew her contentment could not possibly last and every day she allowed herself to prepare for it to burst. In a strange way, she was not surprised it had happened.

"I am assured that Tom loved me," she explained to Jane one night when more tears had flowed before bed. "And we were granted such a perfect time in Kintbury before he sailed. I know that his thoughts would have been of me and our wedding before he died, which brings me comfort."

Jane's papers from her novel had sat dormant for the days following the disturbance and when she finally did go back to her character profiles, it was Jane Bennet who was sitting on top. Miss Bennet was going to be the good one, the beautiful, kind young woman who would assert her moral goodness to redeem the faults of others. Jane had previously doubted if such a person was realistic and if her readers would readily accept someone who could remain as calm as an angel in the face of adversity.

Cassandra had answered this question without even realising. She had proved that this rare breed of woman truly did exist.

# Chapter 37

**1797-1798**
**Life goes on.**

Tom Fowle's death impacted everyone who knew him, each sharing the same opinion that life could be so cruel to deny such a personable young man the chance to make memories with a wife and raise a family of his own. Many of the older generation questioned why God could not have taken them instead, and Mrs Jane Fowle did not last the year before passing away after such a blow. Fulwar and his young family were recalled from their parish in Elkstone to live with Mr Fowle in Kintbury and take over the running of his church.

Mrs Austen was in awe of Cassandra and how bravely she battled to hide her immeasurable sadness. She was philosophical to a fault whilst Mrs Austen herself was so very tired of grief. *'If you lose your reasons for wanting to get up in the morning,'* she wrote to her sister-in-law, Susannah, *'then the time will come when you simply will not get up at all.'*

The letters between the two women were full of bad news these days; Susannah's husband, William Walter (Mr Austen's half-brother) had suffered too. He had started to lose his memory the year before and no longer recognised his family. It was distressing to watch him act so strangely and by February he had lost his senses altogether. It was somewhat of a blessing when he died peacefully in April, yet Mrs Austen and her friend could not feel glad about it. How they longed for some joyful news to fill their pages of correspondence.

Eliza de Feuillide was facing a better time in London, buoyed up by a twist of fate she had discovered by accident. At a dinner party in the city, she was seated next to an old acquaintance, Mr Cruise, who was a lawyer. He knew enough of her history to be aware of her connections with France, and she was updating him on the latest run of events.

"I have received confirmation that my late husband's property in France has been seized by the National Convention. They assure me that they are still maintaining the farm there, but I doubt it will be to the same high standards as before."

"That is a familiar story amongst many of my clients who have interests in France," confirmed the knowledgeable lawyer. "You do know that you can still claim it as your own if you go back there?"

"Yes. I have been told that if I, or my son, present ourselves in person then it will be rightfully restored to us. But how can we do that with a war between our two nations?"

"Yes, I agree. I would certainly advise against travelling during such turbulent times. Perhaps when the war is concluded you can take up the offer?"

Eliza sighed, placing her knife and fork down beside her half-eaten plate of food; she never had much of an appetite when she discussed business at the dinner table. "That will not happen, I'm afraid. I do not have the finances for such a trip."

"That is a pity, indeed," replied Mr Cruise, his mind working overtime to think of how to overcome the problem. He took a sip of wine to play for time, and Eliza wiped her mouth with a napkin, ready to converse with the gentleman seated to her other side.

"I urge you, Madam," broke in Mr Cruise before her attention was lost. "If there is any way you can apply to a relative for help, I would recommend you do so. I anticipate your property will become a valuable asset again one day and you would surely not wish to hand it over as a gift to the Republican Government. Especially considering what they did to your husband."

Perhaps he had drunk a little too much wine, or perhaps he should have phrased it more sensitively, but his boldness provoked an irate response from the Comtesse.

"I appreciate your concern," she replied, with agitation. She had come here for a pleasant evening and was not looking for a deep political debate. "But I beg that you do not take me as a woman with small intelligence. When I tell you that I cannot afford to take the trip, then I speak the truth. I am an orphan, a widow, and have a dependent child. I have no guardian to turn to who can help me!"

Her cheeks flushed and she stared at Mr Cruise, willing him to challenge her. She was sick of a society that put women down simply because they were women.

Mr Cruise was too invested in the matter now to let it go and did not seem in the least perturbed by her rising anger. "There are trust funds which may be able to help in certain circumstances," he explained calmly. "If you wish, I can investigate on your behalf?"

Now Eliza felt bad, and a little ashamed of her show of

temper.

"I thank you, Mr Cruise, but I would be surprised if there was anything you could do. I used to have a trust fund that was granted to me by my godfather when I was a girl. Sadly, the death of my parents and my husband have annulled that."

"How so?"

"I think that is something you should be telling me," countered Eliza, her impatience rising once more at such a tactless question. "Is it not lawyers like yourself who come up with such discriminatory rules against women like me?"

"Lawyers do not make the rules, Madam, we merely apply them."

When the silence between them became uncomfortable he spoke some more. "I do not understand why the circumstances you speak of should close down your fund."

Eliza was surprised. "Nor do I. But that is what I was told would happen. Do you mean to tell me there may be some doubt?"

"What I mean is that there is no automatic reason why a woman cannot apply for her own funds when her guardian dies."

Eliza was confused and felt foolish at so assuredly believing what she did. She had taken the flippant word of another woman in her circle who was also a widow and whom she believed had understood the situation. Now she regretted not checking the precise facts of her own circumstances more closely.

"I would be most obliged if you could look into this for me, Mr Cruise." She leaned in closer as if she was sharing a confidence and he was flattered by the way she smiled at him.

"I would be delighted to be of service," confirmed the

flustered lawyer.

To her gratification, Eliza discovered that she had indeed been mistaken and there was still a healthy sum of money left in the trust fund to apply for as before. Even so, at the age of thirty-five, and with her tapestry of life experiences behind her, she bristled at the thought that she must still seek permission from Mr Woodman and Mr Austen to purchase a new set of clothes.

She wrote politely to the two elderly gentlemen, enlightening them of her misunderstanding and informing them of her intention to resume drawing from the fund. She included a carefully worded paragraph in which she put forward, as diplomatically as she could, her case for independence. Without wishing to offend them, she needed to help them see that she was responsible enough in years to be able to manage her own budget.

The two gentlemen consulted with one another and applied to Mr Hastings for advice. He agreed unreservedly that Eliza could be trusted and so eventually, after several months of battling bureaucracy, the money was transferred into Eliza's name.

The freedom this gave her was exhilarating, and she took multiple trips outside of London without telling anyone where she was going. Her cousin, Philly, teased her often and speculated that Henry Austen was the reason for these mysterious excursions as she had perceptively noted that Eliza was never very far from where his regiment was based.

At first, this was denied, but by Christmas, there was no more need for secrecy and Eliza and Henry announced their engagement. In a letter to Mr Hastings, Eliza praised the affection that Henry had always shown her and raved about how fond he was of her son. She revelled in the fact that after two years of being chased and refusing him, she had finally acquiesced to say yes.

The reaction to this news in Steventon was mixed. No one was in the mood to celebrate a wedding, still raw from having one so recently denied them. They were grateful that the service was to take place quietly and out of reach in London and Mr Austen passed on the family's good wishes via a substantial gift of money paid in contribution to the regimental celebrations.

There was nothing about this surprising union that Henry's family could admonish, yet neither could they rejoice in the secrecy that both parties had displayed leading up to it. Sometimes they were stung that the romance between the two had not been confided in at least one of them, considering how close a family they were. Generally, however, they all understood that after Tom Fowle's death, the pair of lovers would not have wished to flaunt their happiness and good fortune in front of poor Cassandra.

After the wedding, Eliza and her son left their home in London to join Henry in Ipswich, where his regiment was based. Their house at the barracks was pleasant and neat and best of all had a garden which Hastings loved. Eliza quickly became a favourite amongst the officers who vied for her attention at events, and Henry was extremely proud to be seen with his new wife by his side. They were undoubtedly well suited and set out with as promising a start to married life as any couple could wish for.

\* \* \*

A new house was on the cards for Edward Austen too. Thomas Knight II had left all three of his estates to his wife in his will, to eventually pass on to Edward when she died. But such a responsibility as Godmersham Park was too much for the ageing lady to manage on her own, with its long, draughty rooms and countless empty bedrooms. She made up her mind that she would prefer somewhere smaller and sought out a lawyer to transfer the deeds of her Kent estate into Edward's name with immediate effect. She was as fond of Elizabeth, as she was of Edward, and their delightful brood of energetic children would make far more use of the grounds with their little running feet and wind-blown squeals than Mrs Knight ever could.

Edward declined the offer as soon as it was made, refusing to enter into any negotiations that would see Mrs Knight usurped from her rightful home. It took an awful lot of persuading for him to even listen, but over time the respect and fondness he held for the woman who had raised him prevailed, and she was able to talk him round. She assured him beyond doubt that her pleasure in being able to do this was immeasurable, and any pain she might feel at vacating the Park would be replaced entirely with the joy of knowing Edward and his treasured family would be there in her place.

\* \* \*

Jane threw herself into her writing and finished *First Impressions.* Mr Austen was so impressed with his daughter's work that he wrote to a publisher with the intention of putting it into print. It came as no surprise to Jane when the publisher rejected it out of hand, without even reading the manuscript, but she was gratified by her father's faith in her ability all the same. It gave her fresh confidence to retrieve *Elinor and Marianne* and edit it into another finished novel. She placed a thick bundle of pages into Cassandra's hands with the instruction, "I present you with *Sense and Sensibility.* Tell me what you think."

Six months after Tom Fowle's death, Mr Leigh-Perrot invited them all to his townhouse in Bath, where he and his wife spent every season.

*'When you step out from the door you will find everything you desire within five minutes' walk,'* he tempted them in a letter. *'The season is at its liveliest this time of year: who knows who you might meet!'*

Mr Austen politely declined the invitation, citing his preparations for advent as his excuse, but Mrs Austen was keen to go. She was desirous to see if the waters could improve her troublesome health and Cassandra and Jane were equally curious to get away from the silent rectory and experience life in busy Bath.

They arrived late in the afternoon on a chill November day, passing by row upon row of houses where one street was identical to the next. The buildings had all been constructed from the same pale-yellow stone and the rain brightened every residence. Lines of evenly spaced oil lamps shone down on the pavements, with their glass domes turning the symmetrical windowpanes into mirrors. The bustling city was a far cry from the tree-lined lanes of Steventon, which would be dark and full of muddy puddles at this time of day, with nobody stepping outside if it could be helped.

Mr and Mrs Leigh-Perrot lived at Number 1, Paragon,

which was a respectable, three-storey townhouse on a hill. The ladies were greeted by a manservant who had been keeping watch out the window, and their trunks were unloaded whilst the travellers ate supper with their hosts. They talked until the candles were down to their stubs, catching up on the latest news.

Mrs Austen knew Bath well, but her brother and sister-in-law still made sure to advise her of the best routes to take, and the places where she must be seen. "I have sent word of your presence," Mr Leigh-Perrot winked over breakfast the next day, and there were squeals of excitement when the weekly list in the *Bath Chronicle* included 'Mrs and 2 Miss Austen' as new arrivals. It was true what people said - you really were someone important when you came to Bath!

"We shall go and take the waters every day," Mrs Austen decided for her daughters, and they soon settled into a routine. Their stroll towards the Pump Room was crowded and they were quick to learn where it was safest to walk on the pavement to avoid the crazy sedan chair carriers, who weaved back and forth with their passengers peering out eminently from inside.

There were celebrations of colour and fashion wherever they looked, with every shade of muslin on show and bonnets as wide as the shoulders of their wearers. Plumes of feathers flapped about, next to bunches of shiny fruit which were weaved into ladies' wigs. High-pitched tunes whistled in militia regiments, parading through the streets dressed in identical braided red jackets and tall black peaked helmets. Shoppers interrupted their purchases to come out of doors and wave the men on their way. Jane and Cassandra were mesmerised by the deafening crunch of tall black boots on the cobbles, where not a step was out of place. It was a feast for the ears as well as the eyes.

"I see we must take you two girls shopping for some new clothes," sniffed Mrs Leigh-Perrot, not unkindly, yet recognising the inferiority of her nieces' gowns next to some of the more well-to-do visitors to the city. "We shall begin this afternoon."

Cassandra and Jane looked at their mother expecting her disapproval, but she appeared unconcerned.

"Do not fear," chuckled Mr Leigh-Perrot with a twinkle in his eye. "Your aunt knows every shop in Bath; she will see to it that you are attired to be admired."

Jane and Cassandra giggled at their uncle's humorous remark and were surprised again to receive no chastisement from their mother. Rules were definitely going to be different here!

"Come girls, let us take a drink."

Mrs Austen directed them all towards the brightly lit Pump Room which glowed with candles from the crystal chandeliers, even in the daytime. They each took a glass of cloudy, warm liquid from the servers in caps and sat down on a row of finely carved wooden chairs to the side. Mr Leigh-Perrot looked quite at home in his embroidered waistcoat and breeches, stretching his long legs out in front of him to show off his silver-buckled shoes. His wife sat sedately, nodding graciously at anyone who chose to acknowledge them. For a while the party remained silent, sipping their mineral-rich water, captivated by the promenading individuals before them.

When Mrs Austen was suitably invigorated, they headed into town. There were plenty more hazards to contend with out on the open road and it was not just the horses and carriages they needed to watch out for. A new hazard was alive in Bath, unseen in the Hampshire countryside, in the form of three-wheeled chairs which transported invalids from place to place. These contraptions were pushed by valets or footmen: poor, out-of-breath servants who trotted behind their gesticulating masters to try and keep abreast of whichever direction their driver wanted to go. It was common to hear them issue profuse apologies when a stray wheel inadvertently mowed down the train of a well-clad lady.

Each new day in the city was easier to navigate than the last and with fashionable shawls and bonnets to embellish their fresh young looks, Cassandra and Jane soon made themselves at home. Sydney Gardens was their favourite destination in the evenings as it was full of new experiences. They were captivated by the daring acrobats, the entertaining musicians and the fireworks which lit up the night sky with a million jewels.

For shopping, they favoured Milsom Street, with its array of shops selling everything they required, and pretty window displays offering items they did not even know could be bought. They took tea in the notorious Assembly Rooms whilst their uncle played cards, and attended the busiest balls they had ever known. When the weather was too frightful to leave the house, they entertained themselves with tunes on Mr Leigh-Perrot's piano or played cards over endless cups of tea.

There were public libraries too, with shelves packed high with parchment-bound books and Jane felt a new respect for her uncle when he dutifully took her to each one. He graciously offered to share his own books with her at home, standing on his oriental rug to reach past his glass-fronted bureau and pass her something of interest. He encouraged her to write, by clearing a special area for her writing desk where she could work undisturbed, and he ensured she was regularly supplied with paper, quills and ink.

Jane had always thought of her uncle as a silly and pompous man when he visited Steventon, which she now put down to his constant deferral to his dominant wife. At home, in his own library filled with the smart mahogany furniture of his choice, he demonstrated a sharp intelligence and kindness that was different. Some days it was only the chiming of the gold clock on the mantelpiece that reminded them both it was time to dress for dinner, bringing an end to some enjoyable and meaningful discussions.

Jane's mind was soon overflowing with ideas for a new story set in Bath. She invented a character called Susan, around her own age, who would find herself in this exciting place for the first time with her uncle and aunt. Jane wanted to show her readers that the reality of city life was not always as dream-like as it was portrayed in romantic novels, and her mind whirled.

Not everywhere in Bath was charming and they were all careful to avoid the less savoury side of town. The streets populated by the poor ran with faeces and urine, from the stink of chamber pots being emptied directly out of the windows. Quiet alleyways next to rowdy ale houses were used as communal outhouses, with people popping out to relieve themselves before returning indoors for another drink. Mr Leigh-Perrot had been most particular about where they should and should not stray, although he had not elaborated too much for fear of polluting his nieces' impressionable minds. Regardless of that, the stench was hard to miss.

The saddest sight of all was the donkeys. They struggled up the hills every morning to carry heavy sacks of coal. Jane and Cassandra wept over them in the privacy of their bedroom, thinking of the large wooden saddles cutting into the poor creatures' backs whilst they puffed and panted with exertion. They were not treated well at all by their cruel owners who let their ribs poke out through their thinning coats and kept them half-starved. An animal would never be treated like that in Steventon and they hatched a foolish, girlish plan to rescue them all and take them back to their farm.

It was impossible, of course, to change the world, and they knew it would never be practical to do so, but the sorrow they felt for those misused donkeys proved inconclusively that they were Hampshire girls at heart. Bath had been stimulating and diverting at a time when it was needed. It had shown them the prospect of a future in the wider world and briefly put their sadness into perspective.

When the Christmas season arrived, however, they were more than happy to be going home.

# Chapter 38

## 1798–1799
### Old Age and Ailments.

"Who is it now?" Mrs Austen asked of her husband. She was lying down on her couch in the rectory parlour, with James seated next to her on the high-backed chair when a pale-faced Mr Austen entered the room.

"Jane Cooper."

Mrs Austen let out a snort-like sob into her handkerchief. "Oh, Lord! What more will that poor family be forced to endure?"

James was flabbergasted. His mother and father had expressed a whole story of some tragic circumstance between them in a matter of seconds, through a combination of broken words and looks. Their shorthand was something that had confused him ever since he was little, and he wondered if it would be the same with him and Mary if they were lucky enough to still be together thirty years hence.

Mr Austen distractedly placed his letter on the table and slumped down on the opposite chair. It lay there, tantalisingly curled with the address side up, and James longed to know what it said. He could just about make out the familiar hand of his cousin, Edward Cooper, and the edge of a morbid black seal.

When it was clear nobody was going to enlighten him, James spoke up.

"What has happened, Sir? Please may I read the letter?"

"Yes, of course, my boy," his father muttered, pulling himself out of his shock.

James scanned Edward's slanted scrawl. "May God bless her," he murmured, then bowed his head and made the sign of the cross over his chest.

Still lying prostrate, her hand covering her eyes, Mrs Austen was ready to hear more. "Read it to me, James."

James cleared his throat and began, overcome by a shaking in his voice that he struggled to control.

*Sir,*

*I write with grave news. My sweet, dear sister has been taken from us in the most tragic of circumstances. On Thursday afternoon she was returning home in her carriage to her house at Ryde when a horse in a dray took fright and ran directly at her. From what I understand she was violently thrown and stood no chance of survival; the carriage was wrecked. I am told that her suffering was short.*

*Forgive me, Uncle, for burdening you with this news so abruptly, but I am struggling to find the words. I know that you would wish to be told and I trust that you will break it delicately to the ladies.*

*Captain Williams has been written to on the Endymion, but it may yet be some days before he is aware of what has passed.*

*I will write when I know more.*

*Rest assured I remain, Your humble servant,*

*Edward Cooper.*

A long silence followed as each heart was lost in memories of Jane Cooper and the impact she had made on them during her twenty-seven years on earth.

The following week, Mr and Mrs Austen and the girls went to stay with Edward in Godmersham. It had been a visit planned for some time to allow Edward to host them in his imposing new home, but the tragedy of Jane Cooper's accident dampened their spirits. Edward showed them a cutting he had saved from *The Times*, giving an account of his cousin's death. She was now known as Lady Williams, following her husband's knighthood, and as such made society news. Although there was nothing fresh to add that they had not heard before, the family took it in turns to speculate over the negligence displayed by the drayman, recalling similar instances from their own experiences where vehicles had driven on local roads, overloaded and poorly handled.

For Cassandra and Jane, this was their first trip to the mighty Godmersham Park and they were overwhelmed. "I thought Rowling was grand enough," Cassandra enthused as they examined the corridors of rooms.

"I hardly dared believe we would ever stay in a better place than Goodnestone," agreed Jane. "Yet here we are somewhere ten times as grand!"

They skipped up the main staircase away from the black and white tiled entrance hall and floated along the landings, peering into the different coloured rooms with their soft and sumptuous furnishings. When they were settled in their own bedrooms, they spun around with their arms flung out wide, wallowing in the delight of having a whole room each, all to themselves. The views from the windows overlooking the park were vast and even Mrs Austen made an effort to dress for dinner, displaying more energy than she had done at home of late, wallowing less in her long list of ailments and focusing more on making an impression to please her wealthy son.

Mornings were leisurely at Godmersham and breakfast was not taken until ten. Better still, it was taken in the library where Jane and Cassandra could gaze across the rows of shelves and pick out a book for the day, from the hundreds on display.

"Take whatever you wish," Edward urged with a proud and amused smile. And so, they did. After satisfying their appetites with chops and eggs, bread and tea and toasted muffins with jam, the girls retired to their rooms for two more blissful hours of reading.

After lunch the girls played with the children, Mrs Austen went for a lie-down and Mr Austen was shown the different workings of the estate by Edward.

"Aww! Come here, little Dordie," Jane would cry, with arms held wide to wipe away a childhood tear from the nearly-three-year-old George's face. Elizabeth commended her on her magic touch, finding that Little Dordie's tears went as fast as they came when he was in his aunt's arms.

Elizabeth had given birth to four children thus far and her fifth was due any day. The expectation of a new arrival was wondrous and there were toasts all around when squalling baby William entered the world noisily on a crisp October afternoon.

"Why do you look so sad, sweet Fanny?" Mrs Austen asked her granddaughter, who was the eldest of the bunch at nearly six years old.

"Mama told me she had asked for a girl," she whimpered. "And I really wanted a sister."

Mrs Austen sympathised completely. "I know just what you mean," she said kindly, taking the girl onto her lap and rubbing her shoulder. "I had four boys in a row like your mother, and I too remember asking for a little girl." She rolled her eyes in mock desperation and Fanny laughed. "But I was blessed with two beautiful girls in the end. As you will be, I'm sure, if you can wait long enough."

Whilst Elizabeth was recovering from the birth and cosseted in her chamber, Edward took on the full duties of a host. He was a great entertainer and guests came to the house every night to eat tart and jelly, play whist and backgammon and display their musical accomplishments. Cassandra and Jane practised hard on the piano in the daytime so that they would not show themselves up too badly when called upon to perform in front of a room full of noble strangers.

After baby William had been christened in Godmersham Church, Mr and Mrs Austen and Jane took their leave and returned to Steventon. Cassandra stayed behind as a companion for Elizabeth, and to entertain the young children until their mother was fully up and about. It was a familiar task to her by now, and one she accepted willingly. As the eldest unmarried aunt of the family, this role inevitably fell to her.

Back home in Steventon, another child was on its way, this time courtesy of James's wife, Mary. Her pregnancy had caused much concern with the child seeming unusually large. Mary's sister, Martha, came to stay from Ibthorpe to attend to her, along with a nurse who had also been sent, to be on the safe side.

Mrs Austen suffered a relapse in health when she returned from Godmersham and was kept purposefully ignorant of the severity of Mary's condition. She went to bed early with her drops of laudanum. "Don't tell me anything until it is all over," she had pleaded to Jane and so it fell to the youngest sister of the family to bolster her brother's spirits and put on a brave face on behalf of them all.

Thankfully, Mary gave birth to her baby boy without drama and delivered a strong and healthy child whom they called James Edward. Mary rallied enough to be out of danger of dying from childbirth and the child was welcomed as 'Little Edward'. Jane wrote at once to inform Cassandra of the good news, but it was a long time before Mrs Austen was well enough to travel to Deane and meet her new grandson.

Mr Austen resignedly put his wife's ailments down to old age. "It is tedious when you discover your bones no longer function in the same way they did when you were younger," he explained to Jane. "You saw Mr Bond leave here not long ago?" he continued, turning their discourse in a new direction.

"Yes," replied Jane. "We greeted each other out in the yard."

"Well, he was here to tell me that he's finding his farm work too difficult. I'm going to have to hire another man."

"No!" exclaimed Jane. "We can't allow that. We can't allow the likes of Mr Bond to grow old!" She was trying to make light of her father's revelation, but her real emotions had been exposed. "Mr Bond has been here forever. I cannot bear the thought of not seeing him around."

Mr Austen understood her perfectly and felt the same himself. "I quite agree. The man is a treasure. Thankfully he's agreed to continue with the sheep so we shall still see plenty of him."

Jane and her father got on as best as they could whilst Mrs Austen kept to her room, and Jane was promoted to temporary Mistress of the Household. She had fully intended to finish her latest novel whilst Cassandra was away and move her heroine, Susan, out of Bath and into an old Gothic manor in the north of England, but her eyes had other ideas: some days they were too strained to make out the markings of her quill. She told her father it must be due to the dim candlelight, but they both secretly knew that a weakness of her eyes was an alarmingly frequent occurrence.

In place of poring over her manuscript, Jane practised her piano and threw herself into planning the family meals. She hired new maids to take on more work and occupied her fingers by altering Cassandra's bonnets with new trims and feathers. *'I wish I were still in Kent,'* she managed to pass on to Cassandra one day in a letter, her hands thrust deep into thick woollen mittens to keep them warm. *'Everyone there is so rich!'*

Jane and her mother made a poor sight trapped inside the rectory with enough maladies between them to serve an entire village. When Mrs Austen could not eat Jane helped to feed her; when Jane could not finish her letters, Mrs Austen wrote the words to her dictation.

There was no shortage of visitors who came by to wish them well and the Harwoods and the Digweeds called often. Madam Lefroy was dutiful too in her attentions and Jane learned from her father's diplomatic questioning that Tom Lefroy was soon to be wed. He had finished his studies in London, was shortly to return to Ireland, and was to take a wife in the spring. Jane had been too nervous to ask about him herself, aware that her countenance would give her away, yet the quickening of her heart at the sound of his name confirmed what she already knew - she still held feelings for this man who had been one of the most pleasurable acquaintances of her life.

A brief shore leave for Charles Austen was warmly welcomed. Everyone commented on how improved he was in looks and what a perfectly charming and agreeable man he had become. He attended balls and dinners at every opportunity and travelled to visit Edward at Godmersham, the Fowles in Kintbury and Edward Cooper in Harpsden. Edward Cooper was shortly to move his family to Staffordshire and take up a new living in Hamstall Ridware, which everyone hoped would bring him peace and blessings and a fresh start.

Before Charles left to return to his ship, Jane heard him discussing with his father how disgruntled he was by a lack of action and useful service in the navy. Mr Austen proposed to write to Admiral Gambier again, to see what could be done and Jane was reminded of the similar complaints she had heard before from Frank. Once again, Mr Austen's intervention paid off and Charles was rewarded with a promotion to second lieutenant. He was placed aboard the *Endymion* under his old comrade, the recently widowed Captain Williams, which was gratifying for the family. Both men would now be able to share their memories of Jane Cooper on their travels and support one another in their grief.

Frank was faring much better and was presented with his first command on the sloop, *Peterel*. This was a swift and agile vessel which found itself perfectly situated in location to carry a message to Rear Admiral Nelson. The efficiency with which

Frank and his officers carried out their duties encouraged further requests to be made by this notable admiral, who was earning quite a reputation in the British Navy. Frank must have been given a share of his luck because the *Peterel* took foreign vessels of its own around Sicily and Malta, earning a tidy sum of prize money in reward.

Henry was called to Ireland with his militia regiment and purchased the title of captain with Eliza's financial help. He was now paymaster of the entire regiment. In his absence, his wife and stepson went to stay with friends in Surrey to await his return.

Mrs Austen found it hard to bear the anxiety of her sons facing danger and fretted about them constantly. She spent far too much time dwelling on what was happening in the war and her dreams were disturbed every night by visions of some tragedy befalling one or other of her boys.

It was not a day too soon when Cassandra arrived home from Godmersham to brighten up the rooms of the rectory. She smiled with tales of Edward's family and neighbours and told them of her brother's plans to take a house in Bath for the summer to try the new treatments.

"Do you know, girls...?" Mrs Austen decided, sprightlier than Jane had seen her in months, "That could be just the thing I need for my swollen ankles. The water worked wonders for me the last time I was there. I will write to Edward directly and ask if we can join him."

# Chapter 39

**1799-1800**
**The Card of White Lace.**

M r Austen and Cassandra did not go to Bath and waved the happy travellers out of sight from the gravel sweep of the rectory. Edward and Elizabeth collected Mrs Austen and Jane on their way there, and squeezed in amongst them were Fanny Austen (now six) and Edward Jnr (now five). It was the middle of May when they all set off and much was anticipated and talked of on the journey.

Number 13 Queen Square was the location of their residency, with a pleasant, small park outside and comfortable, airy rooms within. The landlady was an amicable woman who brought a little black kitten for the children to play with. The lodgers were soon settled in and Jane and her mother took adjoining rooms on the top floor, while Edward and his family occupied the suite below.

Mrs Austen was eager to call upon her brother as her first outing in Bath and went the next morning with Edward. They both wrapped themselves up against the foul weather for the short ride, but before they could even step down from their carriage outside Mr Leigh-Perrot's townhouse, his servant trotted down the steps underneath a dripping umbrella to save them from getting wet.

"I regret that my master is indisposed at present," he relayed soberly. "He has taken to his bed and is unable to receive callers today."

Mrs Austen wrote to him the minute she returned to her lodgings, urging her brother not to stand on ceremony on her account and two days later she was admitted. This time she took Jane with her.

Poor Mr Leigh-Perrot was suffering from gout and a chill and was wrapped up warmly next to a cheerful fire in his flannels. He could not stand up without the aid of a stick, but his complexion and demeanour were bright enough to satisfy Mrs Austen that he was in no immediate danger.

"I'm sorry I cannot offer you better hospitality," he apologised to his visitors. "I despise being an invalid. I fear my poor Jenny is extremely bored whilst we are secluded from society."

"Nonsense, Perrot," sniffed his wife. "I have told you a thousand times it does not matter. The Assembly Balls will still be there when you are well enough to attend them again." Mrs Leigh-Perrot was as abrupt in her mannerisms as ever, yet it was obvious that the couple were happy to oblige each other's needs.

Mr Leigh-Perrot smiled warmly. "That is why I am so glad my niece is here," he said, reaching for Jane's hand. "I know that you will be a worthy companion for your aunt whilst you are in town. I remember what a pleasurable time you had shopping together the last time you were here."

"Indeed," laughed Jane. "I already have commissions for

stockings for Anna and shoes for Martha, before I even
consider the wants of my sister."

"I think I can help you there," confirmed Mrs Leigh-Perrot,
looking forward to the task before her. She had never
been blessed with children of her own, but she was fond
of her husband's nieces and saw herself as a kindly mentor to
Cassandra and Jane to educate them on the ways of society.

Mrs Leigh-Perrot was the most efficient guide and met
with the party every day. She directed Edward to the best
shops to source his tea and coffee and directed him to the
best suppliers of cheese. She took Jane to the fashionable
milliners favoured by high society ladies and then discreetly
pointed her in the direction of a cheaper supplier in Walcot,
where plentiful accessories could be purchased for a more
affordable price than in the centre of town. By the time the
Austens had marvelled at seeing their names in print as new
arrivals in the *Bath Chronicle*, they felt like they had been there
for much longer than a week.

Mr Leigh-Perrot battled hard against his chill, and it was
not many days before Mrs Austen could meet up with him
in the Pump Rooms. She took a slow stroll after breakfast to
await his arrival by chair which was carried all the way from
his home by two red-faced, puffing men.

Edward tried a variety of treatments in the city, including the latest electric bath. His family were sceptical it
would work but he insisted his health was improving. Once
Elizabeth received word from Godmersham that her three
youngest children were still thriving without her, she too
relaxed into her temporary setting. She relished the opportunity to show Fanny and Edward the sights on her walks
and enjoy how they were admired in their young finery. The

mode of the day was for ladies to wear bunches of fruit upon their heads, and Fanny had a miniature cluster of strawberries to match the larger bunch favoured by her mother.

Jane wrote regularly to Cassandra with eager messages from the children, who were delighted beyond measure at receiving letters of their own from their Steventon aunt. Cassandra wrote of a chaffinch's nest in the garden and the comings and goings of the turkeys in the yard. Jane and her mother dutifully sat with their young charges one cloudy afternoon to help them compose their replies.

It was a pleasurable month, taking in a variety of new places and enjoying the entertainment on offer. They made several new acquaintances whilst they were there and Edward was persuaded to purchase two magnificent coach horses on the recommendation of a friend. Jane filled her notebook with ideas for her novel-in-progress, carefully jotting down the names of the streets and landmarks she passed on her way about the town.

In her final few days before leaving, Aunt Leigh-Perrot helped Jane to choose her gifts. Jane was impressed by her aunt's attention to detail, noting that despite being rich enough to afford whatever she desired, the woman was still astute enough to capture a bargain.

The company of Edward and his party had done Mr Leigh-Perrot good and after they departed he persevered with a gritty determination to leave his house every day. He made it his goal to walk to the Pump Rooms unaided, and when August arrived he was able to get there on foot, using a stick in either hand. Each day he would stay to take the water whilst his wife flitted from shop to shop to complete her errands.

"Did you find the lace you wanted?" he asked amicably on

their slow shuffle back up the hill one morning.

"No. I am not yet decided," replied his wife. "Miss Gregory is expecting a new delivery from London any day, so I shall go back tomorrow and have another look."

The shop she had visited was Smiths, a milliner's in Bath Street. It had only been open for a couple of years and the owners were currently away in Cornwall. In their absence, the shop was being managed by Mrs Smith's sister, Miss Gregory. She employed two members of staff: a man by the name of Mr Filbert, and a young apprentice called Miss Raines.

It was Mrs Leigh-Perrot's habit to build a rapport with the proprietors of her favourite establishments, as experience had taught her how influential this could be. A friendly chat went a long way towards a little favouritism, and she very often found supplies available to her that were not always offered to other customers.

What she was not aware of in this shop, however, was that even though it appeared to be prosperous from the outside, it was not doing so well behind the scenes. Financial difficulties and a broken marriage had taken Mr and Mrs Smith away to Cornwall, and not a holiday as she had been led to believe. Miss Gregory was working under the eyes of two trustees who were keen to turn the business into a profit - lawfully or otherwise they did not care.

"I hope you get your lace today," Mr Leigh-Perrot wished to his wife the next morning before they separated at the Pump Room door.

"I feel sure I will," she smiled cheerily and headed directly to the shop. She was vexed to find when she got there that the new supplies from London had still not arrived, and her disappointment must have been obvious because Miss Gregory went out of her way to gather every card of black lace she could find from the shelves and the storeroom.

"This one is particularly good quality," she purred, unravelling a long stretch from a card and placing it on the counter in front of Mrs Leigh-Perrot.

"Yes indeed," agreed the keen customer. "Do you have something similar but with a more regular pattern?"

Miss Gregory's eyes lit up and she reached for another at the end of the row. "How does this one suit?" she asked pleasantly. "T'would make a fine edging to a cloak in my opinion, although it will work out at two shillings more than the other one."

Mrs Leigh-Perrot threaded the attractive material through her narrow fingers to consider its touch. She weaved it back and forth and held it up to the light. She spent many minutes perusing it and comparing it to the other samples.

"I will take it," she decided. "I have looked around long enough. If I don't purchase something today, I will never finish my cloak in time for the winter."

Miss Gregory chuckled and made a remark to show that she understood. She had been in the same situation herself, she confessed, being unable to make up her mind on something, only to wish later in the day that she had been more decisive. Madam had made an excellent choice, of that she was certain.

She called over to Mr Filbert to wrap up the black lace in a parcel and he jumped to attention at once. He was working at the front desk by the door when he was summoned, counting out some cards of white lace from a basket to put on display. When duty called, he swiftly left the cards where they were and grabbed a sheet of wrapping paper for the customer's purchase, carrying it in front of him, which hid his hands. He whistled a cheery tune as he made his way behind the counter.

Miss Gregory asked Miss Raines to put away the rest of the cards of black lace that Mrs Leigh-Perrot had been examining, which allowed the manageress time to give her customer change from the five pounds she had handed over, and to record the purchase in the ledger. All was done smoothly while Mrs Leigh-Perrot chatted about her plans to call in at the Post Office and then meet up with her husband at the Pump Rooms. Within minutes, the transaction was complete.

"Thank you and have a good day," wished Miss Raines, who curtseyed before the lady and held the door open for her to exit the shop. Mrs Leigh-Perrot could not help but feel satisfied, with the sweet tinkling of the bell ringing in her ear, that she had done a very good morning's work.

Her husband was in a happy mood too when they met up again, fresh from a conversation he had just had with an old acquaintance who was newly arrived in Bath. The couple began their walk away from the Pump Rooms, with all thoughts of lace forgotten.

"Excuse me, Ma'am!" came a cry, forcing Mr Leigh-Perrot to stop speaking mid-sentence. They both turned around to see a middle-aged woman, red in the face, waddling towards them with her ample bosom heaving up and down in time with her steps.

"Miss Gregory!" exclaimed Mrs Leigh-Perrot in surprise.

Mr Leigh-Perrot's irritation was quashed slightly at realising the interruption was from someone already known to his wife, but still, he remained offended by the rudeness of her introduction.

"Did you pick up a card of white lace when you left the shop this morning?" she asked breathlessly, without any of the polite formalities one would expect. "Only there is one missing from the counter by the door."

"Of course not," retorted Mrs Leigh-Perrot. "I took only the black lace away with me. Your assistant wrapped it himself."

"May I see the parcel?" demanded Miss Gregory with an assertiveness Mr Leigh-Perrot found most unbecoming in a woman. "I need to be sure."

"Now look here…" he interposed, appalled at the insinuation being made against his wife, but before he could intervene further, she had already handed the package over. Miss Gregory ripped it open there and then, on the corner of the pavement, and looked totally unsurprised to fish out a thick card full of white lace slipped underneath the black."

"What have we here…?" she gloated triumphantly, holding the item up high.

"It must have been put in there by mistake," concluded Mrs Leigh-Perrot logically, although the shaking of her hands and the redness of her cheeks suggested she was extremely disturbed by the accusation.

"You know that is not true," spoke the cunning shop manager, narrowing her eyes and looking directly into Mrs Leigh-Perrot's face. "You stole it. You're a thief!" She turned abruptly away and trudged back in the direction of her shop, clutching the card of white lace to her chest.

People had stopped to stare at the commotion and Mr and Mrs Leigh-Perrot had not made it many steps further down the street when more footsteps came up behind them.

"It's the man from the shop," said Mrs Leigh-Perrot. "He must be coming to admit his mistake."

"I do no such thing," spat Mr Filbert. "I promise you, I only ever wrapped the black lace. You must have put the white one in the package yourself when you left the shop. Do you take me for an imbecile?"

Mrs Leigh-Perrot cried out in shock and rested against one of the colonnades to prevent a fainting. Mr Leigh-Perrot pulled himself up tall, preparing for a confrontation.

"I require your name and address," threatened Mr Filbert. "You've not heard the last of this by any means!"

"We live at Number 1, Paragon Buildings," responded Mr Leigh-Perrot indignantly. "If you wish to know our name then you must seek it there on the brass plate outside the door!"

It was impossible now to walk the rest of the distance in their debilitating state, so two chairs were called for from the Pump Rooms to carry them home. Mrs Leigh-Perrot retired immediately to her room, which she kept for two whole days, dreading the knock of a policeman on her doorstep.

When five days had passed and no further word of the incident had reached them, the couple began to feel better. Perhaps it had been a mistake after all and now forgotten? Their nerves felt calm enough to accept an invitation to a private dinner party given by some close friends, so it may be imagined what a surprise it was when they returned home from a pleasant evening out to find an anonymous letter had been delivered in their absence. It was addressed to 'Mrs Leigh-Perrot – Lace Dealer' and threatened to reveal exactly what she had stolen to her high society friends. It was obvious that the purpose of the note was for her rich husband to forfeit a large sum of money to keep the matter quiet.

Two days later, a constable appeared at the door with a

warrant for her arrest.

Mr Leigh-Perrot attempted to take charge; he was friends with the Mayor and the magistrate who had accompanied the policeman for the arrest and so, all the way down to the Town Hall, he used his most persuasive words to make light of these preposterous slurs. He accepted the embarrassed apologies of the officials good-naturedly, fully expecting the ridiculous mess would be resolved before the night-time lamps were lit.

It was true that there were inconsistencies in the evidence, accepted the Mayor, and he was extremely sympathetic to Mrs Leigh-Perrot's claims of innocence. But none of that was enough.

"You must go to Ilchester Jail and await trial there at the Spring Assizes," he proclaimed.

Mrs Leigh-Perrot broke down and sobbed uncontrollably. Her husband demanded to speak to anyone who would listen to convince them of their mistake, but his words were futile. The couple arrived in Somerset the next day with either a sentence of death or transportation to Australia looming over them. As the card of white lace was worth more than twelve shillings, the theft of such a sum was classed as a felony.

All of this for a crime the lady swore she did not commit.

Any attempt to keep the matter quiet was delusional and rumours as to what had occurred spread quickly through Bath. *The Times* newspaper announced the arrest in a notice, although their names were - for now - kept anonymous. Mr Leigh-Perrot wrote to Mrs Austen in Steventon before the news broke, as he knew it would shame the family in public. Mrs Leigh-Perrot begged the support of an influential cousin who lived in Lincolnshire.

The jailer at Ilchester was a Mr Edward Scadding, and

by a lucky coincidence, his living had been presented to him by one of Mrs Leigh-Perrot's friends. This made him sympathetic to her repeated claims of innocence and he took her and her husband in as lodgers instead of making her reside inside the jail itself. Mr Scadding's house was small and already overcrowded with his large family, but at least she was saved from the shame of wearing the coarse brown and yellow prison uniform and sleeping on a bed of straw with the other women prisoners.

Mr Leigh-Perrot was supremely protective of his wife's situation and refused to leave her side. He engaged the best lawyers that London offered, regardless of the expense, determined to clear his dear Jenny's name. His own health was still very fragile, and the dirty, squalid conditions of the household did not help. The Scadding family were kind and obliging and their two elder girls in particular were most attentive. They played and sang for their guests in the evenings and attempted to include them in their conversations, but the younger children mostly just stared. They would place their greasy toast upon Mr Leigh-Perrot's knee before running off to play with the dogs, staining his breeches for good. They would be careless with their drinks, knocking puddles of small beer to seep into the cuffs of his sleeves and the smoke from the chimney stained every item of clothing they owned, leaving soot marks impossible to remove.

The food was shocking too, and different altogether to the sophisticated dining experiences the Leigh-Perrots were used to. Neither of them ate beyond what was absolutely necessary, so put off were they by the culinary skills of their host. Mrs Scadding's intentions were to be commended in her insistence on providing them with a plentiful supper, but it did not occur to her how off-putting it was for her guests to watch her lick the chopping knife clean with her tongue, in between chopping the onions and the meat, as opposed to submerging the utensil in some water to be washed.

Letters arrived regularly for the Leigh-Perrots from their friends in Bath to pledge their support. Mr Leigh-Perrot passed their names on to his lawyers so that they could stand as witnesses in the trial. James Austen wrote often to offer his condolences and to assure them that both he and Mary would be there to support them on the day of the hearing. Mrs Austen wrote frequently too, regretting that her own ill health made it impossible for her to travel, but insisting that she would send Cassandra or Jane for companionship whenever she received word to do so.

All of these offers were as gratefully received as they were kindly meant, but the harsh truth prevented any of them from being accepted. Both the gentleman and the lady were so embarrassed by the position they found themselves in that they could not bear anyone else to witness them in their plight.

There was still some good news to cling to, however, with their network of supporters building up a promising amount of evidence against Miss Gregory and her shop. Apparently, it was on the verge of bankruptcy and the trustees who were trying to save it were as corrupt as the people who worked there. It had been a long-standing mission to exploit rich customers through blackmail and Mrs Leigh-Perrot was not the first lady to find extra goods in a package she had not asked for. Furthermore, Miss Gregory and Mr Filbert were not the respectable upstanding citizens they pretended to be and were living scandalously as man and wife without a wedding having ever taken place. Mr Leigh-Perrot was optimistic that all these points would go against them in the trial.

The day of the hearing was on a Saturday morning at the end of March, held in the Great Hall of Taunton Castle. Two thousand people squeezed into the stone-floored room to witness the proceedings and it was obvious from the outset who supported who. The well-dressed and refined set were seated in comparable comfort, as opposed to the common, everyday folk who lolled against the walls.

The amount of publicity the Leigh-Perrots had attracted was humiliating and they were both more relieved than sorry when none of their Austen relations were able to attend in person. James, who had been so sterling in his support, had fallen off his horse a couple of weeks before and broken his leg, Mrs Austen was too unwell to travel, and Cassandra and Jane were ordered by their uncle and aunt not to come anywhere near. 'It would be unbearable to think of all those people staring at such innocent beauties,' Mrs Leigh-Perrot had pleaded.

*The Lady's Magazine* sent a reporter for the event with an artist to record every detail. Someone else came to represent the *Bath Chronicle* and they all confirmed how pale and gaunt Mrs Leigh-Perrot looked, dressed in a light grey pelisse and cambric cravat. The engraving showed her dark brown hair curled down across her forehead, and on her head was a black bonnet with a purple ribbon. She wore a long black lace veil which she pulled back over her head once the trial was in progress. Her expression was tense, and she sat motionless as the evidence against her was read.

When the jury had been sworn in, the first people invited to speak were the three witnesses: Miss Gregory, Mr Filbert and Miss Raines. It was obvious from their answers that they were following a script they had agreed between them, and they were sticking to every word like glue. They never deviated from their carefully rehearsed phrases, and it was working judging by the looks of the jury, who heard a strong case. The prosecution insisted that the prisoner had picked up the card of white lace and concealed it beneath her cloak; Mr Filbert swore he had even seen her do it.

The cross-examination, however, soon broke the story down. With questions being posed to each of them that could not be predicted, their answers were harder to give. The seeking of absolute clarification led to contradictions in their claims and the tightly knit accusations began to unravel.

Doubts were raised such as:

'How could the prisoner possibly pay for the black lace, collect her change and put it back in her purse all with one hand if she was concealing the white lace in her other?'

'How could Miss Raines be certain Mr Filbert had only wrapped the black lace when she had been busy putting away the other cards from the counter at the time?'

'If Mr Filbert was certain he had seen the prisoner steal the white lace and conceal it in her cloak, why had he not stopped her before she left the shop?'

'Was it not all part of the plan to let the prisoner leave and accost her later, so they could then accuse her of hiding the stolen white lace in the package? She had told them where she was going next, so they knew she would be passing by again.'

'Why had there been reports of extra goods being packed

into other customers' packages too? Was this not a similar attempt at blackmail?'

In trials such as these, there was no opportunity to put forward a defence and the task for the jury was to simply decide how believable the prosecution was, rather than consider a counterargument from the accused. The prisoner was only allowed to give a brief statement before the jury deliberated if she should face a sentence of death.

With desperate emotion, Mrs Leigh-Perrot made her appeal. She praised the devotion of her husband unreservedly and questioned why she would choose to tarnish the reputation of the man she held so dear. He was rich enough to give her everything she had ever wanted, and she already had everything she needed in the world. Why then, would she sacrifice all of that to steal a meagre card of lace? Her only consolation as she prepared to meet her fate was that God knew the truth and He would protect her.

Mr Leigh-Perrot wept as she spoke, his tears spreading through the courtroom like a contagion. Muffled sobs fell into white handkerchiefs from every corner.

It took the jury less than an hour to reach their verdict, and cheers erupted to raise the roof when a verdict of 'Not Guilty' was delivered by three o'clock. By midnight the next day, the Leigh-Perrots were back in Bath, ready to receive a steady trickle of visitors from their delighted neighbours and friends who all wanted to congratulate them on their victory.

Mrs Austen wrote immediately to invite the couple to Steventon where she insisted the solace of a break with family would do wonders to mend their broken spirits. Mr Leigh-Perrot replied:

*My dear sister, C.*

311

*Jenny and I are honoured by your invitation and you can be assured that we will visit you soon in Hampshire. For now, I regret we must remain in Bath and settle the bills we have accumulated from that unfortunate trial. Our reputation amongst strangers has been soiled enough by false accusations and we have no desire to add 'Bad Debtors' to our other fantastical faults.*

*Sending wishes for your good health etc. etc.*

*Your devoted brother,*

*JLP.*

"I have never kissed so many people or cried so many tears than in this past week" mused Mrs Leigh-Perrot dizzily, sipping her third glass of medicinal wine in the parlour before retiring to bed, a few days after coming home.

Mr Leigh-Perrot snickered at the thought, although neither of them was in the mood for laughter. They were exhausted by putting on a brave face and keeping up bright smiles. The stark truth was that they were exhausted. Their limbs were heavy, and their heads were sore. They were numb from the shock of what had occurred and it still felt like they were lost at sea on a tiny boat in a storm. It would take them a very long time to recover from what had taken place.

"You're a good man, Perrot," whimpered Mrs Leigh-Perrot with a tremble in her voice through the darkness. "I could not have endured these past months without you by my side."

"I know, Jenny my dear," replied her husband, equally fighting to suppress his emotions. "Nor could I have endured being apart from you."

They continued to sip their wine in front of the flickering fire in silence, each of them battling visions of how close they had come to being parted forever.

# Chapter 40

**1800-1801**
**Farewell to Steventon.**

Even though she had been proven innocent in a court of law, Mrs Leigh-Perrot could not clear her name entirely. Pamphlets were still being purchased weeks later from bookshops across town, reporting the trial's proceedings. Anonymous letters continued to come through the post threatening to expose the couple for all kinds of lies if they did not pay out a sum of money. Worrying as these things were, the strength of support offered to the Leigh-Perrots by their true friends was enough for them to weather the storm and they remained in Bath until the end of the season. If anything, their anger made them even more determined to enjoy the delights of the city where they had done nothing wrong.

In the same spirit as her brother, Mrs Austen extolled the virtues of Bath for herself. It became somewhat of an obsession for her to recall her enjoyment of being there, where the busy daily routine encouraged a person to get up and walk about for amusement. The autumn in Steventon, with its short days and lingering mud and cold, brought a revival of her rheumatic complaints and she sank into melancholic ways.

Mr Austen was growing weary too and his breath no longer seemed to supply his body with the energy it needed. He sought Jane's help with increasing frequency, and she volunteered herself to fill out the parish registers. That meant she could discreetly be on hand to help at every baptism, wedding and funeral. It was troubling for her to witness her father's hands shake when he snuffed out the candles and see how he fumbled with the key when he went to lock the door.

Cassandra and Jane had talked about their parents' ageing many times and vowed to do all they could to help them. Their father was nearly seventy now and their mother was in her sixtieth year. But with Cassandra away more often than home, the larger burden of responsibility usually fell to Jane.

Thankfully, she had the companionship of Martha Lloyd who understood exactly what it felt like. Martha lived with an elderly mother of her own, so when Cassandra went for yet another extended stay at Godmersham in October, Martha and Jane consoled one another.

"I find it incredible that my mother cannot remember where she put something down only hours before, yet can still recall the room she slept in forty years ago."

It was this very topic the two women were discussing when travelling on a raw December afternoon. Jane had been staying with Martha at Ibthorpe, and now Martha was coming to stay in Steventon with Jane. They were both tired and their journey was bumpy and uncomfortable. The wind carried flakes of wet snow which smudged the carriage window and the two women were looking forward to a restorative glass of wine and a long sit down by the fire when they arrived. They each confessed that if they were to lose their fractious moods before dinner, it would be best if the rest of the household made themselves scarce before expecting a conversation.

It was with some disappointment, therefore, that they found Mary and James sitting in the parlour ready to greet them, along with Mr and Mrs Austen looking up expectantly at their faces.

"Goodness, I was not expecting such a welcome," exclaimed Jane, hiding her weariness behind a forced smile.

Martha went over to Mary who stood briefly to kiss her sister before assuming her seat next to James. The two travellers exchanged a quizzical look. This delegation looked serious, and yet there was nobody dressed in mourning and smiles were on everyone's lips.

Jane fumbled with her bonnet and Martha did the same, all the time watched by four sets of beady eyes. The anticipation in the room was palpable. Whatever was going on?

"Sit down, sit down," urged Mr Austen. The girls did as they were bid.

"Before I begin, I must tell you that it is all settled," exclaimed Mrs Austen, her hands clasped nervously in her lap.

Not yet enlightened, Jane awaited more.

"Your father is to retire. We are to leave Steventon within the next half year and settle in Bath."

Jane could sense Martha squirming on the seat beside her.

"Bath," gulped Jane. "We are moving to Bath?"

Her whole body felt cold: colder even than in the coach on the journey. Her head went light, and she feared she might lose consciousness altogether. Her mother was speaking to her with some more words, but they were incoherent. Jane

315

felt as though her ears were filled with feathers, trapping her thoughts inside.

*You do not like Bath, Papa. You have declined to accompany us both times we have been. Why do you want to live there now?*

*You could not wait to come home last time we went, Mama. You complained the whole journey back how your head would never recover from the constant noise. And now you want to reside there?*

Jane must have sat dumbstruck for far too long listening to these unspoken objections because the next thing she noticed was James thrusting that restorative glass of wine into her hand. He looked irritated, which Jane took as a sign she had not responded to the news in the way he had wanted.

Whilst she sipped her drink and tried to compose herself, faithful, loyal Martha filled the silence.

"And your living, Sir," she enquired to Mr Austen. "Who will attend to that?" Coming from a family of rectors herself, she knew this would have been the first thing to have been decided.

"You see him right here!" beamed Mr Austen, gesturing towards his eldest son.

James had the decency to attempt to look bashful, but the preening of his shoulders could not disguise the immense satisfaction he felt at the new appointment.

"We shall move into the rectory here when you move out to Bath," confirmed Mary bluntly, as was her way.

These were the words that brought forth Jane's tears. The absolute trust she had always felt in her parents had been shattered. This matter had been decided whilst both she and Cassandra had been away from home –*their own home* - with no forewarning whatsoever, whereas James and Mary had been consulted from the start. The betrayal was too much.

"Does my sister know?" she managed. "Or Edward?"

"It is so recently decided," confirmed her father, "that you are the first to be told."

*Second*, thought Jane. *Third, if you count Mary.*

"Do you have a house in mind in Bath?" she asked her father, but her mother answered on his behalf.

"Not yet," she crooned. "But you can help with that, Jane. I will write to my brother in the morning and request that we stay with him and your aunt whilst we consider what is about. Imagine what a time we will have looking at all the different properties!"

Jane could imagine only too well.

"We need to begin cataloguing our belongings as soon as we can," Mr Austen informed them, in a softer voice than his wife. "Most of them will be going up for auction, you see. Can I count on you girls to help me?"

"Of course, Sir," agreed Martha diplomatically.

Jane could only look bemused.

\* \* \*

Martha took the brunt of Jane's frustrations for the days following the rude announcement, and it was a while before her own fortitude and patience rubbed off on her friend.

"It was such a shock," Jane repeated to Martha, who did her best to soothe her.

"It was such a shock," she wrote to Cassandra, who took an age to reply.

"It was such a shock," she told her father when he had time enough to listen.

317

"It was such a shock," she explained to her mother, who simply went about her day.

"It was such a shock," she complained to James, who had no patience to listen at all.

She had never been treated in such a way as this before, like a child who they stepped around after a tantrum. The only way she learned to be included in a meaningful conversation was to stop her whining and accept her fate with goodwill.

"I have been forced to move twice in my adult life," reassured Martha when she finally sensed that Jane was receptive enough to take her advice. "Firstly, when my father died, and secondly when your brother married and took over the living at Deane. Both times these changes were unwelcome, but both have brought happiness and friendships that I would not otherwise have known. Embrace the change, Jane. Embrace what Bath offers you. 'Tis the only way."

Jane and Martha began their cataloguing in the library and every day made lists of the books on the shelves. Then they recorded the different items of furniture and counted linen, pans and geese. It felt good to have a purpose for once - a meaty project to get her teeth into – and Jane came around to the merits of moving.

"My father will benefit from the waters as much as my mother," she contemplated whilst stacking a pile of plates in the scullery. "And I am sure the balls in Bath will be more diverting than the ones in Basingstoke, which have become very dull of late."

"Think of all the new partners you will stand up with at the Assembly Rooms," teased Martha with a glint in her eye. "Handsome strangers from places you have never been!"

Jane giggled like she and Cassandra used to do and allowed

herself a happy vision of the two of them parading the streets on the arms of their good-looking beaus.

Jane naturally wrote to her sister as often as she was able, to keep her updated on everything that was going on. She had a hundred and one questions to ask in every letter, but with Cassandra being so far away amid the million distractions of Godmersham, expecting an answer to all of them was pointless.

When news of the move filtered through to the rest of the siblings, they came home, one by one. None of them were prepared to watch their parents leave without staying for one final time in the rectory where they had been raised.

First to arrive was Henry, whose charismatic presence lit up the room like a glittering sun. He breezed in looking supremely handsome and suave, instantly treating Jane like a queen and had big news of his own. Following his Tour of Duty in Ireland, he had decided that the time had come for him to leave the militia and put his days of soldiering behind him. He was opening a bank with a fellow retiring officer, Henry Maunde. They had taken offices in London in the fashionable district of St James, and Henry and Eliza had moved into a house close by, in Upper Berkley Street, near Portman Square.

"Our work is essentially the same as we performed for the regiment," Henry explained. "We are the designated agents for the Oxfordshire's payroll so will maintain it in a similar way as before. But because we are not soldiering, we will have time to seek out other opportunities for investment and grow the business." Henry already knew a thing or two about investments, and if ever there was a man to persuade an investor that his money would be safe, then Henry was that man.

"The best part is that I will be able to spend more time with Eliza," he justified. "I know she is extraordinarily understanding of our separations, as any army wife must be, but I am more than ready to submit to a domestic life at home."

The others teased him and made jokes about sitting with his pipe and slippers whilst Eliza read to him from a newspaper, but Jane thought he was wonderful. How thoroughly modern it was for a man to admit he liked domesticity. How lucky Eliza was to have his brightness lighten up every gloomy day.

"I assume Eliza is happy to be back in London?" queried Mrs Austen.

"Very much," confirmed Henry. "She knows every street as well as I know the lanes of Hampshire and has friends in every borough."

"And the boy?" pressed his mother. "Will he be schooled?"

Henry shook his head and fell serious.

"Hastings is still unwell. I know Eliza had hoped that his trips to the sea would have helped cure him, but sadly his afflictions run deeper than that. He has the best set of physicians attending him in London and Eliza is a most attentive mother. But I fear even that is not enough. His fits come with no warning whatsoever."

"That must be very difficult," sympathised his father, glancing at his own wife who had gone quiet with Henry's emotional speech. He guessed she was remembering (as was he) the fits their own child, young George, had experienced before they sent him away to be cared for by a couple better able to serve his needs. He was still living nearby to this day, well past his thirtieth year, as was Mrs Austen's brother

Thomas who had similar needs and lived in the same house. He was now over fifty.

"Look at us all!" cried Henry, annoyed at himself for dampening the mood. "I did not come here to dwell upon my misfortunes. I came here to help you find a house!" With that, he stood up and reached over to the map of Bath that they had been looking at earlier and encouraged everyone to seat themselves once more around the table and claim the streets they liked the best.

In comparison to Henry, James was the one to suffer Jane's wrath. He was the one she blamed for gloating over his prize of the rectory and for moving in whilst she was being forced out. She wished she could express her spiteful thoughts to Martha to dispel them from her mind, but with James's wife being Martha's sister, she also knew that her friend's sympathies and loyalties would be divided.

On the fourth anniversary of their wedding, James and Mary went back to Ibthorpe with Martha. There was to be a small celebration with Fulwar and his family there too. Jane was invited to make up the party but declined to go, taking advantage of some quiet time at home instead. She helped her father in his study where he convinced her beyond doubt that he was genuine in his desire to move. "It disturbs me painfully to know I am not carrying out God's work in the way I know it should be done. It is time to hand the parish over to a younger man."

Mrs Austen was calmer too with just the three of them. She had received her reply from Mrs Leigh-Perrot who expressed with pleasure how much she looked forward to hosting them all again in her home. Number 1, Paragon was available to them for as long as they needed it, and from this day forward she pledged to seek out details of every property that came up for lease.

When James and Mary returned the following week, Jane's black mood had lifted somewhat, and she was delighted to discover that Fulwar and his family had returned with them.

"I could not let you leave Steventon without coming to express my good wishes to you all," enthused the young clergyman after walking over from Deane the next day. "Will you permit me to stand awhile in my old schoolroom, and take my children on a tour of the grounds? You will never know the influence this beautiful home has had on my life and the happiness I knew here as a boy."

It was a pretty speech by any standard, and it drew Mrs Austen to tears. She embraced her former student and kissed his cheek. Fulwar and his brothers - indeed all the boys Mr Austen had taught - had given her a fulfilment in looking after them that she would never forget.

Mr Austen shook Fulwar's hand, pumping it up and down with vigour. "You too, young Fowle, have long since made your old master proud. What a mighty fine man you have become."

When their memories threatened to embarrass them, Mr Austen did what he always did and sought distraction. "Tell me about your brothers now. How do they do?"

"William is still saving lives, Sir. He is stationed with the army in Egypt as a medic. It is valuable work, but I fear very hard."

"Yes," agreed Mr Austen.

"And Charles has been called to the Bar in London. I am not sure how I feel about putting the laws of the land into his hands," he quipped.

"Get away," laughed Mrs Austen, who had always been fond of Charles Fowle and fancied him at one time a good match for Jane. "All the best lawyers are good talkers, from what I hear."

"In that case, I defer to your better judgement, Ma'am," Fulwar conceded. "My little brother certainly is a good talker, I grant you that."

Whilst Fulwar and Eliza were staying at Deane with Mary and James, the two families had plenty of opportunity to socialise together. Mary was getting quite adept at hosting dinner parties and with Martha returned to Ibthorpe, her other sister, Eliza, soon filled the gap made by her absence.

Jane and her mother were keen observers of anyone they had not seen in a while, and both commented on the change in Eliza Fowle's looks. She had always been the dainty one and the prettiest of the three sisters, but today she looked pale and worn. Mary looked positively blooming standing next to her, which was something neither of them ever thought they would say.

"Cassandra says she has been ill of late," offered Jane, who knew the two were regular correspondents.

"I can see that," agreed her mother. "And I dare say she finds it hard work looking after so many little children when her husband is away," she sympathised. Fulwar looked after several parishes and had taken on the additional duties as Lord Craven's chaplain after Tom Fowle's death.

"I vouch that her looks would be improved if she did not cut her hair so short," Mrs Austen continued to speculate.

"Or if she did not wear her cap so high on her forehead," suggested Jane.

Judgement aside, Jane and her mother thoroughly enjoyed

the company of Fulwar, Eliza and their five delightful children during their stay and invitations were enthusiastically given for them all to visit Kintbury at their earliest convenience. Jane and her mother declined, due to the demands of finding a house in Bath, but Mr Austen confirmed there was nothing he would like more. He agreed without reservation that he would call between the time he left Steventon and the time he arrived in Bath: only the final date and time were left to be fixed.

"We are none of us getting any younger, my boy," he told Fulwar when the arrangements were settled. "Old age makes one want to catch up with friends from the past before it's too late. I am honoured to say that your father was one of the best friends I ever had and if I can share a glass of port with him again and reminisce about our university days, it will bring me more pleasure than you know."

\* \* \*

Usually, when a guest departed, there would be endless weeks of boredom and feeling sorry for themselves at the rectory, because everyone else seemed to be having more fun than them. This time it was different; the impending move was making them popular, and their company was in constant demand.

Mr Bayle, the auctioneer, came by often with a cheery tilt of his hat and a notebook in his hand. He was led by Mr Austen from room to room to value the furniture which now stood in neat and tidy rows. Well-meaning neighbours who had relatives in Bath called daily with details of properties and one day, a gaggle of excited ladies came en masse to buy up the gaggle of geese in the yard.

The most stressful part of packing everything away it turned out, was not in seeing their possessions disappear, but in ensuring the security of what they were leaving behind.

John Bond was the first problem to solve. Mr Austen's old bailiff had been there to greet him on the day he arrived in Steventon and had never worked anywhere else. There was no way Mr Austen could bear the thought of forcing him away. At first, Mr Bond was belligerent, insisting that he had been approached many a time over the years for his services, and he had no doubt he would find work again. Mr Austen was not so sure and after some delicate negotiation with the farm's new manager – a local man from Ashe – Mr Austen slept easier in his bed in the knowledge that Mr Bond was to be kept on tending the sheep.

The other big problem was finding a new curate for Deane. James had just the person in mind and approached the man who had married him and Mary four years before. This was Peter Debary, and it suited James's imagination nicely for this amiable young man from Hurstbourne Tarrant to move into Deane Rectory when he and Mary moved out. He was most perplexed when the offer was refused.

Next, he approached James Digweed. The two had grown up together as children, with the Digweeds living next door in the Manor House at Steventon. Perhaps this was what made Mr Digweed think twice about the offer, as the Digweeds had always been more affluent than their Austen neighbours. The thought of working for a meagre wage in Deane, whilst James claimed the more lucrative position at Steventon, was not enough to win him over and he also rejected James's offer.

That inspired the meddlesome Madam Lefroy to get involved. She was only too happy to enlighten James that her daughter was betrothed to a newly ordained young clergyman called Henry Rice. It was a happy ending for them all, when Mr Rice took up the curacy of All Saints Church in Deane, and Jemima-Lucy was provided with her first marital home.

Charles Austen came home more than once in the final months before the family left. His ship, *Endymion*, was stationed at Gosport awaiting orders for where it would go next, so Charles had plenty of free time. He brought news that Captain Williams was to be wed again, and although this brought back cruel memories of Jane Cooper's untimely death, the family did not begrudge her widow husband the chance of happiness with someone else.

Charles Austen was as good-looking as Henry nowadays and catching up quickly on charm. His smart officer uniform enhanced his tanned, rugged looks and his vibrant personality was welcomed everywhere. Charles's visits home were timed to cross paths with Henry or Edward, and even though the dinner table was surrounded by furniture in all the wrong places and boxes tucked under their feet, these obstacles were invisible when the brothers exchanged their news.

Only Frank was in doubt of not making it back to Steventon before the move was complete; he was still on the far side of the Mediterranean. He was at the end of a fruitful season around Cyprus where his command of the *Peterel* had gained more prizes for the British Navy. He was honoured with a promotion to the rank of Post Captain for his exceptional service, yet such was the unpredictability of communications out at sea, that his family back home knew of the honour quicker than Frank found out himself.

As moving day approached, the rectory was more chaotic than ever, and Mrs Austen was prone to hysterics. It was seen as a blessing from above, when the winds blew in Frank's favour, and he managed to get there in time. Cassandra had not been back many days before him, breaking up her journey from Godmersham with a three-week stay with Henry and Eliza in London. Frank and Cassandra had both inherited their father's calm and pragmatic personality instead of the sensibilities that disabled their mother, so they guided and instructed the final arrangements to their rightful conclusion.

The last days in Steventon saw a flurry of letters fly here and there to confirm dates and times. The first week of May was agreed upon as the time for departure and the family dispersed themselves in a carefully choreographed dance across the whole of the south of England.

Mrs Austen was the first to leave with Cassandra and Jane. They made their way to Ibthorpe to be hosted by Martha and Mrs Lloyd.

Mr Austen and Frank stayed on at the rectory to oversee the auction of their household goods, then travelled to London to finalise any matters of business and call in to see Henry and Eliza. From there they moved on to Godmersham to stay with Edward and Elizabeth.

After resting a while at Ibthorpe, Mrs Austen and Jane left for Bath to move in with the Leigh-Perrots in their townhouse.

Cassandra accompanied Martha from Ibthorpe to Kintbury, where she was welcomed as warmly as ever by the Fowles.

Mr Austen departed Godmersham after two weeks with Edward, leaving Frank behind with his brother whilst he went on to Kintbury to collect Cassandra.

He spent two days in the company of his old university friend, Thomas Fowle, to share the anticipated glass of port, after which time Mr Austen and Cassandra left to join Mrs Austen and Jane.

One month after they had left their rectory for good, the four Austens from Steventon were reunited and ready to find a suitable new home together in Bath.

Only James remained in Hampshire, where the responsibility fell to him and Mary to win over the congregation of St Nicholas' Church. This was what his father had prepared him for his whole life, and he was proud to take up the challenge.

# The Austens of Bath

If you have enjoyed *The Austens of Steventon* and would like to learn what happens to the family next, then all will be revealed in *The Austens of Bath*.

This second novel in the series will accompany all your favourite characters through the next phases of their lives. *The Austens of Bath* will cover the time period from May 1801 until July 1809 when, after that, *The Austens of Chawton* will take up the baton to record the final years of the family's lives.

If you would like to keep up to date with these new works in progress, you can find out more on my Facebook page @ Diane Jane Ball.

# References

I am indebted to the countless scholars who have written before me on the topics of Jane Austen, her family and friends, and life in Georgian England.

Below, I have listed the sources from which I gathered most of my information. They are excellent starting points if you have a particular area of interest that you would like to follow up on, and are categorised into topics.

Many more links, specific to the locations from the book, are also available on my website ***https://diane-jane-ball.com***

## LETTERS AND MEMOIRS OF THE AUSTEN FAMILY

- Austen, C. (1952) **My Aunt Jane Austen**: A memoir. Winchester: Sarsen Press.
- Austen Leigh, R.A. (1942) **Austen Papers 1704-1856**. Colchester: Privately printed by Spottiswoode, Ballantyne & Co. Ltd.
- Hughes-Hallett (2019) **The Illustrated Letters of Jane Austen**. London: Batsford.
- Le Faye, D. (2011) **Jane Austen's Letters – Fourth Edition**. Oxford: Oxford University Press.

## ANCESTRAL RECORDS

- Le Faye, D. (2013) **A Chronology of Jane Austen and her Family 1600-2000.** Cambridge: Cambridge University Press.
- Ancestry. co. uk (2023) **For birth, marriage and death certificates and family records.** Available at: https://ancestry.co.uk
- Find a Grave.com (*2023)* **For burial records.** Available at*:* https://findagrave.com
- Corder, J. (1953) **Akin to Jane: Jane Austen's Family Index of Names and Lists** (Edited and expanded by R. Dunning, 2012) Available at: https://janeaustensfamily.co.uk/akin-to-jane/akin-to-jane.index.html
- Dunning, R. (2014) **Jane Austen Genealogy – The Knight Family Name in Jane Austen in Vermont.** Available at: https://janeausteninvermont.blog/2014/02/20/jane-austen-genealogy-the-knight-family-name-by-ronald-dunning/

## BIOGRAPHICAL ACCOUNTS OF THE AUSTEN FAMILY

- Austen-Leigh, W., Austen-Leigh R.A. (1913) **Jane Austen: Her Life and Letters**. Project Gutenberg eBook (release date Set. 7th, 2007). Available at:https://www.gutenberg.org/files/22536/22536-h/22536-h.htm#Page_49
- Austen-Leigh, W., Austen-Leigh R.A. and Le Faye D. (1989) **Jane Austen: A Family Record.** London: The British Library.
- Byrne, P.B. (2014) **The Real Jane Austen: A Life in**

**Small Things.** London: William Collins Books.

- Chapman, R.W. (1948) **Jane Austen Facts and Problems: The Clark Lectures**. Oxford: The University Press.
- Dunning, R. (2021) **Rebecca Hampson: George Austen's Mother**. Available at: https://janeaustenswor ld.com/2021/11/21/rebecca-hampson-george-austens-mother-by-ronald-dunning/
- Jane Austen Blog (2022) **A Closer Look at Catherine Knight.** Available at: https://janeausten.co.uk/blogs/ extended-reading/a-closer-look-at-catherine-knight
- Nokes, D. (1997) **Jane Austen A Life.** California: University of California Press.
- Robinson Walker, L. (2005) **Why was Jane Austen Sent away to School at Seven?** An Empirical Look at a Vexing Question in Persuasions on-line, V.26, No.1 (Winter 2005) Jane Austen Society of North America. Available at:https://jasna.org/persuasions/on-line/vol2 6no1/walker.htm
- Todd, J. (2013) **The Treasures of Jane Austen: The Story of her Life and Work**. London: SevenOaks.
- Tomalin, C. (2000) **Jane Austen A Life**. London: Penguin Books Ltd.
- Tucker, G.H. (1983) **A Goodly Heritage**. Manchester: Carcanet New Press
- Tucker, G.H. (1994) **Jane Austen: The Woman**. New York: St Martin's Griffin.
- Walton, G. (2019) **James Austen: Jane Austen's Brother** in geriwalton.com. Available at: https://www.geriwalto n.com/james-austen-jane-austens-brother/
- Worsley, L. (2017) **Jane Austen at Home**. London: Hodder & Stoughton Ltd.

# WRITTEN WORKS OF THE AUSTEN FAMILY

- Douglas Editions. (2009) **The Complete Works of Jane Austen:** with extras (including Commentary, Plot Summary Guides and Biography). Kindle Edition.
- Internet Archive (2023) **The Austen Family Music Books**. Available at: https://archive.org/details/austenfamilymusicbooks
- Moore, R. (2018) **Jane Austen: The Complete Juvenilia – Text and Critical Introduction**. Independently Published.
- Oxford University Classics (2021) **Lady Susan, The Watsons and Sanditon**. Oxford: Oxford University Press.
- Selwyn, D. (1996) **Jane Austen: Collected Poems and Verse of the Austen Family**. Manchester: Carcanet Press Limited.
- Selwyn, D. (2003) **The Complete Poems of James Austen: Jane Austen's eldest brother**. Chawton: The Jane Austen Society.
- The Loiterer (2015) **James Austen's The Loiterer & other contents.** Available at: http://www.theloiterer.org
- University of Southampton (2015) **Jane Austen's family music books digitised and online.** Available at: https://www.southampton.ac.uk/news/2015/12/jane-austen-music-books.page

## MARTHA LLOYD

- Elizabeth Staples, "the cruel Mrs Craven", (2019) in

**elizabethberkleycraven.blogspot.com** Available at: https://elizabethberkeleycraven.blogspot.com/2019/0 6/elizabeth-staples-cruel-mrs-craven.html

- Locke, T. (2021) **The Lloyd Family of Enbourne ... and beyond in The Beacon**: August 2021: Walbury Beacon Benefice. Available at: https://d3hgrlq6yacptf.cloudfro nt.net/5f219d3dc1af5/content/pages/documents/augu st-2021-beacon.pdf
- Wheddon, Z. (2021) **Jane Austen's Best Friend: The Life and Influence of Martha Lloyd**. South Yorkshire: Pen and Sword Books Ltd.

## WARREN HASTINGS

- Babington-Macaulay, T. (1851) **Warren Hastings.** London: Longman, Brown, Green, and Longmans.
- Encyclopaedia Britannica (2022) **Warren Hastings – British Colonial Administrator**. Available at: https://www.britannica.com/biography/Warren-Has tings

## EAST INDIA COMPANY

- Encyclopaedia Britannica (2022) **East India Company.** Available at: https://www.britannica.com/topic/East-I ndia-Company
- Dalrymple, W. (2022) **'The Anarchy: The relentless rise of the East India Company'** Kings College, London. Available at: https://www.youtube.com/watch?v=hwd2 6ehENRs

## LOCATIONS

- A Jane Austen Gazeteer (2017) **Kintbury.** Available at: https://ajaneaustengazetteer.wordpress.com/berkshire/kintbury/
- Chapman, R.W. & Cox. B.S. (2022) **A Map of Bath in the Time of Jane Austen**. Bath Municipal Libraries' Collection: Oxford University Press.
- Chawton House (2023) **Chawton House.** Available at: https://chawtonhouse.org
- Hill, C. (1901) **Jane Austen: Her Homes and Her Friends**. dodopress.co.uk: Dodo Press.
- Huxley, V. (2013) **Jane Austen & Adlestrop: Her Other Family.** Gloucestershire: Windrush Publishing Services.
- Jane Austen Centre (2023) **Jane Austen Centre, Bath.** Available at: https://janeausten.co.uk
- Jane Austen's House (2023) **Jane Austen's House, Chawton.** Available at: https://janeaustens.house
- Le Faye (2007) **Jane Austen's Steventon**. Chawton: The Jane Austen Society.
- Townsend, T. (2014) **Jane Austen's Hampshire**. Somerset: Halsgrove.
- Townsend, T. (2015) **Jane Austen and Bath**. Somerset: Halsgrove.
- Townsend, T. (2015) **Jane Austen's Kent.** Somerset: Halsgrove.

## LIFE IN GEORGIAN ENGLAND

- Adkins R. and L. (2013) **Eavesdropping on Jane Austen's England**. London: Little, Brown Book Group.

- Batchelor, J. (2022) **The Lady's Magazine (1770 – 1832) and the Making of Literary History**. Edinburgh: Edinburgh University Press. Open Access ebook edition available at: https://library.oapen.org/bitstream/handl e/20.500.12657/60489/external_content.pdf?sequence =7
- Bath Preservation Trust (2022) **No.1 Royal Crescent. Bath**: Bath Preservation Trust.
- Chatsworth House Trust (2022) **Your Guide to Chatsworth.** Derbyshire: Chatsworth House Trust.
- Hathi Trust Digital Library (2023) '**Search: The Lady's Magazine**'. Available at: https://babel.hathitrust.org/ cgi/ls?q1=The+Lady%27s+Magazine&field1=ocr&a=sr chls&ft=ft&lmt=ft
- Herring, J. (2023) **Jane Austen's Regency World Magazine**. Somerset: Sild Media Ltd.
- Knowles,R. (2023) **Regency History**. Available at: https://www.regencyhistory.net
- Mortimer, I. (2020) **The Time Traveller's Guide to Regency Britain**. UK: Penguin Random House.
- Sullivan, M.C. (2007) **The Jane Austen Handbook: Proper Life Skills from Regency England**. Philadelphia: Quirk Books.

## THE NAVY

- Animagraffs (2023) **How an 18th Century Sailing Battleship Works**. Available at: https://www.youtub e.com/watch?v=4Nr1AgIfajI
- Hubback, J.H. & E.C. (1905) **Jane Austen's Sailor Brothers**. London: Ballantyne & Co. Ltd.

- Southam, B. (2003) **Jane Austen's Sailor Brothers: Francis and Charles in life and art** for the Jane Austen, Society of North America. Available at: https://www.t hefreelibrary.com/Jane+Austen%27s+sailor+brothers% 3a+Francis+and+Charles+in+life+and+art.-a01192242 70
- The National Museum of the Royal Navy (2022) **HMS Victory.** London: Pitkin Publishing.

## THE CLERGY & RELIGION

- Cox, B.S. (2022) **Fashionable Goodness: Christianity in Jane Austen's England**. Georgia, USA: Topaz Cross Books.
- The Clergy Database (2022) **Database - Search**. Available at: https://theclergydatabase.org.uk/jsp/search/in dex.jsp

## FASHION & DRESS

- Cassin-Scott, J. (1971) **Costume and Fashion in Colour: 1760 – 1920**. Dorset: Blandford Press.
- Davidson, H. (2019) **Dress in the Age of Jane Austen.** Connecticut: Yale University Press.
- Davidson, H.(2023) **Jane Austen's Wardrobe.** Connecticut: Yale University Press.
- Fashion Institute of Technology, New York (2023) **Fashion History Timeline.** Available at: https://fashionhist ory.fitnyc.edu/1760-1769/
- Facebook Community (2023) **Attire's Mind** (An informative and vibrant community discussing the messages

conveyed by fashion and accessories over the centuries.) Available at: https://www.facebook.com/AttiresMind
- Yarwood, D. (1961) **English Costume.** London: Redwood Burn Ltd.

## FOOD AND DRINK

- Ford, J. (2014) **Food and drink in 17th and 18th century inns and alehouses** in History is Now Magazine. Available at: http://www.historyisnowmagazine.com/blog/2014/6/7/food-and-drink-in-17th-and-18th-century-inns-and-alehouses#.Y8f2Yi-l3yQ=
- Gehrer, J. (2021) **Martha Lloyd's Household Book.** Oxford: Bodleian Library.
- Hartley, D. (1954) **Food in England.** London: Futura Publications.
- Paston-Williams, S. (1993) **'An Elegant Repast: Georgian Food'** in The Art of Dining – A History of Cooking and Eating. London: National Trust Enterprises Ltd.
- Vogler, P. (2020) **Dinner with Mr Darcy.** London: Ryland Peters & Small Ltd.

## ONLINE SOCIETIES & GROUPS

- **Jane Austen & Co**. (2023) An educational site offering an extensive range of video presentations and events on many different topics. Available at: https://www.janeaustenandco.org
- **Jane Austen Daily** (2023) Jane Austen Daily Facebook Group. Available at: https://www.facebook.com/groups/296923455713211/members

- **Jane Austen Fan Club** (2023) Jane Austen Fan Club Facebook Group. Available at: https://www.facebook.com/groups/2210708105/
- **Jane Austen Society of North America** (2023) An extremely informative site relating to all things Austen. Available at: https://jasna.org
- **The Jane Austen Society** (2023) Newsletters and Reports Archive. Available at: https://janeaustensociety.org.uk
- **Jane Austen in Vermont** (2023) "Random Musings of a Janeite". Available at: https://janeausteninvermont.blog
- Jane Austen's World (2023) *A blog bringing Jane Austen's world and the Regency period alive in indexed posts on hundreds of topics*. Available at: https://janeaustensworld.com
- **Mollands.net** (2022) An incredible collection of e-texts, articles and blog posts related to Jane Austen and her works. Available at:https://www.mollands.net/etexts/index.html
- **The Republic of Pemberley** (2021) A treasure trove of information related to Jane Austen and her works. Available at: https://pemberley.com
- **The Rice Portrait of Jane Austen** (2023) Meticulously researched, and very informative site about the portrait of Jane Austen as a young girl. Available at: https://thericeportrait.com

Thank you to each and every person who has contributed to these resources. This book would not have been the same without you.

# Acknowledgements

We are fortunate in Britain to have many historical properties that fuel our imagination and educate us about the past. I would like to express my thanks to everyone associated with the National Trust, English Heritage and Cadw, especially the volunteers who give up their time to allow people like me an enjoyable day out. The same goes for the museums and properties I have visited linked to Jane Austen and her life: The Jane Austen Centre in Bath, Jane Austen's House in Chawton, Chawton House, No.1 Royal Crescent, Godmersham Park Heritage Centre and the National Garden Scheme for Godmersham Park. Thank you for all that you do.

One of the best parts of researching a book is finding places you would never otherwise know, and there are many villages I have discovered through their connections with the Austen, Fowle and Lloyd families. Lots of them still retain their eighteenth-century charm, and I am especially grateful to the teams that maintain the ancient churches there. Without such history in our midst, huge chunks of our ancestry would be lost.

A huge thank you goes out to the Jane Austen community around the world. Every Janeite knows that there is no shortage of online groups to join, where enthusiasm and photo sharing are contagious. I thank everyone who has ever posted, and particularly those individuals who volunteer their time to act as administrators to keep their groups running. Some names stand out more than others in the inspiration they have given me, so a special thank you to: Samuel Keele of the Jane Austen Fan Club; Adge Secker for his video tours; Hazel Mills for her posts on Jane Austen Daily; Inger Brodey and Anne Fertig for the lectures at Jane Austen & Co.; Attire's Mind for the meticulously detailed fashion posts; Breckyn Wood for the JASNA podcasts; and to 'Laughing with Lizzie' and 'Pinsent Tailoring' who live the Regency life on behalf of us all in their Facebook posts.

I thank all the people at *reedsy.com* for their generous software and valuable guidance that allowed me to format this work to a publishable standard. And to Sarah Wright at Book Printing UK for her advice and reassurance as I sought to get things just right.

On a personal level, I would like thank my friend Michelle, who has always taken an interest in my writing. I hope now it is finished, this book will keep you entertained on those long days you are forced to stay indoors and stimulate your mind while your body is in recovery.

And to Brenda, whose launch of her own long-talked-of family business inspired me to keep going when I thought this project would never reach an end. I am looking forward already to the plentiful supplies of tea and cake we will inevitably consume as I work my way through Book 2.

I have so much to thank my family for; they have been my biggest enablers in this publication.

Firstly, I remember the kindness and generosity of Uncle Stan. Without him, I would never have had the opportunity to spend as much time researching and coming up with ideas as I did. I know he would have been interested in all I have done, especially the parts relating to India.

To Mom, I hope that you will enjoy reading my first novel and it will provide you with many happy hours of distraction. I wish Dad could have seen it, but I think he would have been proud.

To Adrian and Melanie - I hope you enjoy it too. Thank you for keeping me smiling through everything else going on in our lives and for being there day by day. Your enthusiasm to read the finished product is much appreciated.

To Emily and Luke, I want to thank you both for sitting patiently and saying all the right things as I rambled on incessantly about Jane Austen and her world. You must have thought what a crazy person I was at times, although you never showed it.

To Charlie and Bella, who have no idea this book is even happening. Some of my happiest times have been spent squeezing into the corner of your chair to work on my edits and watching you sleep and dream and purr by my side.

To Leo, the whole reason I became a writer in the first place. I never knew how many words I had inside me until you were born, and your short life was the reason I kept going to learn and improve my craft. Thank you.

To Oscar, who has been telling me since he was a boy that I should write a book and never lost faith that I would. Thank you for your sharp journalistic eyes and for your fresh ideas and perspectives which never failed to make my writing better. Thank you for the best walks with Luna around historic sites and for always being there to listen and offer advice when I needed it.

To Tania, who has been part of this book from the start. I

will never forget that meal at The Greyfriar and the moment the ideas began. Thank you for being my first reader, my book club buddy and for designing the perfect book cover. Thank you for coming with me on all my mini breaks and for the countless steps we have trod together around Bath. There will be plenty more of those, I promise.

And to Vincenzo, who has supported me wholeheartedly every step of the way. From helping me with technology to driving me on my field trips, and sharing all the picnics on the go. You never failed to believe what I was doing was worthwhile and although we can breathe a sigh of relief this book is finished, I know you are as excited as me to see what the next one will bring.

Thank you, all.

# About the Author

Diane Jane Ball works as an English teacher and has a degree in English literature - but writing stories is where she's most at home.

Her favourite genre to read is the nineteenth-century novel, and she was first introduced to the works of Jane Austen at school when she studied *Pride & Prejudice* and *Emma* as exam texts.

The idea for this book was sparked by a visit she made to Jane Austen's House in Chawton in August 2021. Initially, it was intended to tell the love story between Martha Lloyd and Francis Austen, but as she researched their backgrounds, Diane discovered that the links between their two families went back much further than she knew.

She quickly realised that the Fowle family from Kintbury were equally as significant to their history, and so Diane adapted her idea to tell the story of the Austen, Fowle and Lloyd families from the beginning. She wanted to show how tightly they were all bound together.

There was far too much material to put in one book by the time she had finished researching, and so *The Austens of Steventon* became the first novel in a series of three. Diane is currently working on the second, *The Austens of Bath,* to be followed soon after by *The Austens of Chawton*.

Diane's own life is one of contrasts. For half of the

week, she lives in the fictional world of Georgian England, accompanying her characters through their daily lives. The other half is taken up with 21st-century technology, teaching English lessons on Zoom.

Diane lives in Herefordshire with her husband and two cats and this is her first novel. You can keep up to date with her activities on her Facebook page @ Diane Jane Ball.

Printed in Great Britain
by Amazon